"A little bit of mercy makes the world less cold . . ."
— *Pope Francis*

CHAPTER ONE
JAMIE

Until death do us part. It's supposed to be *that* simple.

Marriages are supposed to last. Couples are supposed to be able to get through the toughest of times and have each other's back—until one of them takes their last breath.

Problem is, that's not reality. That was my parents', even my grandparents', but not mine.

My marriage was a sham from the beginning. I never loved her. I didn't grow to love her. Not even as the mother of my son.

That probably makes me the shittiest man on the face of the Earth. So be it. I've come to terms with that.

Sighing, I breathe out a long, tiring breath as the documents between my fingers—two pages that outline my divorce—fall, landing on the wooden coffee table in front of me.

It says, I've been divorced for three days now.

I didn't contest much of anything. Julia wanted the house, she got it. She wanted the souped-up cars in the garage, she got those too. The condo in New York, whatever. It's not like I cared for that place anyway. It was all just things, items that could be replaced.

The only thing in my marriage that has ever mattered to me is my son. He's the single reason I married her in the first place. He's the only reason it lasted as long as it did.

As much as I want to regret the last eighteen years of Julia Montgomery in my life, in my bed, I can't—because of him. I have many regrets, but my son isn't one of them. I wish things had turned out differently. Hell, I wish he had been birthed by a different woman, but he wasn't, and there isn't a damn thing I can do to change the past.

Lies. Betrayal. A broken fucking heart is what got me into this mess to begin with. Problem is, I would have thought I'd have gotten past all that by now.

I haven't.

I never will.

I pick up the longneck bottle, the condensation slipping down the amber glass and around my fingers as I lift it to my lips. Downing the contents, I swallow the beer, guzzling every bit of the liquid inside the bottle.

The alcohol isn't strong enough, but then again, nothing is. Not even the strongest whiskey could make me forget those deep-brown eyes, long auburn hair, or fingers that could strum a guitar and make me hard just watching her play. It's her voice that always did me in. I'll never get those sounds out of my head as long as I still breathe. I've never heard anything like it. So perfect, so beautiful, so haunting.

Eighteen years have gone by, and Elise Thomas still owns me like no other woman ever has—or ever will.

Eighteen years later, I still hate her with every fiber in my body the same as I did the day she returned.

"For a man that should be celebrating freedom from *the* bitch, you sure do have a look of doom and gloom written all over that ugly face, brother." I glance up, seeing Trey, my drummer, holding a beer at his side, a dark-brown eyebrow arched up one side of his forehead. "What do we need to do to cheer you up?" His lips tip, already knowing my answer.

"Pussy. I want to drown in that shit all night long."

His lips spread, widening into a grin so big it could put the Cheshire cat to shame. Seth—the guitarist in our band—walks up, drapes his arm across Trey's back then jerks him closer. Trey is taller and leaner than Seth, so when his body leans over, his wavy brown hair falls into his line of sight.

"Then what are we waiting for? Let's go find us some honeys," Seth adds.

It's not like it'll matter. By the time I'm balls deep inside a girl, I'll be too drunk to feel an ounce of pain or guilt, and definitely not pleasure.

My guilt is the one thing I've never understood. Doesn't matter who the chick is, I always regret fucking them, yet I still do it. I wasn't the one that left, though. *She* was. So why is it I'm the one that's always felt like I was betraying her when she's the one that screwed me over?

It's a question to an answer I'll never get.

The last person on earth I ever want to see again is Elise Thomas. She's worse than the woman I married, and that's saying a lot because Julia Montgomery takes the cake on being the biggest bitch I've ever met.

"Text Cole," I order, knowing one of them will do it. Cole Masters is the other member of our band, our bassist, and my best friend. All four of us have been friends since we were in daycare together at the age of three. It's always been the four of us. Cole and I are best friends, Seth and Trey the same. Even though none of us are related, they are my brothers. They've always had my back, and I theirs. They've never betrayed the band or me, and I know they never will. "Tell him to meet us."

We formed Bleeding Hart, our rock band, when we were in junior high when none of us knew how to play any instrument or even how to sing a note. That wasn't the original name of the band, but it's what I later changed it to when I was going through a rough time in my life. We all loved music more than we loved to eat. We knew even back then we wanted to make it big no matter what it took.

And we did.

We bled sweat and tears, but we made it to the big league: record deals, world tours, money, fame, girls. We've even dabbled in drugs here and there, but we also learned that was a dead end and a fast track to losing the career we've worked too damn hard to achieve.

At least I can say I've gotten and kept one of the two things I've always wanted.

"Says he can't, and he'll catch up with us tomorrow," Trey relays. "Says to come over around noon, and we'll work on laying that track for the new album in his studio."

"What's more important than getting smashed with your boys and finding pussy?" Seth asks.

Trey and I both look at each other, a dry laugh coming out of my mouth. "Pussy he already has," I answer. "Let's hit it."

CHAPTER TWO
JENNA

My stomach growls, hungry and angry that I haven't eaten since lunch yesterday.

I grit my teeth, blowing out my frustration. *Fucking Cole.* He left forty-five minutes ago, walking down the block to the bakery to get us something quick to eat. He should have been back by 8:10. It doesn't take *that* long to buy donuts, but knowing him as well as I do, he's balls deep inside the baker as we speak.

Horny bastard.

He's no different from any other man. Thinks with the piece of meat dangling between his legs well before he uses his brain for something useful—like remembering that I'm starving. I whined exactly that half a dozen times before he crawled out of his bed to go get us some sustenance.

I slept here last night after having a "bad night," and now I'm late for work. Luckily, being a senior special agent for the Los Angeles, California field office of the FBI, I'm not required to punch in every workday morning like clockwork. Most days I'm working out in the field with my team.

5

My eyes cut to the top of the toilet tank as my phone chimes with an incoming text message when my arms are midair, securing my long, red locks into a sleek, tight ponytail high on my head. My hair isn't nearly the length it once was, but I still prefer to keep it on the longer side. It normally extends to the center of my back, but while I'm working, I have to have it out of my face.

Letting the strands fall, covering the back of my neck, I lean to my left, away from the mirror, grabbing my cell.

Josh: Where are you?

Joshua Beckett—my boss, longtime friend, and my team's special agent in charge.

Josh: You were supposed to be here half an hour ago. The fuck, Cat?

I've gone by Jenna, my first name, since I was seventeen. Only Josh calls me "Cat," preferring it over my real name. There was a time, long ago, when I hated that he'd call me that, or even worse, "Wild Cat," but over time, I got over my issues with him. We got through them together, and now he's one of my best friends. He's my boss first and foremost, but a friend nonetheless. I hate how he came into my life, but also love that he was the one, because had it been anyone else, I wouldn't have the freedom I do today—or perhaps I wouldn't even be alive.

My head snaps to the open bathroom door that leads into Cole's bedroom when I hear the front door from downstairs slam closed.

Finally. Much longer, and I might've passed out from lack of nourishment.

I write a quick text, shooting it back to the boss.

Me: Headed your way now.

I'll never make excuses. I'm late, and there is nothing that's going to stop the ass chewing he's going to give me when I arrive. It's deserved. I have a job to do, and as one of the two senior agents on the team, I shouldn't be late for any reason.

I didn't bring a change of clothes, and I knew that before I decided to shower at Cole's this morning. I'll have to wear the same clothes I showed up here in last night, the same ones I wore to work yesterday. In my case, every outfit I wear to work is the same. The only thing that ever changes depends on whether I wear a jacket due to changes in the weather or when I have to be present for court proceedings.

I slip my cell down the deep pocket of my black tactical pants as I step back into Cole's master bedroom. After snatching my bra off his four-poster bed, I head out of the spacious room.

Sliding an arm through one of the straps of my black racerback bra, I wrap it around my back and push my other arm through, pulling the cups under my boobs and snapping the hook closed around the front as I take the first step down the stairs. Chills rush down my spine, stopping me dead in my tracks when I hear a voice I haven't heard in years.

"Looks like our boy had *some* kind of night." Trey laughs, and it guts me, instantly stealing the air from my lungs, and at the same time pulls my eyes down the staircase and into the large, open living room below.

My gaze flicks over when I hear a snicker come from Seth's mouth. "I don't think I wanna meet whatever chick he's banging," he remarks, leaning over the glass coffee table, picking up my leg holster and weapon. I cringe, hating someone putting their hands on my shit. It's the FBI agent in me. When I'm at Cole's, I tend to let my guard down when I know I shouldn't. I sure as shit should not have left my weapon out of reaching distance. I know better.

There's a third person in the room with them, and it's taking everything inside me not to fixate on him. It physically hurts me not to look at Jamie. I know as soon as I do, it'll hurt ten times worse.

"No way!" My eyes snap down to Trey's. At some point, he turned around and is now looking up the staircase at me with the same hard, hateful sneer on his pretty face that matches the one he was wearing the last time I saw him. "No fucking way is he fucking *you!*" he snarls.

If I had any doubts whether he still hated me, that just proved he does.

I hear *his* quick intake of breath, the shock rolling out of his mouth, knowing Jamie's finally noticed me. Still, I force my eyes to remain locked with Trey's angry brown ones. He's always worn his wavy locks short but with long strands on top. The front always finds its way into his eyes. It's his signature look, and it still looks good on him. Even with the hatred rolling off him, he's still as good-looking as he was at eighteen-years-old. All four of them are.

"I don't know." I shrug, continuing down the steps, taking them slower than I normally would, not wanting to lose my balance. *He's* here. Jamie Hart is within breathing distance. Everything inside me is screaming to run. But I won't. Not this time. "You'd have to ask Cole. I'm not one to kiss and tell." I force a smile, my brown eyes still locked on Trey.

Cole and I aren't an "item" and never will be. Other than my partner, Malachi Hayes, he ranks up there as one of my best friends. My second-best friend, to be exact. It wasn't always that way. There was a time when Cole was my worst enemy. Never in my wildest dreams would I have imagined we'd be friendly with one another, let alone someone I'd confide in, lean on, and love for the man he is today, for the things he's done and been there for.

"Elise." His whispered voice sends a sharp pain shooting across my back, conjuring up memories I'd rather never think about again. I haven't been called by my middle name in such a long time that I'd almost forgotten what it sounded like on his tongue.

My eyes finally pull in his direction, giving in to the need to see him and hating myself for still feeling the way I do about him all these years later. After everything he's done and said, I still haven't gotten over him. And I still love him. I shouldn't, but I do.

He isn't staring at me. Those indigo eyes that I remember so clearly are looking at something he's holding in the center of his palm. I know what it is without seeing it. It's the silver cross pendant with a single black diamond in the center that he gave me for my fifteenth birthday with the inscription on the back: J and E.

I've never been a religious person, but there is something about crosses that I love. They're comforting in a way I can't explain. Jamie knew I liked them, and to this day, it's my favorite treasure.

Jamie and the guys were a year older than me and a grade ahead of me in school, but I had known them since we were little kids. Growing up in a small southern town in Mississippi, we attended the same Sunday school class. I was infatuated with Jamie from the first day I met him at age nine after my parents moved one town over, buying a new house and enrolling me in a new school.

He knew I liked him because, for him, it was love at first sight too. That's the one thing I always knew was true with us. We were meant for each other from the very beginning. Only when push came to shove, he wasn't in it for forever like I had been.

He believed *her* over me. And that sealed our tragic fate.

"Cole wouldn't come within touching distance of you," Trey spits, pulling my attention away from Jamie and back to him.

"Yet, I'm in his house." I step off the last step, four feet from William "Trey" Thompson. He hates me. All three of them do.

Seth is silent, but the same disgust on his bandmate's face is the same one he has trained on me now. Jamie is still in shock, but the anger is coming. I know that because I know him. His emotions are slow, but when they hit, it's like a Mack truck coming at you at a hundred miles per hour.

"Why are you?" Seth finally speaks up at the same time the door of the one-car garage bangs shut. Cole's back, and I'm going to kill him for them being here. For having to deal with this shit when it's the last thing I ever wanted to come face-to-face with.

"Fuck!" Cole shouts, coming through the opening leading from the kitchen. He stops, taking us all in. "Fuck," he shouts again, running his hand through his short dirty-blond hair.

"You want to explain this, brother?" Jamie barks, his anger finally making its presence known.

I step past Trey, walking in Jamie's direction. He steps backward, retreating from me like he can't stand the nearness. He probably can't. I glance down, hating that he backed away from me. It's like another stab to the heart, along with so many other cuts he's carved into me. Hasn't gotten any easier. Still hurts just as it did before.

I see my black tank top on the coffee table and snatch it up.

It's the sharp intake of air behind me that stops me midair from pulling my shirt over my head. It's confirmation Trey saw the ugly scar that mars the flesh across my back in a nine-inch diagonal mark. Most of the time, I forget it's there. I wear ribbed tank tops most days, but it's rare when someone other than me, Cole, or Malachi sees it. They act like they don't even notice it, even though I'm not stupid. I know they do. I know they hate what it represents. But I can't change the past. They can't change the past. It is what it is.

I yank the material over my head, pulling it down my torso, tucking it into my pants. Then I snatch my holster and weapon out of Seth's hand, quickly strapping it to my right thigh. Finally, I whip my body around, facing Trey head-on, and give him a look that says he better not even think about opening his damn mouth.

"Leave it," I order. "It's in the past, Trey. It stays in the past. Got it?"

He swallows as he nods, shock and guilt, perhaps, coating his olive complexion.

I shoot a look over my shoulder, seeing Jamie's face has hardened into stone.

Lifting my arm, I open my hand, requesting the item of mine that's in his. Instead of giving it to me, he closes his fingers around the cheap piece of jewelry, fisting his hand. It pisses me off, but I'm not in the mindset to fight him over it.

I turn away, needing to get out of here as fast as my feet will go without running. My cell phone chimes with an incoming text message, but I ignore it. It won't be Josh, that much I know. It's either my best friend and partner, or it's one of the boys. Either way, they'll have to wait until I have my shit under control.

"Jen," Cole says my name in a way that sounds like a heartfelt apology.

I'm not mad at him. I know he had no way of knowing they'd show up. He and I don't talk about Jamie or the guys that much. We stay away from the topic of his band. Bleeding Hart has been my favorite band since they formed, back when they called themselves Hideout. I was their biggest fan at one time. Thing is, I still am. Jamie's voice, the lyrics he writes, the music the guys create speaks to my soul in a way nothing else ever has. Individually, all four are talented. Together, they make a phenomenal music group. They were always destined for success, and they found it. For that, I'm so proud of all four of them.

I stop in front of Cole, and his hands clasp around my biceps, lightly squeezing. Leaning down, Cole's lips brush against the shell of my ear, and I have to lock my jaw in order to stop my body from reacting to his touch. "You're shaking." He whispers the obvious.

"I'm leaving," I bite out in a low tone through clenched teeth. If I don't get out of here, I'm going to lose all my strength and break down. I can't allow that to happen, not in front of the rest of them. Cole is a different story. Between him and Malachi, I can't say which has seen me at my worst, but probably Cole. I sought comfort in the one place I never should have—Jamie's best friend. It isn't right. I placed Cole in an impossible situation, but I didn't have much of a choice.

Fear and the need to protect that which you hold most dear will do that to a woman, to anyone.

He leans up, his remorseful face coming back into view. His brows furrow, and his green eyes cloud. "I'm sorry," he mouths, but I shake my head, silently asking him to let it go and to let me leave.

"I'll see you tonight," I force out, my tone nowhere near as light as I would have liked it to come out. My nerves are shot, and I have to get out of here fast. I raise my brown eyes up to his six-foot height, pleading with him to understand in a way that only he can.

There's a part of me that wants to step into Cole's arms, letting him wrap them around me. We may not be *a thing* in terms of sex or an intimate relationship, and never will be, but that doesn't mean I don't enjoy or take from the physical touch and comfort he gives because I do. More so than I have the right to. It's why I was here last night.

When I have a bad day, the only way for me to have a fighting chance at sleep is being nestled in Cole's arms. I should be ashamed of that, but I'm not. It's the only solace I've had in the last ten years since he's known the full truth, and I eat that comfort up every chance I get. The fact that he and Jamie smell so much alike due to the brand of cologne they wear, is something neither of us acknowledges, though we're not *that* stupid, and we both know it.

"I swear to God," Jamie barks from behind me, stealing the tremors from my body. "If you do not take your hands off her, I will rip them off. Stop fucking touching her!" he commands, and I swallow, my throat feeling clogged. For a moment, I welcome his jealousy. It's been a long time since I've felt it, seen it, or heard it.

The thing about Jamie is that his emotions roll off him in stark honesty. He's never shied away from them or hid them. What you see is what you get. What you get is who he is to the core.

"It's not like that," Cole says, tipping his head back in frustration that his best friend would think, even for a second, that he'd want me *that* way. Cole loves Jamie in a way that I used to not understand. The same way Cole didn't comprehend the way I loved Jamie. It's why we were always at each other's throats as kids and teenagers. We weren't friends like I was with Trey and Seth. Cole and I didn't hate each other, but we certainly didn't like each other back then.

Cole is bisexual. He likes the feel of a man's body against his as equally as he loves a woman's. He hid that fact for a long time, but eventually, the struggle of fighting who he is, what he wants, became too much, so he admitted it, first to Jamie and then to Trey and Seth, and finally to me. Apparently, his bandmates already knew. It was with me that it came out as a shock. Not because I didn't approve or respect it, but because I had never opened my eyes to see what had been in front of me the whole time.

Cole's and my spats stemmed from him thinking he was in love with Jamie the same as I was. It was years later that he realized it was his attraction to men in general and the real love he does, in fact, have for his best friend. It just isn't the same kind of soul-baring love I feel for Jamie.

"Sure as fuck looks like it to me," Jamie throws back at him.

"Us too, brother," Seth pipes up.

It doesn't go unnoticed that Trey has remained silent. He's never the silent one in the group. He's usually the loudest and most outspoken.

"They're yours to deal with," I say to Cole, still peering up. "I have to get to work."

Cole's head falls forward again, his eyes landing back on mine. He nods but hasn't moved to release me. Tired of this, I step around him, forcing him to drop his hands from my arms. I don't stick around any longer, and as soon as I'm out of the other three's sight, I bolt out of his garage door and race to my black Tahoe.

I wasn't ready for this. I'm still not ready for any of it, but I know the walls are going to come crashing down around me. It's only a matter of time—and that scares the hell out of me.

CHAPTER THREE
JAMIE

Rage.

Anger beyond anything I've ever felt takes root somewhere deep inside me. For the first time in my life, I have no idea how to handle it. I've never been pissed off like this toward Cole before. Sure, we have our differences from time to time. He's a dick. I'm a dick. But this is something entirely different. This is a feeling I'm not used to when it comes to my best friend—the one person that is supposed to have my back no matter what.

Betrayal.

I've only ever felt it one other time, and it was when Elise left me only to return with a shit ton of lies she expected me to believe. I wasn't that naive or stupid. She thought my love for her would cloud common sense. It didn't. She hurt me in a way that I've never recovered from.

The question is, has *he*?

"I suggest you start speaking." I grit my teeth, trying my damnedest to stay rooted to the spot I'm standing on. Everything inside me is screaming to knock his ass to the ground. He was touching her in an all-too-familiar way. He shouldn't be touching her at all. No one should be touching her.

Mine.

I know she isn't, not anymore, but that isn't something my brain can compute. She was supposed to be mine forever. My fists ball, my fingers closing around the necklace still in my hand, trying to crush the metal. It doesn't work; there is no give.

When I gave it to her at the age of sixteen, I really believed we had forever with each other. She gave me her virginity on her fifteenth birthday. Still, to this day, it's the best gift I've ever been given. I love my son, and he is my greatest achievement, even over my music career, but he wasn't a gift I had ever wanted—at least not from Julia. I hate that fact more than I'll ever admit, but I'll never regret him. I do, however, regret ever stooping so low that she ended up as his mother.

"She didn't betray us, did she?" Trey's voice cracks. He's only ever sounded that way one other time that I can remember, and that was right after we all moved out west.

My gaze flashes to where Trey is standing. His ass drops down to the cushioned box below the stairwell. His face is a fury of shock and defeat. Not something I'm used to seeing when it comes to him. He's the fun, loving, over-the-top one out of the four of us.

His eyes are locked with Cole's. My head swings back and forth between them, trying to understand the silence in their stare down. Cole finally shakes his head, and that only angers me more.

I don't know what Trey's getting at by his comment. *She didn't betray us, did she?* Like hell she didn't. She betrayed me, and that's all that matters.

I'll hate her for it until the day I take my last breath.

"The hell she didn't," Seth counters, and I'm grateful for his intervention.

"No, brother, she didn't." Cole steadily shakes his head, fueling a fire that's kindling deep inside my gut.

"Her back," Trey whispers, his head falling to his hands.

"What does that even mean?" I roar. "What does her back have to do with anything or why she was here?" I direct at Trey, demanding answers from one of them.

"She's going to kill me." Cole sighs deeply, taking a step closer to the rest of us as he finally takes a step into his living room.

"Yeah, well, I'm about to kill you now if you don't start talking. Say something that's going to make me not want to rip your goddamn head off like I do right now."

"There is nothing I can say that's going to make you believe me. You made up your mind about her years ago. And I swore I'd never tell you. I agreed with her at the time, but now I wish I had told you."

"How long?" I question. "How long have you been sleeping with her?"

"I haven't," he bites out, anger shooting back at me. "That is something I'd never do to you."

"And you expect him to believe that?" Seth asks. "You expect any of us to believe that when we watched her walking down the stairs from your bedroom, putting on clothes? Please, by all means, explain that, Masters," he spits, calling Cole by his last name. He only does that when he's pissed.

"I'm not going to tell you, but I will show you." He eyes me as he passes, the glass coffee table the only thing between us and the only thing keeping me from launching myself at him. I could reach out and grab him, yank him to me, but something stops me from doing so. Maybe it's the hope, the need to have him make these raw feelings inside go away.

How he can do that is beyond me. She *did* betray me, and in the worst possible way too. Everything she did had a trickle

17

effect. It's why I am where I am today. Why I am the asshole I am. She did that. Love did that.

"We're waiting," Seth continues.

"Yeah," Cole breathes out. "You'll be wishing you hadn't when it's all over. If you even get to the end, that is." He reaches up, high on the shelf next to his seventy-inch TV and entertainment center. Pulling his hand back, he has a plastic compact disc holder between his fingers. A DVD, I'm guessing, and that pisses me off. I want answers, not whatever game he's playing at.

"I don't have time for your bullshit." I shake my head and turn to leave, done with this. I need out of here before I actually do lay my hands on him because I guarantee you it won't be in a friendly manner. "I'm out of here."

I don't get four steps away when her terrified voice hits my eardrums and cuts all the way down my chest, slicing me open.

"Jamie."

My name on her tongue stops me. My feet are frozen where I stand. Her voice grabs a hold of me, not allowing me to walk away.

She didn't betray us, did she? Trey's words come back to me.

"Jamie," she says again, this time my name comes out more urgent, more haunting than the first.

I turn, coming face-to-face with the television, the screen green and black as if it's displaying some type of night-vision view. It's the girl's half-naked body that has my knees buckling, hitting the hardwood floor.

"I can't stomach watching this again. But a word of advice, it's ten minutes long. Don't stop watching even when the urge to puke hits." Cole passes me, leaving in the same direction I had been heading toward as my eyes remain glued to the screen, unblinking.

Elise.

18

CHAPTER FOUR

JENNA

Eighteen years ago

I'm shaking, and I can't get my body under control. I'm so cold. My feet feel like heavy, solid blocks, weighing more than my own body weight. My teeth clatter together, and I can't make them stop no matter how hard I try. My hands sting, my wrists ache so bad from where the handcuffs are clasped tightly around them, the hard, unforgiving metal biting into my bone.

"Jamie!" I scream for probably the millionth time since I've been here.

I've lost count of the days, maybe even weeks since I've been locked inside this room, chained to only the metal pole that's in here besides *his* work table in the far corner that I can't reach. It's pitch black, so I can't see it, but I know it's there. There's nothing on it, not now anyway. The only time the surface isn't bare is when he brings in items to torture me with.

I don't know how much more I can take.

"Jamie!"

I don't know why I continue to call my boyfriend's name. It's useless. I know he's nowhere near me. Doesn't know where I am or if I'm ever coming back to him. Hell, I don't even know if I'm coming back to him—and that scares me more than anything else.

The door to what I've deemed my jail cell opens, slamming into the wall, jolting my body into alert mode. He's here, no doubt having heard or even seen me on the camera attached high on the wall in one of the four corners of my room.

Bright light assaults my vision, blinding me. I squeeze my lids shut, pulling my chained hands up to cover my dirty face.

A breeze whooshes past me, and then he's slamming something down on the desk ten feet from where I sit on the concrete ground. I don't know where I am, if I'm in a house or a warehouse. I'm guessing some sort of warehouse, but this could be a basement for all I know. Basements aren't common in the South, and I don't know any houses that have rooms with cold, concrete flooring or painted cinder block walls, so a warehouse is more likely.

"Jamie!" I cry out again, knowing it's pissing him off. That was my goal, after all. That's been my goal since the first night I arrived.

He marches over, dropping down on his haunches, his hand flying out and wrapping around my throat. Cool, light-blue eyes train on mine.

"Stop. Saying. His. Name," he yells, spit hitting me in the face. He applies pressure, squeezing me enough to get my attention but not enough to cut off my airway.

"Let me go, and I'll stop saying it," I demand, even though he terrifies the life right out of me. I've never known evil like the man crouched in front of me. I never knew someone could be so cruel, so devious. I'd been wrapped inside a bubble my whole life, naive to the types of things that existed outside my small world.

I'm not the perfect little good girl—far from it. If anything, I was the instigator, the trouble-maker; I pushed every boundary with my parents, my teachers, anyone really.

I've never been a rule follower, and I'll be damned if this monster is going to make me become one. He'll have to kill me first, and he just might. That's not a fear I've learned; that's a likelihood of the situation I'm in.

His hold around my neck tightens, and then he starts to rise, standing back to his full six-foot-five-inch height and taking me up with him, lifting my feet off the ground. It's not like I weigh as much as I did when I arrived. Besides, he's bigger and stronger than any man I've ever met, including my father. My own five-foot-five-inch height is no match for him. He easily picks me up and tosses me around like his personal rag doll anytime he feels like it. Today is no different.

"You think your little bitch of a boyfriend gives a damn about you? Misses you?" He laughs, dropping me back to the cold hard concrete ground. My ass hits hard, but after all this time, the pain doesn't faze me as much as it did in the beginning. "Oh, baby, far from it. He's already replaced you."

"Liar!" I yell back, equally as loud. He hates it when I fight back. I don't think he's used to noncompliant girls. "Jamie," I holler in spite. He would never, could never replace me with another girl. I'm it for him the same as he's it for me.

"Okay, Wild Cat." He takes a step away from me, his black combat boots retreating. I hate when he calls me that pet name. I hate when he calls me by the name I've gone by my whole life. I hate when he says anything at all to me. Pain—emotionally and often physically—soon follows. "I guess I'll just have to enlighten you then."

Seconds later, he's back in front of me, tossing six-by-four photographs at me, hitting me in the face, the arm, my lap, all of them of people—a couple. I pick one up, seeing the face of the boy I long to see again. My love. My Jamie.

Only he isn't alone in the photo. Jules is in it with him, and they're . . .

Oh, my God, I think I'm going to throw up. Bile rises in my throat.

I drop the photo to my lap and pick up another. They're . . . kissing.

I throw it down, grabbing another and then another. It's an intimate shot. They're having sex, and I know for sure I'm not going to be able to stop. I turn my head, my body trying to puke, only nothing comes out because I haven't eaten or had anything to drink in I don't know how long. A day, maybe two.

"No."

"Yes," he counters. I turn back around, my butt inching backward. The thin, now dingy, long tank top I'm wearing does nothing to damper the bite of the cold metal pole that my chains are attached to when my back comes in contact with it.

He wouldn't do that to me, to us. He wouldn't. There has to be a mistake. It has to be fake. He loves me. He's only ever been with me, and I him. We were each other's first, and we are supposed to be each other's last.

"You've been in this dump—my form of Hell—with me for seven weeks, and all this time, he's been fucking your best friend. He doesn't miss you. He doesn't want you. He doesn't love you. You were replaceable."

"No," I bite out. "I don't believe you. You're a liar. You kidnap girls. You're a sick freak."

"Most of that, yes. A liar I am not. His small, teenage dick is probably deep inside her cunt right now, Wild Cat, fucking the memory of you away. Everyone is replaceable. Everyone is forgettable. Even you." He firms his stance, crossing his arms over his large chest. "Are we going to have a good day or a bad one?"

His cell phone rings from one of the pockets of his black denim jeans. He could be beautiful if he wasn't so vile. Even so, I have to admit, his features are nothing like you'd think if you imagined what the bogeyman looked like. Josh has honey-blond hair, light crystal-blue eyes, and a rock-hard body. He's someone you'd picture on one of those muscle or fitness magazines, or even a famous actor in action movies. His features are what's most deceiving about him. Looking at him, you'd never imagine he's a human trafficker.

Snatching his phone out of his pocket, he eyes the screen and then purses his lips in annoyance.

"Fuck," falls from his pouty, full lips. "I'm busy," he answers. "What do you want? I've told you repeatedly to stop calling me. I bought her. You don't get to know anything else about her, where she is, or what kind of condition she's in. She's mine to do as I please, to sell to whoever I want."

Chills ripple down my spine. *Sell?* I never considered he'd sell me. Kill me? Sure, but never sell.

I never even knew this was a thing. Selling people. Who the hell does that?

"I'm sorry. What was that?" His voice becomes low, lethal. His crystal-blue eyes bore into mine so hard that I think he can see straight behind me to the pole my back is leaning against. "Pregnant. You sold me a pregnant bitch? What the hell am I supposed to do with some pregnant cow?"

Oh no! He knows. But how? Only one other person knew. I hadn't gotten a chance to tell Jamie before I was abducted. There is no way someone else could have known.

"Oh, you'll be sorry. Maybe not today. Or tomorrow. But very soon, you'll be sorry you ever contacted me in the first place, little girl." He pulls the phone away from his ear, his eyes still on mine. My chest pounds, fear mounting with every heavy breath I take. "Something you want to tell me, Elise?"

I shake my head from side to side, fearing what he'll do, fearing what he won't do.

He takes two steps back, reaching for something underneath the table. I can't see what's in his hand. He's keeping it hidden behind his back, but I know whatever it is, isn't good.

"Please don't," I plead, unsure of what I'm pleading for. My life? My unborn child's life?

I haven't allowed myself a second to think about the baby I found out about only hours before he took me. I couldn't let myself think about what could happen to him, or her. It's a miracle he hasn't found out before now. I haven't gained any weight. In fact, I've lost pounds. I haven't had the morning sickness I've only heard about. But what I haven't had, that even he should have caught, was my period. I'm fairly sure I've missed two of them.

With his free hand, he pulls the remote from his pocket that controls the raising and lowering mechanism of my chains. Panic starts to set in, taking root inside my chest. *What is he going to do?*

"Don't worry, my defiant little Wild Cat. After I'm done with you, I'm going for her next. She'll pay for deceiving me. I'll even let you in on a little secret. The man I sell her to won't be near as nice as the man I'm going to sell you to. That's a promise."

Her? Does he mean Julia? Is that who he was speaking to? Surely not. It can't be. If she knew I was here, she would have told someone. She would have had me rescued. She's my best friend. We've been best friends since her first day of ninth grade when she started as a new student at Thatcher High School nearly three years ago.

"Please don't," I beg again. The cable reel that's connected to the top of the pole creaks, the chain attached to my cuffs starts to pull upward. "I'll do whatever you want. I'll stop talking back. I'll be good. Please don't hurt my baby," I cry.

I push up on my feet, slipping around to the other side of the pole, using it as a shield. The chain slowly inches up, the slack in it being pulled tighter.

"Please don't." I cry harder, tears rapidly falling down my face one right after another. "Please."

"This is a business, Elise. I thought I'd established that with you already. I can't sell you for a profit if you're pregnant. Pregnant chicks aren't good for business, so . . ." He leaves his words hanging, letting me fill in the blanks. He's not going to allow me to remain pregnant. And I don't know how I'm going to stop him when I've been unsuccessful for weeks in getting out of these restraints, let alone this room. I haven't seen sunlight since he tossed me in here.

His right hand falls from behind his back to his side, revealing a bat clutched in his fist.

Horror.

Dread.

Fear.

Those emotions take center stage.

If he thinks I'm going to stand here and take his beating, his murdering of my child, then he's got another thing coming. In the end, I know I'll only make it worse, but I have to at least try. I may only be seventeen, a kid myself, but I want this baby. I want it with Jamie. This life inside of me didn't ask for any of this. Hell, I didn't ask for any of this. But it's here, I'm here, and I have to do everything within my power to protect it, protect him or her. Protect me.

I'm able to dodge the first blow. Josh's bat connects with the pole instead of my body. The chain tightens, pulling my arms up until I'm standing on my tiptoes. When the second hit comes, my left side takes the full force of the wooden bat; the hard, unforgiving material connects with bone.

I scream, not able to hold it in like I usually do. Then again, he's never been this brutal.

Wrapping my hands around the chain, I hold on for dear life and raise my legs, pulling them into my stomach, doing the only thing I can think of that might protect my baby, knowing deep inside it's futile. Still, it's my only hope. And hope is all I have.

"Here's how this is going to work. If you say the name Jamie ever again, if you think of his name again, you'll remember this moment. You'll remember what I took from you. You'll remember what every blow felt like. You'll feel every single hit like it's happening all over again."

My other side and my back take the next hit, this time harder than the first. Another lands, hitting my ankle and making my legs drop. That's when he's able to connect with my abdomen, over and over and over again, until I can't hold myself up any longer.

"And so help me if I ever hear his name come from your lips again, you won't live to regret it."

More hits follow, a cracking sound with it, making me think for only a second that the bat broke or split in two. That thought goes out the window when a burning, skin-tearing licks across my back have wails I didn't know I could produce flying out of my mouth. This new, searing pain overtakes the blows he's hammering on my body, and it's the last thing I feel before everything goes black.

CHAPTER FIVE

JAMIE

Present

The video ends, and I bolt down the hall and into the bathroom, barely making it to the sink before bile catapults up my esophagus and vomit pours out of my mouth into the porcelain basin. I continue throwing up until I'm dry heaving.

Turning on the faucet, I let water pool into my palm and then bring my hand to my lips, slurping the water into my mouth. I rinse and spit into the sink, then I splash cold water on my face.

Glancing at myself in the mirror, Trey's words from before come rushing back, pounding through my skull. *She didn't betray us, did she?* What he really meant was *we betrayed her.* I betrayed her by not believing her, by not trusting in what we had. I betrayed the only girl—now a woman—that I have ever loved.

My heartache, her heartache, everyone's heartache was always on me. Never her. I did this to me, to us.

I'm still haunted by the look she had in her brown eyes the

night she showed back up, the night she walked in and caught me having sex with my now ex-wife.

The sight before me disgusts me, so I do the only thing that feels right. I let my right fist connect with the glass in front of me, punching through it and through the drywall behind the mirror. It does nothing to stop the memory of my past from assaulting my head.

Eighteen years ago

WHY CAN'T SHE SHUT THE FUCK UP?

All I wanted was to get shit-faced, fuck, and then pass out. That had been the plan since I woke up this morning. It's the same plan as every other day for the past . . . hell, I don't even know anymore. A month? Two months? Three?

It feels like she's been gone much longer than the eighty-nine days she hasn't been here. Disappeared. Left me. No note, or text, not even one damn phone call. She left me. She left us. I was in this for life. Had been in it for life since the second our eyes connected. There was something about Jenna Elise Thomas that I wanted and needed even from an early age.

I loved her. My pathetic self still loves her even though she apparently doesn't feel the same. I never saw it coming. Was I that blind to what was in front of me? The guys don't seem to think so; not even Cole and he couldn't stand my girlfriend.

Can I even still call her that if she didn't bother to break up with me before she took off?

Julia said she'd been planning to run away for a couple of weeks. She'd know. Elise and Jules have been inseparable for the past couple of years. At first, I hated all the time Elise had been spending with the new girl in school. They became fast friends, and it was like I lost half of her time.

I never complained. I didn't have the right to. Elise never said one negative thing any time I hung out with my friends—my bandmates. She and Cole were always at each other's throats, but not once did she ask me to stop hanging out with him or ditch my friends to spend more time with her. She encouraged me more than anyone—my parents, my family, even my band—to practice, to hone my skills as a singer and guitar player. When I wasn't feeling it, she'd push me even more. Every day we were together, she would tell me that I was going to make it big one day. That the whole band would, and she'd be right beside me, watching us in glory.

So why isn't she here with me now?

Why did she ditch me—us? And for who?

That pisses me off so much that my skin burns to hit something, someone, anything in my path.

According to Julia, she met some douchebag at one of our local shows one weekend back in late April and then up and ran off with him a week before school let out for the summer. I missed my high school graduation because I could barely function. At the time, I didn't believe she'd just leave without so much as a goodbye. That would have shown I'd at least meant something to her.

I was convinced something bad had happened to her.

When she never showed up at my house that night, I felt it in my gut. It was like someone had put a vise around my heart, captured it, and was squeezing the life out my body.

And although my heart was ripped from my chest, it wasn't because something bad had happened to my girlfriend. It was Elise's own doing that broke me. Had she taken a gun and fired a shot through me, it would have been less painful than her leaving and not having the balls to tell me to my face.

She got Jules to do it for her, the fucking bitch.

"Come on," she whines from above me. "Move harder, Jamie."

The way she says my name has me constantly swallowing back down the bile crawling up my throat.

With more strength than I think I have in the drunken state I'm in, I push up, lifting off the bed and taking her with me. I pull her off my dick, flip her around onto her knees, and then slam back inside her pussy.

"You want it harder?" I bite out through clenched teeth, pissed off at the world and everyone in it. "I'll give it to you so hard you'll be screaming in pain rather than pleasure."

"Yes," she says breathlessly, clenching her walls around my cock. It excites her the more I act like an asshole. "Give it to me, baby."

"Shut up!" I bark and then slam into her harder. *I'm not hers.* I'm not her boyfriend. She doesn't get to call me that. No one will get to call me that ever again. From here on out, girls are just there for one thing—the heat between their thighs. It's all they're good for because I'll be damned if I trust another one. I certainly won't hand over my heart on a silver platter again to get used and abused and then tossed out like trash.

"So good," she says, ignoring my order. "You're the best, Jamie."

Like I give two shits if I'm the best dick she's ever had. Her pussy certainly isn't the best I've experienced, and in the last several weeks, I've had a lot to compare it to. None of them measure up to the best I've been inside. Not even close.

Elise.

I hate her.

I fucking hate her!

"It's true," comes a whisper, stopping me, and I freeze on the bed, my eyes locked on the bare, cream-colored wall above my headboard.

She's back.

Elise is here.

There is a sharp intake of air, followed by another and then another until I think she's hyperventilating.

Coming to my senses from the shock of hearing her voice, I shove Julia forward and off my dick. I snatch the black top sheet from beneath us, pulling it around me the best I can, and I plant my naked ass on the bed, my eyes meeting hers for the first time in months.

Her fair skin is flushed, red splotches coat her neck and up her cheeks. Tears cloud her brown eyes, running down her makeup-free face. The first instincts that come to mind are to rush to her and comfort her, make the crying stop. But then I remember everything that's happened in the three months she's been gone. I remember every moment of hell that her actions have put me through. All the anger that has manifested since the day Julia made me realize the truth triples.

"Well, look what the cat dragged in." My brows furrow, my jaw tightens, hardening to steel right along with my heart. "Did you think I'd sit around waiting for you to up and return, baby?"

Her hand flies to her mouth, her palm covering it just as a sob breaks loose as her knees buckle and she hits the carpeted floor.

I jump off the bed and yank my jeans up my legs without my boxers.

"How could you?" she asks, her head tipping up to gape at me from where she remains crumpled in the doorway.

Cole's tall frame appears behind Elise's.

"Jamie, what the hell?" He nods down in front of him, and then his eyes grow rounder when he notices Julia in my bed. I glance over, noting a smug grin on her face as she holds the sheet to her chest. It strikes me as odd, but then Cole's voice pulls my attention back to the open bedroom door. Back to Elise. The desire to go to her is still there, but I force it to leave. I will not comfort the bitch that did this to me. She doesn't deserve it. And the horror on her face tells me she's getting back all of the hurt she's caused me—and that's exactly what she deserves.

Hell, I might as well pour alcohol on this wound. I take a step toward my bed, reach for Julia, and pull her into my arms, planting a kiss on her too-thin lips. I watch Elise the whole time, unable to look away even though this is hurting me just as much as it's destroying her.

"Jamie, stop!" Cole yells. I don't know what his goddamn problem is. He seems to hate Julia more so than he dislikes Elise. He's been against us fucking since I started screwing Julia Montgomery. She was Elise's best friend. Even Jules declared Elise had left her too. What better way to say *fuck you* to the girl that damaged my heart than to nail her best friend?

I push Jules off, shoving her back to the bed.

"Jamie," Cole calls out again.

Elise's hands go to her ears, covering them as she casts her eyes to the floor. "Stop saying his name," she pleads, her body starting to rock back and forth, pain etched on her tear-soaked face.

Elise was never the crying type. In the years I've known her, I can count the times I've witnessed her tear up on one hand. She comes off strong, and she is. That was just one of the numerous things I loved about her. She wasn't sensitive like so many other girls. No one messed with her except Cole. They knew not to. They knew she'd beat their ass, and they knew I'd beat their ass right after she did.

I step toward her, squatting down directly in front of her, and pull her hands away from her ears. The spark that's always ignited every time we touch electrifies my whole body, but I fight it, not wanting it.

"She fucks better than you too," I lie, right to her beautiful face, hating myself instantly and not understanding why. She deserves this. She deserves worse. "Go back to wherever you came from. I don't want you. I never want to see you again."

I stand and then step right over her, shoving past my best friend in the process, saying, "Get her out of my house." It's my parents' house, but whatever.

"Wait." The word sounds like a plea and so very wrong coming from Elise's mouth. She's never had to beg me for a damn thing. Until now, I've always been more than willing to give her anything she's ever asked for or, in most cases, demanded.

"Fuck. You," I say, throwing up both middle fingers and not knowing if she can see me just before I take the stairs, needing to get out of this house. I can't breathe with her this close again. I pick up my pace, the front door in my line of sight. If I don't get away from here now, I'm not so sure I'll have the strength to avoid going back in and begging her myself to take me back, make us right again.

She did this to us.

I won't be the one that gives her a second chance, not when she's the one that pissed all over us in the first place.

I won't have mercy.

It'll be a cold day in Hell before I forgive her for the things she's done.

CHAPTER SIX

JENNA

Eighteen years ago

It took Josh seven weeks to break me. He thought it would take another seven to put me back together, mend what he had broken, and mold me into who he wanted me to become. He underestimated me from the very beginning. What took him weeks to achieve only took me seven days to do to him.

"Are you sure this is what you want?" His voice is hard, unforgiving in the manner in which he speaks. That isn't something that has changed from the time I first met Josh to right now, where I sit in the passenger side of his pickup truck, staring at the house of the boy I've longed to see again. It's been nearly twelve weeks since I've been gone; eighty-nine days since I've seen him or anyone else other than the man that took me captive with the intent to sell me to the highest bidder.

"I wouldn't have requested it had I not been sure."

"It's not a good idea. You shouldn't be here, Cat." He rarely calls me "Wild Cat" anymore, preferring to shorten the nickname or call me by my first name, Jenna instead. I prefer either over Elise now. Since I've recovered, hearing my middle name on his lips makes my stomach roll. It brings back memories I'd rather forget ever happened.

I'm not suffering from Stockholm syndrome. I don't fully trust the man sitting to my left but don't distrust him either. We've found common ground, so to speak. There isn't that much difference between him and me. He was born into *this* business. He was raised in it the same as his parents before him.

You learn a lot when you bring a man to his knees, strip him bare. At first, that hadn't exactly been my goal, but a few days after my beating, when I finally opened my eyes and saw what my condition was doing to him, an idea sparked.

It saved my life. It's why I'm sitting beside him now, unchained, no longer his captive like I was back inside that windowless bare room—my former cell.

It was a warehouse like I had thought it might be. A large space in a crime-ridden shitty city five hours from where I grew up. Just one state over, close to the Gulf of Mexico. In hindsight, I think it would have been easy for him to get rid of me, make me disappear to never be seen again had his original plan worked out. Had I not been pregnant. The thing I knew from the moment I read that stick changed everything. Just not in the way I had first thought it would.

"This is exactly where I should be. I need him. I know you don't understand that, and I don't know how to make you, but it is what it is. I've always loved him, and in spite of everything, I still love him. I still want him. There is no way I'd be able to stay away from him, Josh."

Yet, even I have to admit there is something that's holding me from catapulting out of this truck and into that house to find him. It's not that I don't want to, because I do. It's that I'm scared of what I'll find when I lay eyes on him again. Those pictures still haunt me. I can't get the images out of my head, and every time I close my eyes it's the only thing I see. Sleep is futile most of the time.

This is a different kind of fear. This is something inside my gut telling me walking inside that house isn't going to be the welcoming I expect it to be. Like a premonition, knowing I have to walk through it no matter the outcome.

I have to have faith, though, don't I? Trust in what Jamie and I have. After all, love is supposed to outlast everything, stand the test of time. With love, you're supposed to be able to get past all the bad. We may be teenagers, but I know what love is.

"If you're sure about this, then you need to let me take care of her."

Julia.

I never would have thought she'd be capable of such things. I knew she was rich, her parents wealthy. I didn't compute that to mean she had the means to hire someone to kidnap me, get me out of the picture so that she could have Jamie for herself.

Had I not seen the proof with my own eyes, I wouldn't have believed Josh when he told me everything. He had pictures of them meeting together, a recording of their conversation, his insurance policy had she tried anything or gone to the police.

She's sixteen, for Christ's sake, five months younger than me. She'll turn seventeen two weeks from now. What teenager thinks something like this up? What person plans this sort of thing out and then goes through with it? One that's even more devious than the man I'm sharing air with.

"No," I force out, turning my head to survey the side of his. He's still beautiful. He's still hard too. I don't have an ounce of sexual attraction for him. Some might think it's because of everything he's done to me, but I know it's simpler than that. I've only ever had eyes for James Hart. Jamie has been it since the beginning. He'll always be *the one.* "We talked about this. You can't do that ever again. You've changed, Josh. You can't go back to that life. You swore that you would go the opposite way."

Josh isn't evil. He has evil ways, but deep down, he isn't evil to the core. Had he been, he never would have felt remorse for what he did to me. He never would have taken care of me, cleaned me, helped me to heal as properly as he could without taking me to a hospital.

I have a nasty, ugly, angry scar across my back where his bat splintered and dug into my skin as he hit me over and over with it. He thinks I had two broken ribs, and ninety percent of my body was covered in bruises. The bruises are gone, but the markings inside and out still remain.

He asked me for my forgiveness. I haven't given it to him yet, but I want to. I just don't know when that'll be or if I'll ever be able to say it out loud.

"What's one more time?" His head rolls to face me. "You can't sit there and say she doesn't deserve it."

I turn my head, gazing out of the window, back to the house. There's a party going on inside if all the cars and the lights are any indications. Jamie's parents must be out of town.

"I wouldn't put my worst enemy through a minute of what I went through. So, don't. I said, no. Leave it at that. You promised, Josh," I remind him.

"And I won't touch a hair on her blonde head until you give me the go-ahead to do so."

"That day will never come."

"Never say never, sweetheart."

"As long as you keep your word by never kidnapping or harming an innocent person again and rescue those that you can, I'll never tell anyone your identity."

"I didn't ask you to do that, Jenna," he whispers, finally calling me by the name I've requested him to use. I can't stomach my middle name anymore, associating it with all the things that happened while I was held against my will.

"You didn't have to. You want my forgiveness, right? Then I need you to do what you've promised. It's the only way you'll ever get it." I glance back to him, his eyes still on me. "Thanks for bringing me home. Thanks for letting me go."

Present

A DOOR INSIDE MY HOUSE SLAMS, PULLING ME OUT OF A MEMORY I haven't thought of in years. There's no doubt that this morning's encounter is having an ill effect on me. That wasn't the only thing I thought of today. In fact, too many things from all those years ago have clouded my head.

It's why I had to bow out of work early. I wasn't making progress, so it was pointless being there. It's Saturday anyway. It's not like I can't catch up come on Monday. Still, we have a case to solve, and there is always someone that needs saving, but my lack of focus wasn't helping.

Josh knew it. Malachi knew it. Hell, even Kelly, the newest agent on our task force, knew something was wrong. I wasn't acting like myself. When I'm on the job, I'm always focused and able to stay on point. I don't get distracted. Being a federal agent, I can't afford to let my personal life affect my work life. Other people's lives depend on my skill in locating and dismantling human trafficking rings in and around the Los Angeles County area.

Being a survivor of human trafficking drove me down this career path. I know what goes through a captive's psyche. I know their fears, their hopes, their pain.

After I returned home, I finished my senior year of high

school being homeschooled. I did two years of junior college while working a full-time job. Then, one day out of the blue, Josh showed up, taking me by surprise and scaring the hell out of me. It had been three years since I'd last seen him, but there hadn't been a day that had gone by in those three years that I hadn't seen his face in my dreams.

At first, I thought and feared, he'd returned to take me all over again. To finish a job he'd left unfinished.

I was wrong. He was there to recruit me, and nearly fourteen years later, here I am, an FBI agent who works alongside the man that kidnapped her eighteen years ago. Even now, it sometimes seems surreal.

Laughter and joking pull my eyes toward the small opening that peers into my small kitchen. The boys are home. My heart always skips a beat when one of them walks into a room.

"Do you have something you'd like to tell me, Brandon?" I ask, forcing my voice to harden into the stern tone both of them know not to test. It always works. They both stop in their trek to the stairs, turn, and face me.

Daniel's expression drops, annoyance marring his beautiful features. It makes him look older than his teenage years—and I hate it. His dark-blue eyes stand out against his tan skin and jet-black hair.

"Whatever it is, can't you let it go until tomorrow?" he asks but doesn't stop to let me answer. "We both need to shower and get ready for tonight."

"Stay out of this, Danny. This is between your brother and me. Go practice or study for next week's test. Go do something," I order. "It's hours before either of you need to be there. The band doesn't start playing until nine."

Ten Seven is a small dive bar that I own jointly with Malachi. We don't run it, as we don't have the spare time, but it's something we enjoy as a side business that's separate from our law enforcement career. It's not far from a precinct down the block. There are always more badges in there at any given hour than there are civilians.

Amateur bands play nightly. Confessions, my boys' alternative rock band, plays there every few weeks, depending on if one of them is grounded.

I mock a fake laugh, turning on the couch to face them. "That is if you both make it there to play in the first place. So . . ."

I know what he did, and although I'm not mad at him, he still got into trouble yet again at school yesterday. This has to stop. I'm tired of having the same conversation with him over and over.

Danny grabs the rail at the bottom of the stairs. "You're on your own, bro." Then he ascends, taking the steps two at a time, leaving his younger brother down here with me to face the music of his actions.

He blows out a breath of air before stepping toward me, his platinum-blond hair and fair features a stark contrast next to his brother's polar opposite looks.

Damn kids think they know everything. Think they're smarter than everyone else too. In their defense, they're both too smart for their own good. It gets them in more trouble than not.

This is the part of parenting that I hate. I don't like reprimanding either of them, but someone has to teach them to grow up to be good, hardworking men that I hope they'll turn into one day.

"Take a seat." I flick my eyes, telling him where to go, my voice firm when on the inside I am anything but.

Here we go again.

CHAPTER SEVEN

JAMIE

That video gutted me.

Realizing I've been wrong about everything this whole time shredded me. Ripped me apart from the inside out. Leaving every pore on my skin open and bleeding. *We could have been together this whole time.*

I haven't felt the burning sensation that lives just below the surface of my skin in years—but it's back with a vengeance. When I was mad or upset as a kid, it felt like I was burning alive inside my own body. It was painful. I couldn't control it. My parents took me to doctors, specialists, psychiatrists. They all said it was in my head. It wasn't really there.

Bullshit.

I felt it. They didn't. It was real. I can't explain it. I still don't understand it myself, but I did learn the signs. I started to recognize when it was about to happen. I could walk away from the situation to avoid it happening, or I could forge through it. Force it out of my mind, which is what I did most of the time.

Over the years, it's lessened so much that I thought it'd just stopped, went away for good. I was wrong. My skin is hot to the touch, like my blood is boiling underneath. Sweat begins rolling off my body like it's the middle of July in Mississippi instead of the cool mid-January Southern California breezes.

I don't miss those days. I haven't been back home in years. I don't miss that place either. It was a reminder of what I had lost. Only now, I know I was wrong, so wrong that I don't even know where to start or how I got here. I haven't had time to fully process it or figure out where I got off track. I don't even remember when I stopped thinking something bad had happened to Elise and started to believe she ditched me. That she didn't love me as much as I loved her.

This is fucked up.

She was pregnant with my baby when she was kidnapped. She was beaten until she lost him or her. The thought that she had to deal with all of that alone sends a cold shiver down my spine. Only it doesn't cool me off. The heat, if anything, is a cold burn that hurts far worse.

"We're here," Seth says, pulling to a stop alongside a curb and parking his Range Rover across the street from what appears to be a small dive bar. *Ten Seven* is what the sign above the entrance displays in bright-blue neon. Makes me think of the code for when officers go off duty. I have a buddy that works for Santa Clarita PD. We met when he would do security side jobs for the band when we used to do smaller shows back in the day. Now that we're a lot bigger, he's just a friend of the band. "Did you check his phone location to make sure he's still showing in this area?"

After spending time puking my guts up, then smashing a lot of things in Cole's house after he wouldn't answer his phone, it finally dawned on me that I knew the password to his account. That gave me access to the GPS on his cell phone, locating him. He's been at this location damn near all day, but the guys wouldn't let me come hours ago. They wanted me to cool off so I wouldn't do something stupid that I'd later regret.

I haven't. Not one damn degree have I chilled. I have since calmed down, though. I'm not hysterical like I was this morning after watching that brutal, sickening video.

What kind of sick fuck records that kind of shit? He better pray to God I never find him because if I do, I won't stop with the same beating he gave Elise. I'll end his miserable life. He took Elise from me. He hurt her beyond comprehension. He murdered our child.

I honestly don't know how she survived what she went through. And I won't have those answers until I find Cole and then her. I can't lie to myself. I'm scared. I'm scared of seeing her again, knowing I let her down, let us down. She didn't do anything wrong. I did. And for that, I'm not sure if I can ever forgive myself.

Had I handled things differently, I would never have been in a loveless marriage. I would have been with the girl I fell in love with twenty-five years ago. Elise would have been my partner, my friend, my wife.

It feels like my heart is being crushed all over again. Maybe because it is.

"He's still here," I tell them, looking down at the lit-up screen in my lap that shows Cole is inside that bar across from us. From inside Seth's vehicle, I hear music, a live band, but I can't bring myself to reach for the door handle.

I don't know if I can do this.

⚓

IT'S HALF AN HOUR BEFORE I STEP OUTSIDE INTO THE NIGHT AIR. The streets are busy. There are always locals and tourists everywhere in LA. It's not like back home where you know everyone, and they know you, your parents, and even your grandparents.

Here, actors are a dime a dozen, trying to make it big. Celebrities are followed and harassed by the paparazzi. We've been lucky for the most part. We're famous, but our band doesn't appear in the media every day of the week. We can usually go out as we please, with the occasional fan coming up and asking for a selfie for their Instagram page.

We are adored by our fans and usually accommodate their requests. It's only when they get outrageous that we try to laugh it off, so we don't upset them or hurt a fan's feelings. There is an endless line of chicks available for any of us, and we've all been known to taste what's being offered. It's the crazy ones that think it's okay to touch without permission that you have to be cautious of.

So, right now, while my head is all kinds of fucked up, I'm grateful no one is staring at us or racing up, asking for an autograph. I couldn't deal with any of that right now.

The three of us silently cross the street. Trey still hasn't made a sound all day. He seems lost inside his head too, but I can't deal with his emotions on top of my own.

Walking through the single door, I pause just inside. It's bigger than I imagined, judging from the outside. My initial thought was dead on I see as I observe several patrons wearing weapons holstered to their hip—cops. Though, some of the people in here don't appear old enough to be out of high school yet. Must be a young or teenage band playing tonight.

The place is set up more pub style with dim lighting. Most of the tables are full, with people eating and talking. I keep looking around for the man that has one hell of a nerve to drop a bomb like that in my lap, then not stick around to help pick up the pieces.

Goddamn him. He'll be lucky if I don't deck him just for the hell of it.

"Huh," Seth breathes, making me stop scanning the spacious interior, searching for Cole, to glance over in his direction.

"What?" I ask, taking stock of his profile from where he stands next to me. Trey is on his other side, hands in his pockets with his head pointed to the ground.

I guess I should understand why he's taking all this *almost* as hard as I am. He and Elise were friends too. He was more hurt over what I thought she had done than Cole or Seth were. Seth was angry. Cole seemed more confused than not, and now I guess I know why. Well, no, I don't, actually. He questioned the reason behind her disappearance, but even he said it sounded far-fetched. So, the question is, why hasn't he told me any of this before now? And how long has he known the truth?

"That kid," is all he says, nodding to where there is a small stage toward the back. In front of the stage is a vacant dance floor surrounded by tables and chairs. Currently, the drummer and guitarist are the only members of the band taking up space on the stage. The sound is low but steady. Their front man, or woman, is nowhere in sight.

"What about some kid?" I ask, frustrated that this is what has him distracted when we're here for two reasons: find Cole, get answers.

"There's something about him." He pauses, his head cocking to the side. "There's something familiar, but I can't put my finger on it."

"Who cares?" I blurt out, turning my head to scan the room once again. My eyes land on Cole's frame almost immediately but then fall to the woman standing in front of him with her back against his broad, solid chest. *Not sleeping with her, my ass.* Her red hair is down tonight versus when she had it pulled up this morning. The back stops just below her shoulder blades, and the front is in choppy layers.

Damn, I can almost remember what it felt like to grasp hold of those strands while I was inside her.

Cole's arm is wrapped around her chest, holding her to him. Watching them is pissing me off and making my skin singe.

"What is it?" Seth whispers as if to himself, but I ignore him.

"Today, dude, today," a young but deep voice rumbles through a microphone. My eyes never veer from my best friend and the woman I'm still clearly hung up on after eighteen long miserable years without her.

"I'm here. I'm here," another male voice says.

"Took your sweet time."

"It's called a break," he quirks, humor in a voice I realize I know all too well. Suddenly my eyes flick over to the stage where the lead vocalist has taken his spot at the front of the stage behind the mic stand.

"You never said Brandon was in a band." Seth's voice has an accusing tone.

"I had no idea," I admit, watching in amazement. I didn't even know he liked music, let alone knew how to sing or perform. He's never said anything or mentioned this. He's never taken an interest in my band.

A smirk forms on his face, then he leans forward, his lips touching the mic in front of him. "This is called 'Lay It Out.'"

The electric guitar starts, followed by the drums, then Brandon's voice hits my eardrums, eliciting something I'm guessing is pride, or joy, or . . . something. A smile tugs at the corners of my mouth for the first time in I don't know how long. He's good; different from me but good nonetheless.

"Damn," Seth says, my thoughts echoing his words.

"Stop." Elise's voice pulls my eyes away from being in awe of my son's talent. She's still standing in the same spot, too close to my so-called best friend, only now she has a microphone in her right hand. "Brandon," she starts.

"Jesus Christ, Mom! Can't we just play?"

There's a sharp intake of air to my right side, coming from Seth's mouth, only inches away from my ear.

My gaze snaps back to the stage. The young guitar player that Seth was going on and on about just minutes ago looks frustrated. I watch him as his ass lifts off his stool, as if in defiance. Sliding my eyes back to Elise, I see both of them having a silent stare down.

A prickling feeling runs down my body when I realize what the kid called her. *Mom.* She's his mother.

"Brother," Seth breathes, shock evident on his tongue. "He looks just like you." There's a shudder that slips past his lips. "That's what it was. That's why he seemed so familiar. That kid could be your double. A clone. Jamie, that was you at seventeen." He says everything I'm thinking in my own head.

"Daniel James," she seethes, her voice lethal.

My eyes close, shutting my lids tight. I can't watch. I can't look at that stage and see both of my sons up there. *Sons.* Plural. I no longer just have one. I have two.

And they know each other?

What the hell is really going on?

CHAPTER EIGHT

JENNA

I have to lock my jaw to avoid lashing back at him for his out-of-line outburst. He's usually more controlled than this. His brother is the loose cannon, the one that doesn't think before he speaks. Danny isn't like that, or wasn't. Maybe being around Brandon more and more is changing him.

I don't know if that's good or bad. Brandon isn't a bad kid by any means. He hasn't had the upbringing he should have had, but that isn't his fault.

"I'm sorry," he says, the remorse in his voice cooling the heat coursing through my veins. He finally plants his behind back against the edge of the stool, his eyes dropping down in shame, as they should.

"Danny," Brandon chuckles from his spot in the center of the stage. "If you were so hell-bent on getting grounded, all you had to do was say so." Another laugh bubbles out of him, and I have to shake my head. "You know I would have told Jen way before now that you skipped first period yesterday morning to make out with your girlfriend."

"Magdalena," a deep, familiar voice roars from the bar top twenty feet behind me.

Jesus Christ, he had to go there. That boy doesn't know when to keep his trap closed.

"I'm going to beat your ass," Danny warns. It only results in making Brandon bend over in hysterics. Not that he's ever taken his brother's threats seriously. He doesn't have a reason to. Danny isn't afraid to fight, loves it in fact, but Brandon never has and never will be on the other end of his fist. They are best friends and brothers. Have been friends since they were two years of age, even when they were both clueless about the DNA they share.

Maggie stands from her seat closest to the stage, searching for her father, no doubt. That girl will be lucky if he lets her leave home for school after tonight.

"The two of you have done enough ass kicking this week," I remind them, my expression back to seething as I remember the call I received from their principal yesterday afternoon. I can't stand that man, and for some reason, he has it out for Brandon. Not like I don't know why. Brandon cuts up too often, but a lot of it's because he's bored and doesn't have anything better to do with his time, and his GPA happens to be standing in the way of Principal Latham's own son.

Brandon stands upright, back to his full five-foot-eleven-inch height, arms raised in the air, a smirk on his lips. "I didn't touch one hair on his ugly head."

"No, you just instigated it like you always do," I say, placing my free hand on my hip. He shrugs in reply. "Now, are you planning on giving an audience worthy performance, or are you going to keep half-assing it up there?" I ask, getting back to the reason why I stopped their performance in the first place.

"I wouldn't exactly call that half-assing," Brandon smarts.

"Neither would I," Trever—the band's drummer and

Danny and Brandon's closest friend—agrees. He bangs on one of the cymbals with the drumstick in his right hand as if to back up his words.

They are good, not great, but good, especially for their age. Danny is only up there because Brandon is and because it's his brother's passion. He can play guitar and has since he was a small kid. I started teaching him when he was a little boy, but it was never something he loved doing. Trever likes the drums, but he likes the attention he gets from girls from playing in a band more than he does the high you get from creating art. Brandon, on the other hand, is a different story. He actually is *damn* good. The other two hold him back, but tonight he is the one half-assing it up there just like I called.

"You are," I say, speaking directly to Brandon. "Even you know you are. You're better than what I just heard. And I'm not going to listen to anything less than what I know you have inside here," I tell him, pointing to the center of my chest. "So, you have two choices. You can put everything you have into the next song you play, or you can hop off that stage. Choice is yours, bud."

He purses his lips, thinking, his sky-blue eyes never leaving mine, and I know immediately what he wants.

"No," I answer.

"Oh, come on," he whines. "It's my birthday. Don't you love me, Jen?"

"Yes, I love you. I love you more than you will ever comprehend. And I already gave you a birthday present, or have you forgotten *not* getting grounded for that shit you started yesterday at school?" I remind him. Brandon isn't my son, but he's been in my life so long that I often forget that he isn't mine. With Jamie on tour twice a year and his piece of shit absentee mother, he basically lives with me most of the time. He even has his own bedroom at my house.

With everything that happened this morning, I'm not so sure I can keep the charade up much longer. It's not fair to Brandon to have to hide his second life. Hell, it's not fair to Cole either, and now that bag is wide open. It wouldn't take much for Jamie to prod and find out everything I never wanted him to know.

"If you let me sing 'Damaged Heart' . . ." His smile widens, waiting for me to give in. He keeps trying, asking, begging me to give him the okay to add a song I wrote years ago to their playlist. Most of their songs he and Danny wrote together. Brandon is a good songwriter in his own right. But that song isn't just *any* ole song that I've written or had a hand in writing. It's *the* song. It's the song I bared my soul in, in hopes it would help me get over his dad. It didn't. And I know now nothing ever will.

I finally sigh, nodding even though I know he's about to shred me to pieces. He just doesn't realize it. And he won't, because I won't allow myself to break in front of my kids.

Cole grabs me by the hips, pulling me back to his chest, knowing what I'm about to feel and not being able to do a damn thing to stop it.

Give me the strength I need to get through this, I plead inside my head.

CHAPTER NINE
JAMIE

S hit.

"What day is it?" I turn, facing my bandmates.

"It's Brandon's birthday?" Seth questions, squinting at me like I'm the shittiest parent he's ever met. Maybe I am. Sure feels that way.

Trey's head has finally lifted, and if I'd had to guess, he's staring at Elise, a war going on in his dark eyes. I'll have to dive into what his hang-up is later. Right now, I have too many other things pressing that I need to deal with.

"What day is it?" I ask again, the notes from the guitar coming through the speakers. The song grabs me, tugging at my chest even though Brandon hasn't started singing yet, my gut tells me I'm in for a ride. She obviously wrote it if he's asking her for permission to sing it.

Does that mean it's about me? Does she even think about me like *that* anymore? Questions plague me, and I want answers to them all.

"Hell, I don't . . ." he says, taking out his cell from the front pocket of his jeans. I turn back around, needing to watch the kids on the stage. "It's January fifteenth."

"Fuck," I draw out. *I forgot my son's birthday.* What the hell is wrong with me?

"You seriously didn't remember?"

"Fuck you," I spit. "I've had a lot on my mind, and then this morning happened. It's not like you remembered either."

"Not my kid," he deadpans.

There's nothing I can say to that. He's right, and no matter the excuse, I should have remembered Brandon's seventeenth birthday. I've never forgotten it before. In fact, I'm always back home for that reason. I purposely make sure my end-of-the-year tour finishes by the first week in January so that I'm home in time to be with him, celebrating. Only this time, I didn't have *that* home to go to. At least his mother would have been there to make his day special. I can count on that, at least.

Does she know about this? Know about Elise . . . or hell, she must go by Jenna these days. Cole called her Jen this morning, and Brandon just called her that a few minutes ago.

It didn't go unnoticed that she told him she loves him. I don't know what she meant about not grounding him since he isn't her son—at least not Brandon anyway. Regardless of their closeness, that's not something she controls or has the authority to do. Julia would flip the fuck out. There is no way my ex-wife knows my ex-girlfriend and our son have any sort of a relationship. I would have heard about it by now. She would have demanded I put a stop to it.

She made it abundantly clear years ago when she found out she was pregnant that if I chose Elise or ever spoke to her again, I'd lose my son and never see him again. At the time, I didn't want to see the girl I was still in love with, so I never called her on that shit. It's the one and the only thing I ever gave her my word on. God knows I never promised to be faithful to her, and I wasn't.

But now, I need answers. I need them tonight before my mind starts making shit up.

The guitarist, Daniel, or Danny, he's good, talented, but it's easy to tell his heart isn't in what he's playing. Makes me wonder why he's even up there if this isn't his bag. Learning to play an instrument is hard enough. Try being in a band and coordinating music with other people. That isn't something anyone who doesn't enjoy it would want to do. Trust me, I know.

Brandon's voice comes through the mic, low at first, starting the song, singing about a former lover, an old flame from long ago. The chorus is where he shines, his voice sounding broken and raw as he belts out the words and screams of pain that slice me wide open.

The lyrics burn a hole through my chest. There is no doubt in my mind they're about me. I'm not conceited. I don't think I'm every woman's fantasy, though I've been told that countless times. I have, however, only ever wanted to be one woman's whole world.

This song, though, isn't that. This song is about soul-crushing heartbreak. It's tragic, but then again, that sums her and me up perfectly. I knew that before today, but now . . .

I shake my head, dropping it in shame and heartache as I run my fingers through my black hair. My eyes close again, and if I don't get something strong down my throat soon, my knees are going to hit the dirty floor I'm standing on.

"She's coaching him," Trey whispers. If the three of us weren't standing so close to each other, I wouldn't have heard him.

My gaze snaps to the dance floor area in front of the stage.

She isn't watching the band. She isn't even looking at the stage. Her eyes are cast toward the ground. She's listening, and by watching her every move, I see the same thing Trey did. Her movements are subtle, but she's telling him when he needs to increase his tone or when to back off. Trey is dead on. She's coaching Brandon.

Brandon is better than the last song he started. This time his voice is crisper, deeper even. He has a punk flair that I'm actually digging. I like alternative rock, but heavy metal will always be where my heart lies. It's the kind of music I typically listen to, and it's the genre of music I write and perform. This is good, though, really good.

Her hand reaches up, swiping her cheek as though she's wiping a tear from her eyes. Her face appears pale under the fluorescent lights shining down from above the stage. Her chest shudders, and it makes me want to run to her and wrap my arms around her body. I've always hated when something bothered her. She tries hard to hide it, but she's always been shit at masking her emotions. I never understood why she did. It's something I've never been afraid to show.

"Jen," Brandon says through the mic, staring down in front of him after the song wraps up. "Why do you look like I just killed the cat? I totally rocked that." He nods, a smile tugging at the corner of his lips.

"Don't care about that stupid cat, but . . ." Her breath rumbles through the mic she's holding, "Yeah, Brando, you did." I can see her from where I stand. The smile on her face is forced, and from the look on my son's face, he knows it too. She's not lying, though. Brandon performed that song spectacularly. His vocals were made for it if you ask me, though I wouldn't mind hearing it from the lips of the woman that wrote it.

"Uh," he breathes out, his hands clutching his chest in mock shock. Even from here, I know the little shit is faking the expression marring his young face. "Are you saying you don't love Maximilian? He's family, Jen. I can't even with you right now." His eyes snap to his audience. "She hates our cat. Who hates animals?"

"He's your cat that I'm forced to feed and house," she states, but I see the smile ghosting her lips—a real one this time and a far better sight than the stark sadness that was radiating off her in waves only seconds ago.

She nods her head off to the side of the stage like she's telling him something and then walks in that direction.

"This next song is a cover. I don't really like doing covers, but . . . since it's my favorite song, I wanna do it. It's called 'Careless.'"

Jenna disappears off to the side of the stage, walking a quick pace down a dark hallway, and for a moment, my attention is back on the stage. "Careless" is the name of a song we released on an album a few years back. I wonder for a second if it could be mine that he's about to play. The wait isn't long. As soon as Danny strums the first few chords, I know it's my song.

My eyes glance back over. Jenna isn't anywhere in sight, and although I want so badly to stay and hear them perform a song I wrote, the pull to go to her is stronger. I take a step in front of Seth, and a hand reaches out, grabbing onto my wrist, applying pressure.

"Aren't you gonna listen?" His tone rushes out, a hint of anger in every word.

"I need to find her. I need answers," I reason.

"But that's your son, playing our song, man. Don't you want to hear it?"

"Sons," I correct through gritted teeth, snatching my wrist from his grasp. His brows furrow, displeased. I don't give two shits what he thinks. Yes, I want to hear Brandon. I want to hear every song he has played tonight and any song in the future. But there is something inside of me that's pulling me toward her like if I don't get there quick enough, she'll be gone, and I won't get another chance.

If I even have another chance to be had.

CHAPTER TEN

JENNA

That song eats more of my soul each time I hear it. There is a part of me—a small part, but it's there—that wishes I never would have put pen to paper, making it real. That's the problem with being a writer, though; you can't physically refrain.

A story can only live inside your head for so long. Eventually, the pull to tell it is too overpowering. You have to get it out, and then it isn't only yours anymore.

It was nine months ago when Brandon found my journal lying open that he discovered that song. Ever since then, he's been dying to perform it, to add it to their set list. He wishes I'd sing it with him, but what he doesn't understand is that I can't. All the screaming I did while I was captured scarred my vocal cords. I can no longer sing and the sound come out pleasant.

A shudder ripples its way through my body, my breath getting caught in my throat. I rest my forehead against the white-painted cinder blocks of the near-empty storage room. There's a door that leads out to the parking lot behind the bar. The need to escape is sitting on my chest, but I'm trying not to let it win out. I can't leave, not while my boys are out there. I promised Brandon I'd do everything within my power to be here through the duration, and that's what I intend to do.

It's not unheard of that my job often calls me away at all hours of the day and night. I don't have the typical eight-hour day shift like most parents do. I told Josh an hour ago I'd knee him in the crotch if he even thought about asking me to leave should duty call.

For a brief moment, the music gets louder, telling me someone has opened the door behind me. As quickly as the light breeze coats my backside, it's gone, but I'm left knowing someone is in here with me, invading my space. It pisses me off and has my jaw locking.

"Cole," I warn, pressing my palms into the cinder block wall in front of me. I needed a breather. I needed a few minutes to myself to regain my control. I didn't need him following me. Not tonight anyway.

The scent I both love and hate floats up, surrounding me when he stops right behind me. Though in my head, he and Cole smell so much alike, I recognize the real thing almost instantly.

An audible gasp rips from my mouth, my head popping off the wall, my chest expanding at rapid speed when warm, rough fingers caress my hip in a way I haven't felt in far too long. My eyes flutter closed for a brief moment, remembering what his touch does to me. It's the hot July sun scorching flesh. It's tingles coursing through me from head to toe. It's the pleasure of melted chocolate coating your tongue. It's sweet champagne flowing down your throat. It's everything at once, but not enough of it at the same time.

It happens like lightning striking. Like the snap of your fingers.

He flips me around, my back meeting the wall and my front

meeting his chest. My ass is lifted, my eyes become level with the storm forming in his dark-blue ones. His lips smash into mine in a fury of movements, his hard body pressing into mine like he wants us to meld, to blend with the wall at my back.

There are no words, only smacking as lips and tongues fight. My nails dig into his biceps as his fingers bruise the back of my thighs as he holds me in place. My legs squeeze around his waist, needing something more than what I'm getting, but I'm so lost in the way his mouth is burning mine that I'm not even sure what it is that I need.

Suddenly, my legs drop, my feet hitting the ground with a thud, then he's going for the button on my jeans. Need like nothing I've ever felt before takes front and center. My jeans and panties are yanked down my legs. He releases me to do the same to his, and then I'm picked up again, my knees spread open as far as they'll go with my clothing bunched around my ankles. My eyes flutter closed, and in the next second, it feels like I'm impaled, and all the air in my body rushes out, my pussy grabbing hold of his cock, holding on for dear life.

My eyes pop open, doubling in size as my mouth forms an O. *Jesus Christ. I don't remember him being this big.*

"Fuck," he draws out, his breath hot against my ear. "You're so tight."

I don't have time to process his words as the urge for more has me using his shoulders to heave against him so he'll move. *Oh, my God.* That feels so good.

"Shit." His head falls against my shoulder. "You're gonna kill me. Jesus, it feels like I'm being strangled in the best possible way."

Can't he just shut the hell up and let me enjoy this?

"Fuck me, Jamie. Just fuck me," I pant.

His body surges forward, pressing me against the cold wall even more. I'm so hot all over, it doesn't even faze me. He pumps into me, his shaft running up and down over my clit in constant contact. Pleasure zings through me.

"Yes," I say, my voice more breathless than I think it's ever been. "Harder," I command, and then I'm rewarded with exactly what I've demanded.

My orgasm tears through me, every nerve inside me coming alive with pleasure. Teeth clamp down on the skin between my neck and shoulder as he spills himself inside me. I'd somehow forgotten this part of him, how he becomes a biter during his own orgasm.

As quickly as the tornado ripped through me, it's over, and like any storm, damage has been left in its wake.

He drops my legs, his body remaining leaned into mine, his breath coming in and out in pants. I quickly shove him away and drop down, yanking my underwear and pants back up my legs.

"Jesus Christ, Jamie, do you go around fucking every woman without a condom?"

God, I can't believe I just let that happen. What the hell is wrong with me? I'm thirty-five-years-old. I'm not some teenager. I shouldn't be losing my senses at my age.

Stupid Jamie Hart and his even stupider masterful cock.

But hell, I haven't come that hard in years. It felt so good.

CHAPTER ELEVEN

JAMIE

S on of a bitch.

In my defense, seeing her look so beautiful when I walked in, with a body that's matured into the hottest piece of ass I've ever laid my eyes on, everything I came in here to say went out the window. Sadness poured off her in waves, and I just wanted to fix it. I needed to place a smile back on her face more than I needed my next pull of air.

I've only not wrapped up my junk with two women—her being one of them. She's the only one I never regretted that choice with. I shouldn't feel that way right now, but there aren't any pangs of regret registering. What does ring out is why I'm standing here in the first place.

I ignore her accusation and dive right in. "Want to tell me why I have a kid I never knew about?"

There are so many questions that want to fly out of my mouth, but that's the one at the forefront of all of them. Hours ago, hell, fifteen minutes ago, I thought our child died— murdered before it ever had a chance at life. I've spent the better part of today mourning a life that was conceived eighteen years ago. He's older than Brandon by weeks or months. I have no idea.

The heat blazing in her brown eyes simmers out, being replaced with something akin to remorse. She's still the same, mostly. The same tales are trapped in those dark irises if you view them at the right angle. Her lids drop to the ground. "I can't right now." Her head shakes.

"We're having this conversation, Eli—"

"Don't call me that," she snaps back, cutting off my words, the fire rekindling in her eyes as they meet mine.

"Fine," I bite out. "Jenna, we're discussing this, and we're doing it now."

"And I said, I can't." She storms past me, pulling the door open, walking away, leaving me standing here alone, needing answers that she doesn't want to give.

Like fuck, I'm not settling for that. I breathe out, air whooshing out of my mouth, and I go after her. My legs are longer, so it only takes a few seconds to catch up with her, but she's made it down the dark hall and out into the bar as the band finishes up the song they're playing. The same pull as before tugs on me, making my eyes go to the stage as I grab onto her bicep, stopping her in front of me.

"So," Brandon starts, "if you've followed us long enough, then you know toward the end of our set, one of us makes a confession on stage. You know, being Confessions and all." He chuckles, and I can't do anything except stand here, staring at my boy, pride consuming me. I just wish I'd known about this. There is nothing I wouldn't have given to have him on tour with me, jamming with the guys and me.

"It should be Danny's turn, but he's given me this one." Brandon's hand lifts, wrapping around the back of his neck, and from where I'm standing, the light hits his face just right, and I can see his brows furrow like he doesn't want to say what's on the tip of his tongue.

"Ah, shit," Jenna whispers, but my eyes never leave my son's. Jenna's back relaxes against my chest, and her head tips back against my shoulder. Whatever it is, she knows, and I don't have a good feeling about what it is he's struggling to say.

A forced smile spreads across his face as he gazes back out at his audience. Everyone is silent, waiting.

"Just for the record, anything I say up here cannot be used against me. This is my safe place, and for any of you badge toters, you might want to think twice before trying because Jen isn't someone you want to mess with."

"Kid, just say whatever it is," someone I can't see says from somewhere in front of the stage. "There isn't one person in this place with balls big enough to cross your mommy."

Brandon's lips quirk, that comment seeming to settle him some, and I'm left to wonder if it was the older-sounding man telling him it's okay to tell us what he wants, or if it was because he referenced Jenna as his mother even though she isn't.

How well do they know each other? That's another question on a long list of them that keep piling up.

"So, yeah," Brandon starts again as Jenna's hands go up to her face for a brief second or two before she drops them to peer back at the stage where Brandon is standing in front of the mic. "A year ago tonight, I did cocaine for the first time," he admits, and I have to grab something in order to remain standing. Jenna's jean-covered hips are the something my hands latch on to as my son continues with his *confession.* "And I liked it. Well, at first, I did. That quickly led to other things that I won't go into, but," he pauses, seemingly searching the audience, "I got in over my head. If it weren't for Jenna, I wouldn't be standing here today." His right hand reaches up, grabbing and squeezing the necklace he's wearing around his neck. "She saved my life. Then she made me promise to never do it again. I kept my word for all of three months. Shit got tough again, and for a split second, the night I OD'd, almost dying, didn't matter anymore. The promise I made to the one woman that treats me as much like her son as Danny is, didn't matter anymore either. I wanted an escape, an out . . . so I took it. The thing is, the reason behind it all is so stupid."

He shakes his head and sighs, his breath vibrating through the microphone. "Anyway, that's my confession. I'm sorry, Jen," he finishes, his eyes once again scanning the large, open space. My guess, he's looking for her. "I screwed up—again."

"Everyone messes up, kid," the same old man from before pipes up, filling the silence that settled around us.

Brandon's head swings in our direction. I know the second his eyes land on us, recognition almost instant. "Well . . . shit." He swallows. "This isn't going to end well for me. Hey, Dad," he says.

"We're talking about that too," I seethe next to Jenna's ear, my eyes never veering away from Brandon.

CHAPTER TWELVE

JENNA

Eighteen years ago

It's a good thing both of my parents have to be up, dressed, and out of the house by six in the morning—every weekday. Otherwise, they would have questioned why I was out the door an hour before the school bell rang, signaling first period.

Dad is the vice president of an advertising firm, and Mom is a Gynecologist, working at the largest hospital in the metro area. My parents have great careers, they're both hardworking, and they try to instill the same drive in me.

Only I've never wanted a nine-to-five like they did. My passion is music, the same as my boyfriend's. I love to create it, and I enjoy performing in front of others. It's a high like no other—seeing the looks on their faces, knowing I'm entertaining and touching their souls with my words and my voice.

Mom and Dad don't get it. Sure, I want to finish high school, but college isn't for me. I know that, and for what I want to do, I don't need it. Jamie isn't planning on going to college next year, but he does plan on sticking around until I graduate in a year. Then I'm ditching this small town with the guys. We're going to Los Angeles, California.

I'm not too worried about Jamie's band. The guys are talented, even Cole's stupid ass.

Sometimes I wish I had what Jamie has with his band. It's more than just friendship or a group of guys that want the same thing. It's a brotherhood. I haven't found what they have. Maybe when I get to Los Angeles, I'll find what I've been longing for. I can't see myself in an all-girl band. Though, I'm not opposed to that. I've just always gotten along better with guys, more so than other girls.

Julia Montgomery, my best friend, is the exception. We're polar opposites. She's girly, a rule follower, the straight A student. Me? I'm doing good just to keep my GPA high enough that my parents won't threaten to take away my piano or my guitar.

They'll never understand how much I need music. I need music like I need water, food, and air. I have too much anxiety living inside of me. By writing my feelings out, singing them, I'm able to release the stress or fear that's trapped inside me.

Like right now, my emotions are all over the place. One buzzed and heated moment changed everything. I know it's not necessarily a bad thing, just bad timing. We would have eventually made it to this stage in life, but I would have preferred it to have happened later, down the road, several years from now. Definitely not while I'm still a junior in high school.

My parents are going to murder me. I don't think they'd kick their teenage daughter out for this royal fuckup, as they'll see it, but I can already picture the disappointment in their eyes. My mom delivers babies born to teenage mothers every week. She was preaching safe sex way before I completely understood what sex was and where babies come from.

At least I'll have Jamie's parents in my corner if worse comes to worst. His mom is a saint, and his dad is pretty awesome too. That's not to say mine aren't, they're just a lot more conservative than his are. And much less understanding.

I open the bathroom stall door, grabbing the stick I peed on and toss it in the trash can as I head out. The initial bell rings as I step into the hall. First period Algebra—a class I can't ever see needing—is the last place I want to be. It's the last week of school, only four days left until we're let out for summer. The seniors aren't even here. They finished all of their exams last week, so I won't see Jamie until late tonight because he just started a job this week.

I don't know how I'm going to concentrate on school work today. I have too many scenarios running through my head. I don't think Jamie is going to be thrilled, but at the same time, I know he won't be mad. It's not like either of us can blame the other or anyone else. We did this, and the weird thing is, I'm not upset like I thought I would have been when I went into Walmart this morning to buy a pregnancy test.

I don't like disappointing my parents. I know they both work hard to provide me with a good life. I think that's what I'm more stressed about than the baby itself.

Holy crap, I'm going to be a mom.

"Hey," Julia calls out from behind me. My backpack is tugged on, so I turn, grabbing her and pulling her into the bathroom I'd just left.

"I'm pregnant."

The look on her face is one of shock at first, and then horror graces her fair features until finally, a scowl sets in place.

"Is it Jamie's?" she asks, seemingly pissed.

"Duh." I nod my head because if there is one thing she should know above all is that I'd never cheat on my boyfriend. "Of course it is."

"Have you told him?"

"Not yet. I won't get to see him until tonight." I hate that I opened my big fat mouth. I should have waited. No one should have known before I told Jamie. What was I thinking?

"Come on," she says, pulling on my arm. "Let's get to class. We'll talk about your situation at lunch."

"It's not a situation," I deadpan, getting offended that she'd refer to it like it's a problem needing to be fixed.

"You sure about that?" She turns around, her perfectly plucked eyebrow arched as she walks backward to her history class.

I'm positive—but I don't answer her. My emotions are too out of whack, and if I don't keep my mouth shut, I'm going to say something nasty that I can't take back. She's one of the few people, hell, maybe the only person I ever hold my tongue for. We're best friends, but we don't always see eye to eye.

She just better not go blabbing her mouth before I'm able to tell Jamie and my parents. I'd hate to lose her friendship, seeing as how I don't really have that many friends that are girls. The thing about me is, once you cross me, I don't give second chances. Which is probably why friends are scarce in my life.

I don't fuck over other people, and I expect not to be fucked over in return. Trey, my boyfriend's bandmate and probably my closest friend other than Jamie and Julia, says my standards are far too high. But I disagree.

You can't let people walk all over you and then forgive them simply because they said they're sorry. It doesn't work like that. Decent human beings don't screw over their friends, so if I matter, then I shouldn't need to forgive someone because they wouldn't have needed it in the first place.

❦

Present

I'VE SPENT SO MUCH TIME WORRYING AND BEING SCARED OF THIS moment that I never stopped to think about what a relief it would be to not have to guard my secrets any longer. The anxiety and fear that Julia would find out Danny was still alive were always at the forefront of every decision I made.

If she could have me kidnapped, then what would she do to my son?

I couldn't take that chance. When I returned, I'd planned on telling Jamie what I never got to tell him before I was abducted. Even knowing he didn't believe me and didn't want to hear anything I had to tell him, I was still going to find a way to let him know we were having a baby.

But then Julia suddenly came up pregnant too, so I took a step back. I watched her, and even though Josh had told me, I hadn't fully believed she had been the one behind it. It didn't take long for me to see what I'd never seen before—the evil that lives deep inside her. She isn't normal. She doesn't think normal. There's a psychotic nature that shines bright.

To my knowledge, she doesn't know that Josh told me about her part in my kidnapping. She thinks I got away from my captor, that I escaped. I never set the record straight on that detail. I couldn't. I couldn't risk her finding out I was still carrying Jamie's baby.

When Trey told me about her pregnancy and that Jamie was taking her with them to California, I knew then that I could never let Jamie know about his other child. At that time, I hadn't been to see a doctor. I didn't know if my baby was really okay. All I knew, all I hoped for, was that Josh hadn't hurt him or her like he'd done me. I prayed every hour of every day for my baby to be healthy.

Every decision became about my baby's safety and what

would keep him or her safe. It was a week after they left that I finally went to a doctor to get checked out. I was nearly five months pregnant and severely underweight—but my baby was fine. My son was healthy and measuring on point—or so the obstetrician told me.

Julia, or her parents, somehow convinced mine the same as they did Jamie that I'd made it all up. I was never kidnapped like I'd claimed. I ran away, and when I found out the grass wasn't greener, I hightailed it back home.

Julia always did have her parents wrapped around her finger, so I wasn't surprised they'd believed her. Mine, on the other hand, was the biggest shock of all, aside from Jamie not taking my side. Honesty was their biggest rule, and though I broke a lot of rules, I'd never lied to them. Sure, I snuck out from time to time and got caught. I skipped school here and there. I'd even been in a couple of fights before, but every time my parents or any authority asked me something, I told them the truth.

It's why keeping Danny a secret for the past eighteen years has been slowly killing me. I hated doing it, still hate it. I don't like dishonesty. It's a feeling that eats at your soul little by little until there is nothing left. For all I know, there may not be. I haven't moved on. The only reason I've moved forward was because I had to, for Danny's sake. He needed a sense of normality and that's what I've tried to give him.

Believe it or not, I tried to instill the same morals in him that my parents had in me: be honest.

He knows there is nothing he could ever do that would make me give up on him or not back him up. I just ask him to tell me the truth no matter what it is. He knows I hate secrets, though he also knows I have them. Danny knows a lot more than a kid his age should, but I thought if I wanted honesty from him, then I had to give it too. There are a few details he doesn't know, and he knows I'm not going to tell him.

There are some things a child doesn't need to bear on their conscience. It's better that those things stay buried in the dark.

"We're going to talk about everything you said up on that stage, and if you need to do it now, that's fine," Jamie says, towering over Brandon from where he sits next to his brother in a cheap plastic chair against the wall. "But if you're okay, let's do it later when we're home."

Ironically, we're in the same back room Jamie and I had sex in half an hour ago. The boys had two more songs to perform before their set was complete, so I made Jamie cool his shit until they were done.

"I'm fine, Dad." Brandon nods his head once as if to confirm his reply. "In fact, I'd rather never bring it up again."

"Jesus Christ, son. You're obviously not fine if you're snorting cocaine." Jamie's head drops, and his fingers knead into his eyebrows. "Fuck."

"Why don't I know about this?" Cole demands, his hands braced at his hips as his brows furrow. With his gaze fixed on me, his irises darken. He's pissed, that much is evident.

"Why don't *you* know?" Jamie laughs, zero traces of humor in his tone. "Why didn't I know?!" Jamie's head falls to his shoulders, and his eyes close. Cole takes a step forward. "If you touch me right now or come within reaching distance, I will lay your ass out, Cole." Jamie's head shoots up, his blue eyes blazing with fury.

"There's a lot you still don't know," Cole says, trying to reason with his best friend. "I hate how you found out. I know you're pissed at me right now, but fuck you! Everything I did, every choice I made, was for them." Cole points to Danny and Brandon.

Danny's eyes snap to mine, and I know he's about to bail before his ass lifts off his seat.

"Come on," he says to his brother, pulling on the sleeve of his black T-shirt. "I've got to get out of here."

"Sit back down," Jamie says, his eyes never leaving Cole's. My gaze drops, as does Cole's. We both see the tremor in Jamie's hand before he sticks them both into his jean pockets.

"No," Danny deadpans, moving to step in front of Brandon and away from his father.

Jamie's hand flies out, gripping our son's bicep, stopping him from making a beeline for the back door.

I stand, having had enough of this back-and-forth dance Jamie has been doing with everyone since we all walked back here. Trey and Seth have been silent the whole time. The regret in Trey's eyes has only intensified since I saw him this morning. Seth, on the other hand, is still angry, though I'm not sure if it's the same kind of anger he showed me when I walked down Cole's stairs just this morning.

"Let him go," I say. "Let them both go." My eyes connect with Danny's, and the restraint he's showing makes me proud. He's come a long way in being able to control his reactions, his emotions. "Straight home. Is that clear?"

"He's not leaving," Jamie bites out, but Danny snatches his arm free, bypassing and grabbing his brother up from the chair on his way out. "Everyone is staying until I have answers."

"You're not likely to get them tonight, Jamie," I admit. "You sure as hell aren't getting them while those two are here." I nod my head, telling both boys to leave. "I'm not far behind. You both better be there when I get home."

I hear the frustration leave Jamie's mouth, but the boys do as I say, exiting through the back door that leads to the parking lot out behind the bar. Trever can handle the equipment himself or leave it, and they can come back tomorrow to get it.

Taking my phone out of my back pocket, I shoot Anne a text, giving Jamie's mom a heads-up. I'd rather tell her myself than have one of the boys call her or even Jamie himself, though I bet the latter is less likely to happen.

Me: Jamie knows about Danny.

Anne: Oh, dear.

Anne: I thought I'd feel joy if this moment ever came, but I don't. Just heartburn.

Me: Don't work yourself up. I didn't want to upset you. I just wanted you to know.

Anne: Should I fly out?

Me: Jamie doesn't know that you know, at least not yet. And he doesn't have to know. I won't tell him.

Anne: My boy deserves to know the truth, the whole truth, Jen. I never wanted to keep it from him. Had I not been more worried for Danny and Brandon's safety, I would have told him myself. I'll get packed and try to be on the next flight out.

Me: You're welcome to stay at my house if you like.

There's a small piece of me that's glad she won't be staying at the house Jamie used to share with Julia now that they're divorced. I hated when Anne would visit, and she'd have to put up with the *daughter-in-law from Hell* as she often refers to her. Anne never liked Julia, not even when I was dating Jamie, and she was just my friend. I guess she had a sixth sense about her. Anne knew she was a bad seed and tried to tell Jamie that. It only caused a problem between them for a short time. Finally, Anne stopped giving her opinion of his wife to her son.

"How about you stop playing on your fucking phone and give me some answers. Tell me something, anything, so I can make sense of all of this." There's a plea in Jamie's voice, begging me to tell him, and a huge part of me wants to spill everything. Sure, he has a right to know. But it's not like he gave me the time of day when I begged him to believe me.

I take two strides, stopping in front of him and jabbing my

finger into his hard chest. My hurt and anger-filled eyes look up to meet his. "You didn't care enough to give me the time of day eighteen years ago. Everything she told you made perfect sense then, so if you think I owe you a damn thing, then I'm here to set you straight. Go to hell."

I stand here, making sure he understands everything my words just conveyed. Then I walk away just like he did all those years ago.

CHAPTER THIRTEEN

JAMIE

Eighteen years ago

Her grip on my T-shirt tightens as I pull away. Being this close was a very bad idea. My skin burns with need, wanting her to touch me because I know she has the power to simmer the flames. Being this close, all she'd have to do is run her hands under my shirt and up my abdomen. The pain would ebb away, being replaced by the pleasure her touch has always brought me.

But then the memory of the hell she put me through assaults me. I don't want her touch. I don't need her touch. Not today, not tomorrow, not ever again.

"Let go, Elise," I snarl, my eyes lit, blazing down at her. She's nearly a foot shorter than me. I've always got off on towering over her, but right now I feel about as tall as a yardstick. She still has too much power over me, and I've got to figure out a way to sever it.

"Jamie, please. Talk to me. I don't understand why you

"Because I have nothing to say to you. Just like you didn't have anything to say to me for three goddamn months. Now take your hands off me."

The look on her face when she releases me is as if I'd slapped her across the face. There is so much pain in her brown eyes. I have to get out of here before I cave and try to make her smile. The sadness on her face doesn't belong, but then again, it didn't belong on mine either, and she's the one that cast a permanent frown on my lips.

"It wasn't my choice. I'd never leave you of my own free will. You have to believe me, Jamie."

Tears pool into both of her eyes, threatening to spill down her makeup-free face. She looks younger now that she doesn't wear black eyeliner on the top and bottom of her eyelids. Ever since she turned thirteen, it was rare to see her without makeup. Usually, the only time I did was if my parents were out of town and she told hers she was staying at a friend's when really she was sleeping with me in my bed.

I miss waking up to her. I've longed to sleep wrapped around her. Those were the only times I'd ever get a full night's sleep. She once was my peace, but now she's my hell.

"Why can't you stop with all the lies and just admit you ran away? At least admit it to me, even if you want to lie to everyone else. You owe me that much, Elise."

"I've told you the truth. I've told everyone the truth, yet none of you believe me. I was kidnapped!"

"By who?" I ask, not sure why I'm bothering to entertain this conversation.

"A man," she bites out, irritation evident in her voice.

"What did he look like?"

"I'm not going there. It's over. I want to forget it ever happened. Why can't you believe me?" Her voice comes out tired and defeated. She's been singing the same tune for nearly a

77

week now, and I'd imagine keeping up with all her lies has to be daunting.

"I'm done," I seethe, but she takes my declaration as another reason to touch me, grasping onto my forearm, her fingers wrapping around me. "I don't want to hear any more shit out of your mouth."

"Did you even search for me?"

"Why would I search for someone that obviously didn't want to be found? I moved on. Maybe you should do the same."

I snatch my arm loose, her nails clawing me as I turn, not looking back and knowing I never plan on seeing her again after today. I just have to get into my truck and drive away. Drive until my new life takes center stage, forcing me to forget the one that was supposed to be with my forever girl.

Forever. What a load of garbage.

"Jamie," she calls out, and my stride slows, wanting to obey her. "Please don't leave without hearing me out."

"A little too late."

"I would have eventually told you all of it. I just needed time to process it myself. You don't know what it was like." Her breath comes out in a huff.

I peek over my shoulder one last time, knowing it's going to kill me, but I do it anyway. "Should have thought of that before you hit the road."

"I didn't leave you!" she screams, and it's a knife to my gut.

I can't let her break me. I have to be strong. With Julia pregnant with my kid, even if I wanted to let all of this go, it really is too late.

"So you say," I tell her, leaving Elise standing in my bedroom doorway as I walk out of my parents' house. I wasn't planning on hitting the road for California until tomorrow, but there is no way I can stay another minute, let alone another night in the same town as Elise Thomas. Not if I'm going to keep my word to Julia and be with her and raise our kid together.

I don't have a choice. I made my bed, the same as Elise made hers. I never would have fucked another girl had the one that was supposed to be by my side for the rest of our lives not ditched me for some prick.

Kidnapped. A dry laugh bubbles out of me as I slide into the driver's seat of my pickup truck. Never would have pegged Elise to cry wolf. But she did, and now we're both paying the price.

Hope his dick was worth it.

✳

Present

WE'RE THREE BLOCKS FROM MY HOUSE, WELL, MY EX-WIFE'S house that is. That was the first thing that caught my eye when Cole parked his SUV next to a curb in front of a small house ten minutes ago. After Jenna walked away from me, the same as I once did to her, I demanded my so-called best friend to give me the answers I know he's holding on to.

He won't, and I have to remind myself every few minutes that we've been friends for over thirty years. If it weren't for that and needing him to bring me to Jenna's house, then . . .

I blow out a breath as I stare out the window, the heat making the glass fog.

Her house is much smaller than the one Julia resides in. This house is what I guess some people would call cozy. My rental house since I moved out is at least three times as big as this, and Jules . . . hell, her house, my old house, is a mansion compared to this one. It compares in a lot of ways to Cole's small, quaint home. But he's always liked tight quarters. I, on the other hand, needed breathing room from the woman I was married to.

"How long have you known?" I finally ask.

He doesn't answer right away, and I'm starting to think he isn't going to open his mouth when a sigh slides past his lips. "Nine years."

"You've known . . ." My voice cracks, and I have to pause to pull air in through my mouth. "How could you keep that from me? If this were you, and you were sitting where I am, I would have told you, Cole." I drop my arm, then I turn my head to look at him. He's gazing forward, staring out at the darkness we're cloaked in. There aren't any streetlights on—it's pitch black.

He sighs. "You don't get to say that without knowing the whole story. I'd hope if you were in my shoes, you'd have made the same call I did."

That's bullshit. I can say without any doubt, I wouldn't have.

His head rolls, his eyes landing on mine. Regret lives inside his stare, but so does a sense of righteousness. I've never known him not to do the right thing, even when he didn't want to. He's always had higher morals than the rest of us. It was no secret that Cole and Elise didn't get along. They were constantly fighting, but this one particular day, Elise forgot her journal in the cafeteria. Cole could have been a dick and trashed it. Instead, he brought it to whatever class she was in, making himself late for his own.

"If you would tell me, or she would, then maybe I'd start to understand, but right now, this feels like the ultimate *fuck you*. This feels . . . hell, worse than betrayal, man. I don't even have a word for what this feels like. There's a gaping hole in my chest, and I don't know how to begin to fill it or fix it or if that's even possible." I breathe, pulling in a slow breath, attempting to calm my nerves. "I don't know how we move on from here," I admit.

"We can't until you know everything." His chest rises as his arm stretches across the steering wheel. "I don't know if she can tell you everything. Or even if she will tell you. Fuck, brother, I don't know if you should know everything. It ain't good."

I laugh because what else am I going to do? I'm at her mercy.

"I saw that video of her being beaten and tortured. I already know it isn't good."

"That wasn't even half of it, Jamie. That wasn't even a quarter of the fucked-up shit that makes up this whole goddamn mess."

I just shake my head. It's blatant he isn't going to enlighten me. I'm about to get out when there is a rap of knuckles against the window next to me, followed by the back door on the passenger side opening.

"We doing this or what?" Seth asks, sliding in the back seat and slamming the door, Trey doing the same on the opposite side, getting inside the vehicle behind Cole. "She owes you an explanation."

"She doesn't owe him a damn thing," Cole refutes.

"Like hell she doesn't," I bark. How does he not think I deserve answers? If nothing else, the least he could do is tell me why she kept my son a secret. Because I don't care what anyone says, and yeah, I was in the wrong about everything, but I should have known about him from the moment she walked in.

Everything else can go out the window. I should not have been kept in the dark. Hell, Cole should have told me the moment he found out.

"I'm going in. It's the only way I'm going to find out since someone in this vehicle won't tell me a damn thing."

"You know," Seth interjects, "that's real shitty, bro. We're supposed to have each other's backs. We're not supposed to keep shit from each other."

Cole whips around in his seat, his angry eyes blazing toward Seth. "Don't you ever say I don't have his back or either of yours. I get he's pissed. I get he doesn't understand, and he's hurt. I even get that you are too, but fuck you for accusing me of that shit. Fuck. You," he reiterates.

"I'm done with this," I say, getting out, leaving them to argue or fight or whatever. I'm going to get answers. She better be ready to give them because I'm not leaving until she does.

CHAPTER FOURTEEN

JENNA

Eighteen years ago

Tomorrow I'm supposed to start my senior year of high school. This was supposed to be exciting, the mark of our countdown. Only nine months, then I'd graduate and leave this small town with the love of my life. Instead, that's nowhere in sight.

Since I've been back, all I've been called is a liar, a piece of shit, worthless trash.

And now Jamie is gone. He not only left, but he took Julia with him. He chose her over me, over everything that we've built in the last nine years. I thought our love and friendship were unbreakable. They weren't. Whatever she told him, made him believe, it worked. She severed what I thought was impenetrable.

Talk about being sliced open and ripped apart all at the same time. No amount of torture that Josh ever dealt out hurt this bad. My heart is in pieces. My head is messed up. And I still haven't told anyone that I'm pregnant. God, I hope I'm still pregnant.

"Hey! Wait up," Cole says, grabbing me by the elbow and stopping me from escaping.

"I'm not doing this with you too, Cole." I'm so sick of the verbal confrontations with Jamie's friends, his bandmates. They all act like I betrayed them by betraying their brother.

"You let him leave," he says, his tone accusing.

"Let him?" I laugh. "I begged him not to go. And then I begged him not to take *her* with him. No, Cole, I didn't let him do shit. He stopped trusting me, and now he's eating up whatever bullshit she's feeding him." Tears sting my eyes, threatening to spill. I tip my head up, my eyes latching onto the stars scattered across the clear night sky, trying to ward them off.

I'm so sick of crying.

No more, I silently chant before letting my head face forward, my sad eyes landing on his skeptical green ones.

"I admit, it's a hard pill to swallow when you clam up about this supposed guy that took you. You refuse to go to the cops." He goes silent, shoving his hands into his pockets, then his eyes drop to the ground.

What does he want me to say? I'm not going to sway from my conviction. I'm not going to admit something that isn't true.

"I didn't lie to him, Cole. I didn't lie to my parents or to anyone else. I didn't choose to leave him," I say as adamantly as the day I was brought back.

"We've never been friends," he says to me. "Hell, I can't even recall a time that we've pretended to be friendly."

"That's because I thought we had enough respect, or love for Jamie, that we didn't need to pretend anything."

"You think I want what's yours." His eyebrow arches, daring me to tell him he's wrong. "You think I'm in love with my best friend, and you know what, sometimes I think I am too." I nod, agreeing with him. I've always thought that, but this is the first time Cole's verbalized any sort of intimate feeling for Jamie. "But the thing is, I just want him to be happy no matter who he's with."

"He was happy with me," I bite out as I step forward, jabbing my finger into his chest.

"I know." His brows furrow and his gaze drops to where my finger still touches him. "He's not any happier with her if it makes any difference."

"Then why isn't he with me?"

"It's more complicated. He—"

"Hates you," Trey says from behind me, interrupting Cole. I whip around to face him, his dark-brown eyes snapping over my shoulder. "Seth's ready. Let's do this. Let's get out of here."

"I'll be there when I'm there," Cole replies.

"I want to talk to Elise. Leave us." Trey's hate-filled eyes never leave Cole's as they silently war between them. I'm about to say to hell with both of them when Cole mumbles a goodbye, leaving me standing alone with Trey in my parents' backyard.

Cole has lived next door to me since we moved here. Maybe that's another reason he and I don't get along. From day one, I tried to become his friend, but he didn't want a friend that was a girl.

Trey's gaze finally falls to me and something in them makes me take a step back, not liking the look penetrating me at this very moment.

Present

WALKING AWAY FROM JAMIE IN A SIMILAR WAY THAT HE DID WITH me didn't make me feel good. In fact, it made me feel like shit.

I knew this day would eventually come. Everything catches up with us at some point, but I'd be lying if I said I wasn't taken by surprise. I hadn't expected him to show up at Cole's house, even though I've known that was a possibility all along. They're friends, bandmates, business partners, so the joke's on me. I shouldn't have been blindsided. I shouldn't have been there, taking the chance it would happen.

Maybe a part of me—a small part—wanted it to happen. I've always yearned for him to know Danny, to love Danny like I do. But it was a risk I couldn't take. Not with my son's life.

"When were you planning on telling me Jamie was back in the picture?"

"He's not in the picture, Mal," I answer on autopilot. Cutting my eyes to my partner and best friend, Malachi Hayes, from where I sit next to him in the passenger side of his SUV, I cock my head. "How'd you find out?"

There's only a handful of people that would have told him, and I doubt it was either of the boys. I'm betting on Cole. Josh had been at the bar and then conveniently disappeared as soon as Brandon called out his dad on stage.

"You know who." His dark, almost black eyes glance at me for a split second, just long enough to let me feel and see he's pissed off that it wasn't me.

We make quite a pair, Malachi and me. His rich, Native American heritage contrasts next to my plain, fairest of fair skin, though his long jet-black hair matches mine in length. Where he towers over my five-foot-five-inch height with his nearly six-foot-four-inch frame, that didn't used to be the case. He's a little over a year younger than me, and like Cole, he didn't care for me when we were in high school. I know now that had everything to do with the lies my so-called best friend was filling his head with.

"Cole has a big mouth," I snarl.

"You should have told me this morning. I knew something was wrong the minute you walked into the safe house."

Our task force has a house in Santa Monica, nestled among vacation rentals along the beach where women, children, and sometimes even men recover after being rescued from human trafficking rings. Being a victim myself, I know how hard it is to come back home, back to a reality that is no longer the same. I know what it's like to have to rehabilitate yourself alone, and that is something I never want another person to experience if I have anything to do with it.

I'm not a therapist, and I don't pretend to be. That's why we have Jessica—Josh's wife. She is full-time and completely dedicated to the foundation she started fifteen years ago. You see, whereas I was the last person Josh ever kidnapped, Jess was the first. After he let me go, he found her, then rescued her. Apparently, there was something about me that reminded him of her, and that was one of the reasons I was able to get under his skin without even knowing it.

Other than our similar hair color and fair skin, we're nothing alike. She has blue eyes, and I have brown ones. She's soft, sweet, delicate even. You'd think being a certified psychologist that has been through the things she has, she would have hardened her emotions. She hasn't. In fact, she's big on displaying and talking about feelings. I, on the other hand, am not so much for that. I'm more like Josh than I am his wife.

"I should have, but then I would have had to acknowledge it myself." Malachi pulls his SUV in the driveway next to Josh's matching black Tahoe. We all have matching vehicles. "And I wasn't ready," I admit.

He stops, shoving the gear shift forward, but doesn't make a move to shut off the engine.

"Are you prepared for what Jamie knowing could bring?"

I breathe, blowing air out of my mouth.

"No." I shake my head. "But we knew it would eventually catch up to us, and regardless if I'm ready or not, my son and Brandon's safety come first."

Mal reaches his right hand out, holding it up, fingers splayed apart and waiting for me to take it, which I do, sliding my left hand to his, our fingers interlocking.

"You know I'd give my life to protect my godson. That goes for his brother too."

My lips spread, giving him a weak smile. "I know, and you have no idea what that means to me. Thank you, Mal," I say, squeezing him.

There is no one besides Danny that I trust more than Malachi Hayes. I trust him with my life, my son's life, and the boy that I love just like he was my own. I know if the worst of the worst happens, I can count on my partner to protect what I hold dearest to my heart.

CHAPTER FIFTEEN

JAMIE

I hesitate, my fist raised in the air to knock on her door. *What am I supposed to say?* I don't know where to start. Cole is right. I am pissed, but I'm equally hurt. I'm devastated, shocked, torn the fuck up.

I drop my arm, not able to bring myself to announce my presence just yet, my head mimicking the motion.

I know I have no right to demand answers, even if that's exactly what I want to barge in there and do. I've racked my brain for the last two hours, trying to imagine reasons significant enough that she wouldn't have told me about *him*—our son. If she wanted to hurt me the same way I did her, then she's succeeded. But then I keep coming back to that type of behavior isn't like her. Not the girl I once knew, loved, still love.

Pondering all this while standing on the small porch is short lived. My head snaps up when the front door swings open, finding Danny standing before me. I swallow, unable to breathe or form a coherent thought as seconds pass by, both of us locked

He's mine and Jenna's kid, just like it was supposed to be. What wasn't supposed to be was me not knowing he existed.

"Will you get your mom?" I finally ask, finding my voice again.

"She isn't home," he deadpans, crossing his arms and scrutinizing me from where he stands. The porch light suddenly feels like a bright beam of heat pointed directly at me.

"It's after midnight," I say, worry etched in my tone. Being on tour for months at a time, that was the one thing I'd never bend on with Julia. She always had to be home with our son. Apparently, the same can't be said about Jenna, and that doesn't sit well on my chest.

"She has a job." He arches a jet-black eyebrow, challenging me on his reasoning.

"And you're a kid," I counter. This is bullshit. She should be here.

"No," he argues. "I'm seventeen. Far from a kid." His brows wrinkle, irritated, his cheeks flushing with heat.

"You're still underage. You still shouldn't be home alone."

"He's not alone," Brandon's overly cheery but forced voice follows, then he appears next to his brother in the doorway.

It's the first time I've seen them standing so close that I'm able to compare the two. They match in height, but where Brandon is lean, Danny is thicker, bulkier, stronger maybe, and with a look on his face that makes me question if I'd want to go toe to toe with him in a fight. Where Brandon comes off light, sometimes funny even, Danny comes off with a hint of danger behind eyes that are a dead ringer for my own.

"Even better," I say, stepping inside without asking because I'll be damned if I leave either of them in this house alone and unsupervised. Brandon steps aside, letting me pass, but Danny remains rooted to the ground, his eyes watching me as I enter, a silent warning meeting my gaze.

I'll give him this, he's intimidating as fuck. That's not to say I'm afraid of him because I'm not, but I could see how someone else might be. He's got that "don't fuck with me" vibe rolling off him in waves.

What kind of kid did she raise?

I've always taught Brandon not to go looking for a fight, but should one stop in front of you, and you can't get out of it with words, then fight like your life depends on it. In the world we live in today, you can't take chances. Violent acts happen every day, and to good people that weren't asking for it. You have to always be on guard, pay attention to your surroundings.

"By all means"—Danny flays out his arm—"come right on in."

"Danny," Cole draws out from behind me. "Knock it off with the attitude."

Entering from the front door, you step right into the living room. There is no foyer like in the home I once shared with Julia. I wonder if it's a coincidence Jenna lives this close. Did she move out here like we'd planned, and the boys just ran into each other one day? My gut instinct tells me I'm way off, but then I'm clueless about everything.

"I'm not the one that Mom's going to be pissed at." Danny's hard eyes bore into Cole's. I can vividly see there's familiarity in the way they speak to each other—and I hate it. I hate knowing my best friend has known for *years* that I have another son but didn't say one word. I hate that he knows my kid on a personal level, and I don't. It shouldn't have been this way.

"Not like it'll be the first or the last time," Cole replies. I'm left wondering if he's referring to when we were teenagers or a more present time. For some reason, now that my mind has calmed slightly, I do believe him when he swore he's never slept with her. Even if she's a completely different person than she was when she was mine, she still isn't Cole Master's type—and he isn't hers.

She is mine, though. My type, that is. Back at the bar, that spur of the moment, where we both lost all control, and I fucked her back in some storage room against a wall was by far the best lay I've had in years. Not that I'm surprised. She was always *the one*.

"So, where is she?" Seth asks, my gaze snapping to his as he walks inside, Trey following behind.

Danny's jaw locks, walking away, leaving the front door wide open. My eyes follow him, unable to look away. I'm intrigued and terrified at the same time. It's obvious he doesn't like me, and I have to admit that stings. That stings a lot. He doesn't even know me. He wasn't given that chance, and neither was I.

What did his mom tell him about me? I wonder for a brief second.

Does he think I never wanted to be a part of his life?

Does he know I wasn't given the option? An option I would have taken without hesitation. He's my son, dammit. I should have known. She should have told me. So, why didn't she? And how convenient that she isn't here to answer that question.

He stops when he nears the open kitchen, turns, and then places his shoulder into the wall. He looks at everyone except me, taking in the strangers in his home, then finally stopping on Brandon. Glancing between them, it's as if they are having a silent conversation with each other. I'm an only child, but that doesn't mean I don't recognize what they're doing. Cole and I do the same thing. We've known each other so long we usually know what the other is thinking.

"Apparently, work was more important than being here. Instead, she left the children home alone," I say, watching as Danny's eyes change to lethal, his eyes slowly roaming until they land on mine. In a split second, he's off the wall, stomping toward me with purpose.

"Whoa!" Cole rushes forward, placing his palm on Danny's chest, halting his stride. Cole's head swings around, his eyes boring into mine, though I haven't taken mine off the kid that's highly ticked off right now and looking to tear my head off. "Maybe you shouldn't question Jen's parenting skills in front of this one," he grits out.

I raise an eyebrow. A part of me likes that he isn't afraid to come to her defense. A feeling of pride courses through me at the thought.

"He's a little more protective than most kids, brother." That comment seems to make Danny relax. Stepping back, he rolls his eyes, showing his young age.

"Fine. We'll come back to that later." I roll my head until I find Brandon. "You and I are having a conversation about what you said tonight." I stare Brandon down from where I stand next to the fireplace where the television screen is hanging above the mantel, playing a basketball game that no one is paying any mind to. I'm still having a hard time processing the confession that came out of my boy's mouth. Never in a million years would I have expected my son to be a drug user.

"Can we not?" he asks, backing away and taking a seat at one end of the plush couch across from me. There are two full-size couches and an oversized matching chair and ottoman that make up the furniture in Jenna's living room. "Besides, it's a moot point now. It's over. It's done. It's not even a big deal anymore."

"It's a very big deal, son," I say, floored by how he wants to ghost over this. "You overdosed on cocaine, Brandon. Not only did that happen, but I don't know a thing about it? Jesus, son, if you need help, I'm your dad. Why didn't you come to me? We'll find the best rehab center. Whatever it takes."

"He's not a fucking drug addict," Danny barks, his eyes darkening when I glance over. We have one thing in common, that's obvious. He's as quick to anger as I am.

"Language," I seethe, even if I don't exactly have the right to scold him. The thought of Jenna being okay with his easy use of foul words rubs me the wrong way. Sure, she and I talked like that when we were their age, still do, but never would we have dared to speak like that in front of our parents.

A snicker of a laugh rolls out of the boy's mouth that I haven't officially been introduced to—my son. Most likely my oldest son too. Julia had Brandon five weeks early, but even without doing the math, Danny should still be older than his brother.

"Dad," Brandon calls out. "I'm not addicted to drugs. I swear." He laughs, but it comes out more nervous than not. Brandon doesn't have the confidence Danny seems to be built with. "And I don't need rehab. I'm fine, like I said."

"Then why didn't your mother tell me about this?"

Now Brandon's brows furrow, a sudden mood change turning dark. "If by mother, you mean your ex-wife, then that's because she doesn't know," Brandon admits.

"What the fuck?" falls out of my mouth before I can get control over my words. "My ex-wife? That ex-wife is and will always be your mom. What do you even mean by that, Brandon, and what's with the tone?"

Danny walks over to the other end of the couch, removes his phone from inside his front pocket, then sits down. Not paying attention to our conversation as he plays on his phone.

I've lost over seventeen years with this kid, and it's just now sinking in.

Brandon shrugs as if it isn't a big deal. It's one thing for me to hate his mother; it's another for him to say something negative about her. That's unacceptable in my eyes. She isn't perfect. None of us are, but from everything I've seen, she has always tried to be the best mother she can be. It's one of the reasons going through with the divorce was so hard. Brandon deserved parents that loved each other, but that wasn't something he was rewarded with. I know that showed, and I hate that fact. The more I tried to love Julia, the more I loathed her over time.

For now, I'll leave his remark alone. We'll come back to it at a later time. I won't have him disrespecting her now that I don't live in the same house as he does with his mom.

"Happy birthday, Brandon. I'm sorry I forgot." I sigh, hating to admit that to my son.

He shrugs again like it's not a big deal. "It's after midnight, Dad. It isn't my birthday anymore." He gives me a tight smile, and I know without words that it *was* a big deal. I screwed up, and I don't think there is any type of damage control that can fix it. I'm so disappointed in myself right now that I don't have the least idea what to say or do.

"Why do you keep checking your phone?" Cole's brows pinch together, and my thoughts are disrupted when I take a glimpse at my other son. "What's going on, Danny?" he demands in such an authoritative tone that it both catches me off guard and pisses me off at the same time. Cole doesn't have kids. He doesn't even have blood-related nieces or nephews. Brandon is his godson and has always called my bandmates "uncle," yet the way he speaks to Danny is like he actually has some type of say when it comes to this kid, my kid—and that ticks me off.

I'm not the only band member that has children. Seth has two kids—a ten-year-old and an eight-year-old, both girls. His long-time girlfriend, along with his daughters, live in Arizona, away from the glitz and glamour of Hollywood. They make it work, even though he's on tour a large portion of the year and in LA with us as often as possible.

In some aspects, I get it, not wanting to expose your family to everything our lives bring with it. And now that I remember Brandon's confession, I think Seth made the wiser choice, keeping them at a distance.

"It shows Mom is here." Danny holds his cell phone up, waving it in our direction, showing some kind of map application. "But she isn't. And she'd never . . ." he pauses, his eyes dropping to the ground. He's thinking. I can physically see the wheels turning in his head.

"Never what?" I hear fall from my lips.

"Never leaves and forgets her necklace. She always wears it or has it on her no matter what. There's only been one other time she's taken it off, and she would have told me if she was going dark."

Going dark? What the hell does that mean?

I reach into my jeans pocket, remembering that I still have the piece of jewelry I gave her when we were teenagers.

"This necklace?" I lift my hand, releasing the cross to dangle from my fingers.

Unmistakable panic sets in the kid's indigo eyes, making my chest heavy with anxiety. What is it about this hunk of junk that had him so worried about his mother not wearing it?

He pulled up a map on his phone. *Does he have his mom tracked?* I could understand Jenna doing that to him, but not the roles reversed. It's a parents' job to know where their child is at all hours of the day, and I've been known to pull up Brandon's whereabouts a time or two, but never in my wildest dreams would I imagine him doing that to his mother or me. Not that he could. He doesn't have access to my password, and frankly, why would he want to? Children don't worry about their parents the same as we worry about them.

96

Danny jumps up from where he is seated on the couch.

I'm starting to think he does, though, and that's unsettling.

"Why do you have it?" He reaches forward, snatching it from my grasp, taking the necklace from me before it registers it's gone.

"It's a long story," I say.

"Danny," Cole says in a chastising tone. "Stop freaking out. Your mom is fine. I'm sure she'll be back soon from whatever it was she had to do."

"If you're *that* worried, why not just call her," I point out.

"She's an FBI agent," he grits out like that's all the explanation it needs.

"And I'm a singer in a band," I quip. "If my son calls me, I'm going to answer." His jaw locks right before he turns his face away from me. It's then I realize I said "son" as in single, not plural.

Fuuuuck.

There's no way to fix that. Maybe I've only just found out about him in the last few hours, but it doesn't negate that he is my son too. I wish Jenna would have told me before now, like when she first returned home eighteen years ago.

She better be ready to talk when she gets home because, believe me, that's exactly what we're going to do.

FBI agent. Like that trumps our current situation. Nothing can be more important than explaining why she failed to tell me she was pregnant.

I'm suddenly assaulted with an unpleasant memory from my past.

❧

Eighteen years ago

I'm not supposed to leave without her. I don't even know how to leave from here, knowing I'll never see her again. I'm not even sure I can go through with all the threats I've issued.

I've never had this problem before. My bites have always been worse than my bark. If I say I'm doing something, you bet your ass I'll follow through. This is different, though. She was mine for nine years. We made plans, we had our future laid out. There was no mistaking what I wanted and what she wanted. We've always been on the same page—until she ran away.

I never saw it coming. I was blindsided, and it still doesn't make sense. Maybe if I'd allow her to explain, let her get one word in, then I would know why she did what she did. The thing is, I don't think I can handle that knowledge.

I know if I let her back in, even for a minute, I'll never let go. I'd forgive her like the sap I really am, and then I'd open myself up to letting it happen all over again. I can't, and I won't go through that torture again.

I won't—not even for her.

"I'm all packed up." Julia's sugary voice coats my eardrums, making my stomach rumble with unease.

I'm trading one hell for another. I'm at least able to recognize that.

"Then get in the damn truck already," I bark.

"We need to get a few things straight, James," she says, calling me by my given name rather than the nickname I go by. Her tone is as if she's asserting some type of dominance or authority over me. This bitch better learn real quick that isn't the way to earn my respect or my loyalty. I shouldn't have any sort of loyalty to her in the first place, but somewhere along the way, I stupidly fucked her without a condom. I don't remember it, but it's not like I've been *that* sober in the last few months. I've spent more hours wasted or passed out than I have awake and functioning.

And that's all Elise's fucking fault.

"What?" I say through clenched teeth, my patience wearing thin.

"I love you. We're having a baby, and although I realize you don't love me yet, I also know you will." She smiles as if she actually believes the crock of shit coming out of her mouth. "Maybe not today. Maybe not even tomorrow. But once you see our baby"—her eyes glance down to her flat stomach where her hands rest on her abdomen—"you'll love me then, Jamie. I just know you will."

"Not likely, now get in the goddamn truck." She doesn't budge. "Let's. Go."

Her head suddenly snaps up, her light-blue eyes that I once thought appeared sad, concerned, and innocent all in one pin me with a look that's eerie as fuck. A batshit crazy, *I'm fucking psycho*, look to be exact. "You will love me, Jamie. And you'll love our baby almost as much." She steps closer, and it takes everything in me not to retreat. "But if you so much as talk to *her* ever again, even through one of your friends, you'll lose this baby. You'll never see him or her again. I suggest you not test me on this. You won't like what I'll do. Am I making myself clear?"

This bitch just threatened me with my unborn child.

What the hell have I gotten myself into?

I'm trading one hell for another. No truer words have ever entered my head.

CHAPTER SIXTEEN

JENNA

Present

There is something I'm missing and have been missing since we took this case seven months ago. Even Josh is on edge lately because we haven't gotten one damn break. He's the levelheaded one of all of us, but when you go month after month, and every lead is a dead end, well, then even the leader is bound to start showing signs of cracks in his hard exterior.

I won't give up; none of us will. It's why the case was turned over to our team after one of the federal agents disappeared, and the other requested a transfer, scared that the same thing would happen to him.

This job isn't for pussies, the weak minded, or cowards. It takes balls to go after the type of criminals we do—heartless, evil bastards that would sell their own grandmother to the highest bidder if it put more money in their pockets.

This isn't how I dreamed my life would turn out, but if I'm honest, I'm not so sure now that I would go back and change much of it, if any. Sure, I wish *some* things had turned out differently. I wish my son had had a relationship with his father from day one. I wish Brandon didn't have to keep secrets from his parents so that I can keep Danny safe.

At the end of the day, I do this job for two reasons, and neither of them has to do with why I should be in this role. Sure, I'm glad I'm one of the people that gets to help those that have suffered the same and even a worse fate than I did. But that isn't why I get up every morning, why I work late, or why I drop everything when "the job" requires my presence.

I'm here because of Daniel and Brandon. And that's it.

I will not chance something happening to either of them. Those thoughts keep me up at night. Those thoughts make me feel helpless, like I can't breathe.

I never imagined I'd fall in love with my ex's *other* son, but I did. I never stood a chance with Brandon. With Danny, I knew from the moment I read the pregnancy test—I loved him and would do anything for my unborn baby. The day I met Brandon, he was three years old. Still, to this day, he makes me laugh. Of course, he pisses me off just as much as he purposely does things to make me happy.

He's a good kid. Both of them are, and I know I'm lucky to a large degree.

"You gotta break at some point, Jen." Malachi's voice pulls me out of my thoughts. Lifting my head from the computer monitor, I take in his wrinkled brow as he sips coffee from the mug in his hand. Finally, he sighs. "We've been at this for hours, hell, weeks at this point, and still aren't any closer to a breakthrough."

Lifting his other hand, he reaches out, handing me my own steaming cup of coffee. Taking it, I bring it to my lips, taking a small sip and then another.

"They haven't struck in six months . . ." I place the cup on the desk next to my keyboard. My ass has been planted in the same spot since he and I arrived close to eleven last night.

"That we know of," he says, finishing my silent thought.

Glancing at the clock behind his left shoulder, I see it's after seven in the morning.

Damn.

I've been up for twenty-four hours. Not that I'm surprised. Not that it's unlike me, because it's not.

"There's something that we're missing." I give him a pointed look. "And I don't plan on stopping until I figure out what the hell it is."

I twist back around, my eyes falling to the computer screen and the script before me. With my right hand on the mouse, I scroll down and go back to reading the context of the chat we have pulled on a weekly basis from the pit of Hell that is the internet's dark secret—the dark web. The place where seedy people do seedy shit every day.

"It's Sunday morning, Jen. It's time to call it a night. You need sleep, hell, I need fucking sleep."

"So go to sleep," I offer, not glancing back to him. There are several vacant beds if he's that tired. If not, his condo isn't far from where we are. He could leave and be home within a couple of minutes.

Movement from the open doorway catches my attention. Snapping my eyes over, I find Jess, Josh's wife, standing there studying Mal and me, her eyebrows pinched together.

I realize a second too late what it is my overprotective and too in-my-shit partner is doing, the sting from my skin being pricked happening before my brain has time to react.

She has the audacity to look guilty, even though I know damn well she's the one that supplied him with the needle filled with a fast-acting sedative that'll knock me out for at least five to six hours.

I glance back at Malachi, already swaying to the side of the chair. "Goddamn you." My eyes waver, drooping. "I'm going to beat your ass for this, you fuckhea—"

I can't even finish my threat before my lights turn completely out, then I'm gone from the here and now.

CHAPTER SEVENTEEN

JAMIE

Present

I'm startled awake by what sounds like the front door being kicked in. My eyes snap open, and for a brief moment, I forget where I am. Then the night before comes back to me, and I realize I crashed out, waiting for Jenna to return home.

"Mom!" I hear yelled from the railing overlooking the living room. My tired and heavy head glances up to see Danny standing barefoot on the landing in only a pair of black basketball shorts. When his eyes grow large, I swing my head to see why he's so concerned.

He's down the stairs before I'm able to take in the large guy walking in the door. He's tall, and that's an understatement. The man is huge, with long, straight black hair that hangs down his back. When my gaze lands on his face, I know immediately who he is. Don't remember the guy's name, but I'm almost certain it's who I'm thinking of.

"Did you fucking drug her? Again?" Danny emphasizes.

"Watch your fucking mouth," he says, an eyebrow arching up.

I sit up, taking stock of everything as Brandon walks lazily down the stairs. Cole stirs from where he was asleep at one end of the couch. Trey had crashed at the other end at some point hours ago, and Seth is lying on his stomach across from me on the other couch. He's still unmoving, which doesn't surprise me. Seth can sleep through a 5.0 earthquake on the Richter scale.

"Well, did you, Uncle Mal?" he demands, crossing his arms over his bare chest. The boy could put a lot of grown men to shame with his size, maybe even me. I work out like it's my religion, even when I'm on tour, but I'd be willing to bet he's in the gym daily.

Uncle Mal?

Malachi.

That's exactly who I first thought of, though he still looks similar if memory serves me correctly. He's also very, very different from the pissant little kid I remember that used to fawn all over Julia back in high school.

"You bet your ass I did." He nods his head. "Move and let me deposit her in bed."

What the hell is going on? The burning sensation below my skin is starting to sizzle, but I know I need to keep my cool. He may be bigger than me, and he can probably take me, but if he hurt her, so help me God, I will beat him within an inch of his life.

I stand, my teeth grinding in my mouth.

Cole scoots up, his legs dropping to the rug beneath the couch. Trey lifts, then turning, he tosses one arm over the back of the couch, watching Danny disappear behind Malachi as he strides down a short hallway where they enter the last door on the right. That must be Jenna's bedroom. I haven't ventured far from the living room except for when I went down that same hall last night to locate a bathroom to take a piss.

"That's the second time this month," Danny whisper-yells, coming back out of Jenna's room, Malachi following him and shutting the door after exiting.

"What would you have me do, Danny?" he asks, striding back toward the rest of us. Once they are both back out in the living room, Danny turns around, eyeing Malachi as he's being addressed. "Wait until she's gone forty-eight hours without sleep? Or maybe seventy-two is the number before I should step in. You know what happened the last time, and I'll be damned if I let her fuck up like that again. She doesn't have nine lives like she seems to think."

Danny nods in agreement with his course of action.

Under no circumstance was drugging her acceptable.

"Malachi Hayes?" Trey offers, cocking his head to the side. "Didn't we go to school with you?"

His gaze travels over, taking each of us in, except for Cole, which strikes me as odd, seeing as Cole came off more nervous than not when this guy walked through the door.

"Surprised you remember me, to be honest, Thompson," he says, addressing Trey by his last name. Something about his tone rubs me the wrong way, but then again, I never liked this fucker.

"A little hard to forget the scrawny little kid that used to be obsessed with my wife," I cut in.

He snorts, pissing me off. "And here I thought she was your ex-wife." His expression suddenly changes from easy to lethal. "That cunt is the last person you need to bring up in front of me. Remember that, Hart."

I glance at Brandon before training my dark gaze back on Malachi. "Really?" I ask. "In front of my son, you're going to call his mother *that?*"

"Nothing he hasn't heard before." He places his hands on

his wide hips. "See, unlike Jen, I don't sugarcoat shit in front of him."

That makes Brandon burst out in a laugh. "Since when does Jenna sugarcoat anything? Especially around me or to me."

Taking in my son's demeanor, he doesn't seem the least bit upset by the way Malachi referenced his mother, and that has me a bit concerned. We may be divorced, and I may hate the bitch and think she's a cunt myself, but I'd never show that sentiment in front of Brandon. He should have come to her defense like I already know Danny would have if that had been said about Jenna.

"She does when it comes to you," Malachi remarks. "You're just oblivious to it."

"Yeah, okay." Brandon nods, even though it's evident in his tone he disagrees.

"She does, actually," Danny says, agreeing with Malachi. Danny reaches up with his right hand, grabbing the back of his neck, and for the first time since I've laid eyes on my son, he appears vulnerable, and something tells me it's rare for him to let his guard down. He looks like he didn't sleep at all.

After Danny found out I'd taken Jenna's necklace, he spent the next hour in a sour mood, glowering out the window, waiting for his mom to come home. He finally stalked up the stairs to his room, and Brandon soon followed, though I noticed he walked into a different room than the one his brother did. It didn't go unnoticed that it did seem a bit odd, though I guess they are a bit too old for sleepovers, so perhaps Brandon sleeps in a spare bedroom.

"Jesus Christ, Danny, you look like hell warmed over." Malachi's brows wrinkle with concern and disappointment. Seeing other male authority figures interacting with Danny, first Cole and now Malachi, is pissing me off more and more as each minute ticks by.

"I didn't get much sleep," he bites out.

"If you were worried, then you should have called her. She would have answered, and you know that. Hell, you could have called me." He sighs, shaking his head. "You know the only time she doesn't answer her phone is when she goes dark, and when that happens, she prepares you well in advance, kid."

"I'm fine."

"You aren't." He pins my son with the same type of stare I've given Brandon dozens of times when I'm calling bullshit on what's coming out of his mouth. As a parent, I'd like to think I can tell when something is bothering my child. Then again, after what I learned last night—my son's overdose—maybe I'm not as in tune as I thought. "Now go get back in bed."

"Can't. I gotta be at the gym in an hour."

"You step foot in that ring, and he'll wipe the floor with you. Either text him and cancel, or I'll do it myself. And boy, if I have to do that shit, you better bet your ass I'm going to wipe the floor with you the next time you step in a ring with me," Malachi breathes, his face relaxing. "Don't make me tell you again, Danny. Get your ass up those stairs." He raises his arm, pointing his index finger in the direction of the stairway. "And get some damn sleep before I shove a sedative down your throat."

Danny raises an eyebrow, almost like a challenge.

"Touch him, and it'll be the last thing you ever touch again," I say, unable to hold back any longer.

He has the audacity to laugh, and yeah, sure, he's a hell of a lot bigger than he used to be, but that doesn't make a bit of difference to me. I might have found out about Danny less than twelve hours ago, and his mother and I have yet to talk, but that doesn't negate the fact that he's *my* son, and I'll be damned if anyone harms him while I'm around.

Malachi makes a move toward me, rounding the couch, but Cole stands in a second flat, stepping between us.

"Now isn't the time to throw your weight around," he says, his hand flattening against Malachi's broad chest. "He just found out about Danny. Give him a break."

"Last I checked," Danny mouths off, "I don't need anyone coming to my rescue." And with those last words, he turns, heading toward the stairs.

Malachi grabs Cole, fisting the material of his white T-shirt in his hand, and yanks him to where their chests are inches from each other. Taking a step back, I eye them in a different light.

"Really?" Cole gestures. "In front of the kids?"

Brandon laughs, then turns, tailing his brother up the stairs while he tosses over his shoulder, "Like we don't know the two of you bone."

They do?

Since when is Cole seeing anyone? And if memory serves me right, he was just talking about some chick he banged yesterday at the bakery down the street from his house. Sure, he bats for both teams, but he's usually a one-man or one-woman kind of guy. Never is he promiscuous.

I'm not so sure I'm okay with this. Not Cole having a relationship with another man. I don't give a rat's ass about that as long as the guy is good to my best friend. Malachi, on the other hand, seems like a douche, and from what I remember of his obsession with Julia, I know Cole can do much better and deserves better.

I may be pissed at him at the moment, but the rational side of me knows he wouldn't have kept something this vital from me without a damn good reason. I just want to know what that reason is so that I can understand why. Right now, there's nothing inside my head that I can fathom any reason good enough that he'd go along with keeping the knowledge that I have another son from me. I just can't. There's nothing logical, and I keep asking myself the same thing over and over again. *Why?*

"I should ask you why he and your other two bandmates are here. She's going to be pissed when she wakes if you don't get them the fuck out of here."

"*He* isn't going anywhere until *he's* had a talk with her," I bark. "If she's going to be pissed at someone, my bet's on you, seeing as you admitted to drugging her." My blood boils as the words roll off my tongue, wanting to kick his ass for whatever it was he gave her.

Who does something like that? And why is the better question.

Does she really work herself to the bone so often that she doesn't take care of herself? Or was she just avoiding me?

Guess I'm not going to get those answers until she's conscious.

She better get whatever rest she needs because as soon as her eyes open, she's gonna start talking. I'm not leaving here until she does.

CHAPTER EIGHTEEN

JENNA

Twenty-one years ago

I see Jamie standing in front of his locker, inserting a thick textbook, then retrieving another in equal size. He has Algebra next period, so I won't get to see him until school ends at three twenty this afternoon. It sucks. Now that I'm in ninth grade, in high school, I thought I'd get to see him a lot more than when he was a freshman last year, and I was still stuck in junior high.

I only get *maybe* sixty seconds between a couple of classes. Not even our lunch times are the same. I'm always leaving the cafeteria, going back to class when his class breaks for lunch.

Stopping next to him, my backpack hanging around both of my shoulders, I lean against the locker next to his, praying that whoever it's assigned to doesn't walk up, interrupting us.

"Hey," I say, greeting the hottest boy in Thatcher High School. His jet-black hair is short in the back, damn near to his skull, neat and trim, but the strands on top are much longer, and

He closes his locker door, and the lock snaps in place automatically. He grabs me by the waist, pulling my body flush with his own, not wasting a second of our time together between bells.

"What's up with you and that new girl?" he asks, tipping my chin up, so I'm staring him in the eyes.

"What do you mean?" I lift up on my tippy-toes to give him a chaste kiss on his lips. That's all I usually chance while we're at school. There is no telling when teachers are watching. They don't like when boys and girls or even when same-sex couples display what they deem inappropriate behaviors. They catch you, chances are you'll end up in detention, and if that happens again, my parents are going to kill me. It's only the beginning of the year, and I've already had to stay after school twice this month.

"You've never hung out with other chicks before." He squeezes my butt, obviously not giving an ounce of care if anyone sees us. It's one of the many things I love about him. "I don't know. It seems like you've taken her under your wing or something."

"Jamie." I cock my head, looking into his gorgeous indigo eyes. "She's new. She didn't have any friends. I thought I'd be nice for once. Good karma and all; besides, she seems cool. Don't you think?"

"Maybe. But you're way cooler, and I miss my girlfriend hanging out with the rest of the band and me."

"I doubt Cole does." I laugh. "And we both know Seth couldn't care either way. He's just there to play."

"Cole can kiss my ass. You're right about Seth, but Trey likes you. Sometimes, I think he likes you a little too much."

I laugh again. "Trey just likes bouncing girl stuff off me and having someone to bitch to. The rest of you don't ever want to hear it."

"Because we're not bitches with pussies." That earns him a backhand against his toned stomach. He chuckles, and we both know my hit didn't faze him one bit. "I'll tell you what," he says. "Why don't you bring her over with you. You can be all girl friendly and still hang with me."

"You sure?" I know he is. He wouldn't have offered if he wasn't cool with it. Still, I don't want to get in the way or be a distraction when all four of them are working their asses off on new music. They're starting to get local gigs, so they need to spend as much time together outside of school honing their talent.

The bell rings again, signaling we have thirty seconds to be in our next class with our butts in the seat or get marked as tardy. I don't need any more of those either.

"Yes. Now make sure this fine ass"—he squeezes my butt cheek—"is at my house by four. Later, babe," he says, releasing me and jogging down the hall so that he isn't late. Something I need to be doing too, just in the opposite direction as him.

PRESENT

I dream about him more often than what has to be considered normal. It's been nearly two decades, and I still have vivid dreams, or nightmares if you really think about it, about my high school boyfriend. My only boyfriend, seeing as I haven't dated anyone since him. Hell, until last night—

"About damn time." His voice coats my skin, making goose bumps pop up on my bare arms and stilling my thoughts.

He's here.

He's here in my house.

Logically, the only way he would have found out where I live is if Cole told him or if he called Brandon and got him to tell him. Either is likely. Brandon isn't a good liar. Sure, he can withhold the truth, but once something is known, he isn't apt to withstand the pressure. God, I love the boy, but that is where he and Danny differ. But then, I trained my son to be exactly the man he's turning into. Strong. Resilient. Unbreakable.

I have my reasons for being as hard on him as I am, and every one of them is because I love him more than life itself.

I once thought I knew what true love was, but I didn't, not really. It wasn't until I held him in my arms and laid eyes on him for the first time that I felt that undying type of love. A love that would stand the test of time. A love that I would do anything, and I do mean absolutely anything, to protect.

A couple of years later, when I finally met Brandon for the first time—an unplanned meeting on my part—it was like that little blond boy coated my heart in honey. Sure, he was half Julia, but there was so much more than the DNA that made him up. He was him, and instead of being sad or pissed off over what Anne had done, he made me smile and laugh. I think that was the third time in my life that I fell in love.

"Are you okay?" he asks when I don't acknowledge his presence.

I sigh, letting out a tired breath, then I look over to my right. Long seconds of silence pass, but then my eyes bug, and it's only now that I realize he's in my bed—with me. Jamie Hart is lying on his side, resting his head on his hand with his tattooed elbow digging into my mattress.

His flesh wasn't marked by ink back when he was mine. Not that I'm complaining now, because I'm not. They're hot, and as much as I wish I didn't think he was, Jamie's still hot too. Like the shadow stalker that I am, I've memorized every single one of his tattoos. He's a famous musician, so it isn't hard to know when he's gotten new ink when he's in the media and fans post his picture on Facebook and Instagram daily. I know this because I have an alert on my phone for the hashtags #JamieHart, #BleedingHart, and last but not least, #BleedingHartSummerTour. Yeah, I'm fucking pathetic.

"What are you doing here?" I ask, ignoring his question. By the scowl that graces his face, he doesn't like me not answering him. After a beat and he doesn't respond, I ask again. "What are you doing in my house, Jamie?"

"We have things to discuss, don't you think?" He drops his forearm, landing his arm down on the spare pillow next to mine before sitting up.

"Oh, you want to talk?" I turn, facing him, and slide my legs up the mattress, crossing them Indian style. "How about the next time you decide to fuck someone, you wear a condom. You think you could manage that?" A sharp pain slices across my forehead, reminding me of what my stupid, idiotic, meddling best friend felt he had to do, and I wince.

"Are you okay?" There is concern in his voice, and I hate that I like it, and that pisses me off. "For real, babe, are you okay after what that fuckwad did?"

So, he knows Malachi knocked me out. *Just how long has he been here?*

Jamie scoots closer, his warm hand wrapping around my elbow like a blanket. A blanket I don't want touching me. I mean, I do, if I'm honest with myself, and I like to think I am, but it's a touch I can't handle, so I snatch it from his grip and toss the covers off, jumping from my bed as fast as I can move.

I need distance from him. It's too much. Him being here is too much, just like I knew it would be.

He can't be here. He has to leave.

I close my eyes, putting my palm against my forehead and pressing inward, hoping it will alleviate the pain. It won't, and I don't have time for this crock of shit.

Fucking Malachi. I'm going to beat his ass.

It's not the first time he's done this, and I doubt it'll be the last. I'd be mad at Jess too, but she already believes I work too hard, so of course, she helped him when he asked. Hell, she could have been the one that planted the seed to begin with, when I refused to take a vacation last month. She gets tired of me saying year after year that I don't need one. I'll vacation when I die. There are too many sick fucks in this world that need to be put behind bars for me to get some R and R.

"What's wrong?" He's standing only a few feet away when I open my eyes. He's barefoot, and well, I guess I should have expected that since he was in my bed when I woke up.

"You're here. That is what's wrong," I deadpan.

"You're in pain," he states the obvious, and I roll my eyes. "Do you need to go to the hospital? What the hell did he do to you? What did he give you?" he fires at me, taking a step closer, ignoring that the whole reason I jumped out of bed was to flee from him.

"No." I shake my head. "I'll be fine. I just need water. The stuff he gave me dehydrates me, and that's what causes the headache." His concern is unnerving. And not because it's unlike him. It's exactly like the boy I once knew. Problem is, he isn't *that* boy anymore. He's changed a lot. He's jaded. He's a lot more of an ass now than he once was, and he was definitely an ass back then—at times anyway. Now there's more of an edge to him. He's less approachable. "Can you please leave?"

"I'm not leaving until you tell me about *him*."

"You have a son. There. You know about him. Now. Leave." I take a step back, closer toward the door. He's blocking my path to the bathroom, but it's not like I plan on going there to hide. This is my house, not his, and I'm not some weak bitch. I won't hide. I won't cower, but if he doesn't watch it, I will, and I know I can, kick his ass. And if that's what I have to do to get him out of my house . . . well, I don't have a problem doing just that.

Jamie isn't small by any means. He's not Mal or Josh's size, but not many men are. He's six-one, and he works out. He, Cole, and Trey all do. Seth is the only one that isn't much of a gym rat. Jamie lifts weights. He's fit and trim with a good bit of muscle under his clothes. I know this from watching from afar for all of these years. Halfway through all of his shows, he always ends up stripping out of his shirt. He gets hot on stage. Not that I'm complaining about that.

I, on the other hand, have trained with the best. I'm in tip-top shape. I can and have taken down men twice my size.

He takes a step toward me. "I'm not leaving," he says, shaking his beautiful head.

"You are." I nod once. "And you can do it the easy way or the hard way. Your choice."

"What's that supposed to mean?"

"It means you can either walk out the door on your own feet, or I'll help you exit my house. But know this, if I do it, you'll be in a whole world of pain, so . . ."

His lips tip up right before a laugh pops out of his mouth. "Jenna, baby, I'm a lot bigger than you. A lot stronger too."

"Bigger? Sure," I give him. "Stronger? Not likely."

He cocks his head as if to say, *you can't actually believe that.*

"Leave, Jamie. I'm not asking. I'm not ready for this conversation. I'm not saying it'll never happen. I'm just saying it isn't going to happen today."

He takes another step closer, and I step backward. "And I'm telling you, we are having this talk today. Right now," he says, his tone serious.

"You're going to make me, aren't you?"

"How about we stop wasting time arguing and just have it out. Why didn't you tell me about him?"

I force out a breath and then shake my head. "Goddammit, Jamie, I said—"

I stop arguing at the sound of my front door slamming with so much force that the pictures on my bedroom wall shake. My jaw locks, knowing there is only one person in the entire world that has enough balls to burst through my door like that.

CHAPTER NINETEEN

JAMIE

Present

Who the hell is slamming doors? I eye Jenna, silently asking that very question, but like everything else, she doesn't answer me with a damn thing. I'm trying. I'm trying hard not to blow my shit and lose it. After seeing a piece of what she went through all those years ago, getting pissed off isn't how I'm going to fix anything between us. But I can't be the only one giving here. She has to at least give me an inch. I know I don't deserve it, but at the same time, nothing I did or didn't do, for whatever reason, gave her the right to keep my son a secret.

"Daniel Thomas!" he yells, his deep voice booming. "Get your ass down here now. Front and fucking center, boy." The way he calls for my son—demanding Danny's presence—pisses me off, and I raise an eyebrow at the woman standing in front of me.

It takes everything I have not to demand to know who the hell that guy thinks he is. It also doesn't go unnoticed that he barged into Jenna's house without knocking, and that has me wondering if she has a boyfriend and if that's what he is—her boyfriend.

Less than thirty-six hours ago, I was accusing my best friend of fucking her.

Thirteen hours ago, I was balls deep in her, so . . .

I know she's changed, but I don't see Jenna allowing what happened between us last night to happen if she was seeing another man. My fists clench at my side at the thought of someone else touching her. It's irrational. I've fucked countless women. Women I don't even remember for the most part. It's not like I can expect her to have limited the number of partners she's had over the last eighteen years.

I still don't know if what happened to her back then resulted in more than some twisted fuck beating her. There is so much I need to know. And that's something I have to squash for the time being. Just that train of thought alone is making me see red. It's making my skin burn.

"Breckett!" she seethes, her jaw locking right before she pivots, yanking the door open and stomping through. "No one, not even you, gets to come into my house yelling at the top of their lungs. And no one gets to talk to my son like that except for me."

I walk to the door, stopping and placing my shoulder against the frame. The guy she's eyeing up and down with her arms crossed and legs spread almost mirrors the way he's standing in her living room. He's tall. Probably three or four inches above me; he's big too and older. Probably in his earlier forties judging from the touch of white mixed in with his dirty blond hair. There's more gray in his goatee than there is in the strands on top of his head.

He doesn't take his eyes off the landing that overlooks the

living room. "Yeah? Funny. I'm pretty sure I talk to him like that on a daily basis."

"In the ring is different. At the gym is different."

A door opens from upstairs like someone's rushing to get down here, and that's where my attention pulls, my eyes lifting in that direction.

"I'm coming," Danny says nonchalantly, pulling a black T-shirt over his head.

"Danny!" My eyes cut from him to the girl that's following him out of his bedroom. "Couldn't you have finished doing that before opening the door?" she whisper-yells.

His mom lets him have girls in his room?

I'm not sure if I should be surprised or not. There was a time she spent many hours in my bedroom with the door closed and with us doing many things without clothing. As a parent, though, I would have expected a higher standard. Wasn't like I did that shit when my parents were home. We were discreet about it.

"For real, Danny?" she asks, surprise laced in her voice, so maybe I am wrong about this situation.

"Cat," Breckett—I'm assuming, since that's what Jenna referred to him as—drawls out, eyeing her. "You aren't that naive. They've been sleeping together for over a year."

Something about the pet name he called Jenna ruffles my skin. Could be that no one besides me is supposed to call her by endearing words. That one, though, I just don't like. It's not the least bit endearing in my book.

"You know?" The girl cringes, and then a horrified expression graces her face as she jogs down the stairs, trailing Danny.

Jenna's head falls as she pinches the bridge of her nose, then her head shakes.

"Of course, I knew, Mags." Breckett lifts his arm, pointing his finger at my son. "Danny is the one that told me."

A gasp comes out of the girl's mouth, followed by her bottom lip dropping, and then she punches Danny in the arm. "You did not tell my dad!" she yells. Danny just smirks, his eyes never cowering from the girl's father.

"You did what?" Jenna asks, shock evident in her voice.

"I didn't train him to be a pussy," the guy declares, and I glare at him, irked by his comment. "A guy wants to date my daughter, he better have balls of steel. Luckily for you, Magdalena, he does, or you wouldn't be dating him. Might want to remember that, daughter, and consider yourself lucky."

"So, you're *not* gonna kick my boyfriend's ass?"

He laughs, then my jaw locks as my hands ball into fists. That earns me a questionable look from Danny, but right now, I don't care. I don't like this guy, and I really don't like how close he's standing to Jenna or how he's talking to *my* son. It's like he's talking to his own son.

"Girl, I kick that boy's ass daily. You have no idea what he goes through just to date you."

Jenna huffs out a breath, seemingly ticked off by his comment, and if she doesn't shut him up soon, I'm not going to be able to keep my mouth shut much longer. The days of me not being in Danny's life are over. He's my son. I don't need a DNA test to prove he is. I can look at him and see he was made by Jenna and me.

I turn away, needing to focus on something else or someone else because this is Jenna's house, so as hard as it is, I'm trying. My eyes land on Seth's. The way he's scanning Jenna and her oversized houseguest with his head going back and forth between them has me pausing to look at my bandmate. He's scrutinizing them, or the guy at least. A beat later, his eyes grow large, like he just discovered something no one else has.

Cole walks from down the hallway but then stops, his eyes seemingly bugging just as Seth's were a second ago. Seth's expression has turned angry, and that has me wondering what the hell is going on.

"Oh, fuck," Cole whispers, his eyes going from Breckett's to mine and then to Jenna until he repeats the same process again.

"Why are all of you here?" Jenna asks, realizing the rest of my bandmates are here. She eyes Seth and then Trey before flipping her attention to Cole. "And why do you look like a deer caught in headlights? What's wrong, Cole? Better yet"—her head cocks to the side—"why are you wearing your guilty, I've fucked up look right now?"

Danny's eyes squint, and then his head tips to the side. Something is running through his head, but I can't focus on that. I turn my head, flipping my gaze back on the guy I now know is the father of the girl that Danny is dating. That's when I see it. It's like a light bulb turning on. I know who he is, and it's my turn for my eyes to grow so large I think they're going to pop out of their sockets.

It's *him*. He's the guy that I watched yesterday beating the shit out of the mother of my child with a baseball bat. He's the guy that tried to murder the unborn baby she was carrying. He's the one that took her from me.

I don't know why it didn't click when I first laid eyes on him. I saw pictures of him from years ago when Julia claimed my girlfriend willingly ran off with some douchebag that she'd met at one of my band's gigs.

"Jamie," Cole calls out in a pacifying voice that makes Jenna whip around, facing me. I can't take my eyes off him. If she wasn't in my way, I'd have rushed him the second I realized *who* he is.

"Jamie?" she questions, her eyes confused, telling me she has no idea that I know who *he* is. That means Cole didn't tell her he showed us that video.

Fire rages beneath my skin, and I swear to God it feels like I'm about to light up in flames. Breckett's light-blue eyes land on me. I see the recognition when he realizes I know exactly who he is, and that's when his eyes turn ice cold.

"Bro," Cole says, his voice getting closer. "Calm down. Let's talk about this."

"Talk about what?" Jenna asks, confused. "Jamie, what's going on? Why are you so . . ." Her arms lift, waving both of her hands in my direction.

"You!" Seth barks, an accusation in his tone. "You're the guy."

I step forward, about to launch myself at him, when two strong hands grab onto my shoulders, halting me from attacking him. "You don't want to do that," Danny says, his tone low, so I'm the only one that can hear. "Let's take this outside." He goes to shove me toward the front door, but I don't give up that easily. I'm about to kill this motherfucker, and no one is going to stop me.

"Get out of the way, Danny," I order.

"I said let's go outside."

"Does someone want to explain what's going on?" Jenna asks, her voice etched with worry and confusion.

"He knows," Breckett, or I guess Josh Breckett, if the name she called him in the video was his real one.

"He knows what?" she asks, not putting two and two together.

"Please, just come on, and let's go."

"No," I argue.

"I'm asking you to do this for me." That sobers me marginally. What am I supposed to do, refuse my son the first thing he's asked of me? No. I can't, so reluctantly, I let him shove me to the front door and out of it.

"Where are you two going?" Jenna demands, but I don't stop to answer her, and neither does Danny. If I do, there'll be no way for me not to go after that son of a bitch.

Why in God's name is he in her house?

Why isn't he behind bars?

CHAPTER TWENTY

JENNA

"What the hell just happened?" I ask no one in particular once the front door closes behind my son. Jamie was more than just pissed off at the sight of Josh being here. He was livid and disgusted. It was written all over his face. He was seconds from blowing his shit had Danny not asked his father to step outside.

Which is another thing I'm not getting at this very moment. Danny isn't that person. He doesn't buddy up to someone he's just met. If I'm honest, he's a lot like me in that way. He's more reserved and stands back, observing more than interfering.

I don't believe for a second he and Jamie bonded in only a few hours' time. It's going to take a lot more than a few of Jamie's demands to cultivate a relationship with his newly discovered second offspring.

"He knows," Josh says from my left, his voice almost a whisper, bringing me out of my thoughts. I swing my head in his direction, a cold, detached mask settling on his face. He does that when he doesn't want to feel things or when he doesn't want other people to see any amount of vulnerability. He's a master at hiding his emotions. It's not often any of us, even me or Jess, his wife, catches him in any exposed manner.

"Wasn't that Brandon's dad?" Maggie asks. I turn to where she's still standing at the bottom of the stairs. "Why did my boyfriend just force him out the door?"

"Time for you to leave, daughter," Josh says with a *don't even think about arguing with me* stare.

"Who knows what?" she asks him, ignoring his order. Like her mother, she pushes Josh more than most people that know him would even consider, let alone actually do. I find it amusing most of the time, but like her, I want to know the answer to that question too.

There's no way Jamie knows the whole truth about my disappearance or about his ex-wife's part in what happened to me—or us rather. A cold chill ripples through me at the thought of it all. I try not to think about the past, and when I do, I'm quick to shove it to the back of my mind. No good can come of more people knowing all the sordid details of my ugly past.

It wouldn't help matters. That truth would only cause pain, and pain is something no one needs if I can help it.

"Maggie," Josh says in a stern voice, drawing out his daughter's nickname. "Go home." The order is clear, even she knows if she doesn't immediately comply, consequences are likely to follow. She may be a girl, a young and sweet young lady, but she isn't made of porcelain. Josh is damn near as hard on her as he is Danny.

I used to not agree with him. We used to argue until we were both blue in the face about how to raise our kids. Eventually, though, I came around to seeing things from his eyes. I lived through a hell I would never put on my worst enemy, and I barely survived it. It was only pure luck and the fact that I somewhat resembled someone else he could never forget that I was able to get under his skin.

127

That's another thing I don't like thinking about or remembering. Josh is different now. He changed. He isn't the monster I remember him as when I woke up that first day. He is no longer the man that spent weeks trying to break me down into a weak, afraid, and wrecked teenage girl.

He's my boss, my confidant, my advisor, my friend.

"What did I do?" Maggie inquires, trying to work her daughter charms on him so that he'll lighten up.

"Not a thing, girl, but this is an adult conversation and not for your ears." And it works. He sighs, seemingly appearing more tired than I've seen him look in a long time.

"I'm sixteen," she argues.

"Exactly. Now go!" his voice booms through my small living room.

"You're serious, Dad?"

"If you don't want to be grounded in the next five seconds, you'll get out of here and go straight home."

"Yes, sir." She forces a smile, not liking what he's just said to her but smart enough to know she's taken it too close to the edge with him. "I'm out. Love you, Daddy."

It's silent for a long minute after Josh's daughter leaves, no one saying anything but all of us staring at Josh expectantly.

"I'm not getting any younger, you know," I finally say, crossing my arms over my chest when it looks like he's going to continue to keep his lips fused together.

"He knows. Danny's father, Jen. He knows *who* I am." I scrunch my brows, eyeing him and waiting for clarification even though the hairs on my arms are starting to stand. *There is no way he knows certain things.* Things I want to stay buried forever. "He knows what I did. To you." Josh glances away from me as this sinks in. "And judging by the rest of them," he goes on to say. "They all know."

"That's not possible," I whisper slowly, bringing my hand up to cover my mouth as I take in the looks on Seth and Trey's faces. I know Cole knows most everything. I hated when he told me Josh had told him details I would've rather him never voiced.

"Well, then maybe you need to ask Masters." Josh shakes his head. "What the fuck did you do?" he asks, his tone accusing as his cold stare bores into Cole's.

"Jamie needed to know," Cole says, admitting he not only told Jamie, but the guys too, and Jamie believed him. That doesn't make sense. He never, not even for a second, believed me when I begged him to. When I swore on my life that I'd never lie to him, that I have never lied to him, he still didn't believe me or trust me.

So, why is it he suddenly had a change of heart?

"I'm sorry, Jen. But you gotta agree that he needed to know the truth after all this time," Cole says, guilt etched into every surface of his face.

"I told him the truth. He didn't believe me. None of you did." I glance at the other two.

"You showed him, didn't you?" Josh asks.

"What?" I whip my head from Josh back to Cole. "Showed him what?"

Cole nods, his eyes almost ashamed.

"How much did you show him?" Josh questions.

"I'm assuming they watched the whole thing. I didn't stay. I knew I couldn't stomach that shit a second time."

What the hell are they talking about? Watched what?

"Someone better tell me what the hell Jamie saw," I demand, my voice coming out harsh and not giving a damn.

"A video," Trey tells me when Cole and Josh don't offer up an answer.

"A video," I repeat. "What do you mean? What would be on a—" I stop midsentence, realization dawning. There was video surveillance in that room, my cell, but I had always thought it

129

was just so that Josh could watch me when he wasn't torturing me.

"Jen," Josh's voice softens, and it's taking everything in me not to jerk my foot up to his crotch. I've trained with Josh over the years, so it's not like I'm afraid to square off with him, but sometimes a woman just wants to go straight for the easy route.

"Why would Cole have a video of . . ." I can't even say it. I don't want to verbalize it, but they are forcing me to do just that. *Son of a bitch.* I take a deep breath and try again. "What was on it?" I ask in a too calm voice.

"Does it matter?" Josh's brows furrow with irritation, it's obvious he wants to end this conversation. Well, too fucking bad; we're having it.

"What was on it?" I repeat, slower this time. "And why did Cole have it?"

Josh blows out a frustrated breath, the force hitting me in the face, and then he runs his hand over his hair. "He was starting to forget. He was seeing me as the good guy, as a friend, and the only way I knew he'd never forget what I've done was to see it actually happen." He breathes again. "So, I showed him the worst."

God, no. Not that. Anything but that.

"I gave him a clip of a recording that showed me trying to rid your body of the baby; of me trying to kill Danny before he was born," he says, clarifying the details.

"You did what?"

I stop breathing at the sound of Brandon's voice, my eyes snapping to his from where he's standing at the railing on the landing that overlooks the living room, his angry eyes on Josh.

This is not happening.

CHAPTER TWENTY-ONE

JAMIE

I followed Danny to his black Ford Raptor, getting in the passenger side of the cab while thinking this is a rather expensive vehicle for a kid his age with a single mom on a law enforcement salary, but I don't say that. I don't know him well enough to dig into those details of his life, even though that and more is exactly what I want to do. I want to know everything about him from the moment he was born until now. I should have had those years but wasn't granted the opportunity.

I wronged his mother by not believing her, not trusting her, but I still should have been told and given the opportunity to be his dad. I wonder if it would have changed things had I known? Would I have given up Brandon to raise Danny? I have no doubt Julia would have tried her damnedest to take Brandon away from me had I known about my other son and chosen a different path, a different wife.

I would have fought like hell for both of my sons. There is no doubt in my mind.

The question is, why didn't she tell me? I was an ass. I was more than an ass back then, but she could have blurted out, *I'm pregnant,* multiple times before I left. She could have called me. I didn't keep the same cell phone number after I left home, but I know my mom would have given it to her had she asked for it.

"Where are we going?" I ask after he's been driving for five minutes.

"Nowhere in particular."

"Danny." I sigh, shaking my head. "Just take us back."

"No," he deadpans. "You wanted to murder Josh. It was all over your face."

The anger I felt when I realized that motherfucker was the one that took my girl and tried to kill my unborn child comes roaring back, and my body is on fire. "That's exactly what I'm going to do, so turn the truck around."

"No," he repeats. "That would be stupid. You won't get one punch in before he lays you out."

"Thanks for the vote of confidence, son." I turn my head, eyeing him as he stares at the road. He eventually glances at me, sensing my stare. He didn't call me out for calling him son, and a part of me is relieved. "I'm not looking to throw a few punches. I'm going to kill him."

"Mom's going to kill him. Both of them. What video did Cole show you?"

"What?" I ask, surprised. And then, realization hits me square in the chest—he knows.

"I know a lot. More than I'm supposed to know. Mom and I don't have secrets," he admits, but then Danny goes quiet for a few seconds like he's thinking. "There's plenty she hasn't told me, but she's honest about not telling me things, details she doesn't want anyone to know, and trust me on this, she certainly didn't want you to know, so the fact that Cole showed it to you without clearing it with her first, isn't going to go over well."

"How do you know if she didn't tell you?"

"I know she was kidnapped the day she found out she was

pregnant with me. I know she never got a chance to tell you before Josh took her." He glances out of his peripheral. "And before you ask, there isn't much I'm going to tell you either. It isn't my place. It's Mom's, and I won't betray her trust even on things I know that I'm not supposed to know."

"She won't even have a conversation about why she never told me about you. How else am I supposed to find out when she's closing me out?"

"You already know some of it, thanks to Cole, so give her a minute to breathe. But know this, she may never tell you all of it. Do I agree? No, but the thing about Mom is, she thinks she has to protect everyone. You have to understand the weight of the whole world is on her shoulders, and when it comes to protecting the people she loves most, there is nothing she won't do, and if that means keeping things secret, then she will sacrifice everything and anything to do that."

I let his words sink in, absorbing them and trying to understand. I don't, but it's apparent Jenna has raised a smart kid.

"Why are you so cool about this?" I ask, needing to know. "Why doesn't this bother you? If I had never known my father and just up and met him one day, I wouldn't be calm."

"I never said it didn't bother me. Yeah, I know who you are." He sighs and then takes one hand off the steering wheel, running his hand through his black hair. "But I've always known who you are. You aren't a shock to me like I am to you. And I get that you are. It's fine."

"It's not fine, Danny. None of this is fine. I should have known about you from day one. What happened to your mom shouldn't have happened. Life wasn't supposed to have been like this."

"Who are you to say this wasn't exactly how it was supposed to turn out?"

"Because she was the one I was supposed to marry and have a life with. She was the one I was supposed to have all of my kids with," I rush out like I can't get my words out fast enough.

"And then if that had happened, if things had gone according to *your* plan, then Brandon wouldn't be my brother. He wouldn't exist. My girlfriend wouldn't even exist. And do you know how many women would have suffered the same fate as my mom?" He stops talking and glances at me long enough to arch an eyebrow.

"No, but——"

"Uh-huh." He shakes his head. "I don't know how many either, but the chances are high that it would be in the hundreds, maybe even thousands. Shit happens for a reason, man. Life isn't set in stone. Every path changes based on our decisions and the things we do. Does it suck that I grew up without a dad? Sure. And I'm sorry if you take this the wrong way, but I'd take my brother being in existence over that life every single time. It is what it is, and you're going to have to learn to live with it."

"You know what that motherfucker did to your mom, and you're okay with it?" I ask, not guarding my choice of words or my tone. I'm not mad at him, but if there is something I need to understand, then it's this.

"No," he bites out angrily. "That's one of the things I'm not supposed to know, but I do, and I can't change it. Doing something about it would not only cost me my girlfriend, but it would paint her father in a picture that she doesn't need to have of him."

"Are you——" He holds up his hand, stopping me.

"I'm not finished, old man. I will not do that to Maggie, and I won't let anyone else do it to her either, not even you." For a second, I feel guilty because I had been about to blow up in front of Josh's kid without any regard to her being there. "Brandon doesn't know either, and I want to keep it that way.

Whether you like it or not, he loves my mom, and he doesn't need that shit in his head."

"But you do?"

"No," he agrees. "But like I said, it is what it is, and there is no undoing it. I can't unsee what I saw."

"For the record, I'm thirty-six. I'm not fuckin' old." He laughs, and for the first time, I feel like I can breathe. I'm still tangled up in knots over so many things I don't even know which one to start with first, but I'm at least marginally better than I was when I was standing inside Jenna's house only a few feet from Josh Breckett.

"I guess it's easier for me to accept what Josh did because I know who he is today and what he's done to make sure other women don't go through what my mom did."

"That doesn't make it okay. That doesn't change what he did."

"No, it doesn't, but he hasn't stopped repenting for all the bad he's done since he let Mom go. That has to count for something," he reasons with me, but I still don't agree with him. I won't. I can't. There are no excuses for that level of evil. Once an evil person, always an evil person. And if not evil, it still lives inside him somewhere, looking for the opportunity to come back out.

"We'll just have to agree to disagree on that, Danny."

"Cole will be lucky if he doesn't get his ass beat for showing you the video," Danny tells me, not addressing my last comment. His cell phone chimes with an incoming text message, but he doesn't reach for his phone.

"Your mom okay with your use of adult language?"

"No." He laughs.

"Well, I'm not either."

"Don't really care what you're okay with if I'm being honest with you, *old man*," he says, emphasizing this title he's placed

135

upon me. I don't call him on it again. If anything, I'm taking that as a step closer to Dad.

"Yeah, and I wish you'd tell me everything you know if I'm being honest with you, son."

"Like I said before, I'm not telling you. It's not my place. It's Mom's and Mom's alone to decide what she does and doesn't want you to know." He picks up his cell, eyeing the screen, and then places it back down. "The way I see it, maybe you should consider yourself lucky. Even though I wouldn't change knowing the things I do, that doesn't mean I don't sometimes wish I didn't know. Sometimes being oblivious sounds like fucking bliss," he admits.

"Stop cussing."

"Stop telling me what to do," he fires back, but it doesn't go unnoticed that there isn't any heat behind his words.

"That isn't going to happen from here on out."

His eyes flick to mine for a split second. "Don't think I'm going to start guarding my words for you." Then he slows, getting into the left turn lane and makes a U-turn, heading back the way he just came; back to his mother, I'm hoping. She might not want to have this discussion, but it's past due to get everything out in the open. Danny says I should consider myself lucky, and maybe he can say that knowing what he knows, but I can't. There are too many ifs rolling around in my head. I have to know everything, and I need to hear it from his mom.

Be ready, baby, because we're having this talk whether you want to or not.

CHAPTER TWENTY-TWO

JENNA

A t my request, Josh left not long after Maggie did. Brandon was having a hard time looking at him and not getting angry. He doesn't understand, and I'm not sure I'm going to be able to help him with the war raging inside his head. He feels so much more than any other person I've ever met, or maybe he just allows others to see it, whereas a lot of us hide our emotions, guarding them. He's like his father in that sense. I guess I never really realized that until now.

Seth and Trey haven't breathed one word, and Cole keeps avoiding eye contact with me. "I don't get it, Jen." Brandon stares at me with confused eyes, imploring me to explain.

"Yeah," Seth agrees, piping up. "Neither do we, kid." His dark eyes bore into mine.

"Brandon, honey." I look at him with as much sympathy as I can muster. "You weren't supposed to hear any of that. I'm sorry that you did."

"Why would Josh hurt you and try to kill Danny before he was born?"

"Remember how I told you the reason I joined the FBI was

because I wanted to help those that have been affected by human trafficking because I had once been kidnapped and taken against my will?"

"Yeah, of course." He nods.

"Josh was the one that took me."

"What?"

"Brando, it was such a long time ago, and so much has changed since then. Josh being the biggest one of those changes. He isn't that person anymore."

"He said he beat you and tried to kill my brother."

"Maybe you need to watch the video again because if you saw what I saw, you wouldn't be so quick to forgive that sick fuck," Seth says, his voice rising with every word that comes out of his mouth.

"Dammit, Seth. I was there! I lived it and I went through it alone. Who I forgive is my business. I don't need to watch anything. I remember every second of it."

"I want to watch it," Brandon declares.

"Hell. No." I look up, seeing Danny and Jamie coming through the front door. "You're never watching any of them. Trust me when I say you don't want those images in your head."

I'd suspected my son knew more than I'd told him, but I wasn't for sure until right now. The question is, how much does he know, and did someone tell him, or did he go snooping on his own? I'm really hoping it's the latter. I can understand Josh's need to not just tell Cole but to also show him. I get that, and I can even understand why Cole did what he did. I'm surprised by it, though I shouldn't be. He's been keeping a massive secret from the one person he loves most in this world. He did it for Jamie. I know that's the only reason he held it in as long as he did. He loves Jamie's boys as if they were his own sons, and just like Malachi, I know there is nothing Cole wouldn't do to protect Danny and Brandon.

That doesn't mean I'm not upset with Josh or Cole. I am, and I will be for a while. Josh should have told me he still had videotapes from that time, that he kept them. In all this time, that never crossed my mind.

"What do you mean, any of them?" Jamie asks. "There are more than what I saw?"

I was gone for eighty-nine days, nearly three months. There's no telling how many hours of footage Josh has. I don't have to ask him why he kept them. I can take a guess and bet I'm dead on. After all these years, he's still punishing himself for the man he used to be. For the bad things he's done. For the women he's hurt.

I eye Danny, subtly shaking my head. There's no point in telling Jamie or any of the rest of them that answer. I really don't want to know, and I certainly don't want anyone else to see them. I didn't want Danny to know about any of that, and I certainly didn't want those kinds of images in his head—at least not of his mom. There are plenty of ugly things he's seen over the years. I haven't sheltered him as much as I should have, but I always think about the what ifs. Those keep me up at night, and if the unthinkable ever happens, I want him to be as prepared as one possibly can be. It's why I allow Josh to train him the same as he does his team—hard.

Danny shrugs as he finally rounds the couch, obeying my request to keep that information locked away. He takes a seat adjacent to Brandon and me.

"I want to know," Jamie demands, placing his hands on the back of the couch Danny, Cole, and Seth are seated on. His fingers grip the soft material, squeezing it tightly.

"No," I say. "Let it go."

"Let it go?" he repeats, his eyes darkening. "That isn't going to happen, and you know me well enough to know that already."

"I can't stomach seeing another," Trey admits. He's been quiet, sitting alone in the oversized chair directly across from Brandon and me.

"I can't believe you let some sicko around our son, around both of my sons. What the hell were you thinking?" Jamie places both of his hands on his hips.

"Watch it," Danny bites out, his jaw locking to keep from saying something else.

"Jamie." I sigh. "It won't solve—" I stop what I'm saying when my front door opens, my attention leaving Jamie to watch his mother walk in.

Being from the South, this isn't unusual. Anne and I are about as close as two women can get without being blood related. I've never knocked on her door, not even when I was a kid, and she's never knocked on mine.

"Mom," Jamie says in an almost whisper. "What are you doing here?"

Brandon's head pops up, and Danny whips his body around to face her as Anne steps in the door, parking her luggage beside it, before quietly closing my front door. Danny's head dips, his eyes going from her belongings and then back to his grandmother.

"Hey, Jamie," she starts, and it's evident from the stress marring her still beautiful features despite her mature age that she's been warring with herself since last night. I feel bad. I probably should have waited, but I couldn't. It was only a matter of time before Jamie found out about his mom. "I—"

"Grandma!" Danny's voice comes out sounding chastising. "Did you take a cab here from the airport?"

"Yes, Daniel, I did and do not even start." She holds up her hand, but I know it won't do any good. If Danny has something to say, the boy is going to say it.

"Why didn't you call me? I would have come and picked you up."

"I'm fifty-eight years old. If I want to take a cab, I'll damn well take one."

"I'm not okay with that." He crosses his arms over his chest as Anne arches an eyebrow at the same time.

"Can we get back to what you're doing here, Mom?" Jamie asks, the bite in his tone making me cringe. I know he's going to be mad, but Anne doesn't deserve his wrath. She did so much for Danny and me in the early days that I'll never be able to repay her or thank her enough. "In particular, how long you've known about my son?"

"Which one?" Her tone matches his, and I want to roll my eyes. This reality isn't going to go over well with Jamie. I'd forgotten Anne had told me she was coming. The least I could have done was warn Jamie that she knew about Danny. That she knows *everything*. I can only imagine what's going through his mind.

First, he learns I was actually taken and was telling him the truth. That alone had to have been hard to swallow, but then to think the baby I was carrying, his baby, was killed, and then to see him on a stage, playing guitar next to his brother that's only six weeks younger than him? Yeah, that would have been the shock of a lifetime. And now, he's figuring out not only did Cole and I keep Danny a secret, but his mom did too.

"Mom." He closes his eyes, his fingers now digging into the back of my couch. "Please tell me you did not know about him and keep that from me too."

"I'm sorry, son."

"Jen," Cole calls my name, his voice defeated. "Please talk to him already. Just explain it so that he knows why, because I swear to God if you don't, you're going to force my hand, and I'm going to do it myself."

Jamie's eyes are still shut tight, and his jaw locked. Pain and anger marking his handsome face.

The inevitable was bound to happen. I just never knew when, and I'm no more ready now than I was yesterday, or hell, eighteen damn years ago.

I've heard the phrase, "the truth will set you free" countless times. In my case, the truth scares the ever-loving shit out of me. But can I tell him everything? Can I tell him what *she* did?

CHAPTER TWENTY-THREE

JAMIE

I took off when it was clear no one was going to give me the answers I've been begging for since yesterday.

I know I fucked up. I fucked up in the worst possible way, and it cost us years that we can't get back. Memories that'll never formulate. Memories that we should have made together. I can't stop this never-ending feeling of betrayal from manifesting. The girl I'm still very much in love with. My best friends. Hell, my youngest son even and now my mom.

The sun was just starting to dip into the Pacific Ocean when I pulled my SUV into the driveway of the beach rental I'm staying in. It's a twenty-minute drive from Jenna's house and the same distance from my ex-wife's home.

Even divorced, I know that if Julia finds out about any of this, she'll have a goddamn conniption fit that my ex-girlfriend is back in my life.

Reaching above the stove top and opening the cabinet, I pull down an unopened bottle of the best whiskey I've ever tasted—Blanton's Kentucky straight bourbon. Not the cheapest and certainly not the most expensive brand on the market, but for me? It's perfect and exactly what I need to take the edge off.

After I open it, I don't bother with a shot glass or a tumbler. Wrapping my thumb and forefinger around the short neck, I lift the bottle off the counter, bringing it to my lips and tipping it up. The burn can't be felt until the contents hit my gut after guzzling more than I should. I'm going to feel every bit of this in the morning, but that's something I'll have to deal with then.

An escape looks too appealing at the moment to worry about anything else.

My eyes suddenly snap to attention when the alarm on the rental starts pinging, telling me that someone has opened the door. A code has to be entered within fifteen seconds, or the alarm will be tripped.

Walking briskly out of the kitchen, my senses heightened with caution. I step into the living room and then stride to the foyer. The pinging stops because the correct code has been entered, but I stop dead in my tracks as Jenna closes the door behind her.

How did she know my code?

She must sense that question on the tip of my tongue because she says, "You still use the date we first met for everything, Jamie. It was the first thing I tried, and it worked."

She's right, though I've been using that four-digit code for so long that I'd forgotten it was actually a specific date.

"Why are you here?" I ask, not sure if I really want to know her answer. I'd expected Cole or even the rest of my bandmates. I didn't expect her.

"Because you're right." She sighs. "You do deserve answers, so I'm here."

"You're going to tell me everything?"

"I'll tell you some things, but I need you not to press for everything." She holds up her palm when I start to open my mouth to protest. "Like I said yesterday, I'm not saying I won't ever tell you"—she shakes her head—"I'm just saying give me some time to figure out how best to tell you."

"There is no best way. Just spit it all out."

"I can't do that, Jamie," she tells me, again shaking her head. "Certain things about the past are going to hurt a couple of people I care a lot about, and I don't want to hurt them."

I want to demand she tell me who these people are, but my pride is keeping me from going there. The way her eyes are speaking to me, she more than cares about these people she professes to care about. She loves them, and she loves them deeply to want to spare their feelings.

I don't like not being one of those people that she loves *that* much. I used to be, and deep down, I know there's still something between us. It sparked last night, setting off emotions I'd shut off so long ago. Being inside her again, after all this time, only made me realize every ounce of pleasure I've been missing from my life.

When I remain silent, not making any demands, she continues. "That morning, of the night I was taken, I realized my period was late, so before school started, I bought a pregnancy test and discovered I was carrying Danny. The seniors had already taken final exams and didn't have to attend the last week of school, so you weren't there. Thinking back, I wish I'd skipped that day and came over to your house and told you, but I was barely seventeen and in shock, and the school would have called my parents. I wanted time for it to sink in before I had to tell them their only child was having a child of her own."

I feel like shit imagining what must have been going through her mind. I know her parents weren't awesome parents, but they did love her and only wanted what was best. Her mom being an ob-gyn and seeing teen pregnancies as often as she did, I can't be certain she wouldn't have pressured Jenna to get an abortion. She wouldn't have. I know that for a fact without having to ask her. We'd joked about babies on a few occasions, and we both agreed we wanted them and wanted them together—eventually.

"I was planning on telling you after you got off work that night before your parents got home. I promise, Jamie, I was going to tell you."

"I believe you." It's the truth. I can see it in her eyes, and that fact right there makes me want to punch myself in the face. Had I really looked at her when she came back, paid closer attention, I realize I would have seen the same truth I'm seeing now. I was so goddamn stupid.

"Only I didn't make it to your house after school. The next morning I woke up to find my wrists were clasped together inside metal bands. Handcuffs, only a lot thicker," she clarifies. "I didn't know where I was. There were no windows. Only a bare room with a metal pole that went from the floor to the ceiling and a workbench." She shrugs. "The same room I'm guessing you saw in the video Cole showed you. I never once left that room until that last beating, ironically, the one you watched."

"Why did he kidnap you?" I ask.

"Why does any human trafficker take people?" she counters and then exhales a tired breath. "Usually for profit of some sort. Exchange for drugs, sell for money, force them into prostitution. But to answer your question specifically, Josh took a job. He took me with plans to break my spirit and then sell me to whoever was willing to pay the highest amount of money for me."

Anger seeps into my skin, soaking every surface and penetrating my body. "Did he do any of those things to you?" I can't help but ask, both wanting and not wanting to know the answer.

"He didn't sell me. He never made it to that point. I wasn't exactly *easy* to break." Her admission gives me a small amount of relief. I know first-hand that she's a fighter. No one is going to take her down without going to the mats with everything they've got. It's why she always fits in so well with my friends and me. Her mind is strong.

"Luckily for me," she goes on, "I was different from any of the others he'd taken before me, but also—"

"You weren't his first or his last?" my voice booms, cutting her off. How the hell does she willingly occupy the same room with that monster and not shoot him in the goddamn head for what he did to her? For what he tried to do to our son?

"I was his last," she tells me, all too calm for my liking. "What I was saying, or trying to say, is that I was different but just enough like another that he'd taken a few years before me. That was my saving grace."

"What does that mean?"

"Remember Maggie? Danny's girlfriend and Josh's sixteen-year-old daughter?"

"Yes," I bite out. I hate that my son is seeing anyone connected to that sicko. Danny says he loves her, and I can actually understand that type of love at his age. I had it once, but that doesn't mean I can be okay with him seeing her, yet knowing the things her father did to his mother. He's admitted that he's seen multiple videos of the torture Jenna went through. I only saw that one, and I'm itching to rip him apart piece by piece.

"Maggie's mom, Jessica, was Josh's first. We're both redheads, and that's what reminded him of her."

Wow. Fucking wow. How many women has he brainwashed?

"Let me get this straight. He took her, sold or traded her, and now she's the mother of his child?"

"She's his wife. The love of his life, and yes, the mother of his daughter," she says almost to the point of exasperation.

N. E. HENDERSON

"What in God's name did he do to you to make you think what he did was okay? Was acceptable in any form?"

"It's not whatever it is you're thinking," she tries to reason with me. "I'm not brainwashed. I know it wasn't okay. It's still not okay, but what's done is done, and there is no going back in time to change things. Josh isn't the same person he was then, and I like to think I had a little to do with changing him for the better."

"He should be behind bars right now," I roar at her, not understanding why she doesn't feel the same way. "No, he should be six feet underground if I'm being honest here."

"Believe it or not, I understand that logic and why you feel that way. I'd be worried if you didn't."

"Jesus, Jen." I sigh, realizing how I've easily transitioned from thinking of her as Elise to now calling her by the first name she used to hate. "Did he threaten you that if you told me about Danny, he'd come back?"

"No," she answers, no hesitation present.

"Then why didn't you tell me about our son?" I ask, steering away from the conversation about the man I think brainwashed her. I can see there is nothing I can say at this point that's going to change the way she sees him.

"When I first came back, I had no idea if I was still pregnant. Then you wouldn't believe me when I tried to tell you I was kidnapped and that I had not and would not have just up and ran away. You wouldn't hear me out. You didn't want to believe me. Whatever it was *she* had filled your head with," she spits out, her hatred for her former best friend evident in her tone. "You ate it up, and she was the only person you believed. The only person it seemed you trusted."

"I thought you abandoned me—us."

"But you had no reason to believe that or think that. What

148

did I ever do that made you question my love for you, my devotion to us?"

I'm silent for a long pause. She knows the answer is nothing, zero, zilch, and that I'm being a coward by not verbalizing it, so finally, I sigh and then say, "Not a thing."

"Then why was it so easy for you?" she whispers.

I turn my head, cocking it to the other side. *Easy?* Nothing about that time was easy. It was a struggle just to breathe, let alone get out of bed. I spent many days and nights drowning in a bottle of booze.

"Easy isn't what I'd call it. It was pure hell."

"But you still believed every word she said about me."

"I didn't at first. In fact, I was the last one. Except for Cole, and I didn't believe her until . . ." The images conjure up, and I have to close my eyes, clamping down to try to get them to leave. I'll never be rid of them.

"Until what?" she asks, pulling my eyes open once again. Her brows are furrowed, and her brain is turning, wondering what I stopped short of saying.

"Until she showed me pictures of you and him."

"What?" Her mouth hangs open, and her eyes implore mine to explain.

"Give me a minute," I tell her before walking away, going into my bedroom.

I still have the photos. God only knows why I've kept them all these years. They've caused nothing but agony for me every time I look at them. But I guess they're a reminder on bad days. When I question myself, on the days that the pain of the loss of love gets to be too much.

After I take them out of the small, wooden box on top of my dresser where I toss my watch and wallet each night, I turn to find her standing in the doorway, waiting for me. Holding them up, I walk over to the king-size bed and sit down on the mattress. It's a good minute of her staring at me like the items in my hand have the ability to launch themselves at her and bite, but she finally pushes off the doorframe and strides toward me.

When she stops by the bed, she slowly sits, her leg pulling onto the mattress, mirroring the way I'm seated in front of her.

"She showed me these," I say, flicking them out for her to take. She's hesitant but eventually lifts her hand slowly, accepting the two tattered four-by-six photographs, her hand showing a slight tremble. As she scans them, holding one in each hand, her eyes glance back and forth between the two.

She's quiet, not saying a word until finally, her angry eyes snap up to mine. "This is what you based everything on? This is what you accepted that made you throw away the eight years we had known each other?" I go to interject, but she shakes her head. Her brown eyes throwing accusations at me the same as her mouth is. "This is what made you throw away your trust in me?"

"You're smiling at him in one of them, and then you're kissing him in the next. What—"

She jumps off the bed, throwing the photos at me, her anger mounting to epic proportions that have the fair skin on her face and neck turning beet red. "They don't show you that I kneed him in the balls after he kissed me, now does it?"

I was so consumed with the betrayal that it never once crossed my mind. I can't answer her, and she can clearly see what's warring in my mind on my face.

A sardonic laugh pops out of her mouth. "Unbelievable, Jamie." Her head shakes slowly. "You never once gave me the benefit of the doubt. No one did," she finishes, and I feel lower than low.

"Jen," I start. "You're right, I didn't, and I'm sorry." I'm so fucking sorry, and I don't think she'll ever understand just how sorry I am. She meant more to me than anything, even music and my band, yet when she needed my strength, my willpower, I wasn't there for her. I didn't continue fighting for anyone to find her. Even when the last person I ever expected to be in her corner tried to reason on her behalf, I shoved him into a wall and told Cole never to speak her name again. No—she'll never know just how sorry I am because even if she did willingly kiss another guy, I still should have allowed her to tell me her side of it. I shouldn't have taken Julia's word. But then . . . she sure as fuck didn't mention that Jenna pulled away or hit the guy back. She made it sound like my girl was in the arms of another man because she wanted to be with him rather than me.

So, who do I believe? The woman standing in front of me, the one I loved and lost, or the one I married? Julia had no reason to lie. She was as hurt over Jenna ditching her as much as she was sad that she'd ditched me.

Shit isn't adding up, that's for damn sure.

"I can't believe you right now." She turns away from me, disgust in her tone.

She goes to leave, to walk away from me, but I can't let that happen, so I'm off the bed and at her back before she reaches the door. Grabbing her as gently as possible by the elbow, I stop her. Maybe I'm not sure who to believe and who not to believe at this moment, but there is still one thing that I don't get but need to know.

"I still don't understand why you never told me about Danny. Okay, I was an asshole, and I didn't allow you to explain your side of anything. But at any point, you could have blurted out, 'I'm pregnant.' Why didn't you?"

"I was scared!" she yells, and that sobers me completely up. The whiskey I'd drank half an hour ago vaporized from my system. There's a crack in her voice. "I was so scared, even after you left, and still scared when I found out Danny was safe inside of me. I was underweight, but he was healthy. I couldn't chance anyone finding out about him. I didn't even tell my parents until I was eight months along, and the only reason I told them was because I was freaking out, thinking I was going into labor."

"How did they not know? Your mom is an ob-gyn for Christ's sake."

"They barely tolerated my presence. Like you, they only believed her and her fucking li—" She stops short of calling Julia a liar, her body suddenly going as solid as a statue.

"What aren't you telling me?" I ask, that thought pounding in my skull. Why did she abruptly stop like she doesn't want me to know something when all I want to know is everything. Doesn't she see how much I need all the answers she holds? If nothing else, so that I can make sense of it all. She claims she was scared, but even so, she has to know that had she told me about Danny, I would have done anything, and I certainly would have done whatever she needed to feel safe. Even feeling betrayed, I wouldn't have let anything or anyone harm her or our baby.

"I want to take you somewhere. I want to show you something." She takes a deep breath, air expanding her chest before coming out of her mouth in a swoosh. "Will you go with me?"

Still holding her by the arm, my forehead tips down, touching the back of her head, then I nod my yes rather than speak the word.

So many things still unanswered. I'm pretty sure I'd follow her straight into the devil's den if it meant getting the answers I need to know. Even if it means her words will kill me, I'd still go wherever she asked.

I still love her, maybe even more now than I did years ago. Years didn't subdue anything that I feel for her. If anything, my love has grown without me realizing it.

I'm so fucking fucked.

CHAPTER TWENTY-FOUR

JENNA

He wants to know it all. Every detail. Every second I was Josh's captive. Every second afterward when I wasn't with him. He wants those seconds back; I can see it in his haunted eyes.

But telling him all of it . . . I mentally shake my head. I'm not sure I can hurt him in that way. He already knows the past eighteen years of his life, hell, half of his existence, is a lie. I don't think telling him Julia's part would do him any good, and I certainly don't want Brandon to know what an evil bitch his mother is. He already harbors so much pain because she doesn't show one ounce of interest in his life. I'm not willing to destroy their relationship completely, even if she doesn't deserve the son she created in order to keep the man I love and me apart.

There is no doubt in my mind had Julia not gotten pregnant, that Jamie and I would have eventually found our way back to each other a lot sooner than now. Not that we're back together, and I can't say there's a future—not yet anyway. I still harbor my own pain for the way he treated me back then and how he so easily tossed our relationship out the window, all over unsubstantiated evidence.

I'm not sure I can forgive him for that, and that pains my heart because no matter how hard I've tried to stop loving James Hart—I can't. My heart refuses to let him go, even though with him comes so much pain and agony.

"Isn't this a vacation rental?" Jamie asks, eyeing me and then our safe house after slamming the passenger side door closed.

"That's what it's meant to look like," I tell him, rounding the front of my car and stopping until he steps toward me. Glancing at the front, I explain. "It's technically a safe house, but it's so much more than that. When we rescue victims of human trafficking, they come here because they want to. After being released from a hospital, of course," I clarify. "Come on. Let's go inside."

"Am I allowed here?" he questions, following in behind me.

"It's a space that is funded through an independent foundation. The FBI has partnered with the psychologist that runs the house. We oftentimes work here. We have a command center of sorts."

"Why did you bring me here?"

I sigh, stopping at the front door. It's locked. We keep it that way so that Jessica's patients feel more secure while they are staying here. Panic attacks are common occurrences and often a daily part of life behind the solid wooden door in front of me.

Lifting my key, I ask myself if I really want to divulge exactly why I wanted to bring him here. It only takes a second for me to decide that I will. There are so many secrets that he's in the dark on that I don't want to keep anything else from him. I know I should be blatant and just lay everything out on the table, but my gut won't let me get the words out. I wish I could, but after all this time, I still haven't gotten over my fear. It's only turned me into an overprotective mom. No. If I'm honest with myself, and I do like to think I am, I'm beyond overprotective. I'm a word that doesn't exist.

But at least my son doesn't give me too much shit about it, so I do have that to be thankful for.

"When I came back, you didn't really see me. In fact, you made it your mission to purposely not look at me, so you didn't really see the turmoil I was going through. You didn't see how scared or how helpless I felt." I pause, taking a breath. "I wanted you to meet a couple of people that went through similar things that I did. I want you to see them, Jamie. Really see them, and see how going through what they have has affected them."

I finally turn my head, tucking my hair behind my ear to glance at him from where he's stopped at the next to the last step from the small patio. Even though the sun has fully set in the Pacific, I can still see his shadow thanks to the streetlight being so close to the patio. Guilt swamps his face and eyes. I see it so clearly.

Jamie finally steps up, nodding his head and acknowledging my words.

"There's just one thing I need to tell you before we walk in." His head pops up, waiting for me to continue. "No one besides the woman that runs this place knows my name or my team's names. I need it to stay that way, so you can't call me by Jenna or Elise or even my last name. If you have to call me anything, they know me as J."

"Why is that?" he asks, giving me a pensive look.

I turn, facing him. "Just because we're able to rescue them" —I nod my head toward the door—"doesn't mean we always catch the bad guys. And some of those bad guys are so devious that they often come searching for what they consider their property."

"Are you saying these people don't get protection after they leave here?"

His concern for individuals he's never met is heartwarming, but like most everyday people outside of law enforcement, he doesn't see the reality that we do.

"Not all of them, hell, not even most of them are willing to go into witness protection or accept new identities. Most want to return to their lives, and some even want to pretend it never happened. Getting recaptured happens a lot, more than I'd like to admit, and we can't chance anyone knowing our real identities."

"Does that put you in danger too?" He steps closer, almost close enough to be considered invading my personal space; not that Jamie has ever cared about that. He used to consider my personal space his personal space and his alone.

"What's safe about anything law enforcement does? If it isn't the criminals wanting to do us harm, it's the cop haters wishing harm on us, and some follow through on their thoughts." His jaw locks when he realizes the full impact of my job. "Come on. Let's go in."

JESS ISN'T ON THE FIRST FLOOR, I REALIZE WHEN I MAKE MY WAY down the hall and into the big kitchen and then through a much bigger living room area. Only Cat and Mallory are here, one watching TV and the other reading a paperback book. Crissy isn't in sight, so I'm betting she's in a session on the second floor with Jess.

"Hey, girls," I greet them, stopping and placing my hands on my hips. "If either of you sees Jess in the next half hour, will you tell her I'm here?"

"I know you," Mallory says, not paying me a lick of

attention. From beside me, I see a smile slowly gracing her lips, the first one I've seen since we rescued her seven months ago. It looks good on her, and I make a mental note to tell Josh. "You're that guy. The singer from Bleeding Hart. You're Jamie Hart," she declares, a surprised, full-on smile brightening her face and lighting up her brown eyes.

"Yeah," he draws out, not expecting to be recognized. I'm not sure why he wouldn't expect that, seeing as he's a famous musician. "I am." He side-eyes me, and I just shake my head.

"You know," Catherine says, cocking her head, analyzing him, her usually deep, sad eyes scanning Jamie up and down. "D looks just like him, only"—her chin jumps upward—"he's older." She glances over at me. "Is he D's . . .?" Her question is left unfinished, but it's not missed.

She's asking if Jamie is Danny's father, and that wasn't something I was prepared to answer. Nor will I answer, though her guess is spot on. My son has always been the spitting image of Jamie. That used to worry me to no end. Her question is exactly why, and a revelation that I'm not being as careful as I should be. As I know to be.

"Excuse us, would you, girls?" I glance at Jamie, his jaw locked, trying to reel his temper in. "Come on."

"You bring my sons here?" he whisper-yells from behind me, following me into the control room on the third floor. We have the entire top part of the house. The patients know not to come up here unless it's an emergency. Though we have cameras and alarms at every entryway, we still usually keep the doors open in case something happens, and we have to rush down the stairs.

It takes everything in me not to lash out at him. It's not that I dislike him referring to Danny and Brandon as both of his because they are, but I'm not used to anyone else actually thinking they have a say in Danny's life. Josh thinks he has the most say, and I do give him a long leash where my son is concerned, but he's always known where the line is. Danny isn't his, and I've made damn sure he knows that. Same with Malachi, though, with my partner and best friend; he's more of an uncle to my son like Cole is. Even Jess, as much as I know she loves my son for being himself and because of his feelings for her daughter, has always been able to keep Danny at arm's length. Probably because she likes to think of him as one of her patients, the same as she does me, Mal, and anyone that enters this house, with the exception of her husband.

"Danny? Yes. Brandon? No," I clarify. In all honesty, sometimes I wish I had exposed Brandon to all the bad that his brother has been shown. It's not that I don't think he could handle it; it's more that it isn't my right to make that decision. No matter how much I love Brandon, I'm not one of his parents, so that means I don't get to make that call.

Jess isn't thrilled with any of the things I show and teach Danny. She's made it perfectly clear after each of our sessions that her daughter isn't to be brought into the darkness of our world. Josh agrees with his wife for the most part, but that doesn't mean Maggie can't protect herself if need be. She trains with her dad on occasion, but Josh has Danny training her on self-defense, and he works with her on different types of weapons, honing her skills. She's a sixteen-year-old petite badass, if I do say so myself.

"Why would you expose a kid to all of this? I'm not okay with that, Jenna," he says, spitting my name out in an angry tone.

Maybe he doesn't like calling me by my first name rather than my middle one. Though, I don't rightfully care either way. I'll admit, it's still strange hearing it roll off his tongue. But maybe the more he says it, the more he'll start to learn I'm not Elise. I'm not the girl he once knew and loved. The woman I am today is nothing like the naive girl I was back then. I'm wiser, stronger, and I won't tolerate his issue with my judgment calls when it comes to the boy I've raised alone since the day Danny was born.

I turn on my heel so fast he doesn't have a chance to back up. "I will expose Danny to anything I damn well please. If I think it'll make him smarter, stronger, fiercer, you better bet your ass I'll do what I think needs to be done. You don't get to question me. I've raised my son by myself for over seventeen years. He's the same age I was when I was kidnapped. We don't get a choice of the age we are when exposed to the bad in this world. I want him prepared for anything." I jab my finger into his hard chest, pressing forward as hard as his skin will give. "And if this is the path you want to go down, Jamie, then guess fucking what? I've raised Brandon for quite a few years too."

His eyes widen, the fire in his irises lighting up as he stares down at me.

"You're going to throw that back at me? Really, baby?" He doesn't give me a chance to counter or tell him not to call me that endearment. Not because I don't like it, but because I like it too much. Not that I would admit that to him right now. "Here's a newsflash. If you had told me about *our* son, you wouldn't have had to raise him alone. I would have been there. We could have raised him together."

"And what about Julia? What about her threat to take Brandon away and that you would never see him again if you so much as spoke to me again? Huh, Jamie? What about that?"

"How do you know about that?" he asks, but before I can breathe even to give him an answer, the light bulb in his head goes off. "Cole. Fucking, Cole. Why? Why did you tell him and not me? Why did you tell my mom and not me? Answer me those at least."

As worked up as I was getting, his defeated demeanor and his questions that are filled with so much hurt and betrayal are like a bucket of ice water being poured on me, cooling me off to the point of bone-chilling coldness coursing through me.

"And what the hell do you even mean about raising Brandon? Last I checked, he was still being raised by Julia and me." He waits a beat, and when words don't immediately form on my lips, his opens again. "He wouldn't tell me any details of his OD. So that's another thing you're gonna tell me about."

"Making demands won't get you anywhere with me. That's something you need to learn right now. I'm not the girl that bends to your every demand, needs, or whatever. You aren't my number one priority anymore, Jamie." His eyes flash with pain, telling me my words have wounded him. Still, I have a responsibility to keep those I love safe, and that safety sometimes means keeping them in the dark.

"You weren't that girl back then either. Not once since the day I met you have I thought I could bend you to my will, and not once did I want to. But fucking hell, Jen, you've got to give me more. Tell me everything because the what-ifs of all you went through and then everything else you went through after I doubted you are eating me alive. I'm dying inside, and I need answers. I need them all before I blow the fuck up."

"You're feeling guilty, and you think knowing every sordid detail will somehow punish you for not believing me, for not searching for me, for screwing another girl while yours was having God knows what done to her."

"Maybe that is—"

"Ahem." Jamie and I stop arguing when I hear someone clear their throat. Glimpsing to the door opening, I see Jess standing against the doorframe, her arms crossed with her eyebrow raised. "Mallory said you were looking for me," she states, her green eyes going from me to Jamie and then falling back on me, a silent question in them.

"Jamie," I start, glancing back up at him as I take a step

away from his closeness. "This is Doc. She runs the ship here and is the one that helps all the patients recover."

"Victims," she clarifies, earning a glare from me. "J doesn't like the word 'victim,'" she says, addressing Jamie. "Though, that's exactly what they are. Wouldn't you agree, Mr. Hart?" she asks, letting him know that she knows exactly who he is.

"Yeah, I would." He nods, agreeing with her, and that makes me roll my eyes. She clearly wants that response for my benefit. "Why doesn't J like that word?" he asks, directing his question to Jess rather than me, and that irks me.

"Because if she admits to them being victims"—she jerks her head to the other part of the house—"then she has to see herself the same way."

"But she was," he says, cocking his head toward me. "You were a victim just like those girls downstairs were too." His brows furrow.

I never told him what happened to them, but I guess if they're here, then it doesn't take a genius to know why. Doesn't mean I see myself the same. It's not that I never came to terms with my past; I did. Jess and I will always argue over this, but I've grown and changed. I'm not that girl, who yes, was technically a victim. But the thing is, I'm a survivor first and foremost, and that's what I prefer to think of myself as, and every person that comes out on the other side alive and mentally stable.

"I'm aware of what I am and what I'm not, Jamie," I say, though I'm staring straight at Jess, silently willing her to hear my words. I know she means well, but she thinks I shut off my feelings too often and don't see things objectively. She couldn't be more wrong. She is good with all her other patients, but when it comes to me, it's almost like she's on some type of mission to heal me, and in turn, heal herself. I don't know. Maybe it's that I'm the one that got Josh to break. Maybe she

161

thinks she owes me when I don't feel she owes anyone a damn thing.

My cell phone dings with a specific tone, telling me I need to open it immediately. Jessica's eyes tell me she knows whatever it is, involves a case, so her eyes turn back to Jamie, her head following her eyes. "Mr. Hart, would you care to have a chat with me? I'd like to get to know you, and well, J has some work that needs her undivided attention."

Jamie eyes me with a cocked brow, silently asking if the Doc is a mind reader.

"Will you go with her? I shouldn't be long, and when I finish, we'll talk more. There is more I will give you, Jamie. I promise," I assure him before turning and striding up to my three computer monitors without waiting for his reply.

The door closes, the latch clicking in place tells me they left, and if I had time, I'd wonder why he didn't put up a fight. I don't bother pulling out my cell; I can pull up everything I need from the center computer screen.

Firing it up, it's a chat message with an unknown source I've been communicating with for over a month. I only know him as A_ghost_with_no_soul, his handle on the dark web. In the chat is a link. I don't hesitate to click on it. It takes me nearly a minute of reading the screen in front of me to realize exactly what information has been tossed into my lap, and when the light comes on . . .

Oh my God.

I stare at the screen in disbelief, knowing Josh has no idea—but how? How is this possible? How does he not know?

Pulling out my cell phone, I send Malachi a text.

Me: Get to the safe house NOW. Bring no one. Tell no one.

I can't take the chance that he isn't with Kelly or even Josh. This isn't information I want either of our other two team members knowing yet. At least not until I talk it through with Mal. He's my soundboard, the one that doesn't let his head fill with all the what-ifs like I do. He's logical, and that's what I need.

Holy shit, though. What if Josh does know and he just never . . .?

No! I scream inside my head at my thoughts. He doesn't.

Malachi is quick in his reply.

Mal: Be there in five.

Mal: Was already heading that way.

CHAPTER TWENTY-FIVE

JAMIE

I follow Jessica down to the second floor, where she walks through an open door into a spacious office area. My gaze lands on a desk with a closed laptop and a cell phone neatly placed beside the computer at the back of the room. There are two plush chairs in front of the simple desk. On the side of the room closest to the interior door, there is a full-length sofa with a matching plush chair that makes the office feel warm and inviting. Open French doors are directly behind the desk; even though it's dark outside, I know they face the Pacific Ocean. The sheer white curtains flutter in the breeze, and the scent of the sea permeates around me, reminding me of one of the beauties of living on the West Coast.

"It's nice to finally meet you, Mr. Hart," she tells me as she walks away from me and toward the desk that I assume is hers.

"Please call me Jamie," I tell her, watching as she quickly swipes up her phone, checking the screen before placing it back down.

Taking a seat at one end of the gray sofa, I make myself comfortable as she walks back over to me. The doc sits in the chair adjacent to where I am, only an arm's length away. A dark-colored, wooden end table separates the two of us. She crosses her legs and then leans back, making herself comfortable like I did a moment ago. As I take her in, her round eyes land on me. They are a lovely shade of green.

"Doctors work on the weekend?" I ask, though what I'm really wondering is why there doesn't seem to be security anywhere in sight. I'd think a place like this would have several uniformed officers patrolling, making sure the patients, or residents, or whatever they're called are safe.

"I'm here every day. All day during the week and at least a couple of hours on the weekends. My husband and daughter are at an MMA event today. Danny must not be in any of the matches tonight if Jen's here."

"Danny?" I question. "He fights?"

Is that why that prick stormed in this morning, wondering why he wasn't at the gym?

"I'm sorry. I shouldn't have assumed you knew since . . . well, you just met him." Her expression is apologetic. "But yes, Danny sometimes fights in small events. My husband trains him."

At the mention of her kidnapper, woman beater, maybe even rapist, husband, my blood begins to boil. The calm Jenna had instilled in me earlier is now gone, and in its place is a man that has the urge to do some beating of his own.

"Let me ask you something," I say, tossing my right leg over my knee and wrapping both of my hands over my calf, squeezing. "How is it you married the man that stole you, beat you, and then sold you to God knows who? How—"

Her stern voice interrupts my question. "Jenna shouldn't have shared that with you, Jamie." She isn't angry per se, but she isn't happy either.

"I'm going to have to disagree with you on that, seeing as

165

my son is dating that monster's daughter." I take a breath, huffing out air. "So, let me ask again."

"Josh and I aren't up for discussion," she says, beating me to the punch. "My relationship with my husband, past and present, is between us and us alone. I know that isn't what you want to hear as you're trying to sort out things in your head, but it isn't something I'm going to bend on. My life is private," she tells me, her emerald eyes driving home the words that came out of her mouth.

"If you won't explain anything to me, then how am I supposed to begin to understand any of this? It's not logical that Jen is okay being around a man that did unspeakable things to her, to you, and to others. I don't get it, and I'm not sure I ever will," I finish.

"You may not, and that may be something you have to accept if you want her and Danny in your life."

"They're in my life and will remain in my life whether I accept that or not," I stress with utmost certainty.

"Are you sure about that?" Her perfectly caramel-colored, penciled eyebrow arches, driving her question home.

"No one is taking them from me again. No one," I vow.

She relaxes her forehead. "That might not be up to you, Jamie. I've known Jenna a long time. She's stronger willed than any other woman I've ever met. In fact, she could probably match my husband's determination and stubbornness."

"If that sick . . ." I pull in a breath. "If your husband isn't up for discussion, then you probably shouldn't bring him up again." My voice rises. I'm not trying to be an asshole, though that's exactly what I sound like. It's just that if she isn't willing to talk about him, then I'd just rather not hear any mention of him at all.

"Fair enough." She nods, reclining back into the plush chair she's seated in. "Tell me about what's warring inside your head."

"So that you can psychoanalyze me? No thanks. I'm not one of your patients. I don't need you trying to tell me how best I should handle all this newfound information in here," I say, tapping on my temple with my index finger.

"It's not my job to tell any of my patients how to handle anything they might be going through or struggling with. It is my job, however, to help them help themselves. And no, Jamie, you are not my patient, but I am here to listen should you want me to. Sometimes just speaking things out loud is all one needs to sort through their own problems."

"Then I'm just helping myself." I almost laugh. "And if that's the case, what's the point of your job, Doc?" Jesus Christ, I sound like a prick, and in this moment, that's exactly what I'm being. She was once a victim, just like the other two women I met when I stepped foot into this house. I shouldn't speak to her or get defensive like I've been doing.

"In a lot of cases, just listening does wonders for a person's soul."

"I'm sorry," I apologize, my voice more of a sigh than I'd like it to be. "I'm not trying to be a jackass."

"You aren't bothering me with your honest feelings and emotions." She gives me a warmer smile than I deserve. "You aren't hurting my feelings either. This room is safe. If you want to scream or yell or get mad and curse me out . . . you can."

"I don't want to do any of those things." I take a breath. "I have a lot to wrap my head around, and there are still things Jenna hasn't told me that I want to know. Need to know. Yelling at a woman I've just met or any woman at all isn't going to help me or anyone else. I am sorry, Doc."

"In here, you can call me Jessica if you prefer, or Doc is fine too."

"Probably best if I keep calling you Doc so that I don't slip up and call you anything else when we aren't in here." And I don't plan on being back in this room after we leave. I don't tell her that. Her eyes tell me she has a desire to fix people —even me.

"Of course." Her eyes dip, and I can tell she's looking at where my hands are still clamped around my jean-clad legs. "Are you okay, Jamie? Is it okay if I ask you what you are feeling at this very moment?" Her lashes snap back before her brows rise, and her eyes set on mine again.

Do I want to tell her? I war with myself. She's just going to think I'm another nutcase.

"Sometimes it feels like there is a fire kindling inside me and sometimes it feels like my skin is literally on fire."

"I see." She nods.

"And before you tell me it's all in my head"—I hold up my right hand, shaking my head—"just save your breath."

"I wasn't going to say that. I have no doubt that you feel fire below your skin, that you feel like you're burning from the inside out." Her words hit home, catching me off guard. The only person that's ever believed me was Jenna. Even my bandmates somewhat think the doctors were all right and that it's something I tell myself I feel so that I don't face whatever it is I'm feeling.

"Why?" I find myself asking. Jenna's only answer was that she knew I wasn't crazy and that if I say I feel something, then my affirmation was enough for her. Turns out, though, her words weren't enough for me.

"You aren't the first pat—" She stops herself from calling me a *patient*, giving me an apologetic look. "You aren't the first person I've ever met that has made those claims. No one but you can feel what's going on inside your head, inside your body, or even on your body." Her lips tip up, though she isn't smiling at me. "Living through the things I have, I can generally tell when something is real and isn't real for another."

"Who was the patient?" I ask, wanting to know more about this other person.

Her lips thin out as her head shakes in a quick, side-to-side motion. "Doctor-patient confidentiality, Jamie," is all she says before continuing. "Does it only happen when you get upset, angry, or when something doesn't go your way?"

"All of the above," I admit.

"Only those reasons or other times too?"

"Pretty much just those."

"You look like you control it well," she says, a curious beam dancing in her eyes.

"I guess you could say I've learned how. I know what to do to get the burn under control. I can't make it go away, but if I stop and try, I can damper the heat. At least I could until yesterday morning," I admit.

"I heard you were shown something you probably never should have had to see. I am sorry for that." There is no doubt in my mind it was her *husband* that told her that tidbit. As if reading my thoughts, she nods, knowing I'm back to thinking about the man that stole what wasn't his to take, abused Jenna, and then tried to kill our child. "Do you mind sharing with me how you control it? How you stop it from escalating? I'd very much love to know so that it might help others."

I don't have an issue opening this side of me and telling her if it could potentially help someone else with these same issues. It took me a long time to figure out how to manage my problem, so at least divulging the things I try couldn't hurt.

"Sure," I offer, shrugging. "I can do—"

A rumbling sound stops me, and we glance in the direction of the closed door. Living in a house with stairs, I know that sound is someone running down the stairs as fast as their feet will move. The only person on the third floor was Jen. *What's happened?* I wonder, getting up and heading for the door without finishing my answer to Jessica. Someone only runs in a house that fast if they are excited or scared, and the latter has me hightailing it out the door and down the stairs behind Jenna's retreating form.

Is something wrong? Did something happen to the boys or even my mom? I may be upset with her and don't understand how she could have known and not said a word all these years, but if something were to happen to my mom and the last moment between us was me storming past her without so much as a "goodbye" or even "hey, Mom, it's good to see you," I'd never forgive myself, and I already have too damn much I can't forgive myself for to add any more.

CHAPTER TWENTY-SIX

JENNA

Eighteen years ago

It's been fourteen days since my captor wielded a bat against every inch of my body—over and over. From the little bit of information he has divulged, it's been nine weeks, over two months, since I've seen daylight, fresh air . . . Jamie.

I'm still somewhere in his warehouse, or home, or whatever this place is, but I'm no longer locked up. My wrists and ankles no longer have heavy cuffs locked around them. Though it isn't like I'm in any condition to make a run for it. It's only been two weeks since I received the beating that I'm certain will leave not only physical marks for the rest of my life but mental ones too.

My captor and I seem to be at somewhat of a standstill. He says he no longer has plans to sell me to the highest bidder, or any buyer for that matter, but he doesn't know if he can release me. That was our conversation last night. I want to leave this dark, depressing hell. I want to go home. I miss Jamie so much that it often becomes hard to breathe at the thought of my boyfriend or my life before I was taken.

But at this point, I'm not sure when or if that's going to happen. I know I'm making headway with Josh, but his demons seem to have their claws dug so deep into his skin that I don't know if it's possible to get through to him enough to let me go.

My gut tells me he isn't *all* bad. He feels, though he is a master at masking his emotions. He told me about Jessica a week ago, and the way he speaks about her tells me a part of him deeply cares for her, perhaps even loves her. She was his first kidnapping four years ago.

Josh is twenty-one, so when I realized he had started his career as a human trafficker at my age . . . Well, I was speechless. I had no idea what to say to that. I can't fathom this life, his life.

"What made you . . . you?" I find myself asking as Josh changes the bandages on my back. I'm lying on a seemingly new leather couch in a room with a television but nothing else. His place is so minimal, so bare, so plain. There is nothing here with any personalization. No pictures, no plants, no life that I have seen other than the two of us.

"What do you mean?" His voice is rough, less harsh than before, but still deep and as soul penetrating as I thought it was the first time I met him.

I don't know why that seems like a lifetime ago when it wasn't.

When I woke up, cold and alone and damn near half naked in my cell, he walked in as if knowing I had awoken, his tall form looking godlike, or demon-like if you think about it to my crumpled-up one on the ground. I didn't recognize him at first. The room was dim, but when he opened his mouth and his harsh tone bit into me, I knew exactly who he was. He has a voice that no one, male or female, would ever forget. It sends a chill down your spine. It raises the hairs on the back of your neck.

I'd first met him at one of my boyfriend's local shows. The guys had just hit the small outdoor stage and were opening on a song they'd just finished the night before. I was eager to hear it in front of the crowd that'd gathered in the town park for a day of music, food trucks, and fun times with friends.

Julia, my best friend, was supposed to be hanging out with me, but she was nowhere in sight. I'd seen her half an hour earlier, sneaking off with Malachi Hayes, a sophomore at our high school that has a major crush on her. I knew she wasn't really into him, and it irked me that she was leading the boy on. I don't know what she was getting out of it. It didn't make sense, and it wasn't right to let Malachi think she was into him when she wasn't.

I didn't press her on her motives. In hindsight, I guess I should've, but a part of me was relieved. I'd caught her on more than one occasion, watching my boyfriend in a way I didn't like. It was getting to the point that I was going to do something about it, and believe me, she wouldn't have liked me after that.

"What made you want to become someone who takes girls and sells them for money?" I ask, pushing to my knees after he gets up, taking the medical necessities back to the kitchen. The kitchen looks more like the break room at my dad's office than the one at my house.

"It's how I grew up," he answers, walking back in and coming to sit at the other end of the sofa, the middle cushion separating us.

I lean back against the soft, cold leather as easily as I can, pulling my bare feet up and wrapping my arms around my knees. The coolness of the leather feels nice against my skin. It helps to chill the heat inside the wound on my back. It's only when I go to stand up or move positions that it hurts when the leather pulls away from my clammy skin.

"No offense, but I think you grew up awful." It's the truth, and I find myself getting bolder with my words around him. I don't know if that's going to help my situation or make it worse. My parents always told me my mouth was going to get me in a whole world of trouble one day. Maybe that day is now, or maybe that day was three months ago when Josh and I first struck up a conversation.

The memory from that day flashes through my head.

I had been watching the band play from the front of the park closest to the highway, where there's a higher platform with a railing that overlooks the lawn and stage the band was standing on. From up here, there are tables scattered about for picnics and just hanging out. It's a little far from the stage, but I can enjoy the music without being shoved around by other people. Crowds . . . other people—they have never been my thing, so I prefer it up here.

"Hey, beautiful," I hear far too close to my right ear.

Before turning my head to my right side, I take a step away from him. With an irritated expression, I finally take in the guy that's leaning sideways against the worn, wooden railing. He's good-looking, hot even, and with a pair of stunning light-blue eyes that I've only seen on one other person. That eye color is what drew me to Julia that day in ninth grade two years ago.

The hot guy smiles, his lips parting to pearly-white teeth.

Yep. Gotta nip this in the bud right now.

"You're cute and all," I tell him, offering a smile. "But you see that guy up there?" I lift my arm, pointing toward the stage. "The one singing," I clarify. "I'm his and his alone, so . . ."—I give him a once-over—"you're gonna have to find another girl. I'm taken." I smile again and then turn back toward the stage, hoping he'll get the message and mosey on somewhere else. We're outdoors, after all; we're in a park with plenty of space. He doesn't have to invade mine.

I'm caught off guard when he snatches me by the arm, yanking my body flush with his. The guy's lips crash into mine, and his other hand sneaks up the back of my neck and up through my hair, his palm holding my head firm so that I can't easily break free of his kiss—a kiss I want no part of.

When he's done, he lets go, releasing his hold on me and stepping away like what he just did was no big deal at all. "What the fuck?!" I yell, momentarily stunned. Did this actually just happen? The nerve of this man. I'm getting more pissed by the second. He shrugs, ticking me off further, and that move sends me into action. My knee lifts, jamming into his crotch. From the surprised look on his face, he wasn't expecting that and drops to his knees.

"You bitch," he spits out.

I don't stick around to watch him get back up. I race to the center of the park, the place where the stage and heaviest part of the crowd is, thrusting my way to the middle.

Jamie will freak the fuck out and go batshit crazy if I tell him about this. His jealous streak is far worse than mine. I glance over my shoulder. When I don't see the stranger, I sigh, relieved, and then turn my view back to the stage. I doubt I'll see that douche again, so I don't think it's worth getting my boyfriend upset over. That guy just better hope he never comes around me again, or next time it won't be his balls I go for.

That memory makes me want to laugh and cry at the same time. I should have told Jamie. I should have told my parents. Hell, I should have reported it to any one of the number of police officers that were at the outing that day. I was stupid. A stupid, stupid kid that thought she could handle her own problems on her own.

Guess he showed me.

"My parents raised me in that life—this life," he says, stealing my attention away from the moment that changed everything. I just didn't know it at the time. "It's all I know. I grew up watching teenage girls and boys come and go. My folks would typically have two at all times locked in their own rooms in our big house. When I wasn't watching and learning how both of them would break each person down, then I was physically or mentally training in one way or another. From the time I was seven, I was in a gym for three hours a day. My mother homeschooled me, but studies were never the focus on a day-to-day basis. Getting physically stronger and learning every weapon I could get my hands on were my true studies."

"I don't get it, Josh. Why did they do those things? Why would they want their son to do them?"

"I can't answer that question, Cat. I don't know." He laughs, though there isn't a lick of humor in his tone. "The only time I had the balls to ask my father what the girl—I had just witnessed him almost beat to death—had done to deserve to be here, he beat the shit out of me twice as bad as he'd done to her. He eventually told me she wasn't here because she'd done anything wrong. She was here because she was a girl that no one would miss, no one would care about, no one would bother looking for. And because her life was only worth as much money as a buyer was willing to pay for a piece of property."

I don't understand how anyone, good or bad, could view a life, a person, as a piece of property. You don't own a person. At least, no one ought to be able to. It's wrong. It's so wrong. I may be young, but even I know the difference between right and wrong, good and bad.

In the days following the beating that Josh dealt out, we've talked some, and I'm starting to think he isn't as bad as I'd thought in the prior months that I've been here. I'm still wary of him, his motives, and what exactly made him do a one-eighty. I know it has to be the other girl he's mentioned—Jessica. I just don't know if my suspicions about her are accurate or not, and I'm not brave enough to ask that question. At least not yet.

Until that beating with his bat, I'd been pantless since I first woke up in the barren room. Only now, I have pants but no shirt or bra. Yet, I don't think he has any physical attraction to me whatsoever. He never looks at me in an inappropriate way, and maybe that's why I don't feel modest or even embarrassed at the state of undress I've been kept in. With the deep wound I have across my back, a diagonal mark starting from the edge of my back, near my underarm on the right side, and down two inches past my spine on the opposite side, I know I couldn't stand any type of material touching my skin.

"Are you going to let me go?" I ask.

Swinging his head over to me, he replies, "I don't know yet."

The not knowing, the staying in limbo, is what worries me the most. Just because he said he isn't going to sell me doesn't mean he won't change his mind. I can't afford to let that happen, so if making him my friend is what I have to do to survive and get away from this place, get back home, then that's exactly what I plan on doing.

I just pray it works.

Present

MY FINGERS PAUSE ON THE KEYBOARD, HEARING SOMEONE stomping up the stairs.

"What's with douche prick talking with Doc?" Malachi asks from the entryway. "Mallory was all smiles because there is a rock star in the house, by the way." My eyes shirk away from the computer screen, catching his eyes roll as his bulky frame strides in.

"You mean she thinks someone is hotter than you?" I mock a shocked expression.

"No one is hotter than me, and we both know that," he replies, believing every word of the bullshit that just flew out of his mouth. Though, I'm pretty sure Cole would silently agree with him. I don't know why those two won't just give a real relationship a shot. It doesn't make sense. They are both into each other a hell of a lot more than either will admit.

Plopping down in the plush chair next to the desk I'm sitting at, he arches an eyebrow, waiting for me to explain Jamie's presence.

"No idea what they are discussing," I answer vaguely, and frankly, I don't care. Jamie's feelings aren't as high on my priority list as they once were. Besides, I have another pressing matter that takes precedence. "He's not why I called you, Mal."

"Yet, you brought him here, so I know there was a reason." Always pushing me when it comes to the father of my child. Mal knows I'm not over Jamie and that I never will be. He just wants me to admit it out loud and come to terms with it. I don't think a person has to verbalize something for it to be real for them. At least not to me anyway.

"There is a reason, but that isn't important right now; this is." I turn the screen so that he can see it without having to get up from his seat. He doesn't ask me to explain. Malachi prefers inspecting evidence and forming his own thoughts without others' input first. His eyes flash, and his brows furrow the more he scans the screen.

"Why did you have—"

"I didn't," I admit, cutting him off before he asks the question on the tip of his tongue. "This was sent to me."

"By who?" He leans up, grabs control of the mouse, and scrolls down the screen. His attention both on the document and me.

"A source," I say, shrugging.

"You mean the hacker?" His dark eyes glance over, his arched brow calling bullshit.

"Yeah. The hacker." I don't like divulging my sources, not

even to my partner, whom I've come to trust more than any other person. You have to in our line of work. My life is often in his hands the same as his is in mine. "Don't give me that look, Mal."

"How do you know you can trust this guy?" His head cocks, his eyes roaming in thought. "What was his handle again?"

"A ghost with no soul," I say, not bothering to add in every underscore. Flicking his hand away from my computer mouse, I click on the chat box, pulling it up on the screen and nodding toward it for him to see for himself. "I don't know what to do with this information. I need to tell Josh, but I really want to know how he got it in the first place."

"What if *he* is a *she*? What if it's—"

"It's not her." I roll my eyes. "Yeah"—I snort out a humorless laugh—"like that pampered-ass bitch could hack her son's social media accounts much less evade me."

"I know you hate her, Jen. I do too, but you can't underestimate that cunt."

"I'm not. It's not her. I don't know who *he* is yet, but I do know she doesn't have the skills to do this."

This guy is talented—too talented. He silently broke through my firewall five weeks ago when I was researching communications on the dark web and was able to force a chat box onto my screen. He supplied me with valuable information on a case that led my team to a warehouse located at the shipping port where we found Katherine and two other girls half starved and waiting to board a ship that would take them out of this country. If I'd sat on the information he gifted me, we would have lost those girls forever. Katherine is doing well. It hasn't all been roses, and it's certainly been worse for the other two that still remain in a hospital under medical necessity.

"She could have paid someone. You know that just as well as I do."

He's not wrong. She does have the means, but what would be the purpose? She doesn't know I'm here, at least not that I know of. She hasn't attempted to do anything like she did to me. I've kept tabs on her. I didn't have proof back then, so there was no way I could have gotten her locked up for what she did. I still don't have proof other than Josh's word and a still image he showed me once of them sitting in a booth together.

I was wary of his claims for weeks. I didn't want to believe him. Sure, I was angry at her for sleeping with Jamie. I was hurt that he'd so easily taken her to his bed. At the time, I didn't know she'd made him believe the worst of the worst. It wasn't until I was back home and Josh was long gone that I realized she was, in fact, capable of such atrocities. I saw the evil behind eyes I once thought of as sweet and innocent.

That bitch fooled me once. She won't get that chance again.

"Trust me, Mal." I shake my head. "It's not her or anyone she paid to do it. I'll find out who this ghost with no soul is." I laugh. This time, my tone is full of humor. "Maybe even offer him a job. He's good. We could use him on our team, don't you think?"

"A ghost with no soul," he whispers to himself, and I can see his mind turning.

"I gotta get going. I need to figure out when I'm going to tell our boss about this." I push the chair back and stand. Grabbing my keys and phone from the desk, I shove my cell in the back pocket of my jeans and then start for the door.

"Hey, Jen," Malachi calls to me, stopping me before I walk through the doorway and out into the hall. I stop, wrap my hand around the doorframe, then shoot a look over my shoulder, waiting. Malachi glances at the lit screen, the chat box open.

"Yeah," I call out.

His eyes flick to mine. "A ghost with no soul," he repeats, pausing long enough for his words to repeat in my head and long enough for me to wonder where he's going with this. "Soulless." His word comes out slow and like a whisper, a secret being revealed.

"What?"

"Who is the one person you—the genius hacker that you've become—can't even hack. Who did you train so well that you can't penetrate his walls?" His eyebrow lifts, arching high, his head cocking to the side as chills erupt across my arms, the answer coming to me in a flash.

How did I not realize it before now?

Son of a bitch!

I'm racing down the hall, down both sets of stairs, and I'm out of the house in seconds. Jamie may be on his own if he didn't hear me leave. I have a seventeen-year-old's ass to kick, and then I need to find out why the hell he had Maggie and Brandon's DNA analyzed and why he never once told me himself. It's not like Danny to play games, so why did he send me that information showing Magdalena and Brandon are first cousins.

Unless he wasn't the one that took it. And if that's the case, who did?

CHAPTER TWENTY-SEVEN

JAMIE

S he's been quiet since we left that house, sitting next to me in the passenger seat of her SUV. When we walked out, I asked her if I could drive. She didn't hesitate handing over her key ring with the key fob on it, and I was grateful. I didn't want to sit alone in my thoughts. I need some type of control, even if it is only driving us from point A to point B. Now we sit, parked in her driveway behind Cole's Jeep. Danny's truck is next to us on the right, but Brandon's is nowhere in sight. Jenna has been on her smartphone since I pulled out of that driveway twenty minutes ago, the dash reading nine fifteen at night.

Since Brandon's truck is missing, I'm wondering if they are even home. Perhaps they both took their grandmother to dinner, but then again, it's late, and Jenna and I were gone a while. I chose not to go back to my rental house for my Land Rover, hoping the more time we stay in one place together, the quicker Jenna will open up and tell me the answers to the questions I begged her for earlier tonight.

My talk with Jessica didn't help me any. Sure, she said some things that made me pause to think, but nothing helped move me closer toward any semblance of truth. Seeing those two girls with their sad and broken expressions helped by giving me insight into what victims look like. I didn't get to speak to them, but I'm guessing that wasn't the point of the trip. Jenna just wanted me to see the looks on their faces, the emotions they harbor in their eyes.

I did see them, but I was also grateful I didn't have to stare at them for too long. They both reminded me of the eyes I'll never forget—Jenna's eyes when she walked in, finding me balls deep inside Julia. Between the heartbroken look on her face and the guilt I immediately felt, it was too much to deal with. I knew if I met her eyes again, I'd crash and fall to my knees. At the time, I thought I was doing the right things. I realize now that it was because I didn't want to own up to my own wrongdoings. If I couldn't see my faults, I sure as shit wouldn't have been able to see the truth in anyone else either. And that's all on me. I did this to us. I am the one that broke us.

"When my parents found out I was pregnant, they honestly thought that was the only reason I came back home. They thought I'd gotten knocked up by whoever I'd been with those three months I was gone and got scared. I kept my pregnancy to myself until the point that I couldn't anymore. If my mom had thought once that Danny was yours, she probably would have called you herself. I think my dad started to have his doubts, but my mother wouldn't ease up. Whatever bullshit she was fed, she ate it up, and there was no changing her mind. She is probably still holding on to those beliefs to this day."

"You don't know? You don't speak to your parents?"

"I haven't spoken to my mother since the day Danny was born. I haven't spoken to my dad since I left for the FBI academy when Danny was two," she admits, her brows pinching together.

"I'm sorry they didn't believe you." What I really want to say is that I'm sorry I didn't believe her.

I don't say anything else, hoping she'll continue unlocking the doors to all the secrets I can easily see are hard for her to let go of. I can't imagine holding on to things, keeping so much bottled up. Then again, maybe what I did was worse. I closed the door as if my past with her never existed. I had to. It was the only way to keep myself from running back to her.

"I had to get a full-time job, and I did a few months before Danny was born. I forced myself to finish high school early. I knew I couldn't stay at my parents' much longer, not when they refused to believe me. My dad told me he would pay for college if I'd just take the classes. I didn't have anyone to keep Danny while I worked, much less for me to take classes." She pauses, reading something on her phone, then continues, "There was only one person I truly trusted with my son, only I knew telling her was a gamble. The thing about Anne is that I knew I couldn't only tell her pieces of the truth. I had to lay everything out if I had any chance of her keeping him a secret"—her head rolls toward me, her warm eyes landing on mine—"even from you."

"You told my mom, yet you're struggling to tell me?" I breathe and shake my head. "I still don't get it. What were you so afraid of that you purposely kept my son from me?" And why the hell did my mother go along with it? I want to scream that at her, but I don't. While she is opening up, I have to remain calm and listen.

"Danny's safety, for one. Josh didn't just decide one day he was going to steal a girl, Jamie. He worked for people. He worked for his family. And when he brought me home, he disappeared. The person, the people who assigned that job to him, were still out there. I couldn't risk anyone knowing about our son. Luckily for Danny and me, your mom not only believed every word out of my mouth but eventually agreed not telling you was a necessary evil that kept people safe. She didn't want to, Jamie. She has always struggled with that decision. She never told your dad either, and in not doing so, it gutted her even more. She felt in her heart she was making both the right decision as well as the wrong one."

"You still aren't really telling me shit. Okay, you were scared, and you convinced my mom to be just as scared, but don't you think for even one minute that if you had told me, I would have done everything in my power to keep you and our son safe?"

"And what about Brandon?" she tosses out.

"What about him?" Does she think I'd abandon my other son? I wouldn't have done that. I would've loved them both. Been there for both.

"You couldn't have had both. It was better that I didn't make you choose." She swallows then looks away. That's when I know she isn't telling me everything.

"You're holding something back. I know you are, so just say whatever it is and get everything out in the open. We can't deal with shit if I don't know it all."

"I know you're right, but"—her head shakes, telling me she isn't going to give me more than what she wants me to know— "I can't tell you all of it. I just can't, and it's not because of you. There is someone else I cannot and will not hurt. Not like that. Hate me if you want to, Jamie, but I will not budge on this."

"I can't fucking believe you right now. I don't know how you think I'm supposed to understand any of this if you won't talk to me." I clear my throat from almost choking up. "If you keep refusing to tell me, then I will make Cole or my mother come clean. Don't make me go down that road because if I have to get dirty to get to the truth, so help me God, woman, I will."

"Do what you have to do."

She's out of the vehicle before I can say another word. I

didn't miss the challenge in her eyes before she got out, nor did I miss the hint behind those brown irises that let me know I won't like the consequences of my actions if I go through with my threat.

The thing is . . . what choice is she leaving me?

CHAPTER TWENTY-EIGHT

JENNA

Maggie replied to my text, informing me the boys and their grandmother, as well as Cole and the other guys, were at an MMA event out at Seal Beach. Danny hadn't entered any of the matches, so I never planned to attend that one. I had forgotten about it, actually.

With all that's happened in the last forty-eight hours—well, twenty-four for my boy—I wouldn't be surprised if he entered one at the last minute. When my son needs to blow off steam, he fights. At least he fights in a controlled environment, so I can't really get upset about that. Most fighters respect each other, so when he was thirteen and asked if he could do real fights, I didn't even argue with him or try to talk him out of it. He'd already been taking Jiu-Jitsu since he was four. Muay Thai since he was ten. It was only a matter of time before he wanted to take his training a step further.

At seventeen, Danny is a force to be reckoned with. He's earned quite a reputation as a soulless fighter in the ring. He doesn't show emotion. He doesn't hold back. He doesn't let anything distract him from the opponent in front of him. He's fierce and someone not even seasoned fighters underestimate. Some even say he's more ruthless than Josh.

"Where is everyone?" Jamie asks, walking in and closing the door behind him. He sets my keys down on top of the black antique-looking entryway table that's against the wall just past the front door.

"Seal Beach. They'll be home in about an hour." I head to my bedroom without a backward glance.

"Why are they out there?"

"Mixed martial arts event." I sigh, opening my door. "I'm going to clean up."

"It's almost ten," he says, following me, and apparently not getting the hint that I want to be left alone. "The boys have school tomorrow. At least, Brandon does." He pauses for a beat, then asks, "Is Danny in the same grade as his brother?"

I stop, but I don't turn around. Bending over, I untie the laces of my boots before kicking them off next to my closet. "Yes. The boys are in the same grade, and they go to the same school."

"Have they always gone to the same school?" He stands in the doorway, his arms raised above his head. The patch of skin between where his T-shirt is lifted and above his low-rise jeans doesn't go unnoticed. The dark hair that trails down his toned stomach makes my mouth water.

"They've only attended the same school since they've been in high school, since the start of their freshman year." My eyes can't seem to rise above his waist. In my defense, I didn't get a close *look* last night when things between us escalated. I mean, we never actually took off any clothes.

At the sound of his laugh, knowing he's caught me checking him out, I yank myself out of the Jamie trance, shaking my head and bending down again to rip off my socks.

"See something you like, baby?"

I don't look up when I right myself, knowing I don't want to see the cocky smile on his lips. Turning away from him, I pull my tank top over my head and drop it to the floor. Before I take a step toward my bathroom, I'm momentarily frozen at the audible gasp of air that comes from his mouth.

"Oh my God."

It doesn't take a genius to realize what's shocked him. My scar tends to do that to people that have never seen it, which is why I usually limit my state of undress outside of my team members or Cole.

"Like I said. The kids will be home in an hour or so. I'm going to take a bath, so don't expect me to emerge before they get home." I need a long hot soak in my tub. The last couple of days haven't been the easiest.

Jamie reaches me, hooking his arm around my waist and stopping me before I'm able to lock myself safely behind my bathroom door. Pulling me flush with his chest, he squeezes my middle and leans his forehead down on my shoulder. "Now I understand Trey's reaction yesterday morning. I'd forgotten about it. Fuck, Jen, I'm sorry."

"I'm fine. Can you let me go?" I push on his arm, trying to get him to release me. I need distance from him. And I need it now. But Jamie isn't budging. "Please," I say on a sigh when I feel his head shake back and forth, silently denying my request.

His head slowly lifts, and I think he's about to let go when his soft lips land on the spot his head just vacated, kissing my skin. My eyes close when his mouth makes contact, savoring the way his lips caress my neck, softly and gently moving upward. Jamie has always been able to play my body just as well as he can play the guitar.

"I want you. I need you," he confesses.

With his free hand, he pulls my ponytail holder from my hair and moves my locks to the side while the arm locked around my waist tugs my ass to his crotch, my butt meeting his erection.

I've missed this type of affection, this kind of intimacy. What Cole offers is never enough, and I'm starving for the only man that can sate my needs.

I grab onto the doorframe, needing stability. I'm not going to fall; I know he has me, but my knees are weak. I'm going to go down any second if his mouth continues its path across the back of my neck. He pauses when he gets to the center, inhaling, and then his tongue juts out, licking down my spine.

He unhooks my black bra, pulling the material down my arms and freeing my heavy breasts.

"You still bathe with apricot body wash," he says, his hot breath fanning my scorching skin. He inhales once more, drawing my scent in deep. "How I've missed this; missed you."

When he gets to my scar, he runs his finger from the start down to the end, the pad of his thumb slowly and gently memorizing each marred inch of flesh. Even this is hot. It shouldn't be, but it is. I hate my scar, but I'm not embarrassed by it. To me, it represents my survival. My determination and strength to come out of that time frame a stronger, better person.

Finally, his hold on me loosens and Jamie drops his hand below my navel. Bringing his other around to my front, he unbuttons my jeans then pulls the zipper. The material is peeled down my thighs in a slow torture that has my head tipping back, reveling in the pleasure that's already started coursing through my body. It takes every bit of strength I have to lift each leg so that he can remove my pants. I'm left in only a pair of black, cheeky panties.

Jamie's hands glide up my bare legs, and his mouth softly kisses the flesh of my butt cheek. "You always had a great ass, but this one . . ." His voice trails off as he peppers more kisses, his mouth going to the other side, showing it just as much attention.

As a teenager, I didn't work out or exercise at all unless it was a school requirement. It wasn't something that interested me back then. Then I was taken against my will, and no matter how hard I tried to get away from him, everything I did was futile. He was stronger, bigger, and I didn't know how to take him down. Now, working out and training are a part of my weekday life. I'm usually in the gym for one to two hours a night if I'm not working.

My butt may or may not be something I've actively been trying to improve the appearance of for about five years now, and his compliment soars through me. I don't date, even when Malachi tries to get me to come out and be his wing woman, so hearing things like "you're beautiful" or "nice ass" doesn't exactly happen to me every day or even every week. I can't recall the last time I've heard any of those things from the mouth of a man.

He smacks my ass, not hard but hard enough to bring me out of my thoughts and back to the here and now. "Let's move this to the bed."

He stands to his full height, his body behind mine. Jamie leans down, and the soft material of his T-shirt tickles my skin. "You can walk there yourself, baby, or I can carry you. Either way, I'm getting you on that bed, Jen." His voice is hot as he speaks into my ear.

I know I shouldn't let this go any further, but my body is screaming at me for this connection with him again. I shouldn't, I really shouldn't, but . . . what's once more to get him out of my system gonna hurt?

Like I'll ever get him out of my system. What a joke that is if ever I've heard one.

"Jenna," he draws out, a warning, telling me to move my ass or he will do it for me—literally.

Releasing the painted white wood of my bathroom doorframe, I turn on shaky legs and step the short distance to the edge of my made-up bed. The material of my duvet is black and matches my soft sheets.

"Bend over. Hands on the bed."

Peeking over my shoulder, I eye him up and down. "You're overdressed."

One side of his lips tip up. "Want me to lose the shirt?"

"How about you lose everything," I deadpan, and he smirks.

Reaching over his head, his eyes never leave mine except for when his T-shirt is pulled over his head, but once it's off, those indigo irises are back on me just the way I like them.

My eyes drop to his pants, and when my eyes trail up his inked torso, I stop, taking in the scene in front of me. His flesh is beautifully marked with different shades of black. A ferocious lion with its nose wrinkled and mouth open, baring his teeth, is placed center of mass on his chest, covering all of his stomach. Dropping my eyes to the left side of his lower abdomen, I see the lion cub that's supposed to represent Brandon.

No matter how many times I see this particular tattoo in photos, it chokes me up. I love it. The king protecting his baby. The only problem is it's missing a cub—his oldest cub. Danny's place is missing on his father's skin. It should be there; it should have been there from the start. I've always warred with that thought.

Turning around, I sit on the mattress, my eyes seemingly stuck on his toned torso.

As if reading my thoughts, he says, "I've already decided to add another on the other side, Jen." He wraps both hands around my neck and jaw, tipping my head back to look up at him. "I just have to schedule an appointment with my guy."

"You'll never understand how hard it was not to pick up the phone to call you. I wanted to tell you about our son. Every day I wanted to tell you, Jamie. Please don't think this was ever an easy decision."

I know there is nothing Jamie wouldn't do for his children. Doesn't matter if he had one or ten. He'd love them all with every beat of his heart. I never questioned that.

"I can see that. But I can also see that you are still keeping so much from me." He bends down, placing a soft kiss on my lips. Before he pulls away, he sinks his teeth into my bottom lip, and I gasp, not because of pain, but because of the pleasure and longing for this moment. "Doesn't mean you should have, though. Doesn't mean I'll ever be okay with that decision you made."

I regret the time Jamie lost with Danny. I regret the memories I have that he'll never experience, and I regret that Danny lost just as much as his father did. But I don't regret protecting my son or his brother. I'd give my life to protect my boys. At the end of the day, if I had to do it all over again, I'd shred both our hearts beyond repair if it meant keeping Danny and Brandon safe from harm.

His hands drop from my face, going to the button on his jeans. "Lie back," he orders me. "We can talk about the heavy stuff later. We both need this right now."

But do we? I think to myself.

Deep down, I know it's only going to make things between Jamie and me harder.

I may have my doubts, but they don't stop me from doing what he wants—what I want. I lean back, my upper body flush with the mattress and my feet flat on the carpet. Jamie's eyes roam over my body, refamiliarizing himself. It's a heady sight, watching him watch me. It's intoxicating. It's exhilarating witnessing his eyes dilate, liking everything in front of him. I don't remember ever feeling *this* wanted before.

"Do you know how often I've pictured you in my head, looking just like this?" he asks, his eyes flicking up to mine. His pants drop, hitting the floor, his heavy belt buckle making a thud.

Leaning over, he hooks his fingers into my panties and pulls them down my thighs, then off my legs. Bracing one hand on the mattress at my side, he looks down, and with his other hand, he pulls one of my legs up until my foot is flat on the bed. Running his warm palm up my calf, goose bumps start to pebble all over me. Jamie nudges my inner thigh, making my leg fall open.

"This pussy is just as pretty as I remember." A smile tugs at his lips.

I like to think it's more appealing now that I wax it regularly instead of when I shaved it as a teenager. There is nothing worse than the itch the day after shaving to make a girl never want to do that again, but Jamie loved me bare, so I endured.

He leans deeper, closer until his lips come down on mine again, his tongue seeking entrance, and I allow him in. Jamie's hand comes between us, pressing lightly on my chest, between my breasts, and moving in a slow path down. Our tongues dance, and I lift both of my arms, my hands going to his head and running my fingers through the soft strands of his jet-black hair.

"You feel amazing," he tells me, only stopping our kiss long enough to get his words out.

His fingers run over the folds of my pussy, causing me to suck in air. His thumb follows, going through my lips and sinking inside me. This feels so different from all the toys I've used over the years to get myself off, including my own fingers.

His thumb is rough, calloused from playing the guitar for so many years.

"There is no one like you, Jen. No one gets as wet for me as you do."

"Don't talk about other women when a part of you is inside of me," I bark out. Frankly, I don't want to ever hear about him with other women, any woman that isn't me. I went without that form of intimacy for so long I'm not quite certain I remember how to be with a man. The thought of sharing that part of me with someone that wasn't Jamie made me sick. I couldn't do it, yet, he could—countless times, and I hate that so much more than if he'd been faithful to the bitch he married.

Pulling out of me, his thumb coated in my juices, his fat digit runs back up my folds, stopping at my clit. He circles my flesh, adding the perfect amount of pressure. It makes my eyes roll back, forgetting the zap of anger that had coursed through me seconds ago.

"I only want you." His lips slide to my jaw, kissing, nipping. "I only need you." He moves down my neck, his mouth making out with my body. God, it feels good, and I'm so close to the edge. His path ends, stopping at my breast, and then he takes my nipple between his lips, sucking, twirling his hot tongue around me, nipping, and then sucking the pain away.

"Jesus," I literally breathe out and then swallow. My chest heaves. Then sparks fly, and tingles run from my scalp and down my arms, my orgasm bringing me back to life for the first time in a long time.

Just when the spasms die down, my eyes pop open as I feel a much bigger muscle slowly transcending inside of me. I watch as Jamie's eyes flutter closed, enjoying every second as he presses deeper and deeper in my pussy.

"Fuck, you're so tight," he says.

"And you're so big," falls from my lips. Apparently, he likes that admission because his lips slowly spread, revealing his white teeth. Not that it isn't true, because he is. I cried like a little bitch when he took my virginity at fifteen; it hurt so bad from his girth. He's average in length, but he's thicker than any penis or dildo I've ever seen. Being in the FBI, I've seen more than I care to admit.

When he's seated to the hilt, his eyelids slowly open, the dark-blue irises finding mine. "I never stopped loving you. And I never will."

His head dips, his lips finding mine as he pulls slowly out of me before driving back home.

He didn't wait for me to say it back, and I wouldn't have. In all honesty, I didn't have to. He can see everything I feel, everything I'm thinking by looking into my eyes. We've always been able to tell what's going on with the other, and that hasn't changed. I can admit to still being in love with him or not, and he'd know the truth.

His hand holds on to my thigh, pressing it to his hip bone as his dick draws in and out, over and over again, slowly taking me back over the edge once again. I've never had multiple orgasms this close together before. Giving them to myself, I'm always overly sensitive to try for another. In high school, we were both after the chase and the release. We were both too inexperienced for the most part to figure out how to draw the most pleasure from the other. It was nothing like it is right now. This is so much more than I've ever had.

And I'm not sure if that's a good thing or not. This'll make it that much harder to stop, to turn it off. Jamie can easily become an addiction. Addictions are distractions I can't afford. This can only continue for so long.

"Please tell me you're almost there. I don't think I can hold back much longer. You feel too good. Fuck," he pants, and it's enough to tip me over.

"Yes," I whisper. The feeling of free-falling hundreds of feet washes over me. "Yes," I say louder, embracing the sparks, the tingles, the rush. "Oh, Jamie." I tighten my hands around his shoulders, my nails digging deep, needing inside him just as deep as he's in me.

The muscles in my pelvis contract involuntarily, squeezing him. "Jesus," he says, hot air coating my neck as his voice rushes out.

When both of us come down from our high, Jamie falls a little more on top of me, his strength gone. Sweat beads on his forehead, and his breath comes out of his mouth in quick, short pants.

"You're the most perfect thing I've ever had. You know that, right?"

I push on his shoulder, suddenly needing him out of me and some distance away from him. He rolls off, landing on the bed next to me.

Rising up onto my elbows, I roll my head, peering down at where he is lying. "I'm not perfect, and you don't have me. It was just sex, Jamie. And you know what? I'm starved for it, for this, but in the end, that's still all it is. You and I"—I shake my head, and I know it's adding to the heartache I see in his eyes— "are in the past. You broke my heart once, and I refuse to go through that again. You can accept this for what it is or not. Frankly, I don't care," I lie. I wasn't made to not care. Sure, I've changed and I'm stronger than I once was, but the truth is I still love Jamie Hart the same, if not more than I did two decades ago.

"I can't change the fact that I didn't believe you, that I didn't trust you. I wish I could go back in time and redo everything, Jen, but I can't." His voice is a plea and stings my chest.

"Yeah, I know." I sigh, lifting my back off the bed and getting up. "Life's a fucking bitch," I call out without looking behind me as I walk to the bathroom, slamming the door behind me for good measure.

He doesn't follow me, and as I wash, cleaning him off me, I'm thankful. Had he come in here, I don't know what I would have done, but I wouldn't have pushed him away.

I love him, and there is a large part of me that wishes I didn't. I don't want to feel the things that I do for him. But that's the thing about love—you don't choose it; it chooses you.

I towel off, squeezing the ends of my hair that managed to get wet, and then toss the white towel in the hamper before walking back out.

I stop in the doorway, seeing the man that holds more of my heart than I wish he did, lying on his back in my bed. He's changed positions; he's now under the covers with his arm behind his head, and his eyes stuck on the ceiling.

I guess he doesn't plan on leaving, and I'm too spent to argue about it, so I walk over, crawl over his naked chest and slide under the cover with him, snuggling up to his side and chest.

If he's staying, then I'm making the most of it and taking everything I can.

Jamie is silent, and so am I. If it weren't for the backs of his fingers running up and down my forearm in a slow, measured caress, I'd think he'd fallen asleep. His breathing is even, and I'm lost in a trance as I watch the rise and fall of his chest.

He's waiting, hoping I open up and reveal more about a past I wish I could forget. Decisions I wish I never had to make. Secrets I wish I never had asked others to keep.

"Cole found out about Danny . . . ten years ago, I think," I finally say after I had lain fused to his body for a half hour. "He was home visiting his parents after one of y'all's summer tours had ended. I had just gotten to town and picked Danny up from your mom's. He showed up on your parents' doorstep to let your mom know that he was going to take Brandon back to California in three days instead of you coming to get him. Neither of us was expecting him. You told your dad, who'd forgotten to tell your mom, that Cole was home and would be getting your son. Your dad wasn't home, and I was chatting with your mom when the doorbell rang. Danny and Brandon opened the door. Their living room connects to the front door, a lot like mine, so it wasn't a big deal for one of the boys to open the door. I nearly lost my shit when I saw who it was. Cole saw the boys, and then he saw me. He stood there, frozen on your mom's doorstep, staring between Danny and me until anger filled his face. That's when he fled, and I took off after him. I knew he was going to call you any second, and I couldn't let that happen."

"He should have," Jamie says. Looking at it from his perspective, I get that he doesn't understand, that he's angry. Hell, he should be angry, even at me for keeping Danny a secret. Sure, I had a good reason, but that still doesn't mean it was right to keep the truth from Jamie. It's why I couldn't keep the truth from Danny. I at least had to tell my son about his dad and the reason he wasn't around like other dads.

"You live in the limelight, Jamie. Your face is plastered everywhere, and there are no secrets from the media that they don't want to share. Had they discovered you had another child, Danny's face would have been all over TMZ, Entertainment Tonight, E, and the list goes on. He would have been in every tabloid across the country and the world. I couldn't take that chance. I couldn't let the reality that Josh didn't kill Danny come to light. Danny's life would have been in grave danger." I fling myself off him, rolling onto my back. "You can hate me. You can stay angry at me for not telling you for the rest of your life. It still doesn't change the fact that I did what I know was best in order to keep our son safe." And his brother safe, but I leave that part out. There are certain things I know Jamie can never find out. I hate secrets. They eat at your soul, and with every year, every minute, every second that passes, the more you lose yourself. I accepted that fact a long time ago.

"We could have gotten protection. I would have paid anything, gotten the best security out there to protect him and you. You know I would have done that."

I lift up, resting my body weight on my elbow. "I know you would have, Jamie, but the thing is"—I look down at him, wishing he could understand it from my side—"these people take other humans for a living. They can get through security without leaving a trace. I've been searching for Josh's parents ever since I joined his task force. He's been looking even longer. They are ghosts, phantoms until they find something that they're attracted to, that they think will bring a large profit. As much as I'm not trying to hurt your ego right now, you wouldn't have stood a chance, and neither would anyone you would've hired. No one knew about Danny. That was the point. No one could know he was still alive." His eyes squint, trying to read more behind my eyes. "And until I find them and every person connected to their organization, Danny isn't safe. Danny has to be kept hidden from the light, from your light."

"If you think for a second, I'm not—"

"Mother of God!" I cry out, cutting off his words and throwing my back to the mattress, covering my eyes with my hands. *Fuck! Fuck! Fuck!*

"What's wrong?" he asks, raising up on his elbow and pulling my hands from my face.

"You didn't wear a motherfucking condom, again, you ass!" I whisper-yell in case the kids are home.

"Not seeing the issue, babe." His head shakes in quick succession. "We used to fuck a lot without them."

"Which is exactly how Danny came to be." I draw in a

breath, rushing it back out through my mouth. "I'm not on the pill or any other birth control, Jamie." This cannot and will not happen again. I'm not getting pregnant.

"Even better," he deadpans, his voice more serious than I've ever heard it.

"Don't count on it, Jamie. That didn't make a difference the first time. Don't convince yourself it'll make a difference this time either. You're just being desperate and reckless."

I know him well enough to know that subconsciously or not, he thinks if he can get me knocked up again, not only will he get a second chance, but it'll also keep him permanently tied to me.

What he doesn't understand is that it's impossible right now —may never be possible. God, how that thought crushes every hope and dream buried deep inside of me. I don't want that, and if I could control it, I would have been back in his arms way before now. But I don't. This is what it is—just sex.

And I'll tell myself that lie until I'm blue in the face, because the alternative will make this hurt more.

My job is to keep the boys safe. It's always been my job above all else. My wants, Jamie's wants, will always take a back seat to their safety. That's just part of being a parent.

CHAPTER TWENTY-NINE

JAMIE

The questions that I still need answers to haven't stopped pounding behind my eyes just because I spent the last hour with my dick buried inside goddamn paradise. Sure, they were momentary on pause while I was surrounded with her heat, but now, as I lie stretched out on Jenna's bed with her curled up around me, sleeping peacefully, my head is anything but at rest.

I don't know how I'm going to get any sleep tonight when they still plague every thought.

Having her here next to me like this is everything I always wanted. It's everything I've needed for what feels like a lifetime of going without. At the same time, I want to turn her over, grab her by the shoulders, and shake all the answers out of that sexy mouth of hers. But then I also want to enjoy every second with her I get. She was wrong when she said this is just sex. I've had more one-night stands than I care to remember, even a few casual flings from time to time. What we shared tonight doesn't fit into either of those categories. Whether she is ready to admit it or not, I'm a permanent fixture in her life from now on—and in her bed if I have any say in the matter.

Knowing I'm not going to get to sleep, I ease from beneath her and slide out of the bed. After finding my clothes, I pull my T-shirt over my head and pull my pants up my legs. Maybe if I know my boys made it home, then I can at least settle my thoughts enough to get some shut-eye. I seem to have more questions than she is willing to answer at one given time. I worry I'll never be able to pull out the answers to every one of them.

Turning the knob on her bedroom door, I slip out once I've opened it enough to fit my tall frame through.

Soft voices stop my bare feet from padding down the hall until I realize it's my mother and Danny talking. Not wanting to announce my presence just yet, I step to the edge of the hallway but stay in the shadows. It's dim in the living room. The television is off, but the dimmed lights above it are on, creating a warm glow around them. My mom is on the couch, the back of her head in front of me. I don't see Danny, but I know I heard him.

"You want them back together, don't you?" I hear Danny ask. "That's what you're hoping for."

"That's what I'm praying for," she clarifies.

"Why are you so sure he deserves my mom? He threw her away. He broke her heart." His accusations, though one-hundred-percent right, pain my chest. "How does that make you think he should get to have any part of her?"

Because I want it, I find myself answering in my head. Sure, I can agree that I don't deserve her forgiveness. There is a reason I've yet to ask for it. I'm too afraid she won't give it. And why should she? I didn't offer her the mercy she once begged for. Why should she show any to me?

"Because she's the one, Danny. The only thing, the only one that Jamie has ever loved more than Jenna, is Brandon, and now you too. That I'm sure of. They were always meant to be. I think I knew that from the first time he brought your mother over to our house when they were kids."

"Well, I'm not as convinced as you are."

There's a soft chuckle that falls from my mother's mouth. "You will, my boy. You will." Silence stretches for a couple of seconds. "You are so much like your father. I wish you could see it. You feel as deeply as he does; you love as hard, maybe even harder than Jamie. No one may ever love your mom as much as you do, but give Jamie a chance. He'll show you that he loves her like she ought to be loved by a man."

"On that note, I think that's enough talk about feelings and such. Besides, I think your son wants to talk to you, Grandma."

He knows I'm listening.

"I'm sure Jamie does. I know he has questions. I know he's hurt." She sighs. "And I also know I helped cause that pain."

"No," Danny says. "I think he wants to talk to you right now. He's been listening to us for a few minutes now."

"How did you know I was standing here?" I ask, speaking up.

"I have ears," he says as I push my back off the wall.

"No one's ears are that good, son." I step from the shadows of the short hallway, coming into the living room.

"They are if they're trained to be." He sits up from where he apparently had lain his head in my mother's lap. That surprises me. My son doesn't come off as the affectionate type. "I'm going to bed," he declares when I sit down on the other couch catty-corner to the one they're on.

Danny stands, stretching his arms over his head, his T-shirt lifting and revealing a tattoo on his right hip that's mostly hidden by his jeans. I can't tell what the design is, but I can tell it isn't small. He's only seventeen. I didn't get my first ink until I was twenty. Personally, I think he's too young for something he could regret in the years to come. I don't regret my first one, so who am I to judge?

Danny's eyes come down heavy on mine. "If I hear you being mean to my grandmother or upsetting her, I will come back down here and kick your ass." He crosses his arms over his thick chest, his eyes daring me.

"Daniel James Thomas," my mother scolds. "Do not cuss, and do not talk to your dad that way."

Danny's eyes flick over to hers, his eyebrow arching. After a second of silence, my son looks back at me. "I meant every word, old man."

"I know." What else am I to say to that? On one hand, I'm proud that he's so protective of the women in his life—his mom, my mom, his girlfriend. It shows what kind of man he is turning into, and how can I not be proud or not respect that? Though, since his threat was directed at me, a part of me wants to show him that my ass won't be as easy to kick as he thinks. Maybe he is a good fighter, and I hope I get to see that someday soon, but I'm also a father, *his* dad to be exact, and I won't stand for either of my boys to run over me, even the one I just met.

"Night," he offers before stepping past me and heading up the stairs to his room. I'm guessing Brandon must already be in bed asleep. I didn't hear any of them come in, but then, I was busy doing other things, enjoying other things—things I intend to do again when I wake her up in a couple of hours.

After Danny's door closes, I sit back, relaxing against the back of the couch. I'm silent. My mom is silent. Neither of us knows where to begin. Am I hurt? Hell yes, I am. I'm her son. Why wasn't her loyalty to me?

"It wasn't easy, Jamie," she starts. "If that helps any."

"The thing is, Mom, it doesn't. Why did you, of all people, not tell me I had another kid?"

"What did Jen tell you?"

"Why does that matter now? Why can't you just open up and tell me everything that you know, that you know I need to know too?"

"There is nothing a parent wouldn't do in order to keep their child safe from harm. Even if that means hurting them by protecting their life or the life they created."

"Please tell me that isn't the answer you're going with, Mom."

I don't know how much more of this vague shit I can take.

"If you thought keeping certain things from Brandon or even Danny because you believed telling them there was a chance it would get them killed, would you? Would you keep them in the dark no matter how much they wanted to know, begged to know?"

Rather than answer the question she already knows the answer to, I pose another. "Explain how telling me I have a son would get me killed?"

"Not you, Jamie." Her experienced, tired eyes finally meet mine. "Danny."

Something Jenna said. But they are both wrong. If Danny's life is in danger, we get protection. Hiding isn't the answer. Hiding doesn't keep people safe. It just means you're chased and hunted longer.

And that's no way to live.

Danny deserves more. Jenna deserves more, and that's exactly what I plan on showing them if she gives me that chance, and I pray she does.

***

SLEEP ELUDED ME FOR ANOTHER NIGHT IN A ROW. AFTER MY mom dropped that bomb on me—again without any real explanation, mind you—I crawled back in bed and lay there in thought for hours. I finally crawled out half an hour ago when Jenna went to take a shower. I needed coffee, and I heard noise and figured the boys were close to heading to school.

So far, I've only seen Danny. Brandon, nor my mom, has come down the stairs. I didn't think to ask where she was sleeping, but likely it must have been one of the boys' rooms upstairs. It's still weird that Brandon has his own room here, but I've yet to ask why. That question seems less important than the rest.

I'm on my second cup of black coffee as I stir cream into another mug for Jenna. She should be finishing up getting ready, and I want to remind her that I remember how she takes her coffee. There is so much I want to remind her of, yet the sickening feeling I have in my gut makes me keep questioning if I'm going to get to them all.

"Where's your brother?" I ask Danny when he walks through the kitchen, grabbing a Pop-Tart from one of the cabinets, sticking it in the side pocket of his backpack. It doesn't look like Brandon is going to be coming down the stairs. I know they have to leave for school any minute or they'll risk being late.

"Went to his *other* house after he dropped me off last night." His voice has a tinge of irritation in it that makes me think he doesn't like it when Brandon doesn't stay over here.

"You mean his *only* house? The one where he lives?" I don't know why I'm poking him, but for some reason, I get just as irritated when I think about Brandon staying somewhere other than home on a regular basis. Why his mother would allow that is beyond me. There is no way that she's met Brandon's best friend's mother because if she knew Jenna was here, all hell would break loose. Then again, it's not like she isn't going to find out soon anyway. Danny isn't a secret I plan on keeping the way Jenna or Mom or even my so-called best friend has for all these years.

"Considering he sleeps here more than he does there, one might say this is his *real* house."

"Why are you two arguing this early in the morning?" My lips turn up at the sound of her voice. Unlike me, she does sound rested, and her voice is lighter today than it was yesterday, or even the morning before that.

Jenna comes walking from down the hallway dressed in the same type of outfit I've seen her in for the past three days straight. I'm starting to think this is her FBI attire, but then I wonder if she dresses differently when she isn't working. There is still so much I want to know, so many questions I want to ask. I don't, though. Last night was amazing, and I'm not chancing ruining that bliss just yet.

"Why are you letting him sleep in your bed?" Danny crosses his arms over his chest as Jenna stops in front of me, taking the mug I'm holding out to her. "Has he even taken you on a first date, Mom?"

I wouldn't have taken him for the joking type. Brandon? Sure. Danny doesn't seem the type, but then again, I've known my son for less than two full days so . . .

"Can it, smart-ass. Speaking of, though"—she jabs her finger into his chest—"your little ass better not make me a grandmother at thirty-six. We clear?" She nods slowly, indicating that his answer better be "yes, ma'am."

"Crystal." His lips spread wide, showing a perfect row of white teeth. "You'd be at least thirty-seven before she popped the little shit out anyway."

"Language!" she scolds, smacking him on the shoulder. I laugh, unable to hold it in any longer. Danny chuckles. "I'm serious, Daniel James. You knock Maggie up, and I will. Beat. Your. Ass."

"I'm pretty sure Josh would kill me before you got that chance." At the mention of the word *kill,* along with that motherfucker's name, my smile drops, and my jaw locks. Danny's eyes meet mine. "Did I hit a nerve, old man?"

"You think?" I draw in a needed deep breath. Blowing it back out, the hot air blows through Jenna's ponytail from her close proximity.

Danny shrugs. "Maybe you shouldn't sleep with my mom then. Ya feel me?"

"Well," I start, mirroring the same mock smile he's showing me. "If I hadn't ever slept with your mother, then your little punk ass wouldn't be standing here talking shit, now would it?"

"Enough, you two." Jenna looks from me to her son, making her demand clear. "I want you home right after school. You and I have something to talk about." Her eyes squint at our son, having a silent conversation. I don't like it. I want to be a part of everything. That need only seems to be growing, not subsiding.

"Sorry. No can do. I have training at Jackson's until six with Josh," he tells her, and at the mention of his name again, I want to break something. The punk is doing it on purpose. I see it in his amused eyes.

"I don't care. Tell Josh I said you have to report home."

"Can't it wait?" He sighs.

"Maybe that's something you should have thought about before you decided to play little secret FBI agent and hack your own mother. You'll be lucky if you see a computer ever again for that shit. Among *other* things," she adds. Danny rolls his eyes, not taking her reprimand seriously.

"One of you want to clue me in on what you both are talking circles around?" I ask, setting my mug down on the counter.

"No," they both say simultaneously without taking their eyes off of one another.

"Look," Jenna stresses, handing her coffee mug to me but talking to our son. "We are talking about this and that *other* information you sent me yesterday when you get home today, so my advice to you is that you better come clean about everything you've been up to and everything that you know, Daniel. Am I making myself clear now?"

"And all I'm saying is that there are some *things* we shouldn't talk about. Don't you agree?"

"Not anymore. You made that choice when you went snooping."

"Can we all stop having secrets around here?" I say, feeling fed up with all this bullshit. "You can't demand he tell you whatever it is he's keeping his lips shut about when you won't even tell me the real reason behind keeping him from me all this time."

"Back off, Jamie," she says, the heat in her voice as lethal as the hard eyes that flick to mine. "This is between Danny and me. Got it?"

"Not in the least, baby." She ignores me, pulling her phone out of her back pocket, eyeing the locked screen, her brows creasing with concern.

"Can Mommy and Daddy please argue after I leave?" he says, not expecting an answer as he turns away from us. "I gotta get to school."

"Can you call your brother before you leave the driveway?" Jenna asks Danny, still staring at her phone. "He's still asleep, and he's going to be late if he doesn't hustle." *How does she know that?* I think to myself. "If he were here, instead of with *her*, he wouldn't still be in bed."

The jab at my ex-wife's expense has my mouth dropping open, not believing she just said that in front of Danny. I can knock on Julia for a lot of things, but not raising my son right isn't one of them. She had to deal with a lot with me being on tour one to two times a year for the past eighteen years. Even I can cut her some slack if she isn't on top of Brandon, making sure he's up and ready for school on time every day. The boy is seventeen. He should be able to manage that duty all by himself.

"Can we not talk about my other son's mother negatively in front of either of the boys, please?"

Danny snorts, stopping in his tracks and pulling my stare from his mother to him standing at the door I'm assuming leads into the garage. "Guess no one's gonna talk at all in that case."

"What's that supposed to mean?"

He shrugs, not answering. Jenna doesn't volunteer an answer either.

"Yeah, Mom. I'll call him. Love you." He heads back over and leans down, dropping a kiss on her cheek, and in this moment, Julia is forgotten as I watch my son be affectionate with his mom. It fills my broken heart with joy, but it also makes me more aware of all that I've missed. And I've missed a hell of a lot.

"Love you too, baby. See ya later."

Before he's out the door, he glances over his shoulder, his indigo eyes falling on me. "Later, old man."

I nod, my voice caught in my throat. I'm quickly getting used to this, and I'll do anything to ensure it isn't ripped away from me again. Maybe Jenna is right; maybe I'm not using condoms because I'm hoping she'll get pregnant, and that'll ensure I really am a permanent fixture in their lives.

Don't count on it, Jamie. That didn't make a difference the first time. Don't convince yourself that it'll make a difference this time either. You're just being desperate and reckless. Her words from last night slam back into me.

Perhaps. But perhaps I want a do-over too, and not only because I didn't get those years with Danny. I still want the whole package with Jenna. The best friend. The partner in crime. That one person I can tell anything to and not be judged. I can make a mistake and not feel like I'm going to be reprimanded for my failures.

I want a real marriage. A real relationship. I want it all, and I want it with Jenna Thomas.

CHAPTER THIRTY

JENNA

I went to sleep feeling lighter, yet more whole than I've felt in years. I slept peacefully for the first time since before Josh took me. I'd forgotten what that was like. My normal was a couple of hours here and there. I was usually the last asleep and the first awake hours before dawn. I'm not used to being the last one out of bed in the morning.

Jamie woke me up with his beautiful, sexy head between my legs, and then, even though I vowed he and I couldn't happen again, I didn't put up a fight when he lined up his dick with my entrance—sans a condom again. Only, this time, I can't bitch. I watched him sink inside me bare and hard as a fucking rock. Damn, was it good too.

But then I got out of the shower, and a feeling of fear washed over me that I can't seem to shake. Worry etches every inch of my body, and I almost didn't let Danny go to school. He doesn't deserve the crazy, fearful mom that I am, so against what my heart was screaming, I watched him walk out the door.

time I've felt helpless, worthless, desperate; it won't be the last time either, no matter how much I wish for the normal person I used to be to come back to me. Instead, I'm this helicopter mom that feels strung out half the time.

"Hey, Jen," Jamie calls out, stealing me from my depressing thoughts.

"Yeah," I reply as he strides to me, stopping so close in front of me that I have to tip my head back to look at him, a serious expression marring his perfect face. His arms glide around my back, pulling me even closer, and then his fingers thread through my hair. "Can we continue living in last night for a little while longer? Let all the bullshit go for a few hours?"

"Did you run out of questions to demand answers to?"

He shakes his head. "No." Then he leans down, his lips softly meeting mine. His tongue coaxes my lips, needing more of me. I open, letting him in as if I'm already his, giving him what he wants—even if only for a moment. But like reality does, it brings me back to the here and now.

"We don't need to give the boys the wrong impression, Jamie," I say between our mouths, trying to muster up the strength to pull away. "We don't need to get their hopes up." Yet, as my feeble words leave my mouth, I don't pull away or stop my own pursuit, dancing my tongue with his.

I should have followed my son out of the house and left for work like I do every morning. This one shouldn't have been different, except it was. Jamie is here, and I wanted another minute alone with him.

"They're big boys. And I'm pretty sure we're giving them the right impression, baby."

We're not, but fuck me if I don't want to get lost in this fantasy.

Fortunately for me, or unfortunately, his phone decides to ring, breaking the spell I seem to find myself under when I'm locked in his arms. I'm more irritated at the nuisance of getting interrupted than I should be. I need to be grateful. Any more of Jamie and I'll lose all willpower.

He's wrong. The boys don't need to see us together; that'll never be a possibility.

CHAPTER THIRTY-ONE

JAMIE

Fucking perfect. My phone just had to ring, ruining all the good shit happening between us. I see that look in her eyes. She's thinking too hard. She's going to stop this, and I can't let that happen. Not if I stand a chance at gaining her trust, earning her forgiveness, and getting my woman back in my arms for longer than a few hours.

Pulling my cell out of my front pocket, I grit my teeth at Julia's name showing on the screen. *Not now, bitch.* I decline the call, sending it to my voice mail. That's the only part of me she's gonna get. We're done. We're over. The sooner she gets that through her head, the better for all of us.

"I'll be at work all day. Don't really see the point in living in a fantasy, Jamie," Jenna says, taking a big step backward. She isn't getting out of this. She isn't ditching me.

"Nothing about last night or again this morning was a fantasy. Every second I was inside you was real," I remind her.

"And it doesn't need to happen again," she quickly follows, looking away and taking another step away from me.

I take a long step forward, closer to her than I was before she tried to gain distance from me. "Oh, it's happening again," I declare. "In fact, it's going to happen in the next minute or two." My lips spread.

"I'm leaving for work, so no, sorry, my legs are closed. Besides," she exasperates, "it's not right to give your son the wrong impression."

"The boys are damn near grown. They'll be fine." Why the hell is she harping on the boys. They're teenagers, they'll be fine. Perhaps it'll be an adjustment. Hell, it'll be an adjustment for me too. But I want this, and I know Jenna wants it too. It's written all over her face in plain sight. She's doing a shit job hiding her true feelings from me.

"I'm not talking about Danny. He can handle almost anything. It's Brandon you need to be careful with. He already has parental issues. He doesn't need more."

"What the hell is that supposed to mean?"

"That's for you to discuss with him." She sighs. "It's not my place to interfere in your relationship with him."

"Well, how about you explain his OD that no one has yet to elaborate on. That is the least you can do if you aren't going to tell me any more of your *other* secrets. And yeah, baby, I know you're still holding on to things that I need to know, that I have a right to know. Spill, Jen."

"You really need to talk to Brandon, Jamie."

"I'm talking to you. I'm asking you to tell me."

Her eyes close, shutting tight, and I know I've got her. I see the resolve on her face. Finally.

Her eyelids flip open, staring up at me. "You left for your winter tour. He'd just found out about the divorce. He was alone. He hates being alone. In fact, Brandon literally can't deal with being alone for any length of time."

"He wasn't alone. His mother is always there for him."

"Trust me, Jamie. You need to talk to him. Not me."

"Well, he isn't here, and I want answers. And you have them. Why do you know more about Brandon than I do? Why does he have a room here? Why does he sleep over here more than he does at home if what Danny claims is true? Why do I feel like I'm the only one that doesn't know shit about shit when it comes to my life?"

Jenna shoves me backward, away from her, and then takes a breath. "I just told you. He doesn't like being alone."

"And I just said, he isn't alone. He has a mother—"

"She is not his mother!" she yells angrily. "That bitch might have given birth to him, but she has never mothered him." A humorless laugh sneaks out of her mouth. "Well, not unless she's putting on a show for you, that is. Brandon is and has always been her means to getting what she wanted—you."

"You hate her? Fine. I get that. It isn't like I care for her that much either. But like you, she is still the mother of one of my sons. I have to at least give her that. She raised him, she's been there for him when I couldn't be, she has always doted on him."

"God, for someone as smart as you are, you're a complete dumb fuck when it comes to her." She snorts. "Dote on him, my ass. If you call leaving a twelve-year-old home alone while she went off to vacation in France doting, then I guess she fucking dotes on him."

"What the hell are you talking about? She would never—"

"Don't," she fires back, the fair skin across her face and neck blazing with a red tint. "Don't even finish that thought because you are clueless. The day you leave on tour is always the day she flies off to wherever she pleases; Paris, New York, Milan. She leaves Brandon alone to fend for himself. He's why I'm here. He's why I moved across the fucking country. She thought she was toughening him up for God knows what, but what she was really doing was damaging her son. Being alone scares the hell out of him because she's done it over and over and over for years, and you haven't seen it. You're blind or something when it comes to her. That's what I don't get, Jamie."

"She wouldn't." I shake my head, denying her words, though Jenna isn't lying. I know she believes this, but I also know Julia wouldn't do what she's claiming. No mother or parent would. It's not fathomable.

"Keep living in your bubble, Jamie. I don't give a fuck. You wanted to know why he OD'd. Now you know. I can't help it if you don't like the answer, or that, once again, you don't believe me. I've never lied to you. I may not tell you certain things, but I don't lie about it." She takes a deep breath, her disappointed eyes staring at me. "I have to go. I don't want you here when I get back this afternoon."

She's out the door, slamming it behind her before I can formulate words.

Fuck.

What did I just do?

My phone rings again from where I'm clutching it in my hands.

I have to fix this. I can't keep not believing or not taking her words as the gospel. I don't stand a chance in hell of putting us back together if I keep doing this.

But . . . how am I supposed to believe Julia would do such atrocities?

I won't get that answer until I talk to the cunt I stupidly married if I don't answer the phone.

"What do you want?" my irritated voice asks. "Being divorced means I don't have to talk to you anymore. What wasn't clear about that?"

"Thank God." Her words are rushed, like she is panicked. "You have to come home, Jamie."

"That's not my home anymore, Jules. It's yours. Like I said before—"

"Brandon is missing."

Everything in my head stops. This is one of the worst things a parent can be told short of the only other I don't want to say or fathom. My world stops. *Brandon is missing.*

CHAPTER THIRTY-TWO

JENNA

How dare him!

How dare Jamie practically accuse me of lying.

That's exactly why I didn't want to have that particular conversation with him. It should be between Jamie and Brandon. I didn't have a right to interfere, and look where it got me? Back to square one. No. Four paces before that. I'm back to where I was the night I came home and found *her* in Jamie's bed with his dick, my dick, inside of her. Only this time, I didn't crumble to the ground.

If he expects that, then he's got a rude awakening coming. I'm not that girl. I'm not naive or needy. I don't need a man to survive or to get through life. I was doing one hell of a job of that without him, and I'll keep doing it when he's gone.

And after this morning? He will be gone. I'm not doing this. If Danny wants to have a relationship with his father—fine. I'll be supportive, but Jamie better understand that he cannot and will not put our son in his limelight. He can't openly call Danny his son. Not in the public eye. I won't bend on that, not even for

Danny. I don't care that he's damn near grown. I'm not taking that chance. I can't.

The only thing that has the power to bring me to my knees, to crush me, is my boy's safety.

I tried hard not to love Brandon the way I do. I tried to keep my distance, and when we lived thousands of miles apart, I could easily lie to myself and pretend they were just friends.

Problem is, Brandon was never just my son's best friend. I fell in love with my son's brother the first day I met him.

Fourteen years ago

I DID IT.

I graduated from the FBI academy after the longest, most intense five months of my life. There were countless times I wanted to quit. I didn't believe I had what it took to be an agent, and I still may not. I only applied this morning, a couple of hours ago, while I was waiting for the flight that would bring me home, back to my three-year-old that I haven't seen in far too long.

I know he was safe in Anne and Roger's care, but being away from my son and only getting to come back twice to see him in those five months was hell. I may never be able to let him out of my sight again.

When Josh showed up on my doorstep almost a year ago to the day, I never would have imagined I'd be where I am today— a possible FBI agent in the making. He says I'm a shoo-in. I don't know what real pull he has. He has only been an agent for less than two years.

I stayed with him, Jessica, and their one-year-old baby girl while I attended the academy. When I wasn't training with my classmates and teachers, I was training with Josh. He was determined to make me as good as he was in not only firearms but computer intelligence, operational skills, and physical endurance.

I never imagined I'd be as fit as I am right now. I can take down men twice my weight. If that isn't a power trip, I don't know what is.

I'm just praying all those extra hours he spent with me pay off. It's still strange being around him again after everything he put me through. Living in his home, getting to know his wife, I see another side of Josh, a side that I'd hoped for that night he dropped me off and then vanished. He isn't the same person he was, and neither am I. I still haven't figured out if that's a good thing where I'm concerned. Not a day goes by that I don't think about Jamie and what could have been.

I'm not bitter anymore. I was for a very long time, that is until I met Jessica, Josh's wife. She helped me work through a lot. I still have a long way to go, but she is convinced, with time, I'll get over him. I didn't have the heart to tell her I don't believe that. The way I feel for Jamie won't just go away one day. I'll have to learn how to live without him for the rest of my life.

My son helps with that; though, he's too young to realize just how much. He was a godsend really. If I hadn't had him, I think I would have allowed myself to fall into a deep pit of depression that I would have never been able to crawl back out of. Danny is my savior, my lifeline.

And now I'm finally back home to my precious little man.

I raise my arm and knock on the Hart's front door. My body is buzzing with anticipation. I need to see his cute little angel face like I need my next breath of air.

After a few seconds, the door swings open, but neither Annie nor Roger are here to greet me. Instead, I find my eyes lowering to the cutest blond-haired boy I've ever seen. His hair, like

I imagine Danny's head full of black strands, are all over the place on his little head. He aims his eyes up at me, his small little head tipping backward.

"You a pretty lady," he tells me, a lopsided smile on his handsome face. I'm too shocked to form words or thank him for his compliment.

"Momma!" I hear, then look behind him, seeing Danny running toward me. He jolts past his half-brother, his arms already raised for me to pick him up, which I do, squeezing him tight. "That's Bran-din," he says, saying the boy's name the best he can. "He my best friend."

My eyes close, and I hug my son even closer.

"Elise—I mean Jenna," Anne says. "Crap. I didn't know you were coming today. Did you tell me you were coming?" Her voice comes out too rushed and too worried, which is so unlike her, but then so is not telling me Jamie's other son was here.

We had an agreement—her and I. Jamie can't find out about Danny. Hell, even Roger thinks the same thing everyone else in this town thinks; that I got pregnant when I ran off with some random guy I didn't know. Though, in all honesty, I don't know how Jamie's dad doesn't see how much Danny looks like his son.

"No. I thought it would be a great surprise for you and Danny. Seems like I'm the one that's surprised though. Anne," I draw out, "you want to explain?"

"Come in," she says on a sigh, her kind eyes already pleading with me while my fear is mounting to epic proportions that have my heart rate speeding up.

Why is he here?

He can't be here. Not while Danny is here.

Why did she do this?

Oh, God! Did she tell Jamie? Please, no. Anything but that. He won't understand. I mean, how could he? Even if my reasons and fears are valid, I still keep his son's existence from him. He's mad at me now? He won't ever forgive me for this. Not that I think he'll ever forgive me, thinking I ditched him and took off when really, I was kidnapped and tortured for three months.

No. There is nothing I can do to earn that forgiveness, even if I made the only choice I had at the time. Had Jamie believed me, everything would have been different. I would have told him. But then what danger would that have put our son in? Julia is an evil, rich bitch. If she was capable of doing what she did and fooling everyone, what would she have done if she'd thought my son, who she ordered Josh to kill, was still alive?

No. I can't let her find that out, and this is why Danny can't be here when Brandon is. He just can't.

I glance down before stepping inside the house. He's staring up at me, his innocent eyes going from me to the boy in my arms.

"Up," he says, lifting both arms just the way Danny did when he wanted me to pick him up.

"Come here, Brandon," Anne calls, but he doesn't pay her a lick of attention. His eyes are focused on me and me alone.

"Up," he says again.

Hell.

My chest sinks, and my breathing becomes labored.

I know I shouldn't do it, even before I bend down, lifting him up on my other side. Holding both toddlers in my arms, something inside my chest changes, but I don't know what. I can't pinpoint the difference, but I feel it happening. I know something has changed, and there is no going back from this moment.

"You real pretty," he says again, making my lips tip up. Then he practically falls forward, his small little mouth smashing against my cheek, spit and drool coats the side of my face, dripping off, but it's one of the best feelings I've ever had. Tears pool in my eyes, and I know I'm fucked.

***

Present

I EXHALE, BLOWING THE MEMORY OF MY FIRST ENCOUNTER WITH such a cute little boy that unexpectedly captured half of my heart. But that's exactly what Brandon holds in the palm of his hands. If anything bad were to happen to him or Danny, I don't think I'd survive that.

I can handle anything dished out to me. I know I could even handle being captured again. My boys, I couldn't, and because of that, I have to stay focused on them.

My job already takes up so much of my time. I don't have any more of me to give Jamie. I'm stretched too thin. At least, that's what I'm telling myself as I walk up the stairs at the safe house.

Like always, the door is open, but I don't hear voices.

When I walk in, Malachi is standing behind Kelly, peeking over her shoulder with a concerned look on his face. His eyes snap to mine, but I don't nod in greeting or say "morning" like I usually do. Flicking my eyes toward the window, I see Josh sitting at the main station, the one with the three computer monitors sitting on top of the desk. His back is to me, and he has a mug in his hand. It's coffee. He goes through more cups in a couple of hours than is probably considered healthy in regard to the safe consumption of caffeine in that short amount of time.

I drop my purse into the reclining chair closest to the door. It's not unusual for Josh or Mal to fall asleep here from time to time. Jess had comfortable chairs put in a couple of years back.

Crossing my arms, I stare at the back of Josh's head, suddenly pissed off, remembering the photos Jamie showed me yesterday at his rental house.

"Did you know she took pictures of us?" I ask, an uncontrolled snarl forming on my lips.

Josh's mug pauses halfway to his lips. "Yes." He doesn't hesitate to answer me, but he isn't quick to face me.

"Why didn't you tell me?" I don't wait until he answers, having more to get out of my mouth before I combust. "Had I known, I would have understood why Jamie believed her."

After a beat—a beat too long in my book—he twists around and then stands. Disgust mars his mature but still beautiful face. For forty, Josh is in the best shape of his life, and it shows. If I didn't know him like I do, if I hadn't experienced things at his hand, I wouldn't believe he'd have even been capable of such cruelty. He gives his all to save more lives than he ever hurt. He's passionate about this job and takes more things to heart than the rest of us.

"It didn't matter," he finally says. "You gave him no reason not to trust you. Yet, at the first sign, he bailed on you."

"You didn't know that, though. You only knew what I told you."

"The truth," he deadpans. "Yes, you're right, Jen."

"You didn't know you could trust me back then," I reiterate. "You didn't know if I was faithful."

"Hayes," Josh barks, glancing first at Malachi, then he flicks his gaze to Kelly. "McKinley. Get out."

Kelly scrambles, pushing her chair back and making Malachi jump out of the way. Kelly McKinley is a newer agent and doesn't like to get on Josh's bad side. She's more of the "yes" type when it comes to our boss.

Malachi, on the other hand, is slow to vacate the room, his eyes on me the whole time, making sure I really want him to leave me alone with our boss over personal shit that even he thinks I need to let go. Mal hates that I silently pine over Jamie. Hell, I hate it too, but it's not like a person can simply cut off those feelings—at least I can't.

Once the door is closed behind Malachi, Josh's voice booms so loud the people on the first floor can probably hear him. "He doesn't deserve you!"

That pisses me the fuck off, and I lash back. "And you deserve Jessica?" I yell just as loud. Honestly, though, I hope she didn't hear me. She doesn't like addressing the past, and she doesn't like her and Josh being the topic of conversation.

I can picture a scowl on her face, and that's enough to make me regret my choice of words, not for snapping at Josh; he deserved that and maybe more.

Maybe I'll let Danny go train tonight so Josh and I can handle our shit in the ring. Lord knows we're going to need the tension release after this argument.

Josh is silent, and I know my dig struck a nerve. If there is one thing I've learned, it's where to hit him to make it hurt the most, and physical hits aren't the way. Those only work out the aggression we both harbor from time to time.

Josh thinks his way is the only way. He thinks he's right, and everyone else just needs to fall in line with him or get the fuck out. He ends up being right more times than he's not, so I don't give him too much flack unless I know he's in the wrong.

"I know I don't deserve my wife or even my daughter, Cat, but at least I've tried to reverse all the bad shit I've done. What has he done for you?" He strides the short distance to stand in front of me. He towers over me, the same as Malachi does, but it doesn't intimidate me like it once did. "He married her. He forgot about you. He fucked every pussy he came in contact with on tours. You've seen that with your own eyes. And you're worth more. That's all I'm saying."

"You still should have told me."

"We weren't friends. Not even when I brought you home. We had an understanding: I was letting you go free. That was it. We didn't come to have what we do now; respect, loyalty, trust, until many years later."

"Do I need to repeat myself?"

He leans forward, dropping a kiss onto my forehead, lingering with his lips pressed against my skin. Malachi may be my best friend, but Josh is like the brother I never had. He's more than a boss or a former tormentor. Like Malachi, he's family.

He steps back, but his hands remain on my shoulders. "No. But I wasn't wrong to not tell you, and you'll never convince me that I was."

"And you'll never convince me that you should have kept that detail from me." I drop my arms, knowing he isn't going to change his stance, and neither am I.

I can say it would have changed things had I known, but would it really have? Jamie still didn't believe me or trust me, so even though Josh should have shared that information, it wouldn't have changed one thing between Jamie and me. We'd still be right where we are today.

"We'll have to agree to disagree then. Not like it'll be the first time." He sighs, telling me he's finished and doesn't care if I agree with his last statement or not. He turns away from me, walking back to the computers. "We got shit to do today. Port security reported a vessel docking that hadn't been on their schedule. They've checked it out, but I want you and Hayes to go down there and check it out again."

"Consider it handled, but there's something else I have to tell you first. And you aren't going to like it."

"Instead of telling me I'm not gonna like something, just spit the shit out. I swear you and Jess think you have to preface shit with me, and it only pisses me off."

I ignore his half-hearted bitch fit. I know it's true, and he knows it's true, but the fact is, if we didn't preface things, Josh would have had a heart attack well before now. He doesn't do well with surprises. "You know the anonymous guy I told you about that helped us on our case?"

"The one that gave up a tip on the girls?"

"That's the one."

"Yeah. What about him?" he asks, leaning over the desk and moving the mouse between the screens.

"He sent me more information," I say, and then pause, waiting for him to stop what he's doing and give me his full attention.

"Well, you planning on spilling, or did you want me to guess, Cat?"

"It was an analysis of DNA."

He finally stops, looking over his shoulder. "Why would we care about DNA? We aren't in forensics."

"This isn't one of our cases. This is personal information."

His body stills before he twists around to face me, a pensive look on his face as he sits on the edge of the desk, crossing his arms. "Then I suggest you stop beating around the goddamn bush and tell me whatever the fuck it is."

"Brandon and Maggie are first cousins."

"Come again?" His ass jumps off the edge of the desk, his feet bringing him a step closer to me.

"You and Julia are siblings. How is that possible?" My question comes out more like an accusation than I meant it. Logically, I know if that was something Josh had known, he would have told me.

"It's not. Whoever you've been talking to is playing you. And I want to know why, so I suggest you take your ass to that fucking computer and find out who this motherfucker is right fucking now."

"I already know who he is. I don't have all the info, but I will by this afternoon."

"Who is he?" he demands.

I shake my head. "Not giving up my source yet. At least not while your temper is flared."

"You want to see fucking flared? If you don't tell me who the fuck took my daughter's DNA, if they even took it at all, you'll see goddamned flared. Who?"

"Cool your shit, Josh. Maggie isn't in any danger."

"I'll be the judge of that. You start talking now, goddammit, or I'll make you talk, Cat. Don't push me. You know I have the ability to bring you to your knees like no one else can."

His threat isn't one I take lightly. He hasn't made any in years, not since weeks before he released me. I know he's serious. I knew he would be pissed off, and I knew he'd go on the defense. That's why I knew I couldn't tell him it was Danny —not at first. He needs to cool down so that he can see clearly, think clearly. A clearheaded Joshua Breckett knows that the one person—besides himself—that Maggie is safe with is my son.

I step forward and then another until my boots are toe to toe with his. Tipping my head back, I look him in the eyes. "You ever make that threat again, Breckett, and I'll show you the person you turned me into. You're the one that doesn't need to push me."

Threatening Josh has never ended well for anyone. I've never done it before now, but I won't be the one to back down first. He stands in front of me, staring down, his arms still crossed, while mine are planted firmly on my hips.

"You got to the count of three . . . two . . . on—"

The door flies open, and we both turn, seeing Jessica. "School just called. Maggie walked out of class fifteen minutes ago. She left school grounds, and her phone is going to voice mail."

That isn't like Maggie. She doesn't break the rules. That's the one thing I can always count on when it comes to Danny's girlfriend.

What the hell is going on?

And why do I get the sinking feeling I'm not going to like it?

CHAPTER THIRTY-THREE

DANNY

I'm not going to say it was a shock watching my father walk out of my mother's bedroom this morning. I had a feeling that was where he was when I got home last night. Neither were in the living room or the kitchen or on our back patio. But his Range Rover wasn't parked out front, so there was also a possibility he wasn't here. Though I see the way he looks at her, watches her, and it's obvious he's still in love with her.

I haven't decided if I'm okay with that or if I'm not okay with him loving my mom.

I have to give it to him; he's handling it a lot better than I ever imagined he would. It can't be easy to learn you have another kid you never knew anything about, or that the girl you once didn't believe had unspeakable things done to her. I'd imagine that must be hell. I can sympathize with him on the first, but I can't when it comes to how he once treated my mom. What he did, the way he broke her and her heart, is worse than any amount of physical or mental abuse Josh dealt out.

Not that Maggie's dad is a saint or a man that deserved the forgiveness my mom offered him. She and I have never spoken about it. I mean, she just found out that I know Josh was the one that took her all those years ago. I have no doubt it wasn't easy for her to let the things he's done go, but I've never understood, not fully anyway, how she can work with him day in and day out.

I've only known the truth for the past year. I knew there were things she kept secret. After all, she told me there would be things that she'd never share, and she expected me to accept that. I couldn't. It's not in me to accept anything short of the facts, the truth, the whole story, especially where my mother's concerned.

She started teaching me how to hack into computers and databases when I was ten. I thought it was cool, at first . . . okay, so I still think it's cool. There's an adrenaline rush to it. One similar to fighting and winning a match against an opponent on a mat, in a ring, or even closed in a cage.

I don't think she ever intended for me to be as good as I am, as thorough and virtually undetectable as I am. Once I got the taste, I couldn't stop. I spend hours and hours in front of a computer screen when I'm supposed to be sleeping. In a way, it's similar to how my brother got addicted to cocaine last year. Someone offered him something they should have never offered, and suddenly he wanted that feeling over and over again. Like me with hacking, he couldn't get sated enough to walk away.

I don't think that douchebag will ever deal again for the rest of his pathetic, rich boy life. At least he better not, or the beating I gave him that landed him in a hospital for four weeks will feel like a walk in the park if I get ahold of him again. Motherfucker rolls on me, tells someone he knows who was behind his attack, and it'll be even worse. It could end his life.

I run the chain of my black, diamond-studded cross across my lips, over and over as I turn things over in my head. I can't hold it away from my chest for too long. If I do, it'll send a notification to my mom that my heartbeat isn't being detected. And then she would freak the fuck out; much worse than the reaction I had two nights ago when I discovered my father had my mother's necklace in his possession rather than it being around her neck like it should have been.

My necklace, like hers, is in the shape of a cross. There's no reason behind hers being that way that I know of. Maybe there is, and she just never told me. Mine, on the other hand, is because deep down, she knows I border on having no conscience. She thinks having it around my neck will remind me what's right from what's wrong.

It's not that I don't feel because I do. I just don't feel bad for causing pain to someone else. If someone steps in a match against me, they're accepting and asking for any pain I give, the same as I'm doing with them. If it's outside a match or my training, then I'm only doing it if the other person deserved it like that dumbass college guy that sold drugs to Brandon. He picked the wrong guy's brother to mess with. Or the unknown person, whose cell phone I hacked last week, finding kiddy porn. I didn't feel bad when I saw his picture on the news when he was arrested after I sent the files to the local authorities. I certainly didn't feel any remorse when I hacked into my mom's work files, reading through her open cases. It led to the rescue of three women. The only thing that bothers me is that the bastards behind their capture got away.

It's okay though. I know my mom and her team will catch them eventually, but it'll take other girls getting abducted first.

I eye the clock on the wall above Mr. Bell, my English teacher's head, seeing that it reads 9:42. Still the beginning of second period. Brandon didn't answer when I called him from my driveway before leaving home. He didn't answer when I called him after I parked at school and his truck wasn't here. He hasn't responded or read any of my ten text messages either. I was ticked off before. Now I'm getting antsy. Nothing good comes when I get this way. His ass better be in bed with the fucking flu, and if he doesn't respond to the text I'm pounding out now, then so help me God . . .

Me: If you don't respond, I'm going to beat your ass.

Me: I'm not even joking here, bro.

I wait all of two minutes, staring at my cell phone, not even caring if Mr. Bell catches me with it. I'm not Brandon. I can afford to get into trouble if need be. He can't. He also can't miss class. He's zero point four points from being knocked down to salutatorian versus valedictorian if he doesn't mind his p's and q's and stay on top of shit this year. He fucked off too much last year and let things slip. It gave our fucktard of a principal's son a fighting chance for that spot.

I'll be damned if anyone takes that from my brother. I could easily be positioned next to Brandon, but I'm not allowed to draw attention to myself. I never have been, and I'm okay with that. I've never liked the limelight, and maybe that's because my mom's paranoia sometimes rubs off on me.

Like now.

I grab my backpack, leaving class without permission because there is a sinking feeling in my gut that won't go away. I reason with myself that it's never been this bad, never been this debilitating—that's gotta mean something.

"Daniel," Mr. Bell calls out. "Where do you think you're going?"

"Bathroom, Mr. B," I say, opening the door.

"You know you're supposed to ask first, son."

"No can do," I throw over my shoulder. "Gotta go *real* bad if ya feel me."

I don't wait for his reply before I shut the door behind me, striding faster than normal. When I finally make it outside the school doors, luckily, without any teacher or administrative staff stopping and asking questions, I jog until I reach my truck.

Maggie has AP English with Brandon and me, so I know she's wondering where I really went. She's worked her ass off to advance one grade so that she could graduate with me.

She can also tell when I'm lying through my teeth, which is what I was doing when I walked out of class. I don't do it often, but when I do, she and my mom are the only two people that can see straight through me. Probably because, like me, her dad taught her how—just in case anything ever happens to where she'd need those particular skills. Josh doesn't show as plainly as my mother does, but the same paranoia that lives in her also lives in him when it comes to his wife and daughter.

It's why I'm given free rein when it comes to Maggie. He wasn't happy when I told him how far I was planning on taking things with his young and innocent daughter, his only daughter. In fact, he was downright pissed off that I had the audacity to tell him that to his face. I wasn't asking his permission. I was giving him a heads-up so he wouldn't be blindsided. Josh knows there is no one besides himself that she's safer with. He knows I'd do anything, go to any lengths to keep her safe, and for that reason and that reason alone, I'm able to do just about anything without fear that he's going to beat my ass over her at any given time.

Of course, that doesn't mean he doesn't want to. And there are times he pushes our training a little far so that he can get that need out of him. I do the same, so it's not like I can say that much. I struggle with what he did to my mom, and I have to constantly remind myself he isn't that person anymore, but sometimes, my thoughts and feelings get the best of me, and I end up fighting dirty.

It's a win-win for both of us. He gets to lay hits on me for sleeping with his underage daughter, and I get to do the same for the beating he dealt out to my pregnant mother.

Even though I know Josh is a changed man, a better man, my girlfriend is the sole reason I don't do anything permanent to him. She's the only one that keeps me in check—she just doesn't realize how often or why. And she likely never will. Like Josh, I don't want her to know certain shit. She doesn't need her view of her dad tainted with a past he can't undo.

I wasn't lying when I told my father I wouldn't change anything that has happened or didn't happen if given the chance. Maggie and my brother wouldn't be in my life today if things had gone according to my parents' life plans when they were my age.

No one is taking Brandon or Maggie from me. I need them more than they need me. They are my lifelines, like now, when I feel almost to the point of panic, I do what I have to do, knowing my girlfriend isn't going to be happy with me. But it wasn't like I could have dragged her out of class with me. That would have put up too many red flags. Questions would have been asked. They would have called our parents, which is still likely, but hopefully, I'll get to where I need to be before that happens. My mom is going to shit a brick when she finds out too.

Me: Babe, I need you to leave class now. Make up something or just walk the fuck out. Find and get to your dad ASAP. Don't leave his side until I get back to you.

Maggie's reply is almost immediate like she was holding her phone in her hand.

Mine: What's going on?

I remember the day I programmed the term "Mine" in my phone rather than Maggie's name. She is mine, and she'll never be anyone else's. I told her that once when she was five, and I was almost seven. I didn't even understand the true meaning of that word; I just knew it was true.

Me: No time to explain. Just do as I say.

Mine: Umm, no. Where did you go?

Only she and Brandon have the ability to irritate me the way they both love to do. They get a kick out of it and sometimes do it on purpose or even team up together.

Me: So help me God, Mags, if you do not do what I say, I promise, when I get back, I'll make sure your dad grounds you, doesn't let you go to prom and locks you in your fucking room until I say you can come out. Am I clear?

Mine: WTF, and where the hell did you go? Mr. Bell just sent Lane to look for you. Where are you?

I can picture the look on her face without seeing her. I know her mouth dropped open when she read my text, and I know her light-blue eyes clouded with sparks.

Me: Not telling you. I need you to do what I say so that I'm not worried about you too.

Mine: You're scaring me, Danny.

Me: Babe . . . please.

There are very few people that I would beg, Maggie being one of them. I'm just not built that way. I want things my way, and most of the time, I think my way is the right way, the only way, so when people don't do that or argue, I tend to get livid. I think that has a lot to do with Josh's influence on me more than anything.

Mine: Okay, Danny. I trust you, so I'll go.

Me: After you find out where Josh is, turn off your cell completely.

Mine: Why would I do that?

Me: Because I said so!!

Mine: The reason oh bossy one?

Me: MAGGIE!!!!!

Mine: You better not be doing anything stupid.

Mine: And you better answer all my questions when I see you.

Me: Why isn't your ass in your car yet?

Mine: Maybe because my boyfriend is acting like a jerk.

Me: Move. Your. Ass.

Mine: I'M GOING!!

Mine: But you better remember what I said. NOTHING STUPID! Or I'll kick your ass, and don't think I need my daddy to do it for me. I'm perfectly capable of whooping your ass myself, baby.

She actually probably could. One, she isn't like most girly girls. She knows how to fight, and she knows how to use a gun just as well as she knows how to wield a knife. And two, I'd never stop her from hurting me if she really wanted to. We sometimes train together, I teach her techniques the same as her dad does, so I know her strength, but never would I show her mine. Not with her anyway.

Me: Stop texting and get your ass out of school.

If I wasn't in a rush and if my gut wasn't telling me something is wrong, I would have replied back with "promise" instead of my asshole demand. I'm a dick to most people, but I'm rarely one to my girl. Maggie is the sweetest, kindest person I've ever met. She's sassy and even tough in her own right, but she is still an angel. An angel that I worship at her feet on most days, and one I will never let anyone hurt.

While I'm waiting for her to walk out, I check my phone for Brandon's location again. His cell phone location still shows his house the same as it did this morning, and the same as when I checked before I went to sleep last night, because yeah, at seventeen, I suffer the same issues my mother does. I come by it honestly.

I'm not allowed to have access to my mom's account that shows her the location of where we are at all times as well as our heart rate via the tiny device she has embedded in our matching necklaces. She thinks giving me that access is going a bit too far. She doesn't want me to develop the paranoias she has. She's too late for that, which is why I took it upon myself to hack her account.

Hacking an application is easy. Kids can do it, so it's not like she should be surprised if she ever finds out.

When the app opens, I tap the screen on my brother's name and then wait for it to do its thing to locate him.

Her house.

I refuse to call that place Brandon's house, the same as I refuse to call *her* his mother. She isn't; my mom is.

I've never been in that house before. That's one of the only things I ever promised my mom I wouldn't do. She moved us here for Brandon, and upon doing so, she made me swear I'd never go over there, not even the driveway to pick him up. And until now, I've kept that promise.

I toss my cell into the passenger seat of my truck and pull out of the parking lot, seeing Maggie jog down the stairs, heading to her car. I watch in the rearview mirror, making sure she gets in safely before I gas it, going to the one place I have no business being at.

He better be okay. Because if he's not . . . someone is going to pay. And I'm not talking about money.

Fuck, Brandon. Just be okay.

I'd rather beat his ass than him not be physically or emotionally all right.

CHAPTER THIRTY-FOUR

JAMIE

I wasn't so delusional that I thought I'd never step foot back in this house.

My son lives here, so the chances were always likely that would happen, at least until he graduates and goes off to college. And it has been two months since I last walked through the door I am now. The last time I was here, a few weeks before I left to begin my band's fall tour before Thanksgiving, it was to move all my stuff out and into my rental.

Julia begged me not to go through with the divorce, but what was done was done. The paperwork had been filed before the start of my summer tour last year. It was only a matter of time before the documents releasing me from the last eighteen years of hell were final.

"Jamie!" Her voice booms, forcing me to look up, seeing her walking down the stairs dressed in her fancy bedclothes—a red silk nightgown with a matching robe. A robe that's currently open for all of her assets to be on display. Assets, like this house, I bought and paid for. Not that they did her much good. I still wasn't interested. "Thank God, you're home."

"This is your house, Jules," I remind her. "Not mine."

"Brandon didn't come home last night," she tells me, ignoring my reiteration just like the last time I was here. "I figured he was staying out with one of his friends, and when I went to check on him this morning, he wasn't in his bed. His truck wasn't here either. And he isn't answering his phone," she adds, fat tears in her eyes.

"Maybe he had to be at school early or . . . I don't know, maybe he went out for breakfast," I reason, not wanting to jump the gun like a helicopter parent would do. Like she's doing now.

"He would answer his phone. I'm sure of it. Unless . . ."

"Unless what?" I ask.

"Well, you got the papers same as me last week. Maybe our son is hurt that his dad doesn't want to be with us anymore. That could be it, Jamie. Brandon has been so upset all these months while you were away."

Brandon's overdose rushes back.

I know Jenna said it was because Julia left him alone, but I can't see that. There has to be another reason. There is more to it. I know that much. There is a lot more Jen isn't telling me, and until she does, I don't know what to believe.

One thing is clear, though, Brandon's mom does love him. She's worried, even if I suspect she's also using his *sudden* disappearance as a reason to throw me filing for divorce and then going through with it in my face.

There is no doubt in my mind that if I told her I wanted her back, she'd jump for joy. It's not like I ever wanted her to fall in love with me, the same as I knew I could never love her the way she said she loved me.

Hell, maybe Brandon is upset about our divorce. It would explain the overdose. But then . . . he didn't look depressed Saturday night while I watched him confess, or even later that night when I showed up at Jen's house. He seemed fine yesterday morning too. Though seeing me around another woman—one I clearly still have feelings for—well, perhaps that triggered something, and Julia is right.

"Look," I start. "If you're that worried, I'll call his brother." I'm sure if anyone knows where Brandon is, it's him. Those two seem thicker than thieves from the little time I've seen both together. "Just calm—"

"His brother?" She pulls back, staring at me like I've lost my mind, and that's when I realize she doesn't know about Danny. How on earth Brandon never once mentioned it, I don't know. It's like he's been living a different life lately, and I don't even know how long that's been going on. "Brandon is an only child. He doesn't have a brother. What are you . . ." She trails off, lost in thought.

"No. He's not, act—"

"I swear to God, Jamie," she snarls. "If you got one of your little tour whores knocked—"

"It was Jenna, okay?" I shake my head. "Elise," I correct. "I recently found out—"

"She had *that* parasite?" Her tone comes out harsh and seemingly full of hatred.

"Para what?" Did she . . . "You knew?"

Her mouth drops, and her eyes widen like a kid caught admitting something he didn't mean to. "Well . . . I thought she had lost it. I didn't want to say anything. I didn't want to hurt you any more than she had already done."

"You knew she was pregnant with my child"—my voice rises —"and never said one fucking word?"

She crosses her arms. "Unlike *her*, I love you, Jamie. So, let me repeat myself. I didn't want to hurt you. If you recall, she is the one that tore your heart to pieces. You didn't mean anything to her when she left you. Hell, that baby probably wasn't even yours. She messed around with other guys behind your back.

She made you look like a fool. I'm the one that healed what she damaged. Remember?"

"Actually, she knew the day Mom was taken." My eyes snap up, seeing Danny standing with his arms flared out, his hands wrapped around the rail above us on the second-floor landing. Looking down, his eyes bore into mine until they make a slow glide to where Julia is standing a few feet in front of me. "Didn't you?" he questions, his tone dark, coming out like a demand and sounding much older than his seventeen years.

"My God," Julia whispers, taking him in.

"Where is Brandon?" Danny asks, his voice ice cold.

"Is he correct?" I ask, pulling on Julia's arm to get her attention. "Did you know she was carrying my child the day she went missing?"

"No." She shakes her head in rapid succession. "Of course not. How is this possible?" Her eyes slide back to the stairwell where Danny is slowly descending.

"I'm going to ask you again. Where is Brandon?"

"She doesn't know," I answer.

"Wasn't talking to you, old man." His jaw locks, and his hands fist at his sides. "Where. Is. He?"

"Danny—"

"I said I wasn't talking to you!" he shouts, stopping midway down. "I asked her," he says, lifting his arm and pointing to Julia. "I suggest you tell me. I'm not playing here, and you don't want to cross me. Not where he is concerned."

"You need to get out of my house." Julia turns to me, her blue eyes on fire. "Get your bastard son out of my house." Then she stills, her eyes cutting to the side. Suddenly, she whips around, her eyes lifting to Danny's. "How are you alive?"

"Well, obviously, someone didn't do a good job when they tried to get rid of me." His feet descend. "But I'm not here to talk about me. And if I have to ask you where my brother is one more time, you're not going to like what I do next, so I suggest you start opening that mouth of yours for something other than trying to get my dad back into your bed. Because let me assure you. If he knows about me, how long do you think you have before he knows everything? And I mean *everything*."

"Brandon isn't here, like I said. But if you don't leave, don't think I won't call the cops. Get! Out!"

"Go ahead," he says. "Call them. Explain why his phone says he's here, in this house, but he isn't."

"Maybe he left it here when he took off so that no one could find him."

"He didn't. He also wouldn't have taken that off," Danny says, his finger pointing to Julia's chest. Her hand lifts, clutching something from around her neck.

"I don't know what you're talking about," she claims, taking a step away from him, but Danny only takes a longer step forward.

I can see she's lying. The question is, why?

"You're wearing his necklace." Danny's eyes dip to Julia's neckline. Then like lightning, his hand moves fast, snatching the pendant and chain from her body.

"Ahhh," she screams as her hand flies up to her throat.

"Danny!" I yell. But he doesn't pay me any attention, as though he didn't hear me, his focus fully on my ex-wife.

"Did you know there's a tracking device in it? Or did you take it for a souvenir, you sick bitch?"

"Daniel," I bark, not liking the tone he has with her or the way he tore that necklace from around her neck. No doubt leaving marks.

"Last chance. If you're smart, you'll heed my warning."

"No, you'll heed mine. Now get out."

He shrugs, and then what he does next catches me so off guard I'm stunned and frozen to the ground I'm standing on.

He reaches out, his right hand wrapping around Julia's neck, and then he yanks her forward. The sneer on his face mirrors the one I saw yesterday morning. It's the same look Josh Breckett had on his face when he saw me there. Danny's is full of hate to the point I can see the darkness that lives within him. And I don't like it. Not on my son.

She starts to struggle, and that shakes me out of my trance. I take a step toward them.

"Don't!" he yells. "Take another step, and I'll snap her neck so quick she'll be dead before you reach her."

"Danny," I reason. "Let her go. I get you're worried about Brandon, and we'll find him, but you need to release his mother."

"You keep saying that, and you need to stop. She isn't his mother. She isn't a mother at all. She's a—"

"Daniel, don't make me tell you again," I say a bit louder, taking another step toward them. But like he promised, his hand squeezes, tightening even more, making Julia choke, I have no choice but to stop my advance.

"You really don't want to call my bluff, old man. I'm not playing games. I will kill her, and I won't feel one shred of guilt for it. In fact, she deserves it." His voice is eerily calm, too calm. "No. She deserves so much worse. Don't you?" Danny sighs. "Tell me where Brandon is before I lose my goddamn patience."

"I—" Danny's grip tightens in warning, and I fist my own hands just so that I don't lose it and rush forward. "Marina," she spits out, and my eyes widen. "He's at the marina."

Danny still doesn't let go. "Boat number? Which marina?"

"Don't . . . know."

"Not good enough."

"Can't . . . breathe. Jamie," she calls, but I'm unable to do anything but watch.

"Tell. Me."

"Ruler of the Mountain. Let . . . go."

"You knew where Brandon was this whole time? What the hell is our son doing at the marina?"

"He's not," Danny says. "He's at the Port of LA. Isn't he?"

"Jamie," Julia cries, rubbing her neck. "I just wanted you to see that the divorce is hurting our son. Just come home. Brandon, our son, needs us both."

"You really are that good." Danny eyes her, his head cocked to the side. Julia doesn't look at him. Her blue eyes are pleading with mine. "Never understood it. And I wouldn't have had I not seen it for myself."

"Seen what?" I can't help asking, my stare not leaving my ex-wife's. It's a school day. Brandon should be in class, so why isn't he, and why did Julia pretend he was missing?

"She's playing you, old man."

"I'm not. Brandon, my son, our son . . ." She turns to face me, turning her back toward Danny. "Isn't handling the divorce well. He's sad. He's hurting, and you did that to him."

Until this moment, I hadn't felt one shred of guilt about leaving her. In my head, I thought I was doing all of us a favor. I didn't love her, never had. When I was home, we fought. That wasn't healthy for Brandon. I needed to separate from her, to leave permanently. I waited until Brandon was almost grown. I thought he could handle it.

"You're right about one thing," Danny says. "Brandon is hurting, but he"—his finger points at me—"isn't the one hurting him. You are, and you have for a long time. Time for that to end."

Before Julia can react, Danny grabs her, locking his thick arm around her in a choke hold.

"Danny, stop." But he doesn't, and for some reason, I can't move to help her.

She fights. She's kicking and is choking, and like a pathetic man, I stand here staring at them and at a loss on who to help.

This isn't going to end well for my son.

In less than a minute, perhaps less than thirty seconds, she stops moving, her body going lax in his hold.

"What did you do?"

"She's not dead if that's what you're thinking," he says, releasing her and allowing her body to drop to the cold, hard floor. My eyes widen once again as my stomach drops.

"What did you do?" I repeat.

"I knocked her out. She'll be fine. Well, for now, she's fine. When Mom finds out about this, I can't guarantee her well-being then." I stare at where her body lies. She looks lifeless, and a part of me is scared to check.

"That was dumb. That was the stupidest thing you ever could have done. You may be seventeen, but you could face serious-ass charges for the shit you just pulled. She's a woman, Danny. What were you thinking?"

"I was thinking about my brother. Someone you obviously don't think enough about because you let her abuse him for years. God only knows what she was really up to or where she's shipping him off to."

He goes to leave, but I grab him by his bicep, stopping him. "You heard her. She was just trying to get me to change my mind and come back. Brandon was never in any danger, though I get wanting to protect him and—"

"Just shut up. Do you fucking hear yourself?"

"I hear just fine, son, and you better curb the language. Do you know what you've done?"

"I should have killed her, you know."

"Do not talk like that. I don't know what Jenna has told you but—"

"The truth, for one. That's what I know and that's why she

deserves to be sent straight to Hell where she belongs. Ughhhh," he yells, pulling at his hair. "I don't have time to go around in circles with you. I have to get to Brandon. Please just . . . just go find my mom and do not, and I repeat, do not under any circumstances allow her to come after Brandon or me."

"Allow her? What do you think is going on?"

"When you find Mom, tell her that I told you I want her to tell you everything. She'll do it if I ask her. Believe it or not, keeping the truth from you is killing her. It's been killing her for years, but she thought she was protecting Brandon from the truth about her." His head jerks, his eyes on Julia.

"Why can't you just tell me whatever this *truth* is?"

"Because my brother's life could be in danger. Besides, I don't have time, and it's not mine to tell. You want to know, go find her. But I swear to God, if you let her come after me and something happens to her, there won't be another chance with me." Danny's head tips down, looking at where Julia lies. "Go to the place she took you last night. That's likely where she is now."

Danny's eyes linger for just a moment, then he turns, leaving out the front door as quick as his legs will take him.

What the fuck?

Julia moans from the floor, and I'm rewarded with a split second of relief, knowing she isn't dead. Thank God! Something isn't right, though, and I still need answers. Jenna keeps avoiding shit she doesn't want to talk about, yet, she goes in circles.

She's about to tell me everything.

CHAPTER THIRTY-FIVE
JENNA

"Where the hell is she?" Josh demands, his hard but concerned eyes on his wife, though we both know the question isn't directed at her. If Jessica knew Maggie's whereabouts, she would have included that detail.

Turning, Josh stomps over to the desk he was sitting at when I first walked in, grabbing his cell phone before either of us instruct him to do so. Like me, Josh uses the same device as I do to track Danny and Brandon, only he has hers embedded behind a blue topaz ring that she wears on the middle finger of her right hand.

"That's what I need you to find out, Josh. And now, please," Jessica says, taking a deep breath, her eyelashes fluttering like a camera lens shutter taking photos, one right after the other. She only does that when her nerves are on edge.

"I'll text Danny," I tell them, pulling out my cell phone from my back pocket.

"Yo," Malachi says from the hallway before he appears next to Jessica in the doorway. My eyes flick back up, not having unlocked the screen before I heard my partner's voice. "Mags just pulled up. Thought you'd want to know."

"Thank God!" Jess says. Malachi turns his body, facing us from where he stands. Josh nods, and Jessica's body visibly relaxes like a ten-ton weight has been lifted from her chest—and I guess it has. Not knowing where your child is will scare the strongest of the strong, making them feel weak and helpless.

"I need Jen to stay here. You and McKinley head to the port and check that vessel out," Josh orders, his eyes on Malachi.

"Josh, I'm supposed to go with him." It's not that Mal and Kelly don't handle tasks together; it's more that I just needed to go with him right now. I need something that will take my mind off Jamie and what transpired this morning. Being here isn't helping. I need to be in the field where my focus will be on the task at hand and nothing else.

Josh gives me a pointed look that makes my arms break out in goose bumps. "If Maggie walked out of class and Danny didn't call me, then something is wrong."

He's right.

"Got it, boss," Malachi says, his head turning. "Here she is now. Call if Kells and I need to get back." His eyes flick to mine and then down to my phone, a silent message, *call Danny now.* Which is exactly what I do as he disappears from the doorway.

"You have some explaining to do, young lady," Jessica says, crossing her arms.

Maggie appears at the door, stopping next to her mom, with an expression that often mirrors her father's. First, her jaw locks, followed by a pissed-off demeanor rolling off her in waves.

"What are you doing here?" Josh demands, his voice full of venom, but his eyes show just how relieved he really is. "And you better have a damn good excuse for your phone being off, girl. Are you trying to give your mom a heart attack? Why did you leave school without calling me first?"

She crosses her arms and purses her lips before sighing and then starts to fill us in. "Danny ordered me here. I tried to follow him, but I lost him, so I came straight here, figuring this is where you'd be. He said I needed to find you and not leave your side until he gets here."

"Where did my son go?"

Danny left school? I check my phone for a missed call or text message that I know won't be there. And of course, I'm right —*nothing.* I'm too much of a paranoid freak when it comes to my kid. I wouldn't have let a call from him or even Brandon go to voice mail, not even if I was on a case. They are my top priority.

"I don't know, Jen. He was racing out of the parking lot when I got to my car. He wouldn't tell me. I asked."

I press the contact for him in my phone and then bring it to my ear. "When did you talk to him?" I ask her.

"He texted his demands after he left class. Do any of you know what's going on? Brandon wasn't at school before the bell to first period rang, and he didn't show up to second period either. Danny kept checking his phone. Do you think it has to do with him?"

As ticked off as she is, no doubt from being ordered as she says it, she's more worried than she is mad.

"Give me your phone," Josh orders Maggie, holding out his hand while his cell phone is up to his ear, same as mine.

I get Danny's voice mail and my stomach hits the floor as my throat clogs up like I have something lodged there.

"It's Breckett," Josh says into his phone as I'm pulling up the application to find out where my son is. "Hang tight a minute. I need you to get the PD on the whereabouts of two teenage boys. I'll have the locations in a sec." Rotating his cell away from his mouth, he says, "Jen?" like a question, waiting for me to answer.

As I'm waiting for the app to triangulate a location on

Danny, a notification within the same application starts to beep, alerting me to an issue with the device.

I click on it, seeing the device isn't detecting a heartbeat on Brandon and hasn't for close to five minutes. This isn't uncommon. In fact, there are usually multiple times every night, when if he turns a certain way, it'll lose connection because the necklace isn't lying flat against his chest.

The only reason the alarm would sound is if his smartwatch, which is connected, doesn't also pick one up or there is a drastic change in pattern—like when he overdosed nine months ago. His heart rate dropped dangerously low, which in turn notified me and caused me to panic. I knew Jamie's band had left for their summer tour in the UK, so there was a good chance his mother had taken off too. I didn't care though. I would have broken into that house had she been there.

When I found Brandon on his bathroom floor passed out, I called 911 and then started doing chest compressions until they arrived. It wasn't until they had him loaded up that I noticed the pill bottle and the residue of white powder I suspected was cocaine.

His parents being out of town, it was easy to pretend I was his mom with no father in the picture. No one seemed to know whose house they were at, and it's not like every cop in Los Angeles knows who I am or that I was FBI or that I wasn't who I said I was. That gave me time to clean up his mess and bury it. It was the one and only time I crossed a hard line. I let Danny hack into the police department records and the hospital's electronic medical record system, changing things as if they had never happened. I couldn't leave a trace. Shit like that could have followed him for years, or even a lifetime. I wasn't going to let that happen.

I'm not even sorry I did it. Protecting my boys comes before anything and anyone else. It always will.

"What is that?" Maggie asks. "Why is your phone making that awful beeping noise."

"Jess, take Mags downstairs," Josh says, knowing why the alarm is going off and probably thinking it's Danny and doesn't want Maggie to fear the worst.

"No." She plants her hands on both hips. "I want to know where Danny is too."

"You'll get your ass moving, and do as I say, Magdalena, or so help me God . . ." he threatens.

"Come on, Maggie. Danny is fine. Your dad will find him and make sure of that," Jessica promises as I'm thinking almost the same, only it'll be me finding my boys, and if something has happened . . . I can't think like that. Logically, I know I have to stay calm, or I'll panic and not be of any use.

"Fine!" she barks, turning and disappearing from view.

Thumbing out of the notification, I pull Danny's information back up. "He's in our neighborhood, but he's closer to Brandon's house than he is home and . . ."

"And what?" Josh asks.

"He's moving away like he's in a vehicle, which is likely, but it looks to me like he was at, or near Brandon's house not long ago." I glance up. "He knows not to go there, Josh. He wouldn't unless he honestly thought something was wrong with his brother."

"So that alert wasn't Danny." He nods, drawing in a lungful of air. "Then where is Brandon showing?"

"Same as Danny," I say after I've pulled up Brandon's data. "But there is nothing detecting life, like he isn't wearing it. His smartwatch is turned off, and his cell phone is showing Julia's house."

"Hey, Tucker, can you get an officer to head over toward Windshore? I'll text you an exact location. Two of my agent's kids are missing, and we aren't waiting. I need them found stat! You got it?"

I try calling Danny again, putting my phone on speaker so that I can go back into the app to watch his location. Danny's phone goes to voice mail again after ringing enough times for him to pick up.

Why the hell isn't he answering? His truck is on the move. Everything is showing in the same place: his pendant, his cell phone, his smartwatch, the tracking device on his truck. That at least gives me a little reprieve that he's okay; he just isn't picking up his damn phone.

I'm going to murder him myself if this all ends up being nothing, which, God, I'm praying it's nothing. I'd rather kick his ass from here to the other side of the world for him not to be in any danger; only my gut is turning over and over like there is. The panic hasn't been this bad since before he was born when I thought . . .

No, I'm not thinking that; not going there. I can't.

"Just sent it to you, brother," Josh says, having shared Danny's location.

I allow Josh to have access to Danny for this very reason, the same for Malachi. Only they've never had to use it, and Mal thinks I go way overboard when it comes to Danny and Brandon's safety. He thinks they have no privacy, and that isn't exactly true. They keep a lot from me. I just don't let them keep their whereabouts private. And I'm not sure I ever will, even when they become adults. It's something both will have to accept in the long run because I'm not giving it up. I'd become a basket case if I couldn't locate my boys, like I am now, with Brandon's devices not showing like they should.

Josh pockets his phone and then turns to face me, wrapping his hands around my shoulders. "Calm your shit. You aren't any good to them by allowing yourself to get worked up like that."

"I need to leave," I say, starting to back away, but he tightens his hands, not letting me move. "I need to get to where Danny is, Josh. Let go."

"Your ass needs to stay here. I got PD on it."

"He's my son," I argue. "I'm going. Back up," I order.

"Would we ever allow another member of law enforcement to force their way into a case that involves their family?" he asks. "No, we wouldn't, and I can't allow you to either. You aren't thinking clearly. I'm on this; let me handle it. We'll find them."

If it was Maggie, he knows damn well he wouldn't sit back and let someone else take control, not even me. If he thinks I'm going to cower in a corner until someone else sends word that either or both are okay, then Joshua Breckett doesn't know me as well as I thought he did. I can't sit back and do nothing. Even if this is personal, and I know he's right, we wouldn't allow someone else to get involved with any case they were connected to. That just doesn't apply to me.

He can ask, he can demand, he can even try to force me to sit out, but at the end of the day, I still won't. There is nothing anyone can do to stop me from going after my children.

CHAPTER THIRTY-SIX

JAMIE

What in God's name was Julia thinking? Using our son, trying to make me think Brandon was missing, that he was in danger, that he was upset with the divorce . . . all to get me back. Maybe he is upset. I don't know, but I aim to find out as soon as I find him and Danny.

Jesus Christ, Danny. I'm at a loss with him. What kind of man is Jenna raising that he would ever think it was okay to put your hands on a woman like he did back there? And he was so angry, boiling with it. I could literally see his skin on fire. I thought at any second he was going to lose his shit and do something he couldn't take back. I saw it in his eyes. He wanted to end Julia, but why?

And me. What the hell was I doing just standing there, not doing shit? I should have made more of an effort to get my son off my ex-wife, but watching him, in that moment, I thought if I advanced, he'd go through with his threat. I believe my seventeen-year-old son would have killed her.

I don't know what Jenna has filled Danny's head with when

it comes to our past, but whatever it was, he's probably the one person she should have kept secrets from if she was so hell-bent on having them. Danny is still a kid, despite the way she's hardened him up.

If I had been granted the opportunity to be in his life, I would have made sure he had everything a child needed to grow up with the innocence they ought to be allowed to have for as long as possible. The world today is both beautiful and ugly. Jenna should have kept the beauty more prominent.

After Danny left, I stood there like a moron for all of a minute, watching the open front door he raced out. I was stunned, and I didn't have a clue what to do. It took Julia groaning from the floor to pull me out of my frozen state.

I dropped to the floor, lifted her, and then toted her to the couch, where I gently laid her down. She was okay, at least that's what I told myself when I hightailed it out of the house before she regained her consciousness. I was more afraid of Danny's thoughtless acts than I was of my ex-wife's health. That's shitty, but there is no love lost there, and I can't fake that shit any more than I already did.

She admitted to using our son for her own gain—but did Brandon go along with it? Of course, he had to have, or he would have called me or said something, or I don't know, would have been here.

The way Danny acted, it was like he thought his brother was in danger, but this was his mother's doing. Maybe she got Brandon to go along with her farce. Or maybe, after he saw me with Jenna, everything hit home that his parents' relationship was really over. Maybe he was the one that talked his mom into that shit himself.

Though, if I think about it, I'm not so sure that makes sense.

I'm too out of the loop when it comes to things outside of my band. I hadn't realized that until now. I faked so much with

Julia for so long that I started pulling away, and I guess I pulled away from Brandon too. Jesus, I'm a shitty father.

No more. I shake my head as that vow pierces my thought.

Jenna is about to tell me every detail, and from now on, I'm going to be present for everything. I'm going to be an attentive father to both Brandon and Danny. And even if I die trying, I'm going to make that woman mine again—I don't care if I have to cancel my next tour or the one after that. It's not like any of us need the money. It's just what we love to do.

Taking the stairs two at a time, I hear voices shouting or arguing, but I don't pause before charging on.

"There you are," I say, stepping into their FBI makeshift office, or whatever it is they call this space on the third floor of the beach condo they use as a safe haven for the women Jenna's team rescues. She and Josh stop speaking, both of their heads turning to face me. My fists ball as I take in the close proximity he is to her. And does she look scared or wary of him? Fuck no! And that makes zero fucking sense to me.

I want to beat his ass. I want to hurt him, hell, I think I want to murder him for what he did to her, for what he tried to do to my unborn son.

Jenna is standing in front of him like he's a colleague, her boss, her goddamn friend. Maybe he is her boss, but if she thinks he's a friend, she's got a warped sense of the meaning—which he most certainly caused. How else do you explain their dynamic? He kidnapped her. He beat her. He'd planned to sell her like she was a used car for Christ's sake.

"Jamie," she barks. "I don't have time for you. My son isn't answering my calls and . . . fuck!" She shouts. My eyes flick from her face to her body, her arms, to the cell phone clutched in one of her hands. She's visibly shaking, and I momentarily lose my train of thought, the mission I'd been on when I drove over here.

"Shit," Josh says, pulling my attention. His brows are pinched together in concern, and then he grabs her. "Come here, Cat," he says, wrapping her in his arms. "I'll find him. He's going to be fine. You need to have more faith in Danny than you do right now. He's strong, he's—"

"He just choked Julia out is what he did," I say, cutting him off.

Jenna's eyes go wide. "What?" She pulls away from Josh's chest, and that makes the fire coursing through me simmer a fraction. I don't like him touching her. I don't like him being in the same room as her. "He did what?" she rephrases. "When? Where?"

"Half an hour ago. Julia's," I tell her. "She called me and said Brandon was missing. She was freaking out, so I went over there. Danny—"

"Missing. What do you mean he's missing?"

"He's not." I shake my head. Sighing, I run my hand through my hair. "She is the reason he was supposedly missing. I guess she concocted that story to make me think Brandon was upset about the divorce. Or hell, maybe Brandon is, and she was going along with it. It's not like she wanted it to begin with."

"Oh, my God." Jenna starts breathing hard and in shallow pants. "What has she done?"

"Nothing," I say, my brows creasing as I take a step forward, wanting to reassure her, but she steps away. "Danny forced her to admit it was all a charade."

"Jesus Christ." Josh's jaw locks as he glances away in thought.

"Please tell me she doesn't know Danny is your son. Tell me you didn't tell her that, Jamie," she pleads.

"Danny looks almost identical to him, Jen." Josh sounds resolute. "It doesn't take a genius to put two and two together, and we both know she isn't the dumb, rich bitch that she pretends to be or that he believes she is," he says, his hard eyes land back on me, throwing out an accusation.

"Look," I start. "We have other shit to worry about, like Danny assaulting her."

"Good for him," Josh says, stunning me momentarily.

I shouldn't be, but I am. I know he's partially the reason Danny is as hard as he is. He did that to my son, and Jenna allowed it. What am I supposed to do with that knowledge? Does she even realize it?

"You didn't answer my question," Jenna says.

"Yes, she knows," I tell her. "Like he said"—I jerk my head in Josh's direction—"Danny looks just like me."

"No. No." Her head starts shaking in rapid succession, her brown eyes wide and on me. "No."

Just then, Josh snatches her elbow, pulling her to his chest, his thumb and forefinger wrapping around her jaw. "Look at me," he orders. "You will get it together right fucking now, or I'll have Jess come up here and sedate you. You are no good as the petrified mom you are right now. Lock it the fuck down, Jenna. Lock it down now."

"Let her go," I bite out, my fists balling at my sides. "So what if Julia knows? She was bound to find out I have another kid. She'll deal with it. Though, it doesn't matter. We aren't married. She isn't my wife anymore. I don't really give a fuck what her dumb ass thinks."

"She's a fucking psychopath, and you played right into her hand," Josh spits out, a snarl on his lips.

I laugh, unable to hold it in. "If she is, then what does that make you?"

Jenna pushes at his chest, his fingers releasing her.

"A reformed sociopath," he answers without hesitation, then a smirk forms on his lips, making me wonder if Josh is being honest or fucking with me or a combination of both.

"Josh!" Jenna shouts, her eyes flaring like she disagrees with his words. To do what he did, you have to have some form of mental disorder, right? "This isn't the time or the place for this stupid shit. I have to find Danny." Her head cocks. "Was Brandon with him?"

"No," I reply, shaking my head. "But that's why Danny was there; he was looking for his brother." I sigh, running my hand through my hair again. "Jeez, Jen. What was Danny thinking?"

She twists, facing me, but she's still too close to the man that did unspeakable things to her. "He was probably scared out of his mind thinking about what she was having done to his brother. That's what he was thinking. If that bitch so—"

"Are you not hearing anything I'm saying to you? Danny assaulted a woman. He wrapped his hand and arm around her throat and squeezed until she passed out."

"And she's lucky that's all he did," she retorts.

"You're actually condoning this?" I ask, baffled. "No matter how you feel about her or what happened in the past, you're okay with his actions?" This is unbelievable.

She drops her phone to her side, taking a step in my direction. "It's nothing compared to what I'm going to do when I get my hands on her. If she so much as hurts a hair on either of their heads, I'm going to put a bullet in that bitch's head, do you hear me?"

"Jenna!" Josh and I say at the same time, only mine comes out shocked, whereas her name on his lips sounds more like a threat.

"I have to find them." She lifts her cell again as her head tips down. "I have to find both of them now. Something is wrong. I feel it. I felt it this morning. I should have never ignored the signs, but I thought . . ." Her voice chokes. That's when my eyes drop, seeing her hands shake.

"I'm going to call my buddy. He sent officers to Danny's location. They are probably there by now."

"He's stopped. Well, his truck is. It's been in the same location for nearly five minutes. But the sensor in his necklace is moving away from his truck location. He's in another vehicle."

"You track him?"

"I track both of my kids!" she spits back, her eyes never moving from her phone. "I'm out of here." She looks over her shoulder, her eyes glancing up to Josh's face. "I'm going to follow him. Call me when PD gets to his truck to update me on what they find."

"Wait. I'm coming with."

"No." She places her hand on his chest when he steps forward. "I need you to find Brandon. We have no idea where he is."

"Jules said he was on a boat at the Port of LA. That's where Danny was headed."

"That's where Hayes and McKinney were headed," Josh says, almost to himself, his eyes cutting to the side in thought.

"This isn't good." Her bottom lip trembles before she smashes her lips together to stop it. "Call Mal," she tells him, then without a glance to me, she attempts to bypass me out of the door, but I step in front of her, halting her escape.

"Would you please stop and tell me what's going on?" I plead with her.

"You don't believe anything I tell you, Jamie, so no, I won't stop to clue you in. I have to find my boys before your wife does something we all will suffer for."

"Tell me what that means," I demand.

"Julia was the reason I was taken!" Her voice booms, catching me off guard, not expecting the high pitch in her tone, making it feel more like a punch to the gut than a slap to the face. "She planned it. She paid him to take me, to torture me, to rid my body of my son."

"Wha—"

"Don't speak, Jamie. I don't care what you have to say. It's true. All of it, but if you don't believe it, oh fucking well. I have other shit on my plate, like finding the boys before she does to them what she had done to me."

She shoves me out of the way. I'm too stunned by her words to stop her or catch myself before I fall into a desk, nearly knocking the large computer screen off.

"What Jen said is true," he says, his tone laced with heat as he types a message out on his phone. Pushing myself off the solid wooden desk, I can see he's sending a text from where I'm standing.

"I'm supposed to believe the woman I was married to for eighteen years, the mother of my son, orchestrated a kidnapping at sixteen? How do you expect me to even begin to wrap my mind around that?"

He's silent for a long beat, doing something else on his phone now. Once he's found what he's looking for, his head pops up as he flips the screen of his cell to me. An eerie feeling coats my spine, telling me whatever it is he's showing me, I'm not going to like it once I figure out what it is.

"It's an audio recording. See, Julia was the first job where I met my employer in person. Usually, things were done via computer, but she was adamant about not leaving any digital trail."

"She was sixte—"

"Whose daddy is a rich fucker," he says, cutting me off. "Whose daddy gave her access to unlimited funds with no questions asked."

It's true. Mitch Montgomery is one of the wealthiest businessmen in the world. He moves every few years. I used to wonder why Julia's parents ever ended up in Mississippi, to begin with. When you're that rich, you can live anywhere. He could have easily paid for homeschooling and had for a number of years. I think that was why Jules was so shy when she first started ninth grade. She had never experienced public school or other kids her age. Her social skills had been severely stunted until she made friends with Jenna. And even after that, it took several years for her to begin coming out of the sheltered little shell she'd lived in her whole life.

As those thoughts, those memories filter in, it makes his claims all the more unbelievable. I can't fathom what he's saying or what Jenna said before.

It's not possible.

Those words ring out again as he presses play on his phone.

CHAPTER THIRTY-SEVEN

JOSH

Eighteen years ago

"Can I help you?" I say to the little girl sliding into the booth across from me. Her massive amount of hair-sprayed hair is hiding her face from my view as she peers down, her chin tucked while placing an oversized designer purse on the bench of the booth.

"Yes," she finally answers, her head popping up. "You can get rid of someone in my life. Permanently," she whispers, her voice so low I barely heard the last word from her mouth.

"Excuse me?" Surely, this kid isn't the person I agreed to meet to discuss a job.

She slides a photo across the table. I see it, though my eyes never leave the eyes of the young girl eyeing me, whose light-blue eyes strike me as matching my own. Evil lives inside her, the same as it's seared into my soul. Though, I can't imagine this hoity-toity bitch has seen the things I have. I bet she grew up pampered and sheltered from the ways of the world, getting spa

"Her name is Elise Thomas. Jenna Elise Thomas," she clarifies, "and I want you to take her. Sell her to the meanest, cruelest buyer you can find."

"What did she do to you?" I almost want to laugh. Is this little cunt for real?

"That doesn't matter. I have the money to pay you. That's all you need to know." Her perfectly manicured eyebrow that doesn't match her bleached hair arches.

"Uh-huh, sweetheart. You want me to accept this job then I'm gonna need a little more info than that." I don't take women that come from stable homes. Women whose families give a damn if they don't show up are too much trouble and not worth the extra profit. I certainly don't take children, and the girl in this photograph is still a teenager, the same as the little blonde bitch sitting across from me.

"Let's just say she has something I want, and unless she's removed from the equation, I don't stand a chance in hell of getting it." She pauses, then adds, "And I always get what I want."

She's a spoiled fucking brat if I've ever met one. The type that'll go whine to daddy if she doesn't get the newest, the coolest designer crap on the market and then throw a hissy fit when some other bitch shows up with one just like hers.

"This about a boy?" I ask.

Her brows furrow, and her lips purse. "This is about you taking care of a problem. I was told you're the best, and nothing would ever come back on me. Is that right?"

"I'm not in the market of stealing little girls," I say, bored and about ready to ditch this place, this town, this state. I don't have time to play games. I have to find my next project, get her trained for whatever master pays the highest, and get paid. Same shit, different day. I was raised to take over my parents' trade business, and I'm damn good at it. There's no one better at this than I am. I don't have a conscience. I don't feel remorse for stealing the lives of pathetic women that had no life to begin with. If anything, I do them a favor. I give them a purpose.

"I'll double your fee."

"No."

"I'll triple it," she seethes.

With that kind of money, it would get my parents off my ass and give me a break from the mundane of my everyday hell . . . My fingers start to drum on the table as I stare at her, the silence between us palpable. Still, there's a lot of risk.

"She's a troublemaker. It wouldn't be such a far-fetched thing that she just up and ran away. She hates following rules and . . ." A sinister smile stretches across her face. "With my help, I can have her parents, her boyfriend, her limited number of friends believing just that. I'll have them eating out of the palm of my hand in no time. This will be easy for you. I'm the one that'll do all the hard work."

There is nothing easy about kidnapping a person—any person. You have to plan everything to a *T*. The littlest mistake or mishap can fuck everything up and get you caught.

"Do we have a deal?" she asks, her light-blue eyes sparkling as she digs through the purse that's placed beside her on the bench seat. Before I answer, she pulls out a box wrapped in what seems to be birthday wrapping paper encased in neon-green ribbon.

"What's this?" I ask as she slides it across the table, releasing it when it's placed in front of me.

"Your birthday present, of course." Her lips tip up on one side. Carefully watching her, I lean back on my side of the booth, throwing one arm over the back of the red, worn padding. "The money," she whispers.

Of course. This bitch couldn't possibly know that today is, in fact, my twenty-first birthday. Not that I celebrate them. My folks never coddled me. Birthdays were just like every other day in my world growing up—not significant.

"A little sure of yourself, aren't you? What are you, fifteen?"

Her nose scrunches up. "Sixteen. I'll be seventeen next month."

"I need two weeks to plan," I tell her, accepting a job I have no business taking, but the quicker I get out of here, the quicker I get away from eyes that are way too eerily like my own.

"That's not gonna work. I need her gone today. Right after school to be exact. Why do you think I said I needed this rushed and you here immediately? I didn't ditch class for the hell of it. I need her gone."

"I'm the pro here, little girl. I'll say when. I'll say where. Got it? And before you open that little trap of yours, you better be careful. Wouldn't want me to take the wrong little bitch, now would you?"

She rolls her eyes like my threat doesn't faze her, then she leans forward, a smirk on her lips. "There's thirty thousand dollars in that box. You telling me you're gonna walk away from it just because you don't have time to plan. She's one girl. How hard can it really be?"

A lot harder than she realizes. When you don't plan out things thoroughly, it leaves too much room for error. I wasn't raised or trained to make errors. *But thirty thousand dollars . . .*

"I'll make it work, but you're gonna have to get your hands dirty too, princess. I need you to bring her to me."

"Won't be a problem. You tell me where and I'll deliver."

Her lips spread, and her eyes light up like it's Christmas morning, and she's just run into the living room seeing piles of presents that are just for her and her alone. She's a selfish little brat, but there is more behind her eyes than that. Her soul hasn't just been touched with a bit of evil; she's soaked in it.

But the bitch is right—I can't say no to that kind of money. No one in my shoes would.

Present

I POCKET MY PHONE, NEEDING TO GET OUT OF HERE AND OUT there to find Danny. If that cunt is involved, there is no telling what she'll do now that she knows I never handled Jenna's pregnancy like she thought.

"Jesus Christ. She really did that?"

"She was the one that told me Jen was pregnant. You watched the video I gave to Cole. That's who called."

I can see the wheels turning in his head, realizing not only is his ex-wife responsible for Jen's disappearance, but she did it so that she could have him. I'd be willing to bet she got knocked up on purpose to solidify her place with him. Even with Jenna out of the picture, he could have dropped her, and probably would have, had she not granted herself a permanent place as the mother of his child.

"Why didn't Jen do something?" he asks. "If you had proof, why didn't she use it to put her away?"

That's a question I've asked her over and over throughout the years. She knew about the recording. It's how I got her to believe me that it was her best friend behind the whole charade. She would've used that evidence against her had Julia not up and become pregnant. Jenna's emotions weren't in the right place, she wasn't in the right frame of mind, and I should never have divulged that information. Problem is, I couldn't let her walk in that house, back into those lives without knowing all the facts I'd gathered after I decided not to go through with the deal. It's not like I needed the cash. My parents didn't know about all the cash I'd banked on the initial job. When I let her go, it was twenty-four hours before I was supposed to show up at the shipping docks to ship my captive off, like clockwork, just like the ones before her.

I disappeared before they got wind. Though I never had feelings for my parents, not like I do for my wife or daughter. The way Maggie sees Jessica and me is completely different from how I saw my parents. I always thought it was because they raised me to not have a conscience, to not love or hate, to just exist. In the last hour, it dawned on me why—they weren't my real parents.

"She couldn't do that to Brandon," I finally answer. "She couldn't take his mom from him. And well, there has always been a part of Jenna that still doesn't want to come face-to-face with what your wife did to her."

A part of Jenna has always been in denial. She knew the facts, heard them even, but in the back of her mind, she never actually dealt with that realization. When you're scared and as young as she was, faced with protecting a life that wasn't even born yet, you'd do anything, make yourself forget or believe another version if you think that's what is best at the time.

"She isn't my wife," he spits out.

"Funny," I tell him, "because you still take her side like she is."

He doesn't have a shot of hope if he keeps questioning Jenna versus taking what she says at face value. Every time he questions her or doesn't immediately believe her, I can see the pain on her face, in her eyes.

"Do you not see how crazy all of this shit sounds?"

"No, actually, I don't. I've seen a lot more fucked up than this. I didn't start dealing with evil when I joined the FBI. I created the evil that's out there. Took pleasure in it, in fact."

"Saying shit like that isn't helping. I want nothing more than to stick a hot iron rod through your gut."

"Good. You should." My cell dings with an incoming message.

Lark: Truck's empty in the middle of the road. Beat up too. Keys still in the ignition. I have a team en route to take the vehicle apart for clues. Do I need to keep this shit under wraps or not?"

Me: Keep a lid on the media as tight as possible. Let me know when you have something.

Lark: 10-4.

"Come on," I say, pocketing my cell again. "If you can stomach being in a vehicle with me, then you can come while I go find my little sister."

"Your sister?"

"I'll explain what I can when we're on the road, but it isn't much, except come to find out, your wife and I are blood."

"Stop calling her my fucking wife."

"Brother-in-law, ex-brother-in-law." I shrug, walking past him. "You coming or not?" Frankly, I don't give a shit. He can stay or come. If it were me, I wouldn't be able to sit still or calm while my kid was missing.

Danny fucked up going to that house. Why the hell didn't he call me?

CHAPTER THIRTY-EIGHT

MALACHI

Thank fuck Kelly wanted to take two vehicles. With everything I have turning over in my head, I don't want to be cooped up in a car with her. She's a nosy little thing, and at twenty-three, damn near fresh out of the academy, she's trying overly hard to bond with her fellow teammates. I get it, though. Once upon a time, I was in her shoes. I wasn't always under Josh Breckett. I joined his team only five years ago after Jen spent nearly that long talking me into it.

I didn't understand how she could work alongside him after what he'd done to her. Then again, I was still struggling with why she'd want to work with me after the part I unknowingly played that got her taken in the first place. Still to this day, it bothers me. I haven't gotten over it, and I doubt I ever will.

The sound of my cell phone ringing from the cup holder between the driver's seat and the passenger's seat steals me away from the ugly thoughts flicking through my head. Without taking my eyes off the road, I snatch it up, answering the call without looking to see who it's from. "Hayes," I say.

"You really just gonna leave without so much as a bye this morning?" Cole's angry voice both excites me and pisses me off. My dick can't tell between the two as it jolts to life beneath my tactical pants.

"You were asleep. I have a job." And I don't really want to talk to him right now. I could kick myself for not checking the name on the screen. Had I known it was my on-again, off-again, fuck buddy, I would have sent his ass straight to voice mail.

"Could have woken me up," he says, sounding butt hurt over me slipping out of his bed and out of his house, leaving his sleeping form undisturbed. And here I was thinking I was being nice, considerate even when I left at four this morning to sneak in an hour-long workout before heading to the beach house to check on the girls and start my morning before everyone else filtered in around eight.

He's so confusing, and he fucks with my head without even trying. One minute he's hot, and then next, cold as ice. He flops back and forth. Doesn't know if he's gay or straight or bi. Everyone else knows he likes both males and females, but he's yet to admit the truth to himself. Hell, I thought I liked pussy once, but now I know I was only trying to force myself to be someone I'm not. Doesn't hurt that cunt did a number on me either. Makes coming to terms with my sexuality that much easier.

Cole is a different story. He thinks he's supposed to like one or the other. He doesn't get that it's okay to want what the heart wants, regardless of gender. If I could get that through his thick skull, maybe we'd actually get somewhere one of these days. Until then, I'm stuck just being a fuck here and there, just like every other random fuck is to him—and I'm getting sick of it.

"Look, I ain't got time for your shit." Hell, I'm at work, on the way to check out some vessel that showed up at the harbor that wasn't on the schedule to dock. That just doesn't happen. It screams red flags. It screams shady as fuck, which is why the coastguard was notified, and they informed us.

"But you got time to fuck me and then take off while I'm asleep," he deadpans, bringing me out of my thoughts about the ship.

"Isn't that what you want? I mean, you're okay with bringing a lay around your band buddies, but not the guy you're into."

"That's not fair."

"They know, Cole. None of them are stupid. Everyone knows you like dick just as much, hell, maybe even a little more than pussy."

"That's not the point. I couldn't before. Bringing you around would bring up questions. You and Jen are partners. It would have come out, and then what?"

Maybe he has a point. Maybe I'm the one butt hurt that he keeps dodging this thing between us and not taking it further than just sleeping together. I know he likes me. We're both into each other, but without spending more than a night or two a week together, we're never going to be anything more.

And I want more, dammit. Call me a fucking girl, but I want a real relationship. I want someone to come home to. I want a life partner that's got my back like I got his.

Before I can respond, the sound notifying me of another call beeps through my ear. When I pull the phone away from my ear, seeing who it is, I know I have to wrap this shit with Cole up.

"Danny is calling me," I say, putting the phone back to my ear. "Stop questioning everything you want. We can talk about our shit tonight, but if you aren't ready for that, tell me now. I know what I want. I know who I want. It's time you figure out what it is you want."

I pull the phone away from my face, answering Danny's call

before Cole has a chance to respond. If he wants to talk, really talk, then he'll text me later. If not, then we'll keep walking around the same shit he's been skirting around for the last seven months.

"What's this about you walking out of school this morning and scaring the shit out of Maggie?" I ask. I would have called him earlier, but I had to get down to the harbor before that ship leaves. According to harbor patrol, it only has a small load to deliver and wouldn't be here long.

"You have to get down to the Port of LA now," he says, his voice sounding desperate.

"Danny, what—"

"Brandon is on a ship called The Montgomery. You gotta find him, Mal. Please." His voice cracks, alarming me as I put my SUV in park.

"I'm here now. What do you know about that vessel, and what the hell is Brandon doing on it?"

"No time to explain," he tells me as I hear the sound of metal crunching metal. "Just find my brother and find him now," he pleads, not an ounce of his normal self coming through the line.

"What the fuck, Danny? Explain," I demand. "And what is that? What's happening? Where are you?"

I don't have time to pull up the app Jen gave me access to that tells me his location at all times. He doesn't sound like himself, and I know something is wrong. If my gut wasn't clenching up, I'd know just by the sound of his voice that something isn't right.

"Brandon's mom is planning something. I don't know what, but she is the reason he's on that ship, and we both know if she is involved, it isn't good. Mal, you have to get to him. I can't."

"Where are you?"

277

"If I tell you, you'll come for me instead, and you won't make it in time. Just go get Brandon. Please."

Tires screech in the background, and chills break out all over my skin.

"Danny," I seethe, his name coming out like a warning. "What is going on?"

"I don't think I'm coming home. And——" A gunshot goes off, followed by glass breaking, and I stop breathing. "Just tell them I love them in case, okay?"

"Fight," I force out of my mouth. "Fight, Danny, because your fucking life depends on it."

The line goes dead, but I can't allow myself any time to think. If I do, he'll be right. I'll come after him instead of saving his brother. Without another thought, I bolt out of the driver's seat. Seeing Kelly stepping out of her car, I yell, "Get harbor patrol on the phone. That ship doesn't leave until every square inch is checked."

Not wasting any more precious time, I take off running, propelling my legs to move as fast as they'll take me, praying for the second time in my life. *God, let Danny survive whatever she does to him.*

***

Eighteen years ago

I LIKE GIRLS. EVERY GUY I KNOW LIKES GIRLS, SO OF COURSE, I like them too.

Some of my classmates even have girlfriends and lost their virginity back in middle school, but not me. I'm picky. I've always been a picky person. I've never made friends easily. I never felt like I fit in with the white kids or the black kids. There weren't even any Asian kids in my school until last year, but she's a girl. Being a Native American Indian, I stick out no matter where I go. Until the start of my sophomore year at the beginning of this school year, I had long hair that stopped at the top of my lower back. I figured if I cut and styled it like other white kids, it'd be easier to make friends. It wasn't.

And every day, I feel more and more alone.

I work harder than any other kid I know. School is another thing that doesn't come easy to me. I've struggled for as long as I can remember, having to repeat third grade. That was the worst year of my life. Not only was I older than the rest of the kids, but I was much taller and bigger than any of them too. Other kids always seemed more scared of me than not, but I don't understand why. I'm nice. I do what I'm told when I'm told to do it. I don't cause trouble; I certainly don't go looking for it either.

I didn't know how to talk to girls any better than I knew how to approach other guys—at least not until recently. I met a girl in my computer science class at the start of our second semester. She didn't pay me any mind the first half of the year, but now, she won't leave me alone, and the strange thing is, I don't want her to. She's pretty, and like me, she often feels like an outcast herself. She moved to our small town almost three years ago, but I didn't meet her until this year.

Turns out she's friends with the girlfriend of one of the band member's of this local band I started following a few months ago. From what Julia says, the girlfriend, Elise Thomas, gets jealous a lot, so she isn't able to hang with the band while they're practicing. That's why I'm at her house now.

She has the biggest house I've ever seen. Her parents must be really rich. She told me last week her dad is a businessman, and her mom is always vacationing. She said that's going to be her life one day soon too. Married to a successful man so that she could explore the world and have the best of the best of everything.

Her idea of a good life and mine differ, but I don't dare tell her that. I like that we spend so much time together. If she knew that I wanted to go into law enforcement one day, well, I don't think she'd want to be my friend anymore. I may be sixteen, and I may struggle with schoolwork sometimes, but one thing I know for sure is I want to do something meaningful when I become an adult. I want to be proud of myself, and I want my parents to be proud of me.

I liked how my mom's eyes lit up when I told her about Julia. Mom thinks I should ask her to be my girlfriend, but something about that idea doesn't excite me. It's the opposite, really, but I like having her as a friend. So far, she's a good friend, like right now. She's here about to help me get over a hurdle—even if the thought makes me want to vomit.

"Are you sure you're okay with doing this? If you're not, you can—"

"I'm not the virgin, Malachi. You are." She bites her lip as she crawls from the head of her bed to the foot, stopping in front of me. Pushing up, she looks me in the eyes. "And I want to help you with that problem. I do this for you, and then you can repay me with a favor later. That's fair, isn't it?"

"I guess . . . Are you sure though?" I ask. I don't want her to think I'm taking advantage of her.

"Jeez. Would you just fuck me already?" She falls onto her back, landing on her bed dramatically.

"Get on your knees."

"No. I want to be on top." She smiles up at me, her diamond-blue eyes playing coy. "I'm more experienced than you. I can make it good. I promise."

"It's my first time. Shouldn't it be the way I want it?" An

image of a boy, sweaty and shirtless, holding a guitar pops into my head.

"Don't you want to look at me while you fuck me?"

No. But I do know who I want to picture. With her facing away from me, that'd be much easier to imagine. He has blond hair too, though it is much shorter, and he's a lot bigger than her petite frame.

My parents would think it's wrong, me liking other boys rather than girls. That's why I have to do this. I have to lose my virginity to a girl. Julia is the only one I can hold a conversation with, so it's gotta be her, and she's willing. She wouldn't have suggested this if she wasn't into me, so I can make myself be into her too.

"Rather look at that hot ass you have back there," I tell her to cover up the real reason.

"Fine. You just remember a deal is a deal."

Yeah, okay, whatever that means. I don't know why she's so hung up on a favor for a favor. She was talking about the same thing when I was complaining about still being a virgin two days ago. But hell, if she remedies my little problem, then I'll do whatever it is she wants.

CHAPTER THIRTY-NINE

JAMIE

How did I not know?

How did I never see it?

Were there signs and I missed them, or did I gloss over them because I was too messed up over the belief that the only woman I ever loved betrayed me? Was my head really *that* fucked?

I've questioned the words out of her mouth twice since learning she was taken against her will. I can't keep doing that, but I also don't know how to make myself stop. Nothing I hear makes sense.

How was I *that* blind?

Jenna never gave me a reason to doubt her or not trust her. So why did I fall for Julia's lies so easily?

If I hadn't heard Julia's voice on that recording, I'm not sure I would have believed anyone's claim that my ex-wife was capable of such atrocities. I actually thought she was a good mother. Sure, I never loved her, but I also never gave her false hope. She knew from the day she told me she was pregnant that

I'd marry her, take care of her and the kid, but I didn't love her, and I'd never grow to love her.

Is Brandon even mine?

That thought makes me sick to my stomach. But if she's capable of doing what she did to Jenna, then it isn't so far fetched that she would have gotten knocked up by someone else and then told me he was mine. It's not like she needed my money. At the time, I didn't have any. I wasn't famous. I wasn't poor, thanks to my parents' support and all of the band living together that first year. *Was it just me she wanted?*

As much as I never wanted to create a life with her, it's the one thing I'm praying isn't a lie. Brandon is mine whether we share DNA or not, and I'll be damned if I let anyone take him from me.

Either of them.

Both of my sons are missing, and Jenna isn't answering her cell. Josh assures me she's fine and we'll find the boys, though his eyes don't seem as sure as the words that came out of his mouth a little while ago.

I try Jenna's cell once more. She didn't give me her phone number, and I didn't exactly ask. I sent myself a text from her phone last night after she crawled out of the bed to go into the bathroom. She'd just answered a text, so her phone wasn't locked. I didn't want to chance her refusing, so I took it upon myself to do it without her permission.

I was shocked, hurt even, when I learned she already had my cell phone number pre-programmed into hers. She could have called me any time—but she didn't.

I press end when she doesn't answer.

I can't blame her for being angry with me. Not about me stealing her number. If I were in her shoes and it was her not believing the words out of my mouth, I'd be mad too. I'd be more than mad; I'd be hurt. I'm never going to win her back at this rate, not if I keep listening to my head versus my heart.

I locked it up so tight all those years ago. I don't know how to unlock my heart. It's fused shut. It won't budge. But if I don't figure out a way, and figure it out soon . . .

"Malachi has Brandon."

"Is he okay?" I ask from the passenger side of Josh's Tahoe. "Where are they?"

We left the scene where Danny's truck sat in a parking lot of a gas station down the road from the exit to the interstate. His Raptor had some damage at the front and rear. Josh told me it was likely that he was boxed in, and that's how they got his truck stopped.

"Don't know. Jen said for me to meet her at her house, so that's where we're headed now."

If Malachi has him, then he's got to be okay. Surely his mother wouldn't have harmed her own child. Even with what she did to Jenna and to Danny before he was born, I have to hold out hope that she couldn't do that to her own son.

That thought is my head talking and not my heart, not my gut. If Julia was willing to harm someone like she did eighteen years ago, then maybe she is capable of doing harm to the boy she gave birth to.

I glance out the window, watching businesses blur as Josh drives faster than the posted speed limit. Had I known all of this a couple of hours ago, I'd have strangled Julia myself.

"Did she say anything about Danny?"

"No."

Why did I let him leave? Had I not, or had I followed him instead, maybe I could have prevented him from getting taken who knows where by God knows who.

I pray he's okay.

CHAPTER FORTY

JENNA

The feeling like I can't breathe is starting to be too much to handle. My throat has closed, making the ability to speak impossible. It's why I had to send Josh a text letting him know that Malachi was en route here with Brandon.

When my partner called, letting me know Brandon was physically okay, I had a brief moment of relief. Then everything fell apart when he told me Danny called him. My gut told me something awful had happened. I had just refused to face it. I didn't want him or anyone to tell me Danny was gone; someone had taken him.

Not that I didn't already know. My fist tightens around the platinum jewelry in the palm of my hand.

I was leaving Julia's house when I got the call, having spent a good half hour searching for clues but coming up empty-handed. I tossed her bedroom, not considering the fact I could be destroying evidence that could aid local police in finding my son. The thing is, when it comes to your family, your kid everything you're taught as an FBI agent, as a member of law enforcement, goes straight out the window.

I know I'm too close to this. I know I should step aside to allow those that can be objective to lead the way in locating him. But that's the other thing. Because I'm so close, because I know what I went through, I can't physically remove myself from this mission.

Josh won't agree with me, and he shouldn't. I know if it were his daughter in this situation, nothing short of a bullet stopping his heart would get him out of the way. Josh didn't change his name when he applied for the academy. He couldn't. Had he done so, there would have been too many red flags that would have led to a deeper background check into his history. Had the agency known of his former life, he never would have been accepted. It's the same as me, really. Had I divulged our true connection or what I'd gone through, I wouldn't be in the FBI. A missing person report was never completed by my parents, so there was never a record.

We both skated through. Had we not, I wouldn't have any of the knowledge I do today. I wouldn't know statistics, except for the forty-eight-hour rule of thumb. Then again, that's what civilians know. The reality is the first couple of hours are crucial. The longer someone goes missing, the lower the chance of finding them unscathed, or at all is more likely.

I will find my son. One way or another, I'll find him—and I'll find *her* too.

"Jen, sweetheart, why don't you sit down," Anne says, her voice making me flinch.

I'm a walking time bomb if I don't get my shit under control. I've been pacing back and forth, working on wearing a path through my carpet in front of the mantel. Mal should have been here by now. When he called, I was leaving Julia's house.

Being as she lives three blocks over, it only took minutes to get home.

That was nearly half an hour ago. Where the hell are they?

I can't think straight. I don't even remember the last thing I said to Danny before he left for school this morning. What if I never see my baby again?

"You don't have to put on false bravado. I know you're scared. You have every reason to be scared, Jen."

"Panicking, being afraid, letting my emotions get the better of me," I say, "isn't going to find my son. I have to get myself under control, or I'll be of no use." A shudder flows out of me. "I can't fall apart. I do, and Danny is as good as dead, if not something far worse." On the inside, I am panicking, but there's no point in saying that out loud.

"Nothing is worse than death." She pats the cushion next to her, beckoning me to come sit down. "There is no one stronger than our boy. He'll make it out of this. You just have to have faith."

There are many, many things worse than death. She doesn't get that. What happened to me was a walk in the park compared to the things I've seen done to others. Even at Josh's worst, he was still merciful compared to others. She's wrong. So very wrong. There are too many things worse than death. And I can't stomach any of them being done to my son.

"Anne, that's where you're—"

I stop pacing, then my head snaps to the window in my living room that faces the front yard, having heard two car doors close. My eyes are unblinking, and my heart pounds, waiting to see if it's them.

Josh's body is the first I see coming up the concrete path to my front door, followed by Jamie behind him. It beats me why they're together. Josh never mentioned Jamie being with him, but I guess it makes sense. Brandon is his son, after all. In hindsight, I should have contacted him when Mal called me. I've had his number stored on my cell for years, and even if I hadn't, it's not like I don't have it memorized.

Josh opens the door seconds later, walking in. "How long before Hayes gets here?" he asks as Jamie steps inside, closing the door behind him.

"Should be anytime now." My eyes connect with Jamie's dark-blue ones.

"Any word on Danny?" Jamie asks.

I shake my head, unable to say the words. Feeling a slight tremble of my bottom lip, I suck it between my teeth, biting down to make it stop. I'm losing the battle of my control. Realizing that, I squeeze my hand tighter around the object in my hand and ball the fist of my other as I turn away from the three people in my house.

"Don't ask me to stand down or let local police handle this," I say. "He's my son, Josh. And—"

"I won't," he quickly follows, interrupting me.

"Good." I nod about the time warm hands wrap around my biceps. He doesn't have to speak a word for me to know Jamie is the one behind me. The heat from his hard body seeps into my back, making every fiber inside me want to relax into him. It's remarkable how a body can recognize and know another person simply by the way they touch you. Then again, maybe it's the process of elimination. Josh wouldn't touch me like this, and Anne is an inch shorter than me.

God, how I want to give in to his comfort. It's as though his body beckons mine, knowing exactly what it needs. I can't accept it. I won't. I'm wasting time, just as it is waiting for Malachi to get here with Brandon. He's the only source of information I have.

Jamie's forehead dips, connecting with the back of my head. "I'm sorry about this morning."

"Not. Now," I say, locking my jaw.

"He told me to find you and not let you come after him," he continues.

"Try and stop me, and you'll—"

"I'm not. That's not my thought at all," he says, his forehead rubbing from side to side against the back of my head. "I'm telling you what I know. That's what you need, right? All the details. I should have stopped him or followed him when he took off. If I—"

"Wouldn't have mattered," Josh cuts in. My eyes snap up to see him stopping next to me. His light-blue eyes are cast down. "I trained that boy. If he was hell-bent on leaving, you didn't stand a chance in making him stop or following him if he didn't want you to."

"I should have tried," Jamie says, his hands tightening around my arms. The slight shake of his body doesn't go unnoticed.

Josh's fingers wrap around my wrist, then he lifts my hand. He isn't saying anything, but I hear the silent request loud and clear. My nails release the skin they were digging into, and my palm opens, revealing Danny's necklace. "Where did you find that?" he asks.

"Middle of the highway. Three miles from where his truck was abandoned."

"Danny snatched the one that Brandon wears off Julia's neck this morning," Jamie tells me.

There's my answer for why I never got a notification that something was wrong. It goes to show you, you can take every precaution with your children, but nothing is foolproof. I thought I had their safety down to an art. I thought they were safe.

How was I such a fool?

"Turn it off, Jen. If you're hell-bent on being part of this, turn the mom part of you off," Josh commands.

"I can't turn one off to turn the other on. Right now, I'm both. It is what it is," I say, swiping my cheek. I hadn't realized I'd teared up.

In part, Josh is right. I can't be an emotional mess. I have to stay focused, and Malachi needs to hurry the hell up. I need Brandon here so that I can locate Danny. Without him, I'm dead in the water.

"We'll find him, babe." Jamie's hands squeeze my arms. I haven't told him, but him being here, touching me, is helping. The worry, the nausea, it won't go away until Danny is back, and I know he's safe. If Jamie's warmth wasn't seeping into me, I could easily see myself falling apart. Maybe I am stronger and wiser than I once was, but that doesn't mean I'm hard. I've never mastered turning my feelings, my emotions off. What I can do is use them to fuel me instead of hindering me.

The sound of a cell phone ringing brings me out of my thoughts. Jamie's hands fall away from my flesh, and I'm instantly cold. Turning, I see him pulling his phone from the front pocket of his jeans.

His eyes squint before he says, "It's not a number I recognize." Instead of pulling the phone to his ear, he answers it and then taps the button on the screen to put the call on speaker. "Hello."

"I told you, Jamie," she says, chills breaking out all over my skin. My eyes instantly lift, connecting with Jamie's. "I warned you what would happen if you went back to *her!* Did you think waiting and then divorcing me would change things? It didn't, husband. I. Told. You."

A sense of dread and fear coils inside my belly before words form on my lips. Then the call ends as soon as I start to reach for it in Jamie's hand.

I will find my son.

I will bring him home.

And I will make that bitch wish she'd never met me. After I'm done with her, she'll be lucky if she doesn't end up six-feet underground instead of locked up in a confined six-by-eight prison cell.

CHAPTER FORTY-ONE

JULIA

Twenty-one years ago

Daddy really did it this time. He moved Mom and me to some small town, backwoods no-where-ville. There isn't even a mall in this stupid town. The closest one is over an hour's drive away. I just know I'm going to die of boredom in the first week.

My first day of ninth grade starts tomorrow. The schools here actually started a week ago, so now I have a full week's worth of schoolwork to catch up on. I've never attended a real school before. I've been homeschooled all my life. Daddy thinks I need to cultivate social skills, that apparently, I'm lacking.

He can kiss my ass.

I don't need social skills; the ones I have are fine. People just have to learn to do what I say when I say it. His staff shouldn't be allowed to question me or go running to him, tattling on me. They're the ones that need life lessons—which is exactly what the last nanny is getting right now.

Daddy doesn't know that I know the password to his

computer, which is also the same for his email. For a powerful man, he can be so dumb. Works out for me, and now I know the interworking of his *real* business, not the one the IRS thinks he does. Sure, he really is a lawyer and an investment banker, but that isn't where the majority of his money comes from or what pays for the lifestyle we live.

Of course, that lifestyle sure took a nose dive when he moved us to this dump called Mississippi, USA. Paris, New York City, even that year we lived in Chicago was a gazillion times better than where we live now.

Though . . . I cock my head to the side, taking in the shirtless, ripped body on a small platform built to be an outdoor stage. His tan skin is mouthwatering. The way he holds the microphone stand, leaning his body forward, is hot.

"Well, hello," I whisper, even though no one is in hearing range. I suck my bottom lip into my mouth, pinching the meat between my teeth as I eye him up and down. He's downright delicious.

Maybe this small town isn't so bad after all . . .

Maybe I'll give it a chance—for him.

When I want something, I don't stop until I make it mine, one way or another, and that boy right there *will* be mine.

Present

JAMIE HART WAS ALWAYS GOING TO BE MINE. HE WAS NEVER *hers*. Elise, or Jenna as she goes by now, was simply borrowing him.

I thought she'd learned that—apparently not. No worries. Another lesson is in order, and this time, they'll both understand the length I'll go to make something mine.

Jamie will regret divorcing me. One way or another.

"I told you, Jamie," I explain into the phone attached to my ear as my eyes stay locked with the seventeen-year-old boy my men tied to a metal chair. The ropes around his wrists have to be burning his skin by now. He hasn't stopped tugging on them since he was forced to sit down fifteen minutes ago. "I warned you," I continue into the phone. "What would happen if you went back to *her!* Did you think waiting and then divorcing me would change that? It didn't, husband. I. Told. You."

Pressing the button to end the call, I then power the burner phone off. I'm not stupid. I can't take the chance that the authorities are monitoring his calls. I didn't get this far since taking over the family business after my brother disappeared by allowing my personal feelings to interfere with a job.

"You don't actually think you'll get him back now, do you?" he asks, his indigo eyes so much like his father's I almost want to cut them out. Hell, his everything is just like Jamie, from the hair to his lips, broad shoulders, and defined body. Though, where Jamie lacks, this kid does not.

"Well, if I don't, that stupid bitch won't have him either, and he won't have her. He's mine, or he's no one's."

After Jamie filed for divorce last summer, my mind started playing tricks on me, or so I thought. I knew about the other women. I knew he slept around every chance he got. But had he been seeing her on the side without me knowing? I had him followed for months early into our marriage and then again after I received the divorce papers. Nothing ever came that led me to suspect he was seeing his ex. Had it, I would have nipped that problem in the bud before now.

I threatened Jamie years ago, using our son as leverage. I thought for sure that was enough to keep him away from *her*. He obviously didn't take me seriously. Who knows how long he's been planning to dump me only to run back to that worthless trash?

If it weren't for my family's money, Jamie and his bandmates would have starved to death when they moved out to LA nearly two decades ago. They wouldn't have made it big if I hadn't helped them get there. It was my father's connections that landed them their first record deal. But are they grateful? No. The opposite, actually. Especially Cole.

I tried but was unsuccessful in getting him kicked out of the band. That was a stipulations on their first contract. Jamie wouldn't sign it, not without his stupid little best friend being a part of the deal. It was either all of them or none of them. The record company liked their music too much to allow the band to walk. The contract was signed before I knew what had changed.

I wasn't happy. Cole was the single reason the rest of the band never accepted me as anything more than just the girl their friend knocked up.

Did any of them really think Jenna could have taken them to the top? God, no. She would have been eating out of dumpsters right along with them. I made Jamie Hart famous. Not. Her.

My focus was off. I was distracted for far too long. This is all Daddy's fault, if I think about it, or my brother's. If Joshua hadn't ditched his responsibilities, then my father wouldn't have made me step in and learn the interworking of our true business —the nitty-gritty side where we capture teenage girls and boys that are attractive but don't have any family that would bat a lash if they suddenly disappeared. Homeless or runaways are the perfect target. Then sell them to the highest bidder.

Daddy will be retiring next year, and he wants his only grandchild to step into the shoes my brother vacated years ago —and I want to get back to living the way I was always meant to.

"Aren't you going to ask me what I plan on doing with you, boy?"

"Don't see a point." He shrugs. "I won't be here long enough for you to do much."

Stepping in front of him, I react to his blatant disrespect by slapping him across the face. A slow smile forms on his red lips, making me want to do it again. How dare he—

"Ma'am?"

My eyes snap to Carlos, a man that's been employed by my father since I was in my early twenties.

"What?" I seethe, irritated by the interruption.

"The cargo ship. I just got word there are cops all over it, and the package is no longer secure."

"Brandon is gone?" I question, not caring if Jamie's other son hears me. It's not like he'll ever see the light of day again. "Where is he?"

"Don't know. A Native American guy put him in an SUV and then took off from what I was told."

Malachi. I dismiss that thought, not having thought about him in years. Though, now that I'm older, wiser, I should have taken care of him years ago too. He was a loose end I never tied up. Thing is, I couldn't have had him taken along with Jenna; too much suspicion would have been raised. First, a girl goes missing and then another kid? Hell no. Luckily for me, I was able to scare that boy into silence. Had my father found out about Malachi's involvement, he would have shipped me off to suffer what should have been Jenna's fate to begin with. After he found out I had contacted my brother for a job, he was furious.

No, I couldn't have done a thing about Malachi. Whoever has Brandon must be a local cop, or hell, even FBI. In the last hour, I've learned enough to know I messed up. When Jenna came home, I should have made her permanently disappear like I thought I'd done in the first place.

Seems she's stepped up in the world by becoming an FBI agent. And lo and behold, Josh Breckett, her superior, looks identical to an older version of Joshua Montgomery. Not that he ever knew his real last name. My father had him raised by two of his employees, giving him their last name, Brown, instead of the family name I was rewarded with. I guess he changed it when he disappeared.

"Find him," I order.

"Lose my brother already?" Danny says.

Turning back around, I say, "I wouldn't gloat if I were you. You're in a worse predicament than my son was."

"Considering he has you for a mother, I don't think I am."

"I have plans for my son. And if I don't get him back, well, then those plans may fall on your shoulders." A slow smile of my own crawls up my lips.

Maybe I don't need Brandon anymore. It's not like that boy ever had the stomach for the things that would be required of him. He wasn't raised like my dear ole brother was, even though I did try to toughen him up. I made him stay home alone from time to time, starting from the age of ten. The little shit is scared of his own shadow. Sometimes I wonder if I was given the wrong baby at his birth. Brandon and I are nothing alike.

Perhaps Danny is a suitable replacement.

CHAPTER FORTY-TWO

BRANDON

I always knew my mother didn't care that much about me. She wasn't like any of my friends' moms that doted on them, came to school functions, took them shopping with her just so that they could spend time together. The only time mine would show any interest in me whatsoever was when my dad was present.

She has this weird obsession with him that I've never understood. Honestly, I don't know why he stayed married to her as long as he did. I'm sure it was mostly because of me, at least that's what my brother often says.

If I had it my way, my dad would have left my mom years ago and taken me with him. Watching him around Jenna the few times I've seen him with her, it's obvious he's in love with her. I've always known she loves him, but until I saw them together, I never realized why.

Sure, I knew they dated. I mean, they had to have since she got pregnant with Danny before my mom got pregnant with me. But I would never have thought my dad cared so deeply for another woman when it was clear as day he didn't love my mother.

It doesn't make sense why he chose to marry mine over Danny's. If I loved someone half as much as I can tell my dad loves Jenna, I wouldn't hesitate in making her mine.

Jenna hasn't told me much about the past, only bits here and there. Danny has always been my best friend. I don't have a memory of any time that I didn't know him. I grew up thinking he was just a kid my grandma kept during the summer. Him calling her grandma too should have clued me in, but I just figured he was that close with her. Unlike me, he lived and grew up in Mississippi. He saw her more than I got to, so I never questioned it.

It wasn't until we were twelve that I found out Danny and I are brothers. Apparently, he'd always known my father was his father too, but Jen made him promise never to tell me. As much as I hate it, Danny kept that promise to his mom. He wasn't the one that told me—she was. It was a slipup, she hadn't intended for the truth to come out, but once it was said, it couldn't be undone.

She was mad. No, she was furious when she found out my mother used to leave me home alone during the months my dad would be away on tour with his band. Jenna uprooted her whole life, with my brother in tow, to move to the other side of the country for me.

That still seems so unreal, but for the first time nearly four years ago, I finally felt like I had a real home with a real family. Jenna has been more of a mom to me in these past few years than my real mother ever has.

I shouldn't be so shocked by what transpired today—but I am.

"You know what you gotta do, right, Brandon?" Malachi

says, slowing until his SUV comes to a stop at the curb in front of Jenna's house.

"Yeah," I say, not wasting a second of time before unbuckling my seat belt and opening the passenger side door.

"Even knowing what I'll do if I get there first?" he asks, his voice tinged with doubt.

I pause before sliding out of the seat onto the grass at the edge of the curb to look over my shoulder. "I said I was ten minutes ago. Stop trying to rehash something that isn't there. You can hang that bitch from her goddamn neck for all I care." Without another word, I step out of the vehicle, slamming the door shut without looking back. Mal takes off before I take a second step through the grass toward the front door.

My own mother drugged me last night. I woke up about an hour ago with zip ties around my wrists. I had no idea where I was, but the slight sway of the room made me think I was on a boat. It was a minute later when the smell of the sea wafted up my nose, confirming my suspicion. It only took seconds for my memory from the night before to come back.

After we dropped Maggie off at her house, I got a text from my mom, ordering me to come home right away. I groaned, but after taking Danny home, I drove the few blocks where the houses quadrupled in size until I reached the house I hated, despised really.

When I got there, she was nowhere to be found, not that I checked the whole house. I decided to shower while I waited for her to make an appearance. After pulling on a pair of sweat pants that I'd planned to sleep in and a T-shirt, I still hadn't seen or heard from her. I was just about to text my brother after she wasn't in her bedroom or the living room or kitchen. If she wasn't there, I wasn't about to stay there any longer than necessary. Especially after learning what Danny discovered last week, I wanted to be the last person on my mother's radar.

The door swings open just as I step off the lawn and onto the concrete patio that leads to the front of Jenna's house. Her slender frame comes flying out of the house, and I almost stumble when she collides with me. I hadn't expected this reaction, though I shouldn't be surprised.

Grabbing both sides of my face in her hands, she peers up to me. "Are you okay? Please tell me you're okay, Brandon," she begs, her voice cracking and sounding less like the fierce redhead I know her to be. From my height, the four inches I have on her, she appears more vulnerable than I've ever seen, ever thought possible coming from her. The woman standing before me isn't the same one that's grounded me more times than my parents put together. She isn't the one that threw out threats of blackmail if my principal didn't ease up on my case.

This woman is scared, terrified. That makes me pause, realization finally seeping in—Danny is worse off than I'd originally thought when Malachi filled me in.

She doesn't have any time to waste. I don't have any time to waste. If my mother is capable of doing sick shit to most of the women my father has had sex with over the course of eighteen years, what's she planning on doing to my brother if she learns my dad is also his dad?

I have to find him before it's too late.

And I pray to God it isn't already too late.

CHAPTER FORTY-THREE
JENNA

H e moves past me, my hands having no choice but to drop from his face as he slips past, going inside. Turning, I'm on Brandon's heels as I step back inside my house. Julia had just hung up when I heard Malachi pull up. I needed to see and touch one of my boys, and I thank the heavens that Brandon is okay—at least on the outside, he is. Emotionally, he's a wreck. I can see the clouds rolling in through his diamond-blue eyes.

Fact is, I can't worry about Brandon's emotional state right now. Not if I want to find Danny before she does damage beyond repair if she hasn't already done so.

My son is strong, both mentally and physically. Even though I keep reminding myself of that, it doesn't seem to take. I'm still his mom, and he's still my baby. As a tear drops, cascading down my cheek, I swipe it away, pretending I'm not on the brink of breaking.

I will find Danny.

I will.

"Brandon," Anne gasps as her hands go to her mouth, and visible relief seeps into her mature eyes.

Jamie is in front of his son within seconds, cupping his hand around the back of his neck and pulling him forward, embracing him as though it'll be his last. The thing is, I'm not so sure Jamie realizes that could have been a real possibility had Malachi not gotten to him in time.

Thank God Danny called Mal when he did, or I could have lost both of them. On the one hand, it stings a little that my son didn't call me, but on the other, I get why he didn't. I would have panicked and been focused on Danny only. I wouldn't have had the forethought to put my emotions aside or look at the situation objectively.

Speaking of Malachi . . . Why didn't he come in? I saw him speed off as soon as Brandon was out of his vehicle. Does he know something I don't? Does he have a tip that he failed to share with me, his partner, his best friend, the mother of his godson?

"Where—" I start to question Brandon, but I'm cut off by the look in Jamie's eyes when he pulls away from his son, his eyes cast down.

"What happened to your wrists?" Jamie grabs both of Brandon's hands in his, lifting them. They're red and swollen with marks from zip ties. His right wrist has dried blood on the top.

"When I woke up and realized they were bound together, I tried to get the binding off."

"I don't know what the hell is going through your mom's mind." Jamie's head shakes.

"That she's a sick bitch," Brandon replies.

"Brandon, she's still your—"

"Dad," Brandon cuts him off. "You have no idea, and I don't have time to explain it. If we don't find Danny, she's gonna . . ." His voice cracks as he trails off, not able to complete where his sentence was heading.

"Hey," I call out, stepping next to him. Lifting my hand, I place it against his cheek and turn his head to face me. "We are going to find him, but I need your head clear. I need you focused, okay?" Tears cascade down my cheeks as I say this to him. My head has to be just as clear if we're going to pull this off without getting detected. "You know Danny's password, right?"

He nods, slipping out of my hand once again. Stepping around his dad, he steps to the coffee table, sinking down to his knees in front of Danny's laptop. I follow, picking mine up and sitting down on the oversized chair behind him.

"You're going to hack the traffic cams, aren't you?" Josh asks, but by the look in his eyes, he already knows the answer.

"It's the fastest way to find him," Brandon says, his fingers typing across the keyboard.

"Wait. What?" Jamie questions, disbelief in his voice. "Why do you have to hack them? You're an FBI agent. Can't you just get access?"

"Not without a warrant," Josh says.

"We don't have time to go through the proper channels, Jamie. The longer we take to find him, the greater the chance we'll never see our son again." I don't glance in his direction. I can't. Looking at Jamie or anyone else in my house will only make the emotions hit harder. Time isn't on my side. I can't be the panicked mother that on the inside is sitting in a corner, rocking back and forth because she didn't protect her little boy. I can fall apart later, once he's back. And he will be back, dammit. If it's the last thing I do, I will find him, and I will bring him home. Can't say the same for Julia. If I get my hands on her, she will take her last breath.

Cop or not, I will end her sick reign.

"I'm there. You ready?" Brandon asks.

"Enter. I'm ready."

The clicking of keys is the only sound that penetrates my ears as I work to cover Brandon's trail. With Josh's connections, we could've had a judge's order within a couple of hours, I'm sure of it. But as each minute ticks by, I feel as though I'm losing my son—and I can't lose Danny. I can't. I won't. Every second matters.

I can't allow myself to think about all the possible things she could be doing to him. Knowing she's aware he's Jamie's son alone is enough to send my mind reeling.

Even though I prepped Danny for this, nothing can really prepare a person for the types of things another person is capable of doing to the human body and mind. Sometimes the mental strain is much worse than the physical.

If anyone can handle it, it would be my son—but he shouldn't have to.

We're coming, Danny. Just hang on.

That bitch is going down, one way or another. It's one thing to do what she had done to me; it's another to mess with my boys. She will pay for that. She will pay with her life, either behind bars or six feet underground. There is a part of me that wishes she would get a taste of her own medicine: captured, tortured, sold. I hate to admit that, and I never thought I would feel that way.

Rules, ethics, the goddamn law went out the window when she took my son.

Now I want blood.

"Got it!" Brandon yells as the smacking of metal has my eyes popping up, seeing his laptop shut.

I'm out of the city's traffic system in less than thirty seconds. Closing my own laptop, sucking in a breath, I look up, seeing him sitting back on his heels with a cell phone cradled in his hand, his fingers moving across the screen. My eyes suddenly snap to the mantel, seeing both cell phones I'd taken out of Danny's truck still sitting on top of the painted wood surface where I'd placed them when I got home.

Whose phone is he using? Who is he texting?

"Brand . . ." I start to say, his name coming out of my mouth slowly.

His head pops up, his blue eyes meeting mine. "Malachi is less than ten minutes out. He'll get there before you do." Brandon stands as my mind comprehends what he's saying. "There was a reason Danny didn't call you, Jen. He doesn't want to risk you getting hurt. He doesn't want my mom doing something."

There is a pleading look in his young eyes that shouldn't be there. He's asking me not to leave, but that's a request I can't fulfill, and one he should never have asked in the first place.

I shove my laptop off of my lap. It lands on the cushion of the chair I'm sitting in. Standing up, my brows scrunch together. Before I say a word, he moves fast, stopping in front of me and snatching my wrist up in his strong hand. "I can't let you."

I'm so stunned I just stand there eyeing Brandon. His eyes leave mine for the briefest of seconds, roaming over to his dad's. Then he drops a bomb on me that I wasn't expecting. "She's made every woman he has ever slept with disappear."

CHAPTER FORTY-FOUR

JAMIE

She's made every woman he's ever slept with disappear.

S He. As in me. That's who Brandon referred to a second ago. The room is deathly silent with all eyes on my son, even my mother's, alarm etched on all of our faces.

"What are you talking about, son?" I ask, finally finding my words, my brows scrunched together.

"Mom!" he almost yells, turning around to face me. My eyes drop for a split second, seeing that he didn't release his hold on Jenna. "She knows about all the women you've slept with while on tour over the years. She has you followed, or did, maybe still does. I don't know. Danny didn't have notes on any of that."

"Danny didn't have notes," Jenna says, repeating him, her voice soft. "Notes on what? How do you know any of this?" There's a long beat before she adds, "Are you sure, Brandon?"

"Yeah, I'm sure." He sighs, lifting his right arm and running his hand over his blond hair. Normally, my kid doesn't leave home without styling his tresses perfectly. He's done his own hair since I taught him at the age of five. He's always taken pride in his appearance, but today he looks disheveled and unlike his normal put-together self.

I still don't know the details of why his mother had him held on a boat, but whatever he's been through has taken a toll. That doesn't sit well with me. He's supposed to not have a care in the world. He's supposed to be happy, yet the look in his eyes at the moment is the furthest from that.

"Danny was keeping things from me," Brandon continues, enlightening us. "I saw it in the way he started to avoid eye contact with me and in the way he would shrug things off. My brother isn't exactly the shrugging type, so . . . I hacked his computer."

"If you hacked Danny," Jenna says on a sigh, "then Danny let you hack him."

"I know." Brandon glances back over, nodding. "We were going to talk about it last night, but then my mom told me to come home, so . . ."

"Brando, we're going to talk about what all happened last night and today and anything in-between once we get Danny back," Jenna promises. "But I have to leave right now. I'm sorry, but I have——"

"Did you not hear anything I just said? She makes women disappear after my dad sleeps with them, and the last I checked, he's currently banging you." His voice comes out rushed.

"Brandon," I scold, half sighing at his choice of words in front of my mom, his grandmother. Not that it'll faze her. I slept in Jenna's bed last night, after all.

He tightens his hand around Jenna's wrist, not paying me any mind. "I can't let you go. Danny wouldn't want me to either," he adds.

She places her free hand on top of his, prying her captured wrist out of his hold. "That isn't your choice. You aren't the adult here, Brandon. I am. Danny is my son, and there is no one that will keep me from going after him."

"Jen, please," he begs, dropping his shoulders.

"It makes sense, you know?" Josh chimes in, grabbing all of our attention, though his eyes are trained on Jenna. "I didn't put it together until now, even though you told me she was my biological sister a few hours ago. Without me running the show, finding the girls, and molding them, someone else had to do it. The people I thought were my parents obviously are not." He shakes his head. "Hers were. I'm sure *her* father had someone else doing the capturing and training, but I guarantee she did the selling." Josh's eyes go from Jenna to Brandon and then back to Jenna again. "I'd also be willing to bet her plans for Brandon were to make him my official replacement. Get everything back in the family, so to speak."

Jenna gasps, pulling in air through her mouth as his words sink in. *Was that Julia's plan?* It's hard for me to fathom that being something she would do, but then again . . . I didn't really know the woman I married.

How could Julia be planning on forcing Brandon to become what Josh used to be—a monster, the devil? Her own son. How could she do that?

No sane, loving parent would ever put something like that on their kid's shoulders. That thought wouldn't even cross their minds. Hell, they wouldn't be part of that life in the first place to make that call.

How was I married to some sick monster, capable of despicable things?

"Yeah, that's exactly what she was planning." Brandon's head tips up as he pulls in a deep breath of air. Dropping his head, his eyes finding Jenna's, he pleads once more. "Please don't go."

"Brandon, I love you, and I love that you want to protect

me, but that isn't your job. It certainly isn't your call to make. I'm going after your brother. There is no telling what Malachi will walk into or if he's prepared. Mal and your mom have a past. One that isn't pretty. He won't be thinking with a clear head. He has a vendetta, a score to settle, and that's too dangerous of a position he's in. It could get him or Danny or both of them killed. Do you understand?"

"I'm going with you," I declare as Jenna steps away from my son. I really should call him hers too. She's taken care of him in the way his mom should have. I get it now, why she calls both Danny and Brandon her boys. They are, and I wouldn't have it any other way.

"No, you're not, Jamie. I have——"

"You should take him, Jen. He's her sole obsession," Josh says, interrupting her.

"For once, I agree with your boss," I bite out, unable to call him anything else.

If I'm the one Julia wants, then let's give her just that. I need to see her. I need to confront the things she's done over the years. If what Brandon said is true, she has to be brought to justice. I'm not proud that I cheated on a regular basis, but I never lied to her. She knew from the beginning I didn't love her, and she still chose to be with me. I didn't sign up for psycho either, and God, there is no telling how many women I've been with over the years. If I'm responsible for any of them, or all of them disappearing, being hurt, sold, I don't know what I'll do.

I can handle a lot. I have handled a lot, but I don't know if I have the strength to handle that reality.

CHAPTER FORTY-FIVE

JENNA

*H*ow did I miss this?

I knew Julia's obsession with Jamie ran deep, but I just thought she wanted him on paper, wanted the life he could provide. I thought being married to him was enough to satisfy her. I've had her watched from time to time, but nothing was ever reported back that was out of the ordinary.

If she's been doing this for years, having Jamie watched, and then . . .

There is no telling how many women Jamie has been with in the last eighteen years. It wasn't something I ever wanted to think about, so I didn't. I knew he fucked around, all of them except for Seth do. It was par for the course while on tour. I was just glad none of them were into drugs, though they've all been known to dabble throughout the years, but nothing heavy, nothing they couldn't walk away from at any given moment.

Cole once told me it was easier for Jamie to be drunk or high when he had sex with someone that wasn't me.

Even though I knew Julia wasn't getting it from Jamie, it was still a hard pill to swallow that he was out sleeping with other women. That was the main reason I didn't follow him or the band after the shows I'd go to a couple times a year. I couldn't remain in the shadows had I seen it with the naked eye. I wouldn't have been able to stomach it either. Maybe this was a mishap on my part. If I had been watching harder, paying closer attention, I would have seen someone else following him. I would have caught on to what Julia was having done.

Why in God's name did Danny not tell me any of this if he knew? I know him well enough to know he wouldn't have come to me without hard evidence, but in this situation, that's exactly what he should have done.

How he knew, why he was meddling in that type of thing baffles me. I'm not sure it really should. His mind can't be still; he always has to be doing something. Breaking things down or breaking them apart only to rebuild them again is something he loves to do. Figuring out the behind-the-scenes things has often been like a drug in itself. He won't stop or give up until he has answers. It's why I know he'll make an excellent FBI agent or any law enforcement personnel one day. That's just another reason I've tried to train him as hard as I have.

Perhaps in doing so, I've created or instilled things in him that I shouldn't have so early on. He may be strong, he may have a good head on his shoulders, but he's still a kid, and a kid is what he should have gotten to be. Instead, I was honest with him and told him too many adult things that he shouldn't have heard. That's on me. This is all on me. My fear for his safety, Brandon's safety, might have placed my boys in greater danger. I should have taken her down before now, or at least taken a chance that justice would have prevailed had I gone to the authorities when I returned.

Fear is the one thing I'm tired of living in. After today, after I get my son back, and I will, things are going to change. No more hiding. Danny and Brandon's friends don't even know they are brothers. Everyone thinks they're best friends, even Maggie, much to Danny's dismay. If he had his way, she'd know the truth, and I have no doubt that when she reaches an age when she isn't in high school and living with her parents, my son will tell her. Although after this, Danny might not keep his mouth shut.

He allowed his own brother to hack his computer. That didn't happen by chance, and that tells me Danny is growing impatient or tired of the circumstances we're in. It didn't go unnoticed that he isn't upset about Jamie finding out the truth. He's happy. I'd be lying if I said a part of me wasn't happy too.

Relieved and happy was what I woke up feeling this morning. Danny joking with his dad warmed my soul for the first time in so many years, but . . . facts are still facts, and nearly two decades of lies don't just vanish once they are laid out on the table. If anything, it'll be harder, and it'll take longer to find the trust Jamie and I once had—if we can even find it at all.

"Malachi isn't answering," I say, placing my cell phone down between us in the center console.

"What do you think that means?"

"Don't know." I sigh. "At least he had sense enough to call in backup. Kelly, another one of our teammates, sent Josh a text that Mal informed her, and she's currently en route. Josh called his buddy at the police department, so there are additional officers that will meet us there."

Anne and Brandon went with Josh back to the safe house. They'll be safer with him than alone at my house. There is no telling what Julia knows or doesn't know. Josh has to protect his family first and foremost, as well as the girls living there.

"Do you think Danny will be okay?"

"I can't think about the what-ifs, Jamie. If I do, I'll panic, and I won't be any use."

It isn't easy putting those thoughts out of my head. In fact, it's the hardest thing I've ever had to do. Losing Jamie wasn't even this bad, and that ripped my heart out. This, not knowing if my son is okay or even still breathing, is a slow suffocation like nothing else I've ever felt.

Losing Danny would kill me. And I'm not ready to die yet. I haven't really lived so . . . I refused to let my mind run away. I'll face what I have to face, but not a minute sooner than I have to.

"How did I not know any of this was going on right under my nose?" Jamie asks, his face turned away from me, gazing out the window from the passenger seat. A deep, shuddering pull of air goes in and then swooshes out of his mouth.

"You're on tour twice a year. When you're home, you and the guys are always in the studio working on new music. You've always done things that put you and Julia together the least amount." I take a breath. "But hell, Jamie, even I didn't see that coming." *But I should have.* I don't say that last part out loud. It's a failure I don't want to admit to myself, much less anyone else.

"What she did to you, to us, what she was going to do to Brandon and who knows what she is doing to Danny, it feels like I'm drowning, and as soon as I almost break the surface, I'm drug down deeper again."

"I know the feeling," I say.

"How did it happen?" Jamie asks. "The day you were taken, I mean." His head rolls to the left, his eyes landing on the side of my face as I continue looking forward, driving.

Fuck. This is the part I didn't want to tell him. The part I hate remembering, but then again . . . I have to remind myself if things hadn't happened the way they did, then Malachi and I wouldn't be the friends we are today. Sometimes when bad things happen, good things forge from them. My friendship with Mal is one of those things.

Even racing across town at the speed I'm going, I still have at least five, maybe seven minutes before I reach the area the traffic cams last picked up the vehicle that took Danny. I might as well tell him the last piece since he's so hell-bent on wanting answers.

I can't blame him. If the roles were reversed, I'd want to know too. Thing is, if our roles were, in fact, actually reversed, I wouldn't have doubted him; I would have let him explain his side of everything to me. I wouldn't have walked away from Jamie like he did me.

So, there's that.

And the hurt from that is still there, still damn near as strong as it was back when I went through it. Maybe that's what he doesn't understand. Doesn't get.

I can get past a lot. I'm not so sure I can forgive that though.

Eighteen years ago

I'VE BEEN IN AN INTERNAL PANIC ALL DAY. *I'M PREGNANT* HAS BEEN on a loop inside my head since this morning. I should have waited until this afternoon to take that stupid test. Not like there was an urgency to pee on a stick, but no, I just *had* to know. Now that's all I can think about. Probably failed my world history final because I couldn't concentrate. I have no idea what I jotted down on that paper.

My parents are going to kill me. At least it'll be over the baby and not my grades, so I guess that's the bright side of this.

God, I'm so stupid. We're stupid. A freaking baby? I don't know anything about babies. I don't even have siblings.

I'm toast.

Is it legal to kick your teenager out of the house?

Would my parents do that to me? This morning I didn't

think so, but now I'm not so sure. I mean, I'm still their baby. Surely, they wouldn't. I'm only seven-freaking-teen.

Maybe Jamie and the guys will want to move to LA sooner. Of course, I don't know how we're going to support ourselves and a kid too. How will they be able to write and practice with a baby in the way? I may be limited on my knowledge of babies, but one in a house with loud noises probably wouldn't be good for him or her.

Him or her, I think as I'm exiting the building, walking out of school for the day.

There's a living person inside me right now. Holy crap. Holy freaking crap. A person. I don't know if I'm ready for this.

I need to go find Jamie. Normally, I'd go home and change before going over to his house, but I can't hold this in any longer. I'm about to burst just like I did this morning when I saw Jules. I would have called Jamie from the pay phone in the commons area during lunch, but this isn't something you tell your man over the phone. This is something you tell him in person like a big girl, like an adult, which I guess is what I'm about to be sooner rather than later.

I'm about to step off the sidewalk to head toward my car in student parking when I suck in a blast of hot, humid air. A car pulls in front of me, abruptly stopping exactly where I had been about to step. Stepping backward, I see it's Julia's silver BMW, but when I bend at the waist, peering into the passenger side window, it isn't Julia behind the driver's seat. It's Malachi Hayes.

The window rolls down, and his head rolls toward me.

"Umm . . . yeah?" I ask, prompting him when he doesn't say anything.

"So . . . Jules needs you." He glances away from me and out the windshield, his chest expanding with air before he swallows and then turns his head back again.

Jules wasn't at lunch or last period, making me think her

mom or dad must have checked her out of school early, but if he has her car, which is weird since she doesn't let anyone drive it, not even me, maybe she didn't get checked out. I'd say she ditched, but that's more something I'd do, not her. In the three years we've been friends, I don't think she's skipped school once.

"O-kay," I draw out and glance around. "Where is she?"

"Get in. I'll take you to her."

"I have my car. You can tell me, or I can follow, I guess." I really don't need this right now. She knew I was going to see Jamie as soon as school ended for the day.

What could possibly be so urgent that she needs my help?

"Yeah . . . uhh . . ." There's a slow shake of his head, and he looks unsure. I don't know him that well, and he always comes off awkward, so perhaps this is just him, and the strange demeanor is his normal. I don't want to come off like a bitch or mean, so I have to force my face to relax so that it doesn't scrunch up, scrutinizing him. "It's really important. She asked me to bring you to her. She's freaking out and doesn't want her parents to find out where she is."

"Is she okay?"

"Yeah. No. I don't know. Can you just get in and let me take you? I promised I would." His voice sounds so much like a plea that I start to feel bad for him. "It shouldn't take long," he adds.

"Sure. I guess if it won't take that long."

Opening the door, I slide into the seat, placing my backpack on the floor between my legs. He presses the gas pedal before my seat belt is buckled. Glancing up, there is sweat on his temples.

"So, what's the urgency?" I ask, my nerves pricking at my skin.

"She doesn't want me to tell you."

"Either you're gonna tell me, or you're gonna take me back

to my car." I twist in my seat to face him. "Spit whatever it is out, Malachi."

"She's at a free clinic on the other side of town," he rushes out as his hands squeeze the steering wheel, turning his knuckles almost red on this tan skin. "Sh-she . . ." He stutters.

"Why would she be there?" I ask, my mind turning as the words come out of my mouth.

"I don't know. She didn't tell me. She asked me to go with her, and then when we got there, she started crying and begged me to come get you." His face jerks toward me in a fast motion. "That's all I know."

"Okay," I respond, the words coming out slowly as I press my back into the seat, relaxing.

Could she be pregnant too? But if so, or she thought that was possible, why didn't she mention it this morning when I blurted the words out that I am.

It's awkward in the small space of Julia's car. He doesn't have the radio on either, and the silence just makes it that much worse. A few minutes into the drive, I dig out my notebook and a pencil from my backpack so that I have something else to do to occupy my time. It's at least a fifteen-minute drive. It doesn't matter if he's going to the north side of the capital city or the south side, it's about the same distance.

I shouldn't be as annoyed as I am, but I can't help how I feel. She's my friend. I'm supposed to be there for her when she needs me. But the thing is, I need Jamie right now. If something happened to Jules or something was wrong, then why didn't she mention anything before she disappeared today?

Instead of getting lost in finishing the song I started last night, I stew on that thought for the entire ride, only getting more annoyed as each minute passes.

"This is the end of the road," Malachi says, stopping the car.

"Huh?" I glance up, my eyes taking in the nearly abandoned strip mall parking lot. I know this area, but it's not that often I'm in this part of the metro area. It's known as the "rough part of town" for a reason. The news reports at least one homicide a week just in this area alone. Carjackings and robberies are a daily occurrence. "Wait." I cut my eyes to Malachi's. "Where is Jules? I thought you said she was at a clinic. I don't see a doctor's office or any medical place around here."

"Out of the car," he demands.

"Excuse me? Hello. Did you not hear what I—"

"I guess you didn't hear me." He leans over, reaching across me to open the passenger side door. Then, as he's leaning back up, Malachi presses the release button on my seat belt. "I said get out of the car. Now!" he hollers, making me jump back at the harsh tone in his voice.

"Dude, chill," I say. "What's going on? Where is Julia?"

"Get out, or I'll shove you out," he barks.

I jump out, grabbing the top handle on my backpack and pulling it out of the car with me. Without looking back at me, he pulls off with the passenger side door still open, but it soon closes on its own as he increases speed to the end of the parking lot.

I keep standing in the same place as he turns left, leaving me here alone.

"What the hell just happened?" I say out loud, letting my bag drop to the asphalt that's in dire need of being repaved.

It's late afternoon, but still early enough that the sun will be out for another hour. Looking around me, I don't see one business that appears to be open. There is only one vehicle in the abandoned lot—a truck at the other end.

Taking a deep breath, I sigh, blowing air out long and slow.

What am I going to do now? Is Julia even here? If this is some stupid joke, I'm going to beat someone's ass.

It's not like I have a cell phone. I can't call anyone to come pick me up.

Glancing all around, I finally spot a pay phone. Problem is, it's directly in front of that truck, and I really don't want to walk over there. What if some creep is inside? This neighborhood doesn't exactly scream safe, and from what I see on the news sometimes, even I'm a little scared just being here.

I squat down, then I dig into the front pocket of my bag. After finding a couple of quarters, I close my fist around them and then stand, pulling my bag onto one shoulder.

I have no other choice. I have to use that phone. At least I know if I call Jamie, he'll answer, and he and the guys will come get me. It's still daylight, after all. I'll be okay. There is no way Malachi dropped me off with the purpose of completely ditching me. This is just a joke. He and Julia are around here somewhere. I'm confident in that.

Just a joke, I remind myself.

But that joke was on me, and I'd soon find that out.

CHAPTER FORTY-SIX

MALACHI

Present

The memory of what I helped Julia do is still fresh on my mind. Most mornings, I wake up in a sweat from living that afternoon over again in my sleep. I used to have to pour alcohol down my throat so that day wouldn't be the last thing on my mind. Thing is, that's exactly what it was anyway.

According to Jenna, I've paid for that sin time after time, and I shouldn't still be haunted by it. But I am, and the dreams are never going to stop. Had I known Julia's plan, I never would have been part of it. I thought we were playing a joke. Make Jenna—well, Elise back then—think she was stranded on the south side of town, in the bad part of town. I acted like I'd left, but I didn't go far, just far enough that she couldn't see me, but I could always see her.

I had my eyes on her when a guy came from around the corner of the building. She had her back to him while she was putting coins into a pay phone. I watched in horror as he placed one hand over her mouth while his other wrapped around her waist. She struggled as I sat, doing nothing. I learned years later that he chloroformed her to knock her out.

It still amazes me she forgave Josh like she did. If I were in her shoes, I don't think I could have done the same thing. I sure as shit wouldn't have forgiven me like she did either. Not that I'm not grateful she did, because I am. It's just that the guilt from all those years ago is still as thick today as it was then.

After she was taken, I didn't go to the authorities like I should have. Instead, I tracked Julia down. Still to this day, I don't know why I did that other than I was scared shitless. I thought because I'd been the one to drop her off and force her out of the car, I'd get into serious trouble. After I told Julia my fear, she grabbed onto it and never let up.

She said we'd both get into trouble, but me more so than her. Then the next day, she started to claim there was no proof she was even involved and that all the blame would fall on me if I told anyone. She was right in that sense; it would have been my word against hers.

Thinking back, I was the biggest idiot to not have been able to see more than a few inches past my goddamned face. I allowed her to scare me into silence, and by doing so, I was the worst of all. I could have told her parents, the authorities, her friends. I could have told anyone, and then maybe Jenna wouldn't have gone without the love of her life for close to two decades.

Not that I believe he deserves her, but she does deserve all the happiness in life. She's owed her happily ever after—even if it's with Jamie Hart. Danny needs a father, and Brandon needs a mother that actually loves him.

I shouldn't be surprised that bitch was planning on shipping her son off to only God knows where. Stopping her and finding Danny is something I have to do.

Looking at my smartwatch again, I decide I can't wait for Kelly or PD to show up. The sooner I get inside, the sooner I can end that bitch once and for all. One way or another, Julia is going to be brought to her knees. If I have anything to do with it, it'll be by way of a bullet to her skull.

Just one headshot is all I need.

Releasing my weapon from its holster, I wrap my hand securely around the metal as I ease the front door open. I parked a block away so that I wouldn't be easily seen. After doing a three-sixty scope around the building, I only saw two vehicles parked nearby.

Going inside without backup is dumb. Rookies even know not to make this stupid of a mistake, but tell that to another person who has someone they love in danger. Being a federal agent goes out the window. Being a logical man goes out that window too.

Time may not be on my side, and that's not a chance I'm willing to take. Knowing Jenna, she's already gotten the location out of Brandon, so she'll be en route. Backup will eventually get here. I just want to be waiting for them.

Slipping inside, I'm careful to close the door without making a sound, then I listen for any noise as I look around, taking in my surroundings. All the buildings in this area are virtually abandoned and dilapidated. The one next door is about to tumble down, and this one isn't much better. The paint on the interior walls is peeling, and there are water stains all over the ceiling. The fixtures have all been removed or stolen. The only light is from the bare windows allowing natural sunlight inside.

Hearing the sound of footsteps coming toward me, I quietly but quickly step inside the office across from me, fusing my back to the wall next to the opened door. Less than ten seconds later, a shadow crosses the threshold as someone passes by.

I'm not able to holster my weapon without the lock clicking

in place; doing so would possibly give up my presence. It's better to catch him off guard, so as I step out from the empty office, gun in hand, I raise the butt of my weapon and then bring it down on the back of the guy's head. Julia's henchman or guard goes down with minimal effort on my part. With my left hand, I reach out, catching him around his chest before he makes a noise by hitting the ground like a sack of potatoes.

After dragging his deadweight into the empty office that I vacated moments ago, I lower his body to one of the corners, hoping he stays knocked out for as long as it takes backup to get here. Kelly should be here any minute, Jenna too.

I head out, walking cautiously in the direction her guy was heading before I clocked him in the head.

I have no idea if he's the only person here or if Julia is even here. In all honesty, as long as I'm able to get to Danny and get him out of here, she can wait another day or two. As much as I would enjoy every second of filling that bitch with lead, Danny's safety is my top priority.

To my right is a closed office door. I wrap my hand around the knob, turn it slowly, and then glance inside. It's vacant, same as the other, so I ease it back closed and continue on. Seconds later, I stop, hearing a grunt from somewhere in the building. As I listen, I peek behind me to make sure my back is covered, and no one is going to jump me like I was able to do to one of her men—or one man as I'm hoping he was.

What sounds like a slap has my head whipping back around in the direction I started.

"How long has she been seeing *my* husband?" Julia's witchy voice sends chills down my arms. I don't know how I once thought it was sweet and innocent. Perhaps to someone that doesn't know firsthand what she's done, they would hear a different tone.

"According to public record, you aren't married to *my* dad

anymore." Danny's deep baritone voice has a rush of air swooshing out of my mouth as relief washes over me. *At least he's alive.* And he's here.

Glancing up to the ceiling, I say a silent *thank you.*

There is a room, twenty feet ahead of me, most likely similar to the other two offices that line this corridor.

"Jamie isn't your father!" Another grunt, and I'm guessing by the pain that hits my gut, it's coming from Danny. "You were supposed to die."

"Guess life's a bitch, huh?" Danny says. I'd smile at the way he's talking back if the situation wasn't so bleak and he wasn't in danger. The kid has always had a mouth on him. Being brought up where you aren't sheltered from anything will do that. Only time will tell if Jenna made the right call with him. He's a good kid. A smart kid, and I can see him with a future in law enforcement one day.

"Jamie is mine. Not hers. He was never hers."

I stop inches before the entryway. Neither of them can see me, and I can't see inside.

Every moment from my past tries to flicker through my head at this very moment. All the times Julia filled me with lies, threats, hopes, all trying to fight to the forefront of my mind.

Breathing in and then back out, I shake all of them from me. This isn't about me, the things Julia did, not even to Jenna. Danny is inside that room, and my gut tells me she's not planning on letting him walk out of here. There are two options for her: ship him off and sell him or kill him. That sick bitch is going to do the latter. I know it. I feel it.

In her mind, Danny shouldn't exist. She ordered his execution over eighteen years ago, and Josh failed. Whether he failed on purpose or by accident, he didn't accomplish what Julia requested. She'll have to finish the job, and I can't let that happen. Danny is my godson. I love that kid like he's my own, and I'll love him until the day I die just the same.

Slowly inching forward, I peek inside, halting when I see a person sitting upright in a dirty office chair. At the sight of Danny's wrists bound by zip ties, secured to the arms of the chair, my jaw locks, and I see red. *That fucking bitch.* I draw in a slow, steady breath of air, trying to calm my nerves. Getting worked up like this isn't going to do Danny any good.

Blowing my breath out, I ready my weapon in my hand and then step into the entryway, gun raised and pointed in front of me. My eyes scan, quickly finding Julia inches from where Danny sits.

"Step away from him. Now!" I order.

Her head swings around as her blue eyes widen with surprise, then her bottom lip drops, opening her mouth.

"I said step away," I repeat, my stare not leaving hers.

"Malachi," she says, crossing her arms as a slow smile ghosts her lips.

I could take the shot now. I should take the shot now. She can't leave this place alive, and if I don't take her out now, I won't get the chance once backup arrives. She deserves death, but a part of me wants to see her handcuffed and carted off. Knowing she's locked up behind bars, imagining the things other inmates will do to her has my trigger finger hesitant.

Locking her up would be a lot worse for her than death . . .

"Mal! Behind—" Danny starts to say, but Julia backhands him.

I understand his warning and whip around, only I'm not quick enough before my body seizes up, and I'm momentarily paralyzed. It's like experiencing a leg cramp, only it covers every inch of your body, and I go down, hitting my knees. My weapon falls from my hand, dropping to the ground, and there isn't one thing I can do about it.

"Malachi!" Danny yells, but I'm unable to look away from the guy in front of me. He's not the same man I took down minutes ago; that much I'm able to recognize.

"Do something other than tasing him, you stupid ass!" Julia's voice comes out harsh, an order to this guy. Dread washes over me. I should have shot her when I had the chance. Now, I'm done for. It's over, and I didn't save Danny.

CHAPTER FORTY-SEVEN
JENNA

I arrive at the location Brandon found, seeing Malachi's SUV parked as well as two others. Multiple buildings, all looking abandoned, are scattered around this area. I have no idea which to go in first. Mal should have sent a text or called to let me know. I can probably rule out the one Malachi's vehicle is next to. He wouldn't have wanted to give away his presence, so he would have parked farther away.

I decide to park next to him. Glancing in my rearview mirror, I see Kelly's car heading toward me. I don't shut off the engine, leaving it running just in case.

"Stay here, but keep your phone near," I tell Jamie as I open the driver's side door and step out of the SUV, careful not to make any sounds as I ease the door closed.

He doesn't listen, getting out too. I don't have time to argue with him, and I certainly don't need him preoccupying my mind when I know Danny and Malachi need me.

"Like hell I am. I'm coming in with you."

"Jamie!" I seethe out of frustration as I watch Kelly park.

"Just stay here, out of my way, and don't argue," I plead with him to understand.

"Our son is in there——" he starts.

"Exactly! And my focus needs to be on him, not you." I turn away, scanning everything, trying to see if there is anything that would indicate occupants inside. I don't have an infrared thermal scanner, which would help in this instance.

"PD is three minutes out," Kelly informs me as she's getting out of her car. Her blonde hair is pulled into a ponytail, and she's already equipped with a bulletproof vest around her chest. Something I should have put on but opted not to take the time to do.

"I'm not waiting, you with me or——" A gunshot somewhere near us goes off, stopping the words coming out of my mouth. In the next second, I whip around, spotting the building the sound came from. Without any other words, I take off, jogging in that direction.

Kelly can wait for backup, or she can follow. It's up to her.

Racing into a building after shots are fired, even with a weapon drawn, is one of the stupidest things an agent can do. I know that. Every cop and law enforcement personnel knows that, but like any human, when someone you love is in danger, logic and protocol go out the window, and adrenaline and emotions take over.

A third shot goes off as I yank the door open, entering. It's an office of sorts, at least the front area I'm in is. I can go right, or I can go straight. Not overanalyzing, I go right, down a hallway of offices.

Coming to an almost stop when I see the glow of unnatural lighting and then a body. I raise my weapon, pointing it in front of me. My eyes connect with Malachi's, and I instantly know something bad has happened. He's on the ground, the front of his body face down, but his head is lifted, and his eyes are wide.

I know my partner, my friend, well enough that I recognize the look. *Get your ass in this room, now!*

There's another body, a man I don't recognize, who is also lying on the ground near Malachi, but he's unmoving and flat on his back. Blood pools from the area around his head. Chances are he's dead, and if not, Malachi is at least conscious enough that he can handle this guy.

When I take a cautious peek around into the office entryway, I gasp, seeing my son on his knees with his bloody hands wrapped around Julia's neck, squeezing the life out of her.

I'd like to say there was at least a moment of thought behind my actions, and maybe subconsciously, there was. Aiming precisely, I pull the trigger, nailing my target in the side of her head. There couldn't have been a more perfect angle on that shot. Had my son been a little more to the left, I wouldn't have had a shot.

Danny freezes in place, his eyes wide but never leaving Julia's lifeless body.

I vaguely hear my name shouted from someone, but that isn't my concern at the moment. I jump over Malachi, bolting to where my son remains frozen in place.

"Danny," I call out, dropping to the ground next to him. His hands are still around her neck; all his strength, his power, has left his body.

Gently, I wrap my hand around his wrist closest to me, tugging. He releases his hold, and her body crumbles to the ground. Blood splatter mars his beautiful face, shooting pain throughout my chest.

I couldn't allow him to kill her, make him be responsible for taking another person's life. It doesn't matter if she deserved that fate or not. Danny is still a kid, my kid, and I couldn't do that to him. I have no doubt in my mind that he would have killed her, and he would have been in the right. None of that matters, but the aftermath would have. Danny feels deeper and harder than most. He doesn't come off that way, but he's my boy, and I know him better than anyone. Julia was still his brother's mother, and even though she didn't deserve that right, that honor, she still was.

God, I hope Brandon forgives me for this. If he doesn't . . . I close my eyes, shutting that thought out as I wrap my arms around my son, fusing his head to my chest, offering what comfort I can.

"Jenna!" Jamie shouts, then an audible gasp pounds through my ears. "Oh my God."

I make myself keep my eyes closed. I can't look at Jamie, not right now. If I see him upset over her, I'll lose it, and I'll never get over that. In reality, it is something I'll have to face. She was the mother of his son. He had to care about her on some level. As much as that shouldn't bother me, it does, and I'm not sure if that's a reality I can get past or overlook. I know Jamie, and over the last couple days, I've seen the hope in his eyes. He wants us back to what we once had. A part of me does too, but after all the time, years wasted, and living in fear, it's not something I can shut off at the snap of my fingers—if I ever can.

Sometimes a damaged heart isn't so easily mended.

CHAPTER FORTY-EIGHT
JAMIE

Seconds after Jenna bolts inside the building that's fifty or so yards across from where I'm standing, I shake myself out of the trance I'm in to run after her.

A total of three gunshots went off. The first two together and the last at least ten seconds later, happening at the same time Jenna made it to the entrance.

Danny is inside that building. I can't lose him when I just found out about him.

"Sir," the blonde, who I can only assume is another federal agent by the letters stamped on her bulletproof vest, calls from behind me. "You need to get back into Jenna's vehicle now," she orders.

That's not going to happen, but I don't bother to tell her that. She can follow, or like Jenna said, she can stay and wait for the backup that's en route.

I'm not staying out here while Jenna goes in there alone, walking into only God knows what. If anything happens to Danny, I don't know what I'll do.

Yanking the door open, I practically jump inside, scanning

all around. "Jenna!" I yell, pausing to listen. Sounds are vague, but I can't make anything out except for the direction they are coming from. That's the way I head.

Another gunshot fires, only this time it's much louder now that I'm closer.

Malachi is the first thing I see, his body face down. I stop, taking in the sight in front of me. His back rises and then falls, so that tells me he's breathing. Hurt, obviously, but alive. My eyes dart over, seeing another body, then I glance back over to the entryway, taking a step forward.

"Jenna!" I call, taking her and Danny in, then my eyes drop to the ground. When reality hits and I realize I'm staring at a body, at Julia unmoving and blood everywhere, I gasp, sucking air into my mouth. "Oh my God." My hand goes to my face, my eyes unblinking. *She's dead.*

A sense of relief floods my system, but I don't know if it's because Danny seems to be okay or if it's because my ex-wife is no longer part of this world. She's gone. She has to be. I can see her open eyes from where I stand, yet there is no life residing in them.

Stepping over Malachi, I make my way to the other side of my son and drop down next to him like Jenna is on the other side. Now that I can see him, take stock of every inch, worry inches in. Danny doesn't look as okay as I thought. His dark-blue eyes are unblinking, watching Julia's lifeless form on the ground. Blood covers his face, and I pray it's Julia's and not his.

Jenna has her arms wrapped around him, and when I peer down, I see cuts, blood, and marks on his wrists. My eyes widen, and my breath comes in sharp. *What did she do to him?* Looking over, I eye her with disgust, disdain. If she wasn't already dead, I'd kill her myself. Danny's wrists are in worse shape than Brandon's, like he pulled himself from his restraints.

Reaching down to the hem of my T-shirt, I yank it up and

over my head. Using the material, I wipe at the blood on his face, trying to get as much off him as I can.

"I'm sorry, Danny. I'm so sorry," I repeat, not knowing what else to say to my son. "Is he okay?" I look to Jenna, waiting for a response.

"I'm the one that killed her," she admits, tugging Danny closer.

"I don't care." I shake my head, dropping my shirt, discarding it now that it's ruined. "Is he okay?" I nod toward Danny. He is my only concern. That bitch can rot where she lays for all I care.

"He'll be fine. Eventually." She eases up on her hold on Danny, then releases him as she drops down on the back of her calves. That's when I grab him, pulling him in for a hug. When he doesn't balk, my body relaxes.

"Stay with Danny," Jenna says. "Malachi is hurt. I need to check on him." I nod, tightening my arms around my son as she gets up.

"It's over," I whisper.

I never thought I'd have to tell my son his mother was dead, and I have no idea how Brandon is going to react to that news. He already knows the things she was planning, the things she's done . . .

Jeez, all those women. I don't even remember half of their faces, let alone their names. I certainly don't know how many there were. I cheated, and I knew it was wrong, even while I was doing it. It didn't matter why or that I didn't love Julia or that I didn't even remember saying vows to her. Cheating was wrong. Yet, I still did it, and look what happened.

Still, she was Brandon's mother.

I'm not sad that she's gone. I'm not upset that Jenna was the person that killed her. I'm pissed off that Brandon has to live knowing all those things his mom did. I'm furious that she wasn't the mother I thought she was. I'm angry that I didn't see any of this happening right under my goddamn nose, my roof.

There are so many things I have to atone for, and I don't know if I'm even worthy of the amount of forgiveness I need not only from Jenna but from my two boys, those women, their families.

Fuck . . .

CHAPTER FORTY-NINE
JENNA

Malachi was shot twice, once in the shoulder and once in his abdomen. Luckily, no major organs were hit, but the bullet that entered his abdominal area is lodged near his kidney. That requires a trip to the OR, which is where he was taken forty minutes ago for surgery.

"Can't you get them to discharge me already?" Danny asks, his voice full of frustration and anger. He's mad because he thinks Malachi wouldn't have gotten hurt if he hadn't have shown himself to Julia when he went to find his brother.

Maybe there is some truth to that, but then Julia would still be alive, and none of us would be free. Her death gave me solace. I hate my son went through what he did, that he witnessed a person killed inches from him, but I would do it over again without question.

"You haven't been cleared." I sigh, breathing a long breath out. "Danny, just rest. All of this will be over soon, then we can leave."

"Can I at least put my clothes on?"

"They were covered in blood, so no. Josh is bringing you

clean ones." Danny and Malachi arrived at the hospital via ambulance. My son's injuries looked superficial to the naked eye. Physical damage, yes. Emotional injuries can't be seen or mended with a bandage. I insisted he be checked out. I'll probably insist he speak to someone.

Jess isn't going to like that it won't be her. As Maggie's mom, she's too close. Danny needs an outsider, someone he can be completely open with. Sure, he has Maggie, and he has his brother, but they are still kids just like him.

The glass door slides open, and both of our eyes snap up, seeing Jamie entering. We're still in the ER, and only one person is supposed to be allowed back here. Jamie's irises go from me to Danny and then down to his hospital gown-covered waist. When we first arrived, the techs had Danny discard all of his clothes. I didn't stay in the room, but Jamie refused to leave our son's side. I have no doubt that he saw the almost matching tattoo on Danny's hip.

I don't know what's going through Jamie's head. I'm sure he has questions, like how long has he had it and why. I can't answer any of his questions. I can assume, and I'd probably assume correct, but none of that is my place. That's for Jamie and Danny to talk about when our son is ready.

"I told Brandon," Jamie says, shoving his hands down in the front pockets of his jeans.

"Where is he?"

"How did he take it?" Danny and I both speak at the same time.

Brandon's reaction, his feelings, is one of the things I'm most concerned about, other than the outcome of Malachi's surgery. There is nothing I can do for Mal, so I have to put him out of my mind for now and worry about my boys.

"In the waiting room with your girlfriend," Jamie says, addressing Danny. "They both want to come back here."

"Then let them," Danny stresses.

Jamie looks to me. "It's fine. I can go out and let one of them come back."

"I talked the nurse into letting them both come back. We just have to come out."

I nod, pushing my elbows off the side of the hospital bed and then standing. Grabbing my purse, I pull out Danny's cell phone and hand it to him. "If you need me, call or text me. I won't be far."

His head tips up and down before falling to the pillow behind his head on the raised bed. When his eyes go toward the ceiling, I make my way around the bed, passing Jamie to leave.

I hate not having control, and that's exactly the way I feel about my son and Jamie, about Brandon and Malachi. I'm not used to all these feelings. At least before, when the truth was hidden, not spoken about, I had a semblance of control. Thinking back on that, it was just a lie I told myself.

I feel Jamie catch up to me as I go through another set of sliding glass doors to enter the waiting area. I pause when I see multiple people stand. I wasn't expecting everyone to be here, but I shouldn't be surprised.

"How's our boy?" Anne asks, clutching her chest.

"He'll be fine," I assure her and then turn my attention to the kids. "He wants you both to go back," I tell Brandon and Maggie, though my eyes never stray from Brandon's.

Maggie bolts, taking off behind me without being told twice. As Brandon passes, I reach out, wrapping my hand around the bend in his arm. He stops, our bodies both facing opposite directions, and I have to tip my head back to look up. "We need to talk."

Leaning down, his mouth hovers inches from my ear. "We will," he whispers so only I can hear him. There is no hurt or anger detected in his tone.

"Okay," I breathe out, my voice as low as his.

"I love you, Jen. Thank you for saving my brother." Brandon's lips press against my cheek for a quick moment, then he steps away, walking past me.

I close my eyes and then feel Jamie step behind me, his body heat warming me. His warm hands wrap around my biceps, the same way he did earlier when we were at my house.

"Seth is bringing Cole. When I talked to him, he lost it while I was on the phone with him," Jamie says. Relaxing my body, I fall against Jamie's chest, nodding to let him know I heard him.

Cole cares for Malachi, deeply, in fact. I'm sure he's taking it hard. I think that was another reason Cole kept somewhat of a distance, never allowing himself to commit or even think about any type of long-term relationship with Mal. This outcome scared the shit out of Cole. The thing is, life isn't predictable, and it certainly isn't guaranteed. Sometimes we get a lifetime with people, creating a mountain of memories. Other times, we get a small window of time with someone and then live a life with loss, and not getting enough memories.

Time is precious.

"Jen." I open my eyes, seeing Trey standing in front of us, his hands stuffed in the front pockets of his pants with his head bowed. "Can I have a minute?" His brown eyes lift, but his face stays pointed to the ground.

"Can't it wait?" Jamie sighs, squeezing my arms.

"Sure, Trey." I take a breath, stepping away from Jamie.

This moment has been a long time coming. Might as well get the last piece of the past done.

Eighteen years ago

"He was happy with me," I bite out as I step forward, jabbing my finger into Cole's chest.

"I know." His brows furrow, and his gaze drops to where my finger still touches him. "He's not any happier with her if it makes any difference."

"Then why isn't he with me?"

"It's more complicated. He—"

"Hates you," Trey says from behind me, interrupting Cole. I whip around, facing him, his dark-brown eyes snapping over my shoulder. "Seth's ready. Let's do this. Let's get the fuck out of here."

"I'll be there when I'm there," Cole replies.

"I want to talk to Elise. Leave us."

Trey's hate-filled eyes never leave Cole's as they silently war between them. I'm about to say to hell with both of them when Cole mumbles a goodbye, leaving me standing alone with Trey in my parents' backyard.

When his gaze finally falls to mine, I see something in them that makes me take a step back, not liking what I see deep inside irises I once trusted. Three months ago, I had blind faith in my friends. I'd known the guys for years, I trusted them, and I thought they had that same trust and faith in me. I thought they knew me like I thought I knew them.

But I'd been wrong, so wrong.

"What do you want, Trey?" I cross my arms, tucking my hands between my biceps and sides. "Come to gloat one last time? Come to throw whatever false hate you have back in my face before you leave?"

Trey not taking my side stings, almost as much as Jamie not standing next to me, not believing me. Trey and I were friends, or so I thought. We hung out together, we had lunch at the same time, and we've always ended up in at least one class together since my freshmen year.

Trey takes a step forward, and I retreat once again.

"I wanted to say my piece before I never have to see you again."

"You want to talk. Jamie doesn't, and Seth hasn't said two words to me since I've been back. How is it that Cole is more on my side than you or Jamie?"

"Cole isn't on your side. He's on Jamie's, like Seth and me. What you did to Jamie is unforgivable. And now—"

"Now what?"

His jaw locks, and his eyes tell me he would shoot fire from them if he could. "Nothing."

"You're standing here, so it obviously isn't nothing. Just spit it out already."

"You didn't just leave him; you left me too. How could you do it? How was it that simple?"

"Jeez. Do you even hear yourself?" I step forward, my backbone finally reappearing despite everything I've done to tame it since returning. "If you were really my friend, you'd know I wouldn't have walked away on my own, of my free will. I didn't leave him, or you, or my life here. I was kidnapped, Trey."

"Stop!" he yells in my face, inching closer to me. "Stop lying and just cop to it already. At least give Jamie the truth before we leave."

"He left yesterday, and I told him the truth."

His head shakes. "No, you didn't. I know when you're hiding something, and yes, Elise, you are hiding something."

"Maybe so, but it isn't that."

"Then what is it? You have my ear, tell me."

"Doesn't matter," I say, shaking my head. I can't tell him about the baby. I can't tell anyone, not yet, at least. "You didn't have my back on the one thing you should have, Trey, and neither did Jamie."

"We didn't have *your* back?" A humorless laugh slips out of his mouth. "That's laughable."

I start to turn away from him, done with this conversation, when I pause, thinking. *I could show him the evidence on my back, but then what?* Whatever hook Julia has into Jamie and Trey, they'll come up with another false explanation. Maybe that's the reason I came home. Maybe I got myself beat and couldn't hack the "real world," so I cut tail and thought I would be welcomed back with open arms.

I turn my head, glancing over my shoulder, but Trey isn't looking at my face. His eyes have dropped, and his brows are scrunched together. I'm wearing a tank top, and the scarring is still inflamed across my back. It goes to the edge, less than an inch from my armpit. The way his eyes are scrutinizing me, I know he sees part of it. Whether he knows what he's looking at or not, I can't tell.

"None of this is laughable, Trey. When I came home, I expected my friends to still see me as the person they saw, the person they knew me to be a couple of months ago, just weeks, really. Not once have I ever given Jamie or you or my parents a reason not to believe me."

"If you're holding something from us, then you're lying, and if you're lying about one thing, then you're lying about everything. You didn't just betray Jamie." His voice starts to rise, the anger in his tone escalating. "You betrayed all of us when you left. You betrayed me!"

"No, I didn't!" I yell back, but before all the words are past my lips, fire erupts across my cheek. For a split second, I'm stunned, and it takes longer than it should for me to realize he hit me. From the expression displayed on his face, he's surprised too.

Trey isn't a fighter, at least never that I've seen. He doesn't get worked up like Jamie. He doesn't argue like Cole. He and Seth are alike in that way.

"Go to Hell, Elise," he says before turning and walking away from me without an apology.

Present

THAT WAS THE LAST TIME I SAW TREY UNTIL TWO DAYS AGO when I walked down the stairs at Cole's house, thinking it was Cole coming back with breakfast.

Thinking back on that day eighteen years ago, it still seems unreal. I'm still stunned by Trey's action because I know that wasn't him. He doesn't hit people. He's not an abuser. He just reacted to his anger, and that's not me making an excuse for him. What he did was wrong. He doesn't need me to tell him that to know he was in the wrong. Even if I had done everything he thought I did, he still would have been wrong to lay a hand on me like he did.

"That was the first time I ever hit a woman." His head swings toward me. "The only time I've ever hit a woman," he clarifies, then he hangs his head, looking back to the ground.

I couldn't make myself go far in case Danny calls for me, or there is news of Malachi's surgery, so we're sitting side by side in the corner of the waiting room. I haven't taken a peek at Jamie, but I know his eyes are on us. I've always been able to tell when they were. It's a comfort I hadn't realized I missed until now.

"I felt like shit afterward. I know that doesn't make it right, but I did." Leaning back in the dull, gray chair, I let him continue. He obviously needs to say his piece. "After Cole, Seth, and I left that day, we stayed overnight in Dallas before continuing on to LA. I got into my first fight that night. I purposefully started it. I wanted to get my ass kicked, and I did."

"If you think telling me that makes me feel any better, it doesn't, Trey."

"No, that isn't it. It's just . . . Hell, I don't even know." He shakes his head. "You were right, you know. You were my friend. You weren't just the girlfriend of one of my best friends. We were friends too, and I didn't have your back like I should have."

"It's not that you didn't have my back. I told you, over and over, that I wasn't lying, and not even for a second did you question if I could be telling the truth. You, Jamie, the others, you all based everything off a picture and what Julia claimed. How long had you known me? Years longer than you knew Jules, yet, you took her word over mine. I'm sorry, Trey, but from where I sit, not only did that sting, it might as well have been a punch to my face, the first hit, not the slap the day you left."

He nods his understanding, or maybe he agrees with me.

"I saw that scar on your back that day. That day at Cole's wasn't the first time I'd seen it. I didn't know that's what it was, but I knew it was something. It caught my attention that day."

"I know."

"Seeing that video really fucked me up. I haven't slept. I can't eat. What you went through and then . . ." He blows out a long breath. "I messed up, and I have no excuse. I should have been in your corner, not hers, and I'm sorry."

"Look," I say, placing my hand on Trey's shoulder. "If it's forgiveness you're wanting, that's easy. You have it, but if it's the friendship we used to have, I don't know. I can't give you that, Trey. I'm not the same person I was way back then, and I can't promise we'll ever be that close again." I take a breath and then blow it out, squeezing him. "But I don't think Jamie plans on walking back out of my life anytime soon, so . . . maybe we'll get to know each other and see where that goes. It's the best I can give you."

"Did you forgive Jamie too?"

"Not yet."

"Are you going to?"

"I don't know. He's in a different category than you are. He isn't so easy to forgive or forget. And I haven't allowed myself to go there with him—not yet anyway." But I know it's coming. Question is, am I ready to admit things, want things, and then am I willing to allow myself to have them? I don't know yet. Maybe too much has happened. Maybe my heart is beyond repair.

Or maybe I just don't care about any of that anymore.

Yeah right.

I let Jamie Hart back in within seconds of him touching me for the first time in years. I wouldn't even begin to know how to push him away, and if I did, I don't think I have that much strength to see it through.

The heart doesn't play fair. It doesn't see logic or what's good or bad for you. It feels until it finds a connection. Once that connection is made, it locks in place.

That's Jamie and me. He's sealed up permanently inside that cavity in my chest. My heart has no plans of ever letting him go. I can give the reins over, allow my heart to guide me, or I can turn away, but then I'd just be even more miserable, in more agony than I have been for the last eighteen years.

And who wants that kind of life?

CHAPTER FIFTY

JAMIE

I debated whether or not I should tell Brandon that it was Jenna that took the shot that killed his mother. I almost chose to keep that detail from him. He's still a kid, and I didn't want him to resent Jenna in any way. I know she did what she had to do, and I'm glad she did. While Danny was being loaded into an ambulance, she told me why she shot her. If she hadn't, then it would have been our son who took Julia's life. That's a weight I never want on his shoulders, so for that reason alone, I'm glad she did it.

Julia deserved worse. A lifetime rotting in a cage would have been preferable after learning the things she was going to do to my sons.

In the end, I decided there'd been enough secrets. I didn't want to add another to the pile, so I told him everything. All that I knew anyway. I haven't gotten to speak to Danny alone, and Jenna never brought up the last couple of hours before she rescued him. If Danny wants his brother, Jenna, me, or anyone else to know, then I trust he'll tell us.

I'm not going to be the one to force him to talk about it if he doesn't want to. There are certain things I'd like to forget, never think about again. My ex-wife is one of those things.

She's gone.

She's dead.

She can never hurt anyone I associate with ever again, and that's all I care about when it comes to her.

Enjoy Hell, you fucking bitch.

The sound of the sliding doors that lead from the outside into the ER open, pulling me out of my wasted thoughts on someone that doesn't even matter anymore. Seeing Seth and then Cole, I stand. My head swings around, seeing Jenna and Trey still in a private conversation, so I turn back around, waiting for them to reach us.

"Is Danny okay?" is the first thing out of Cole's mouth. Concern is etched across his face.

"He's fine. He'll be released anytime now," I inform him as Seth stops next to us both.

"And Mal? Are there any updates?" Cole swallows, bracing himself for my answer.

"He's in surgery, but that's all I know right now." I glance over, seeing Jenna and Trey stand, their mouths moving, but their eyes are on where we stand.

"How bad is it?" I turn my head back around, witnessing Cole's shoulders tense up. The pain he harbors behind his green eyes cuts me deep. All I want to do is reassure my friend that everything is going to be okay, but I can't do that because I have no idea if that's true or not. The guy was shot multiple times, and I don't want to give him false hope.

"Hey," Jenna whispers, stepping in front of me. Taking another step, she walks into Cole's personal space, wrapping her arms around his waist, embracing him. "It's going to be okay," she assures him, talking into his chest. Her head tips back, looking up at him.

"How do you know that?" he croaks out.

Stepping back, Jenna pauses at my side. "Because he's strong. He's a fighter. And because he's Malachi. He has to be okay. That's why." There's a quiver to her voice that's just now surfacing. I want to reach out, but she's been through a lot today. We all have. I don't want to push us or cause her any more pain, so I stand still next to her.

My attention goes to the double doors farthest away from the waiting area. A tall man with milk-chocolate skin, wearing a long white coat, pushes his way toward us.

"Is the family of Malachi Hayes here?" the man asks, stopping.

My gaze drops to the script displayed on his white coat: Marc Thornton, MD. Trauma Surgery is listed beneath his name.

"We are," Josh speaks up.

Jenna's left hand finds my right one, interlocking her fingers with mine.

"You're all his immediate family?" The doctor arches an eyebrow. "Pardon me for asking, but none of you look related, and it doesn't say he's married in his record."

"You're damn right we're his family," Josh says. Reaching into his pocket, he pulls out a badge. Flipping it open, he flashes his federal ID. "He's one of my agents. That makes him family."

"All right then." The doctor nods. "Surgery went well. We were able to extract the bullet and mend the damage. With rest and physical therapy, he should recover just fine and be back to one hundred percent with time."

"When can we see him?" Cole asks.

"About an hour, I suspect. He's still sedated. We're about to take him to recovery until he wakes. I can allow one person to come in the room once we have him settled if one of you wants to."

"Cole, it should be you," Jenna says.

"You sure?" His brows wrinkle as he chews on the side of his cheek.

Taking a step away from me, Jenna stops in front of Cole, looking up at him. Lifting her hands and placing them on each side of his face, she says, "We only get one life. It's up to us to make the most of it. Either vow to commit to him now or walk out of this hospital and never see him again. You can't do both, and you can't keep stringing him along."

"What if it's too late and he doesn't want me?"

"You won't know the answer to that until you go see him and you talk to him."

He leans forward, pressing his lips to her forehead. He lingers against her until he sighs out a tired breath. Feeling the bone tiredness throughout my entire body, I want to do the same, but then her words hit home, and something else blossoms deep within my chest.

We only get one life. It's up to us to make the most of it. Do those words pertain to us too? I wonder.

"If it's decided," the surgeon says. "Then you can follow me. I'll take you back now."

"Yeah, I'm going," Cole says, taking a step away from Jenna.

Everyone is silent as he and the doctor disappear through a set of double doors that leads into the other part of the hospital and out of the emergency room.

"I should probably call Mal's parents," Jenna says.

"I'll take care of it," Josh informs her from where he and Jessica stand next to one another. Both of her hands are wrapped around one of his with her body pressed close like she'd fuse hers to his if she could. I'm not sure I'll ever understand the two of them, but I guess that doesn't matter. I don't have to. If Jess loves him, then she loves him.

And if Malachi Hayes is the guy Cole likes or loves, then all I care about is what makes my best friend happy.

"Thanks." Jenna nods, a forced smile spreading across her lips. Glancing at me, our eyes lock for a couple of seconds before she turns, walking away. There's a sadness in her brown eyes that tugs me to go after her.

I'm going to get you back, baby, one way or another, or I'm going to die trying.

CHAPTER FIFTY-ONE

JENNA

Malachi is going to make it.
Danny and Brandon are fine.
Everything is okay again.

But is it? Three days ago—the morning I woke up at Cole's like I do every now and again—my path was set, and I'd come to terms with that life. Jamie wasn't mine, still isn't mine. He may have been divorced, something I'd known was coming since the day he filed the papers. Cole had been so eager to tell me months back. I guess thinking it could change things and that I'd consider telling Jamie the truth.

I didn't share the same enthusiasm that Cole did. If anything, his pending divorce just made everything worse, harder even. He was available, but not. Not for me anyway.

The threat to my son's life still existed. I'd long stopped searching for evidence that Julia had ever done anything like what she'd done to me. I thought it was a one-time thing simply to get what she wanted. In a way, it was. Even though she had Jamie on paper, she didn't have him in any other way.

I should be relieved that it's all over now. Danny is free, so to speak, but instead of feeling like I can breathe again, I feel like someone has a plastic bag over my head, suffocating me.

I shouldn't feel partially responsible for all those women that Julia either sold or murdered, yet I do. It's not logical, but if I'd continued, never stopping the eyes I had on her, then maybe I would have realized what was happening and could have stopped it.

I don't even know how many women it was, or if it was only the women Jamie had relations with. Maybe there were others too. He's a rock star, yes, but I wouldn't consider him a whore. Not like the stories you hear about bands' after-parties. Sure, those happen, but Bleeding Hart was always tamer in that way than other bands.

I remember Josh once telling me how he had to capture and sell a minimum of four girls a year. If that still rings true, then how many is that over the course of eighteen years? It's less than a hundred. That number might sound low in the scheme of things, but it's still a lot of women that were ripped away from their homes, their lives, their families.

"Hey, Jen, wait up," he calls from behind me as I'm heading down an empty hallway somewhere in the main part of the hospital. I left the ER, needing a moment alone.

I pivot, facing him. "Don't, Jamie." I hold up my hand, my arm outstretched to stop him. "Go be with the boys or wait in the waiting room. I just need a minute alone."

His eyes linger on mine for a long beat, then he blinks and starts looking around in every direction. Wrapping his hand around my wrist, he begins walking, pulling me along with him.

"Jamie," I whine. Doesn't he understand a minute alone means just me, alone with myself, him not included?

I guess not.

Opening a closed door, he peeks his head inside. A second

later, I'm tugged in the dark room with him where he closes us inside.

Glancing around, I'm thankful it isn't the janitor's closet. It's a small space, an administrative office most likely. There is a desk with a desktop computer and a phone. That's about it. It's mostly bare, with a paned glass window behind the desk. With a storm brewing, it doesn't cast that much light in here despite no curtains hanging.

Releasing my wrist, his hand lifts, gently cupping my jaw and cheek. His head dips, and then his lips are on mine, kissing me. What starts out soft and sweet quickly turns hard and heated. My mouth opens, beckoning his tongue inside all on its own without my brain's permission.

The mental power he still has over me is astonishing. It's both thrilling and annoying. But we want who we want, right?

Still . . . I can't have him distracting me. I need this time to set myself straight and clear my head. I don't think clearly around him.

Pushing on his chest, I pry my lips from his, instantly missing the way he makes me feel from just a kiss.

"Stop," I say breathlessly.

"You want me the same as I want you. Just admit that much to yourself, at least."

"Doesn't mean we should act on it."

"That's exactly what it means," he argues. "I know this is crazy, but we are who we are, and neither one of us stopped loving each other. We can do this. We'll never be able to slow down. Don't you remember the first day we met at Sunday school? By the time the hour was over, you were my girlfriend, and you stayed my girlfriend until I lost you."

"You mean until you threw me away when you decided to believe someone else over me."

"I can't change the past, and . . ." He closes his eyes as his fingers run through his dark hair. Seconds pass with only the sound of his labored breathing between us. When those indigo eyes reopen, he says, "Danny told me a couple of days ago that he'd choose his brother existing and going through every second of what he's dealt with by not having me in his life than growing up how Brandon did with two parents. I didn't get it at first, but now I do. He's right. If things hadn't happened the way they did, I wouldn't have the two sons I have today. They wouldn't have each other. And you know what? I'd go through the last eighteen years without you and Danny all over again so that those two could have each other."

He's not saying anything I haven't thought myself over the last couple of years. I didn't begin getting close to Brandon until I moved to California. When I first met him, I thought I'd fallen in love with that little guy, but I was wrong. It wasn't until I started waking up in the mornings, making sure both boys got off to school on time. When I started being the one that signed his report cards. When he started asking me for advice.

I don't need Brandon to call me "Mom" to know that he is my son in every way except biology.

"I love you, Jen. And I want both of my sons to have a mother that loves them as much as you do. I want Brandon to have the mom Danny has."

"He already has me."

"Do I?"

I turn my head to the side, not knowing how to answer his question. Sure, I want him, and I know he wants me. But all the time lost, how easily and quickly he doubted me, just doesn't up and vanish now that we are free to be together again. I trusted him wholeheartedly, and he didn't return that trust in me. I don't know how to get past those things. Perhaps in the big picture, they shouldn't matter anymore, but they do.

"You hurt me, Jamie. You shattered my heart. Are you

asking me to just forget that and let you back in like it never happened?"

"Of course not." His brows crease. "I was young and stupid, and that's not an excuse, but it's the truth. I was eighteen, barely older than our boys are now. I have to live with the fact that I nearly cost us a lifetime together. I can't go back and change things. I don't think you'd want me to either. Everything shapes us into the person we are, and I'm not the same person I was then. I'll spend the rest of my life making up for the time we lost. I'll cancel the summer tour, hell, the fall and winter one too. Just don't say no to us . . . trying."

"Trying what?"

"To be a family, to being together. Hell, at this point, I'll take friendship if that's all you're willing to give me. I just want you in my life any way I can have you. I can't go through even one day without you again—at least not in some way. Please, Jen."

"Trust has to be earned, and you don't exactly have a good track record, you know."

"I didn't love her. It'll be different with you and me. I don't want to be with anyone else but you."

I place my hand flat on his chest, thinking. Wrapping his hand around the wrist I have hanging at my side, Jamie lifts my arm, bringing it up until my skin meets his lips. He peppers light kisses down the inside of my forearm, and I can't stop the smile that tugs at the corners of my mouth.

"You want this the same as me. Just admit it." With his other hand, he places his warm palm against my cheek with his thumb under my chin. Tilting my head back, he goes on, "It's you. Only you from here on out."

"It's only ever been you for me," I whisper, unashamed that I'm admitting that to him.

"What?" His eyes flicker as his head tilts.

"I haven't had sex with anyone but you, Jamie."

His mouth drops open, but no words fall out. Something inside me sings, knowing I've stunned him into silence. It only lasts a second or two. It's not something I'm exactly proud of. It is what it is. It's sad really, because I've spent so many years longing for that intimate connection that I've only ever wanted with Jamie.

"I know this is probably going to sound shitty coming from me when I've been with . . . well—"

"Yeah"—I hold out my hand like a stop sign, shaking my head—"let's not go there. You've slept with other women. I know. It doesn't have to be discussed or brought up again." He nods.

"Hearing you say that, knowing I'm the only man that's ever been inside you, makes my dick hard." In an effort to drive his words home, he steps into me, pushing my body into the solid wooden door behind me, and then presses said hard dick into my stomach.

Damn him.

My eyes flutter closed, savoring the feel of him against me. He always did know how to use his body to get anything he wants out of me. Not that I have room to talk. I used to as well.

"You know you want this, baby."

My eyes pop up, and my eyebrows lift. "Pretty sure it's you that wants this," I say, pointing at myself.

"Oh, I do." He smirks. I'm tempted to lift my knee, but then I'd screw myself too. Or, it'll prevent him from screwing *me* in this office that we're so rudely occupying.

Pushing off me, his hands go straight for the buckle on my black tactical pants, and then the button is undone, and the zipper is pulled down.

"Jamie," I warn, kicking myself for putting up this much of a fight when I'm bound to lose. Ignoring me, he pushes the material and my panties down my legs before doing the same to his. "We're in a hospital and in an office that anyone could walk in at any time."

"Don't care."

Grabbing me by my thighs, he lifts me up, aligning my body just right.

"I don't suppose you've invested in any condoms, have you?"

"When in the last couple of days would I have had time to buy condoms I never plan on wearing?" Without waiting for a response, he presses between my thighs, entering me slowly.

"Ahhh," I breathe, sucking in air. The intrusion isn't something I've gotten used to, probably won't for a while at least.

"Are you ready to let love win?" he asks, unmoving as he looks into my eyes.

"Did I really ever have a choice?" I counter, squeezing him as I ask.

"There's always a choice," he bites out. "But why fight something that we both want?"

Let love win, he says, like it's that simple.

Instead of answering him, I lean forward, snatching his lips up with mine. We have a lifetime to see if love will outweigh all the baggage the two of us bring to the table. I do want this. I want this just as bad as he does, so maybe we'll finally get that happily ever after we both deserve.

Only time will tell.

There is no doubt in my mind that if you want it hard enough, and if we both put in the effort together, we can find the *us* that was always meant to be.

EPILOGUE
JAMIE

Redemption can be found in forgiveness. The agony of regret doesn't have to last a lifetime if you're able to let the past go so the future can prevail. At least, that's what I've told myself for the last nine months.

My ex-wife is dead, lying six-feet underground. The only reason I know where is because I went with Brandon to her funeral. He didn't want to go, but Jenna talked him into it, telling him he needed closure. In a way, I did too. We all did. Watching that casket be lowered into the ground, I was overcome with relief, feeling eighteen years of tension leave my body in a matter of seconds.

Her parents didn't show for the burial. No one was there except Brandon and me, along with Josh and Kelly, the other agent on his team that I met months back. He didn't come because Julia was his sister; he came as FBI in case Julia's father —his father—tried anything.

A couple of days after Danny was released from the hospital, he shared all the information he'd gathered. Josh took that to his superiors, and another team was assigned the case, which has since been closed. Five weeks ago, the FBI had enough evidence against my former father-in-law, proving his involvement in human trafficking. It's all still appalling that those things were being orchestrated so close to home.

Mitch Montgomery is currently locked up, pending a trial. As luck would have it, the judge denied bail, considering him a flight risk. That's the only reason he's still behind bars. Hopefully, he'll stay that way. Julia's mother hasn't been located, and from what Jenna has told me, there isn't a trail or lead on her whereabouts, making me wonder if something happened or if she's even alive.

In the nine months following the day everything happened, I'm no closer to liking Josh than I was when I found out what he'd done to Jenna. I've accepted him in hers and Danny's life, but that's as much as I can do. He and I will never be friends, but I won't interfere with the relationship they have with him. Though there is a part of me that feels sorry for him, or maybe it's Jess I feel bad for. Maggie learned the truth, despite her parents wanting to keep her in the dark. She isn't letting the past go as easily as the rest of us did.

She may be seventeen now, but she's still a kid too. In time, she'll grow to understand, or at least, accept the bad things that happened before she was ever born. After all, that's what brought her parents together, to begin with.

Danny wanted her to know the truth, so now she does. Everything that happened changed his mental aspect. He didn't like hurting her or causing a ripple between his girlfriend and her parents, but he felt clearing the air completely was the only way all of us could move forward.

The boys, and even Maggie, started their senior year of high school a month ago. My band canceled both of our tours set for this year. Next year is still undecided. Jenna didn't ask me to cancel them, but I wanted to be home. I wanted time with my family. Seth was on board from the minute I told the band I didn't want to do a tour. Cole, nor Trey, put up much of a fight. I think we all needed a break.

I bought the beach rental months ago. Jenna and the boys moved in last month, and I couldn't be happier. She sold her house and is taking a leave of absence from the FBI. I doubt she'll quit, and I wouldn't ask her to, but I don't think she wants to work in the field any longer. At least not anytime soon.

"Are you sure you're ready for everyone to come in? If you need more rest—"

"It's fine," she says, cutting me off. "I'd rather get it over with and then rest afterward." A yawn creeps out of Jenna's mouth. Her droopy brown eyes tell me she's more exhausted than she's letting on.

From where I'm lying on my side next to her—damn near falling off the hospital bed made for one person—I tighten my arm around her shoulder, then lean in, brushing a kiss to her temple.

"You did good today," I tell her and then glance at our daughter as she nurses on her mother. She came barreling into the world fifteen minutes ago. This is something I didn't get to do the first time around, not even with Brandon. Julia didn't nurse for whatever reason. I can't even remember why anymore. "She's beautiful, just like you."

"You do make beautiful babies." Jenna chuckles, looking down at our little girl.

"Can't argue with you there, except we made this beautiful princess together."

There is a knock on the closed door that pulls my head away from my girls. Before I can open my mouth, it creaks open, and Brandon walks in, Danny following behind him.

"I thought I sent you a text that said to give your mom ten more minutes."

"Five, ten, not that much of a difference," Brandon says, coming to stand at the foot of the bed as Cole and Malachi slip in the room behind the boys. Mal gently pushes the door closed, then plants his back against it.

"Dad," Danny says, stopping on the side closest to Jenna. "The two of you have hogged our sister long enough. It's our turn."

It wasn't too long after everything happened when Danny and I had a heart-to-heart. I admitted seeing his tattoo, in which he simply nodded that he heard me, not going into details. I've since added to the one covering my torso, placing another cub to match the one on Danny's hip. After today, we'll both have another tattoo to add, only this one with a pink bow on the girl lion.

"Which one of you wants first dibs?" Jenna asks, speaking to Danny and Brandon.

"I want her," Brandon says enthusiastically with his hands outstretched. His head swings toward his brother's.

"Go ahead," Danny urges him, letting Brandon be first to hold their little sister.

Brandon walks around the corner of the bed, stopping next to his brother. Once she's in his arms, the biggest smile I've ever seen displayed on his face spreads wide, warming my chest.

They're going to be great big brothers.

"So," Cole starts, taking a step closer to the bed. "Which one of us gets to be her godfather?"

Malachi holds up his hand. "Before you tell us, we've already hashed it out. Whichever one you don't pick can't get butt hurt, so . . . who did you pick?"

His eyes are on Jenna. She glances my way before speaking, a smile starting to ghost her pink lips. "We want you both to be her godparents."

"Really?!" they both say in unison.

Jenna and I talked about it a few nights ago. With Cole being Brandon's and Malachi being Danny's, why not? It only makes sense. They've been a couple since Malachi woke up after surgery. Cole didn't wait ten minutes after his eyes opened to ask him. I couldn't be happier for them.

"Both of you were the only choice," Jenna informs them.

"What's our goddaughter's name then?" Malachi asks.

"Sophie Anne," Danny says, speaking up.

We only just decided on a first name last night. It was a name that Brandon threw out, and all four of us loved it.

"Speaking of Anne," Cole says, his eyes flicking to mine. "Where is your mom?"

"Her flight got delayed in Dallas. The boys are going to meet her at the airport in"—I flick my wrist, looking at the time on my smartwatch—"an hour." I look over, making sure they both heard me even though they were on the group text when I told their grandmother to expect them to be waiting for her. "You two should head that way soon."

"Hand my sister over," Danny orders. "I at least get to hold her for a few minutes." Taking her from Brandon, he steps back until his calves touch the couch, where he gently lowers until he's seated. "Hey, Soph. I'm going to warn you now, so there's no confusion later. Your life is probably going to suck when you hit your teens, just so you know."

"Before then, if any little douchey punks start coming around," Brandon follows, making me laugh. Jenna rolls her eyes as her lips purse.

"Why don't we go get Anne," Cole says, gesturing between Malachi and himself. "Give the boys a chance to love their sister before all the long nights start."

"What long nights?" Brandon asks, his nose scrunching up.

Jenna and I laugh while a smirk forms on Malachi's lips.

"Just that she's probably going to make both of your lives

hell far faster than the two of you will do to hers," Cole tells them. "Let's go," he calls out to Mal. "We'll be back, and then that beautiful little angel is mine."

After they leave, Brandon takes a seat next to Danny to play with his sister's fingers.

"Thank you," I whisper, leaning over and kissing my girlfriend on the lips. "Thank you for giving me the family I always wanted."

Interlacing our fingers, she glances at the kids and then turns her head so that her forehead touches mine. "This is our story, Jamie, and I wouldn't change one thing as long as I get everything we have in this room right now. I love you and the kids more than I can put into words."

"I love you too, baby."

She twists her body, angling to the side, snuggling in closer to me as her eyes close.

Our love story may not be conventional, but it's ours, and it's full of love and passion and forgiveness and mercy. We found our way back, and I can't imagine getting here any other way.

ALSO BY N. E. HENDERSON

SILENT SERIES:

Nick and Shannon's Duet

SILENT NO MORE

SILENT GUILT

MORE THAN SEIRES:

Can be read as standalones but not recommended

MORE THAN LIES

MORE THAN MEMORIES

DIRTY JUSTICE TRILOGY:

DIRTY BLUE

DIRTY WAR

DIRTY SIN

THE NEW AMERICAN MAFIA:

Must be read in order for the complete story

BAD PRINCESS

DARK PRINCE

DEVIANT KNIGHT

STANDALONE BOOKS:

HAVE MERCY

BOXSETS / COLLECTIONS:

Silent Series

More Than Series

Dirty Justice Trilogy

ACKNOWLEDGMENTS

My loyal readers and new ones, thank you for reading this story and my other books. Thank you for supporting me, loving my stories and characters, and for being a friend. Thank you for the honest reviews for leave.

Sandy, Heather, Clara, Maddy, and Selena thank you for beta reading Have Mercy while I was writing it. You all helped me in so many ways and because of it, I was able to write this book quicker than any of my others before it.

Charissa, thank you for being the second set of eyes on Have Mercy and spending hours editing this book and helping make it better. Thank you for continuing to boost my confidence while I was writing this story.

Tesha, thank you for being my third set of eyes. You have a way of breaking my stories apart and commenting on ways you think it could be tweaked.

Ellie and Rosa, thank you for polishing this script and being my fourth and final set of eyes on this book. I am so thankful you accepted me as a client and willing to put up with every time I email you saying, it's not finished yet. I still need more time.

Beth and Melissa, thank you for proofreading and so willing to help make this book better.

Emily, thank you for the amazing new cover. I love it so much.

To my friends in my Reader Group—thank you for supporting me. Thank you for your friendship, and thank you for your feedback on my books.

ABOUT THE AUTHOR

N. E. Henderson is the author of sexy, contemporary romance. When she isn't writing, you can find her reading or in her CanAm Maverick, playing in the dirt.

This is Nancy's eighth book.

For more information:
www.nehenderson.com
nancy@nehenderson.com
tiktok.com/@n.e.henderson
instagram.com/nehenderson

Made in the USA
Middletown, DE
02 June 2022